SENTII

Written and created by

J. Alexander

Copyright Notice

This novel, its contents and all works in the Sentinel Universe are copyright of
J. Alexander -
© J. Alexander Sentinel All rights reserved.

You may not, except with J. Alexander's express permission, distribute or alter the content.

MEMENTO MORI

"Born is Light, bred is Darkness.

Gifted is Life but all ends in Blackness"

The Mantle's Dialect, epitaph one. The Maker's first words to Humanity.

PROLOGUE

In the world of Reath one born without magic is said to not have been truly born at all. For in this world magic gives birth to everything. It builds empires and bestows crowns; but it can also reduce those to their knees. But this day was unlike any that had come before it in the last five thousand years. For something greater than 'magic' or 'power' had awoken; death and despair had finally become starved with a gorging hunger.

The Mantle teaches us that Humanity was the Maker's perfect imperfection. Among Gods, Titans, Dragons, and Demons, it was Humanity that would rule this world. With the gift of magic, it was Humanity that brought the other races to their knees and forced them into retreat.

Nevertheless, a truth that only the maker himself would dare remember must be revealed. Darkness will ever exist where there is light and the web of history must be unravelled.

As the Sun God begins his duty from his perch in the east, the Lights of Heaven crack the skies signalling the Maker's blessing for a new age to begin. The aurora stirring the wind high above the land and atop the mountain peak of Etnor to mark The Dawn.

The Third Age of man is coming to an end. Sealed away by a mystery equal to that of the cosmos, a young mage stirs and stimulates his mind in a dimension of his own creation. With the darkness on the horizon his eternal prison is soon to crack and shatter at their arrival.

CHAPTER ONE: THE BLACK CIRCLE

"It's only a little further, brother," said the adventurer, lifting his leg for the final step onto the peak of the snow-covered mountain. "The artifact is within our reach."

"This cold has been relentless! The winter here is…unnatural," replied his companion, eyes trekking cautiously from side to side in suspicion.

"The traces of magic here are overwhelming."

"I sense nothing ahead. One would have thought a legendary sword of such power could be sensed if it were nearby. But that just means I made the right choice asking my valiant brother to accompany me on this perilous quest, the reward for which would satisfy even an adventurer of your renown," spoke the first with a merry tone.

"Indeed. No ordinary adventurers would have survived the ascent. To think you would have attempted this quest alone troubles me," spoke the second. "Although, I'm not sure you or your companions' enchantments would have driven back the storm. It is not natural weather we faced today. This harsh and cold winter blizzard is the result of magic, a spell that has covered the entire mountain in winter."

"Magic cast over the entire mountain!? Is that even possible?" stated the first. "Even you couldn't do that."

Another six or seven adventurers joined the two who had already reached the expanse at the mountain's peak. Although they could not be heard over the sound of the snow storm, each breathed gasps of relief at their successful journey and cursed the rough blizzard that had bombarded and battered their day's ascent.

"Thank you, Ythar!" shouted one. "If not for your enchantments we would have lost more than just the two we did back there."

"Yes! Thanks, Ythar," said another.

"How strange," began the strongest of the adventurers, "the snow-storm is calming."

"Typical," the adventurers muttered in unison.

Ythar turned to his brother with caution. "Robin, don't let your guard down."

As the snow settled into the blanket already disturbed by their traipsing feet, they noticed that the peak of the mountain was not as vacant as they had thought a moment ago.

"What on Reath is that?" asked Robin. A bleak outline became more and more visible. They all looked upon a great sphere, one third embedded into the summit. It bore no markings or significant design on its surface to imply its origin. It was simply an all encompassing black akin to the darkness of the night sky.

"I have seen spheres like this in ancient text. They are a thing of myth. The aftermath of a spell used to seal away the most dangerous of creatures. A prison for a God," said Ythar, identifying the object with his vast knowledge.

"It's the result of a magic spell. A prison for what?" Ythar examined it further. "Whoever made this was seriously powerful, and whatever they made it for… they really didn't want it getting out."

"Hey guys, over here!" called another member of their group draped in furs and pelts from the other side of the sphere, "you need to take a look at this!"

"Oh…" Ythar took in the sight of the violent rupture in the prison's wall. "Whatever was in there isn't in there anymore." He moved closer to the rugged sides of the metal, running his fingers over the jagged edges as if reading words off a page of parchment.

"But this thing looks ancient," said Robin. "Whatever it was is surely long gone by now."

Ythar snapped his hand away from the sphere and looked at his brother in warning. "Who gave you this quest, Robin?"

"Huh? It was some Mantle emissary with more Aur than sense. Even for a legendary sword the reward would be enough to keep us rich for the rest of our lives," said Robin. "Why?"

"The seal on this prison was broken only moments before we arrived." Ythar tensed, his shoulders becoming heavy with unease.

Ythar was the first to notice. His abilities as a mage far surpassed that of his brother and the other adventurers with them. His senses could pick up on even the slightest changes in atmosphere. He could feel the weight of a gaze burning into his back. Robin and his comrades snapped to, spinning to join Ythar. They glared at the creature who had now revealed itself to them. It was no beast or monster with vying wings or gnashing teeth, but a simple, robed, humanoid figure with something at his side.

"A human? Who are you? How am I not able to sense your presence?" said Ythar swiftly to the one he had not sensed. "Are you the prisoner of this cell?"

Looking back at them through deep blue eyes the man did not speak but Ythar was aware of the danger. For a mage of his calibre to not sense the nearby stranger was more than troubling. He took heart that his swift mind and level head approach would make sure he would command this situation, as he had countless times before.

"This plaque on my chest-plate means I am an adventurer, and I am tasked with retrieving an artifact from this place. To raise your sword against us would result in serious consequences. You would be made an enemy of every guild in Ares. That said, we have no desire to engage in a meaningless conflict, so it is in everyone's best interest for you to hand over that sword. You are overwhelmingly outnumbered and outclassed; I'm sensing no magic from you at all." Ythar spoke politely and clearly, confident of his authority over the mysterious man.

The cloaked stranger made no advance. He merely raised his left hand slowly, revealing what looked to be an eastern style sword of ancient origin, his black fingertips clenched softly around it.

"T-that's it! That's the sword!" Robin pointed in accusation. "You had best hand that over to us."

"Robin, wait." Ythar raised his hand across his brother's path, "something about him is not right."

"Never mind that. We can take it from him by force." Robin began forward, ahead of his brother. The adventurers accumulated behind their temporary leader and awaited his orders, their eyes narrowing on the potential threat.

"That sword you carry is our quest to retrieve. We have lost some of our own today climbing this treacherous mountain. We will not leave without it. Hand it over to us and we will do you no harm," assured Ythar.

"This sword belongs to me. Possession of it is my right, and mine alone," spoke the man beneath his dark robes. His words did not hiss or dart across the wind to cut their ears with hostility or threat. They were, perhaps, the warmest thing they had felt today. In his voice was reason and coercion, the pitch of his tone danced toward them kinder than that of those sung from a lyre.

"I fear my words will not change your mind. We will have that blade, but worry not, I am not without mercy. I will not kill you," assured Ythar as he entered a stance for battle, unsettled at the magicless stranger before him.

"Perhaps…" began one of the adventurers, "maybe that blade truly is cursed, and that it will do us more harm than good to possess it."

"Are we not hardened to this cruel world?" began Ythar inspirationally. "Curses and creatures mean nothing before the might that is Humanity. We have come this far, steel yourselves!"

"But I will!" stated Robin as he began forward.

"No!" Roared Ythar, the realisation of their folly all too late.

A moment had not passed. Neither Ythar nor Robin had so much as blinked. What could have been a man, a God, a Demon or just a wretched nightmare now stood in Robin's next stride with the sword it held resting against the adventurer's forehead.

"I-I-I," Robin gasped, "I-I c-can't m-m-move."

The sword that was barely pressing against his forehead remained in its sheath. Whilst Robin could not sense the magic or the presence of the creature that stood before him, he could sense the overwhelming weight of death. There was one, irrefutable, undeniable fact: if he were to move, he would die.

Perhaps it was the blow from the sheathed sword that defeated Robin, or perhaps it was the pure, unfathomable realisation that had the stranger put in an ounce more effort into his attack he would have been obliterated from existence. The difference in their power was so great Robin posed less threat to the mysterious stranger than that of the smallest insect.

"Robin!" Ythar launched himself erupting with his magic power. "Lightning magic: Storm of the raging God!" From the aura of magic that surrounded Ythar's clenched fist, a golden-yellow clasp of lightning engulfed his hand and plummeted towards the stranger. It vapourised nothing but air and snow. Ythar caught sight of the black after-trail of the creature as it dispatched each adventurer with ease using only its fist and feet. The stranger now stood between the jet-black prison and Ythar.

"Do not worry. They are not dead," said the stranger warmly, showing Ythar the same courtesy he himself had been offered.

"Nothing," Ythar stammered, "nothing at all. No magic. No power. No presence! What *are* you?"

"A simple human. Nothing more, nothing less," said the stranger.

"Impossible! No human can move that fast without magic! And that sword you carry, the longer I am in its presence the more I sense it consuming me. I am sure now, that if I were to have it, it's power would be mine! I can hear it calling out to me. I can hear it calling out to me! To wield its power for my own! Whatever the cost, I must have it!"

"I am not sure. No one besides me has ever held this Shirasaya," stated the stranger.

"But it calls to me. It whispers to me through magic. It beckons me to wield it. I must have it! GIVE IT TO ME!" demanded Ythar uncharacteristically as a lust for power began to consume him.

"There is no coming back from the Shirasaya's taint. It is a burden only I can shoulder," said the stranger. "But if you think yourself strong enough to wield it, come."

Ythar launched himself like a rabid bear, less refined and masterful than before. He poured his magic into his strikes, each one blasting the mountainside to smithereens as they failed to connect with its target. With one hand lightly holding his sheathed sword, the stranger skilfully dodged, deflected and danced around the powerful adventurer's attacks. A simple punch to Ythar's abdomen was enough to force the formidable adventurer to his knees in submission and hurl a tankard's worth of blood from his mouth.

"Such great power and such beautiful magic. You truly are a magnificent adventurer," declared the stranger as he looked down to his opponent free of hostility or threat. "I hope once I have saved the world, we can have another battle."

Ythar hurled again, but this time it was more a hurl of pure and utter shock as he began to slump from his knees into unconsciousness. "Wha-?"

"I sensed the waking of a great evil some moons ago," said the stranger as he looked up to the deep, blue sky. "The Dawn approaches and the Old Gods rise. This world has gorged on magic for too long. You ask me what I am? I am the curse of all things in this world. I am the one who stands alone from all the races. I am the watcher of the darkness in the night. I am the Sentinel."

CHAPTER TWO: ARES

Beneath the vast blue skies of Reath where the gleam of the two moons can be seen even in the glorious daylight. A beautiful, ambient shine caresses Reath in its embrace, igniting hope and vanquishing despair across all kingdoms. In the middle of this world, between vast seas and great mountains where the moons converge to bless the land with their subtle embrace, lies the great province of Ares. It is in this land where the glitter of the moon enriches all it touches. Imbued with this pure Moon Dust the crops grow fiercer and plentiful, the waters run faster and stronger with minerals pulled from the earth and life flourishes.

Ares is an isolated island, but its size is so large people once thought nothing was beyond its shores. With the acceleration of technology through magic and invention, the possibilities became endless for both Humanity and the demi-human races they created. But Ares was only the beginning. Beyond it, over a sea whose depths could submerge a Titan whole and swallow kingdoms if the mood so wished it, was a whole other world with mountains that touched the sky and forests so dense and full of life one could live an entire mortal lifetime without identifying all the species of creatures and plants that lived within it.

Ares was split into four kingdoms after the first age of men. Eos, the central and most influential of the four, shares its name with the capital city, The Capital of all of Ares. The Northern lands, cold and hardened, inherits its name from the stoic Ice Titans of Old: Erba. To the East, the Kingdom of Haraura, the country of slaves and crime that connects to the eastern world. And to the South, where the farmland stretches for eternity in the most beautiful landscape of all, the kingdom of Myphos.

In Eos, the scurries of tattered boots and bare feet fill the emptiness of the back lanes and alleyways as the street urchins scamper to safety, their day's haul of bread, fruit and finery swept away by the nimbleness of their fingers. Surrounded by the tall, imposing stone walls they were like mice among remnants of old shops and canopies that lined the old streets. Anything to line an empty stomach and prepare for another night in the vast, unpredictable city.

Another slow and uneventful day would pass for the guardsmen unlucky enough to be posted on the city's walls where presence is scarce. Even the birds rarely dare to fly above the battlements for they too would fear their height. Coming and going beneath them would be all manner of creatures, human and demi-human alike. Traders, merchants, travellers, slaves, adventurers and all sorts of magical beasts capable of human speech were welcomed by the great city. Turning away guests was against their custom.

But not all was vast and imposing and strict and established. Well, actually, the Mantle was exactly that. A faith built upon the assurance that the Maker loves humanity above all else, and will return to us once more during a certain prophesied event. Those who dedicate themselves to the Mantle to become sisters and priests vow a lifetime of devotion, celibacy and faith to the Maker above all else but not all the rooms within their temple are warm and loving. Adorned in habits and veils the mothers of the Mantle are mothers to all. Through their kindness and their wisdom they serve their Father within his walls, but also journey both near and far to teach the values of humanity throughout the world. The delicate and forbidden smile of a sister, can light up the darkest of streets in Eos and guide those who need it to salvation.

Ares, where the first civilisation of humanity was built, held a connection to magic that man would never understand, and so it became the centre of the known world. This great kingdom has grown far from what its founding ancestors created it to be. As with all things exposed to humanity it slowly became corrupt and immoral where the strong prosper and the weak are trod underfoot.

Humanity is weak. Gods, Dragons, Titans, Demons, and the beasts of their creation crawl out of exile in answer to the call of the deep taint. Soon an unimaginable cataclysm will devour all life in this world. For this is not a world where the ordinary lives, only the spectacular and bizarre, the unimaginable and the profound all exist in this illustrious world. Just as it did a millennia ago, a true darkness emerges to consume all that the Maker once loved.

On its West coast, where the sun sets, lies an enormous peninsula that protrudes the vast Western sea with condescension. Standing for almost five thousand years, the Capital city of the Kingdom of Eos stands strong surrounded by its impenetrable walls of stone. A centripetal hub for trading, questing, and mage-craft, the greatest country in the world has built the greatest capital. Home to the most powerful and influential merchants, Barons, Lords, Mages, Military Leaders, and researchers, Eos commands respect. The origin of the world's oldest and most prominent religion has allowed the temples of the holy church, The Mantle, to cast their teachings and beliefs far and wide from within Eos. The walls of the city itself whisper the words of their Dialect so that all feel welcomed by the Maker.

Its most prominent feature, more impending than its golden walls that stretch to the skies or the beautiful women who work the night and call Eos their home, is a monument that emanates power and dominance above all else. The Temple of Nexus, home to the all-powerful Sentinels, the strongest warriors and mages of Humanity. The Sentinels policed the Kingdoms of Ares and beyond with the ancient power that humans used in their struggles against darkness during the dawn of the First Age. The temple takes the form of a large, square tower around five hundred paces wide on each of its four faces, stretching into the sky as if to pierce the heavens as its walls constrict into a spear head. Even the Kingdoms in the skies would find themselves anchored if they dared snare the temple's tip. Its enormity reached out to all in Ares. Here, deep in their gilded halls and resting in seats of power on a level far above the ground, eleven of the current twelve Sentinel Heleics, the Dodecatheon, discuss their looming future.

CHAPTER THREE: THE KINGDOM OF THE SENTINELS

The Hall of Council was vast, adorned with such jewels and gems that no sum of aur could possibly justify their beauty. Empty suits of armour surrounded the room looming with their immenseness, like castles in form, yet gentle, with a scent of preservation and protection. The finest torches perched from the walls housing fierce cobalt blue flames that roared with magic; they would not waiver at the touch of wind or water. The unmistakable emblem that represented the Sentinel order is embossed around the room, two perched dragons, back to back, with their wings displayed mightily. Housed around the room in various forms, the emblem was also masterfully etched into the centerpiece of each Sentinel's chest-plate.

The large twelve-sided table received all but one of the Sentinels, including the twelfth Heleic who held the ultimate title of Arcon. The table was thick and unbreakable, able to withstand anything but a titan's stride. To convene here was the greatest of honours.

"The magic you are all too keen to damn and dismiss is one of great importance to humanity. It could be the tool to our salvation, our chance to rise above even the greatest threats of Reath," spoke a velvety voice lined with coercion as the sunlight roared through the stained-glass windows onto his shimmering, silver armour.

"Need we recant the Tale of Ankou? The great champions of humanity whose lives built the very foundations of human civilisation? The very magic bestowed upon us by our ancestors to preserve humanity so that it will not perish?!" spoke the Arcon, leader of the Sentinels.

The young Heleic spoke again but this time with more rasp and defiance in his tone, "Preserve? Perish? We are Humanity! We are the guides of this world. We must lead humanity to a brighter future. To power and to wisdom! To survive? That is not humanity's place. We have slayed Gods, felled Titans, hunted Dragons with our very power. All those who sit at this table have accomplished unimaginable feats!" he exclaimed as he began to wander the table in awe and admiration, decorating his peers in praise before turning his attention back to his Arcon. "Our leader, the great Arcon himself, who guides the people of humanity's first Kingdom and builds our renown across all the world, slew one of the three heads of the mighty Dragon God: Kitanu. You did not merely survive. You paved a way forward for your people and inspired them with strength and power," he finished passionately.

"The line we walk is already too thin, Thusien. We are not equal to the Sentinels of old who founded this order. We are not like the tyrannical king who ruled Ares after the great war. We must not think ourselves to be equal to a force that we cannot comprehend. Our ancestors made that mistake and humanity barely survived. What you speak of is a matter for the Maker and the Maker alone to decide," spoke the Arcon.

The great room was silent as the ten Heleics surrounding their dodecagonal table, fixed their attention around the Arcon. They saw him as the most powerful man who existed in all of Ares. They were unable to take their eyes off him so as to not incur his wrath.
The Sentinel Arcon, their leader: Arcon Dariel Kalus, the very

Sentinel who battled the Three Dragon Gods of the southern province. To look upon him in this world was not something that was done alone by the eyes. No. To look upon a creature of power was something else here, in the world of Reath.

The eyes would show little more than flesh and frame. Instead one has a feeling, one that stems from the head as the heart channels a power through your chest and into a weight on your shoulders. A sense that you look upon a creature that knows only to kill. Primal instincts that warn you that your very being is threatened. Fear that freezes your soul, the weight of your limbs unbearable for your body to burden. The Arcon had a signature etched into his very presence; His unique magic power. One accustomed to battle and wisdom can identify them with ease in another. The trained see more than the untrained. These men, the most proficient mages of the Sentinels, their names known across all the world, awaited the Arcon's next words to answer the quandary of their peers.

"Thusien, your knowledge of magic is unlike that of any I have ever seen," the Arcon spoke with grandeur as he rose to his feet and began to encompass the table, all eyes following him as he did. "Mages from all across this world have come to seek your counsel on matters beyond their comprehension, myself included," he gestured to his own star metal platebody. "That is why you, of all people, should know that the conversion of one's life energy in the form of 'blood magic' is a taboo that we, as the Sentinels of Reath, cannot condone". He spoke firmly as he completed his circulation and rested upon his own great throne with his hefty arms. "It is our duty, our *privilege* to protect humanity from such darkness and those who would wield it. We are human. To believe otherwise would truly disgrace us in the eyes of the Maker. To give in to such temptation would endure a hardship for humanity that would not allow them to exist on Reath any longer."

The Arcon, blessed with this power, looked through the largest window in their hall, far into the distance, with a knowledge he had yet to share. "There is a darkness coming for us all. If we do not unite under one allegiance of humanity, not even the Sentinels will survive...therefore," he drew on his immense power to deliver his verdict, the walls and the ground trembling as his voice carried through the dense air so that they could hear, "this council will not be swayed by its advantages as we cannot ever accept the cost for such power. I hereby prohibit you from conducting any research on this matter and that any accumulated evidence or research be handed over to the council for review, immediately." With his decree, the Arcon looked directly at Thusien, burning past the simple concept of vision and deep into his very soul. "Do not evade your duty. Your time is almost upon us."

"Very well," said the Heleic with a downcast look, quickly forced into a smile. "I shall remove the idea from my mind and terminate any leads. Thank you, Arcon Kalus, for collecting the council from far and wide to discuss this matter." Thusien bowed respectfully as the council disbanded from their great table.

"Thusien, a word if I may?" The great Arcon beckoned his young protégé as the other council members began to remove themselves.

"Of course!" replied Thusien.

Arcon Kalus was a giant of a man, his long grey hair and beard masking his many facial scars. Though old, somewhere in his late eighties, this colossal figure had the physique of a beastly young man. His silver armour was trimmed with gold, as all Sentinel attire is, concealing his muscular frame. His chest and pauldrons protruded into the air with their enormity. His dragon-beard cloak rustled to the ground. Kalus gestured to Thusien to proceed ahead of him, the two being the last to exit the Hall of Council and to traverse the magical walkways down into the main Great Hall of the Nexus. The two began their walk through the temple.

"You know I must show no leniency when the council is unanimous," Kalus began. "It is never my intention to bludgeon beliefs into you, and because of that I have allowed you to pursue a future in magic in whichever field you desire. But I fear that this exposure to the vast knowledge of this world has prompted you to delve into the deepest secrets of magic from which no man should ever hope to surface." Kalus rested his hand on his young protégé's shoulder,"please, now that it has been dismissed, direct your efforts towards teachings that we can praise. Let us reverberate your words through our halls so that the world can hear them and be lifted by them. Now, more than ever, darkness must stay outside of our walls."

"It is true that I have searched for the answers to our power, perhaps now I should lay those questions to rest in light of your visions of impending darkness…" Thusien looked away so as to avoid the Arcon's eyes. The two walked in contemplative silence through the Hall of Echoes, where trophies of their history stood proud. The skull of the great Titan U'ruk who ravaged the lands for decades, the swords of Tiberius the conqueror who drew his ambitions on laying siege to the whole Continent as he brought his armies from the west. One of the heads of Kitanu, one of the fiercest dragons to ever terrorise the land from the skies.

"It is together that we are stronger, and together that we rule," the Arcon said as the two prepared to separate. "Your power will soon far surpass mine. Your generation of mages will be a great and powerful one. Once I have passed on all of my teachings to you, it is no doubt that you will become the next Arcon in my place. There are few contenders but I believe that in your care, both you and Vosk will drive the Sentinels to greater heights. It is a shame he could not be here for your meeting."

"It is as you say, Kalus," Thusien said, the master deceiver, "You have not yet taught me all I have needed to learn," he finished, eyes widening slightly. The two parted ways as the younger Heleic was joined by his disciple, who lurked in the dark shadows in wait for his master. Silently the two exited the great halls and began for the lower chambers of the order.

"I only pray that it is not too late," Kalus murmured in the wake of his one day successor. "For this darkness to breed in our very walls would bring doom on all the world."

CHAPTER FOUR: AT THE MERCY OF KINGS

Crisp air breathed through frozen winter grass upon the hallowed earth of great Ares. Sunlight lowered its warmth onto the bustling city to relieve it from winter's cold breath. The Sentinel Arcon sat in a spectacular throne forged of the same mysterious metal Sentinel armour was created from. Before him sat an audience of the King's representatives of the land of Ares.

A king means a great deal. Land, power, influence, riches and much more came with the title. It could be heredity by rule of succession unique to the predecessors' will, but more prominently bestowed by the Mantle, the holy church of Ares. As the province of Ares was so vast, no one person could govern it all, no matter how great their power. Around two millennia ago, Ares was split into four kingdoms, and a king was made to reign in each, all under the guise of equality. In recent years tensions have built and friction has amassed, but only mere sparks have yet to scorch the eye.

Representatives of kings from North, South and East knelt before the Sentinel King as they had done in his halls a hundred times before. In Eos, home to the all powerful Sentinels, the King of the West ruled above them all.

"We have substantial evidence of Southern Kingdom raids all along our coast lines, my lord! Some attacks have taken place as deep into the mainland as Bryn!" spoke the representative of the Eastern Kingdom, The Kingdom of Haraura.

"It is all lies, my lord," protested the representative of the Southern Kingdom, the Kingdom of Myphos. "They spin desperate tales to conceal their own treachery! We have had villages burned! Crops and wagons for trade stolen, agricultural towns wiped off the very face of Reath with nothing remaining other than tales. The Eastern Kingdom seeks to weaken our forces in preparation for invasion."

"We, too, can substantiate Myphos' claim," said the Northern Kingdom, the Kingdom of Erba. "Countless assaults on coastal outposts combined with sieges on trade routes and missing persons, all with evidence that Haraura is to blame."

The three representatives were men of power and status themselves. Asked to represent their respective kingdoms by their king personally, they must be competent enough to defend themselves on travels and educated enough to conduct with the fathering Kingdom of Eos. All trained as mages and warriors they knelt before an exhausted Arcon in the plain, grey armour that represented their ruling house; before a Sentinel, all armour was bland.

"Rest assured your evidence will be reviewed," the burdened Arcon replied. "If the Kingdom of Haraura is indeed committing these crimes against our united kingdoms they will be punished accordingly, and both we and the Pontifex will review the position of the throne. But remember..." None of the three emissaries' dared interject, "I am not your king. You are separate kingdoms and free to act as you please, but within reason to your neighbours. I will not order your king's summon. Diplomacy must prevail before any action can be taken. If word comes to me that retaliation has come absent of my judgement, not even your kings will protect you from Eos and all the Sentinels within. You are to return and inform your rulers that special care needs to be applied to your neighbouring kingdoms. For when you need them most, your underhanded treachery will have cost you a price in which you cannot hope to recover."

"Y-yes, my Lord!" They all responded swiftly to his powerful words before bowing respectfully, turning for their escape.

This time, it was the Arcon's turn to meet with someone in their own throne room, an experience rarely allowed and granted. A day in the life of the Sentinel Arcon is a tasking one, but no audience within Ares is as arduous as this. Of the millions of people in all of Ares, he would take caution with his words around his next appointment. Away from the Nexus temple, he found himself in the holy church that stood almost as prominent as the Sentinel Order, overflowing with influence and faith.

The Arcon met with the wise Pontifex of the Mantle, a man believed to be personally held in the Makers embrace. This spectacular temple of the divine and holy was the fruit of the Mantle, the predominant religion of Reath worshipping no immortals or false Gods, but the one, true Maker. Although spectacular and magnificent, something deep in its foundations twitched in the eye, suspicious of its benevolence.

"The Maker watches over us all, Kalus," spoke the plump, middle-aged man with an air of all-encompassing knowledge and purpose.

"I only pray that in his warm embrace the darkness dares not surface, Piaus. I have cast my sight into the flame of our Nexus and seen the great darkness that is to come. As it was aeons ago, it has been prophesied once more."

"Prophecies and Myths hold no flame to the burning sun that is our Maker," Piaus gestured above himself. "Whatever it is to reveal itself, trust that he watches over us and with his gaze, guides humanity," faith present in every word.

The Arcon sighed. "Perhaps you are right. Should my faith in the Maker's support outweigh my fears of mankind?"

"The Mantle exists to serve our maker and in our faith we are rewarded with his guiding light. Alas, the church cannot hope to undertake the task whilst the Sentinels question their purpose. As you have a path, we too, have our own. Which, however much you may wish to deny, may not have us walking down toward the same fate as one another," the Pontifex spoke with an unwavering wisdom, the force of which stung at the Arcon's ears.

"You are quite right," Kalus said. "Through the darkness I can sense a great evil on our horizon, yet my vision, cast so far into the unknown, has lost the ability to see the space around me. I comb my mind over troubling matters in our own home and beneath it all, I cannot sense what it is that fills my mind with unease. That is why I have come here, Piaus. Do you feel it? Not in the distance over the horizon, but here, beneath our feet?" Kalus stripped himself of all authority before the Pontifex as he beseeched the other man..

"I know why you have come here," Piaus spoke softly, gazing around the room. "One spends so much time in the darkness that when he finally sees the light it is blinding. So much so that the light can be interpreted as evil and that darkness is good."

Piaus summoned into his right hand a pure golden flame. "The Maker gifted me with golden light, so that I may help all those consumed by darkness. It is also why most believe me to be so close to the Maker."

The emblem forged by the light was so bright it cut at Kalus' eyes with its authority and divinity. Kalus turned himself to examine the emblem unique to the mantle that could be found all over the Pontifex's garb. Mounted in the centre of the Pontifex's mozzetta that draped over his pale soutane and on the tips of his stole was the emblem of the undefinable, All knowing, All-seeing eye. Radiant and pure, accompanied by his graceful and divine hands, the symbol was unique to the Mantle.

"I assure you; I only see darkness beyond these walls, not within them," Piaus said, a faint smile creeping across his face in an attempt to comfort the Arcon. "The two moons are upon us and the magic is rich tonight. It will be a clear evening for thought and quandary."

"We may not always see eye to eye, but I always find comfort in your wisdom, Piaus," Kalus said. "How do the defences of Eos fare at this time of year? Thorough inspections have been completed on our end."

Deep below the City defences both a phantasmal and arcane etching of magic runes and energy encircled the vast city. This was known as a magic circle but, of course, on an enormous scale summoned by a huge collection of mages.

"The defences of this City have never gone neglected on our part. The magic circles and seals below us have been restored and renewed for another year, at least. It is one of the few joint enterprises that Sentinels and the Mantle share since our forefathers separated them aeons ago. We take pride in such stewardship," Piaus announced. "There has also been rumour that you have gathered your high council from far and wide. Is this in preparation for the upcoming Congregation of Kingdoms?" asked Piaus curiously.

"There are few proposals that need to be heard by their ears," the Arcon said, "but there is need for the Kings of Ares, the Sentinel Heleics and the Pontifex himself to gather and discuss the future. In the coming weeks I hope to accomplish this."

"I see. It is always troubling to see the great Heleics of the Mantle gathering. The whole world follows your movements. The eyes of the people are perhaps the keenest. They worry something is awry."

"And so they should," Kalus nodded. "For if there is darkness to come the Sentinels cannot hope to defeat it alone."

The two pondered each other's words and then bid each other farewell, the Arcon bowing respectfully and the Pontifex with a simple nod in response. The Arcon bowed only in respect of their Maker through the one chosen to be closest to him. The Arcon turned from the Pontifex and left.

In Ares, the only human that stood near in stature to the Arcon was the Pontifex, but Piaus' influence and scheme ran far further and deeper than any of that of the Sentinels. In the Mantle's birthplace of Ares, religion has always been prominent and overpowering. In terms of pure overwhelming presence in this world The Mantle was superior, with billions of followers stretching across all of Reath. There was no greater religion.

The Sentinel continued onwards for quite some time, the marbled floor a sea of stone intricacy disappearing beneath his long strides. The Mantle went about its daily business, flourishing from the donations from the wealthy of Reath. Anyone who wished to have their sins forgiven or have the maker watch over them in life and after death could simply pay their way to a kind afterlife. This was a place of God. Children decorated the halls with good deeds; matrons and priests served as strong as they could. The Arcon's daunting presence was almost lost in these halls, met with nothing other than soft smiles and warm gazes. His animosity stripped from him he was just another man in the community of the Maker. The great gilded doors of the temple swung wide, inviting the gullible and desperate into its halls to seek salvation from the maker.

The Arcon left and began his journey back to his own great temple. As he walked across the expensive, intricate cobble as hard as dragon-scale and just as rare, he pondered his exact purpose at this very time in history. Upon these great walls, where the entire city expands and runs away as if it stood as a Kingdom in itself, he trailed in thought and became lost in his own mind until he realised he had indeed found his way home.

Deep beneath the Sentinel Chambers in the Nexus Temple, stone stairs spiralled downwards. Where the cheers and accomplishments of the halls above could not reach, cold, ancient catacombs lay. Forgotten centuries ago by a heroic Arcon, one of the great Heleics prepared an ancient ritual of death, power, and corruption. A ritual that would change the world forever leaving scars too deep to ever be forgotten.

Thusien held immense focus on the ritual and paid little attention to his loyal disciple as he neared completion of his preparations. They were in a large room with a rough stone flooring. This ancient catacomb was forgotten and unused for hundreds of years before Thusien stumbled upon it to discover its dark secrets. Torches mounted on the walls gave light whilst near the ceiling there were magical flames of cobalt blue that lit the space in its entirety.

The room was tall and long, decorated with artefacts and bookcases that stretched from one extremity to the other. Each gave a thorough historic account of the Sentinels' history from when the order was conceived. Dilapidated and covered in centuries of dust and cobwebs, disturbed only by Thusien's keen fingers, there were texts from kingdoms far beyond Ares where humans had made homes in dense jungle so hot there was no need for clothes and lands so dry the earth was like a golden sea beneath your feet which ships still sailed and yeh one could drown in the absence of water. This knowledge had accumulated here in the old Nexus library long ago when the

Sentinels were revered as champions and saviours. Now, with their history forgotten or too hard to believe, they are nothing more than peacekeepers and false kings.

"Kalus has returned."

Thusien looked up at his disciple, "He is here. It is time, Raiku." He returned his attention back to the artifact in front of him.

"What is it?" The apprentice asked, a young but powerful Sentinel mage.

"I do not know. There is no record of its true name," Thusien replied. "It is no tool of humanity and I sense…huge amounts of power emanating from its core. It has spoken to me and whispered its truth. A truth that I must answer. Lingering, deep within its heart I know that it's secrets will give us a power that we have never imagined."

The object was about waist high and perched on a substantial iron pedestal. It appeared to be very heavy but also effortless to physically lift. It resembled a timer that one would flip upside down whilst baking a cake but differed slightly. Where the glass would normally pinch there was an ethereal black orb and the liquid was a scarlet red. It looked to be blood, but it lacked the viscosity; it seemed much heavier and more gloopy but worryingly, above all, felt…alive.

"The preparations are complete," Thusien said, summoning himself. "All that is left is the incantation from the pages of the old text." His sacrificial blood dripped from his hands to the stone floor, the archaic runes around the pedestal revealing themselves drawing power from the forbidden magic. Thusien stood firmly, in a stance of power, his eyes closed to seal off the vision of the world. As he concentrated, he began to cast his mind into the void to look upon all the magic he knew, his catastrophic power building.

He released the power. The artefact responded to his call,

erupting with a crimson red aura that engulfed it. The liquid inside began to flow. Thusien remained still, his blood and body almost at its limit. With every cell in his being, he poured his life's energy outward at the artifact and the ground beneath them trembled. Ares itself shook so that all could feel it. Menacing and evil, the incredible power was horrific.

To the normal people of the city of Eos, it was as if a dragon perched atop the great temple, glaring down upon the city in pure hatred, destruction, and death, Those beneath it were held hostage at the mercy of infernal dragon fire with a pure sense of hopelessness and despair consuming them. Cowering, the people could not will their bodies to move as the pressure of impending doom came upon them.

To those whose mind's and magic's were trained, they could feel Thusien, one of the twelve Sentinel Heleics, become much more than a mortal man. There was not a soul in all of Ares that did not feel the air quiver, the wind escape, and the ground tremble. As the magic concentrated around a focused point, the people could only stand fixed to the spot as the pressure pinned their very beings in fear. The books of the library shook violently in their oak homes around the walls of the laboratory, the papers rattling furiously as If caught in a storm. The vials of liquid clattered, and the apparatus began to crumble as Thusien exerted his magic power into one, focused spell.

Finally, the artifact absorbed all his power and erupted in a pure, sinister magical energy. Like a hurricane pouring into his body, Thusien raised his hands either side of him, the power building with every millimetre they moved, until, finally, he held them outstretched. As Reath itself began to halt its rotation, he brought them together in a mighty blow. From his hands emanated the deep red musk. Like a rushing wind, it flew like a wave from him, outwards across the world, and all became black.

The spell poured throughout the temple rushing and crashing off the walls, blasting through the heavy oak doors and collided with the warriors that occupied it from top to base. The musk hunted some fifty Sentinels within their sacred walls like prey, binding them as it began to consume them, their skin peeling and cracking at the exposure to the tremendous cursed magic. Their bones began to splinter from within, bursting the vital streams of blood inside them. As their skin became like brittle parchment, they finally fell to the floor, lifeless, their souls claimed by Thusien's ancient spell.

As it passed, the air cleared and returned to its natural state. With a grand total of around three hundred Sentinels in all of Ares, fifty, including all of the present Sentinel Helencs, had been consumed and destroyed.
But those who remained were not unaffected. The intention of the spell was to enhance, using the life energy of those Thusien had deemed unworthy. What remained were no longer Sentinels.

The animals of Eos began to settle once more and the people of the capital found themselves confused but unharmed as they rose to their feet.

Thusien breathed in as if he was taking in thirty-five years of air in one go. What he had done was something unimaginable. But what stood in the catacombs now was no longer human. He had become…something else.

"The Sentinels are mine now," and with that, the golden temple turned black.

Its pearlescent shine vanished into an endless darkness becoming one with the night. Strong stone walls wailed as if the mortar that held them had withered and collapsed. The cobalt blue glow of the Sentinel flames that had resided in the plinths for centuries had now turned a scarlet red. Huge doors flew off their hinges and crossed the room, crushing through the old wood furniture and apparatus as the Arcon poured through in a fit of unquellable rage.

Raiku was quick to intercept him with his two legendary daggers that housed themselves horizontally on his lower back. With his new, enhanced power he took it upon himself to test his strength against the strongest and most tremendous of all the Sentinels.

"What have you done!?" the Arcon roared as he approached. High above them, in the great hall, the Sentinels congregated in mass, summoned by their new leader. But there were those who had survived and not been affected by Thusien's spell. Fused into inhuman creatures, the corrupted Sentinels ravaged at their pure peers. Any of those within the walls that had not been corrupted by Thusien's taint were butchered hopelessly. They could not stand against their enhanced brethren. Bloodied and sinister, the corrupted Sentinels understood their new purpose as the ground beneath them began to shake. In their very souls they became a slave to their new leaders' will.

The Arcon burst through the floor and emerged into the great hall flying past his throne and crashing into the star metal vault door behind it, before falling to the ground. From the crater in the centre of the room, Thusien and Raiku floated upwards with an aura of crimson red surrounding them, landing on the ground. The Arcon raised himself and recovered from the previous attack to face the entire enhanced Sentinel Order alone.

Thusien raised a hand softly and with his magic, repaired the damage to the temple effortlessly, placing each stone back in its rightful place as if it was never disturbed.

"I was sure to create a sensory link to the members of the council meeting during our discussions. Without them, I don't think I could have released enough power to activate the artifact," Thusien said.

"What have you done?! Where did you find such a thing?!" roared the Arcon, desperate for answers and consumed by a hopeless sense of betrayal.

"It was always here," Thusien said. "It has always called to me, ever since I was a boy taking his first steps in these halls. It has whispered to me since, inviting me to find it. Only now, on this day, could it have been activated."

The Arcon was stricken with grief. This entire plan had been in motion for so long and he could not sense it. His failure had cost the kingdom untold misery and he was unlikely to live through to remedy it. "I have…failed you," Kalus said to the usurper.

"No," Thusien said, "I will indeed take your throne, Kalus, but we will become so much more!"

The Arcon's eyes widened. He summoned an enormous sword to his right hand that looked impossible to lift. In his left he summoned a great mace, capable of crushing even the mightiest of creatures. The corrupted Sentinels were already upon their former leader, their undeniable power amplified by Thusien's blood magic ritual.

But the Arcon was not only for show. He tore through them with conviction and chivalry to cleave a path to his intended target. With the ground crushed beneath his advancements it was truly a sight to behold, the might of the Sentinel Arcon; he should not be underestimated.

His colossal mace, with its five outward protrusions high in the air, hurtling down towards Thusien to crush him in his entirety. It stopped, dead, the force of it creating a gust around them. Raiku had stepped before his master and caught the blow with one, effortless hand, his Sentinel power released with a deep crimson glow of aura erupting from his eyes.

"I see you still do not understand, Kalus," Thusien said triumphantly. "We are the true Sentinels," he whispered as Raiku sent the Arcon flying backwards with a blow, crashing into the great Vault doors once more.

"Even with all this power… The Vault will not answer your call," Kalus said, blood creeping down from his mouth, his ruptured insides bursting. "It will only answer to my soul."

"You are right," agreed Thusien, approaching him. "But you must understand now, I have the power to strip that authority from your very being." With that he reached outwards and began to consume the Arcon's very form, twisting and snapping him as his life poured out of him and leapt into Thusien's soul.

With the Arcon dead and the purging of the remaining uncorrupted Sentinels, Thusien stepped over his former master's lifeless body and reached out his hand. The great Vault doors, who answered only to the Arcon, began to grind open.

CHAPTER FIVE: THE YOUNG MAGE

A deep blanket of snow suffocated the autumn leaves into the cold earth, allowing only starved trees and bold shrubbery to escape its grasp. The night covered the landscape like a veil, the golden stars looking at Reath with sorrow, weeping their golden tears across the cosmos. The twisted treeline was scarred of battle and pain through its years of unrelenting torment. The skies were grey and darkened by the evil that had manifested itself slowly in the absence of justice and peace.

Atop the great peak of Etnor, the great mountain of the south, a strange, young man finds himself unwelcomed by nature as it twists and turns away from his presence. In his wake, at the very summit of Etnor where only the strongest of creatures could overcome the harsh winds and perilous freezing temperatures, behind a blizzard of snow looked to be some form of mechanical, metal sphere. This impervious and concealing device had been destroyed outwards with what looked to be a huge blast of magic that had strewn shrapnel and debris across the top of the mountain.

From the battle that had followed, the mountain had suffered further at the hands of the powerful magic wielded by humans. But, as the young mage descended the northern face of the mountain the unnatural cold and snow began to melt away, as if the eternal winter there had finally ended.

The days soon passed as the young man walked north, cloaked in deep black with the ancient sword he carried wrapped in old, discoloured cloth draped over his back fastened by a small, fraying rope. As if he were drawn to something, he paced evenly on an uninterrupted journey towards, where weeks ago, the great Temple of the Sentinels had fallen and their purpose in this world changed forever. Now, no longer the stewards and protectors of humanity in the realm, but the strikers of fear and oppression to any who stood in the way of their progress.

In this crisp, cold winter, nature itself began to beg the young man for relief as he walked uneventfully through the countryside like a vagrant at a passing monarch's feet. Although the man was dark and mysterious the birds soon began to bathe him in symphony. The willows and wisps and fairy's and spirits danced in the wind beneath the sunlight as his presence allowed for such. Whilst it was true that this young mage carried upon his shoulders an unbearable weight that would surely lead to death and destruction, they found that harmony returned in his presence. The sun shone its magnificent rays a little brighter and the skies above smiled through with a gleeful grin. He asked nothing of nature, but it demanded everything from him.

Just ahead, a little in the distance, the cobbled countryside path merged into that of the Capital's southern trade route between Eos and Myphos, a branch of the enormous tree of commerce that held the financial powers of Ares together. The young man caught sight of a small farming village, the sun cleverly showing the last of its light on its simple thatched roofs as if a sign for him to head toward.

Straw lay scattered across the derelict gatehouse, bulging through the windows and seeping through the doorways of what was once a place to greet the entrance of merchants and their beast drawn wagons. The cobbled ground relaxed as he paced across it with his gentle steps, his soles warm from the journey. He stopped before he came to the first building and analysed his thoughts.

'Hmm?' he thought to himself as the sun guided him before relinquishing its light bearing tasks to that of the torches of flame that protruded the stone walls. The oxidised bars slid roughly against their bound locks as workmen and shop owners closed their establishments for the night, leaving the streets quiet and the noise to a dull background din.

The village itself had seen better days, with its dormant temple and its trampled walk-ways, it seemed almost like an excavation site. The few buildings that stood looked as if they were soon to join their fallen brethren and be reclaimed by the earth. A dull roar echoed from the top of the path. 'The Bulls B lls' was the gracious lettering above the double oak doors that labelled the tavern, the convenient absence of the 'a' from the sign seemed appropriate to its fellow, rundown establishments. The young man wandered towards the tavern, victim to its inviting roars. As he climbed the three cracked steps of slabs to the door, he revealed an arm from beneath his long, dark cloak to make the sacrifice, his black fingernails wrapping around the iron handle. The dull roar had evolved into a more uncontrollable cataclysm of shouts, moans, grunts, and music. The Heavy door slowly opened as the noise poured out through the gap as if a fleeing beast had just narrowly missed him. Upon his entrance he remained unnoticed as the horde of drunken patrons ignored the new arrival as they continued to sing the tale of 'Borak, The Crusher'.

"He took his wench and then behence, came crashing down the harbour!"

As Borak's hometown it became obvious of his fame. The walls were littered with paintings of him being showered in gold and gifted women and farm animals for his many heroic achievements. The fact he was tortured to insanity and then castrated with his own hammer 'Thud' bore no indentation on his legend as they celebrated his adventures some forty years after his gruesome death. A giant of a man, who stood at almost seven paces tall, Borak towered most men. It then became apparent that one of Borak's sons, Bork, was at the heart of the festivities, hoisting women into the air while drinking wastefully through a gold-plated tankard.

The young man could not describe this feeling of warmth. He felt he had been alone in the dark for so long that he had forgotten what warmth humanity could create. He was lured into this atmosphere and it brought him joy. He smuggled himself into the busy tavern and blended in with the crowd of occupants both human and demi-human alike and the other passing travellers that had also fallen victim to its merry jeer. The tavern was a typical, natural stone structured building with the inner skeleton of large, wooden beams and joists. Craftsmen of the town, and sometimes the owners themselves, set to work to create hospitable and welcoming establishments not only to house the locals, but to entice travellers that it is *their* business they should custom. With a central hall that doubled as a reception area and bar with a high standing landing above them as the walkways for the second floor and chandeliers made of turned wood with candle-wax sticks in their mantles the atmosphere was warm and welcoming. In the day, a family could congregate and feed themselves from the hefty cured meats and delicious vegetables and stews whilst the evenings gave way to mighty contests of drink and the privilege of landing a kiss from a beautiful woman. Even those unaccomplished could buy their way into company for the night in one of the tavern's many rooms. But the watering hole seemed to be busier and more bustling than intended. Hordes of men and women had gathered for the festivities, true, but the attitudes and disregard for safety was more than these patrons would usually succumb to. The young man, cloaked in his robes of black, made his way through the festivities and by sheer luck, or destiny, found a small drink-lending ledge on the wall where it was inclined for someone to lean. Edging his way in he caught the attention of a waitress with his right hand, his deep, ocean like blue eyes captivating her from beneath his hood.

"A tankard of mead, please," he spoke handsomely, not that she would hear. But with her years of expertise and heightened senses, her furry, cat-like ears twitched at his sounds and she was able to make out his order. Dropping his only gold coin into her hand when she removed one of many tankards on her tray to him, he smiled politely as she wandered on, resentful of her other duties.

After watching the festivities transpire for the duration of half his tankard to be drained, Bork caught sight of the robed young man who had positioned himself discreetly in the background.

"You there, in the hood! Come and test your might against 'ma right hand!" shouted the drunken son of Borak, as he gripped his own bulging biceps in challenge.

"Hm? Me?" asked the young man as he snapped out of his daydreaming and found himself back in the noisy tavern. He had been noticed by the perceptive giant, "oh, uh, no. It's okay."

"Bahaha! No need to be so frightened, ma boy! I'll go easy on you!" roared Bork, son of Borak.

"Get in there!" shouted a drunken patron as they all came together to push the young man onto the stool opposite Bork. "Yeah, give it a go!" shouted another.

Defeated en masse, the young man allowed himself to be pushed forth by the patrons, his eyes dashing to the sight of the pile of defeated opponents who drank away their defeat with overflowing tankards and crushed spirits. The hoisting of women was clearly his victory celebration as he put the two down to his side in preparation for his new challenger.

The mage chuckled at the encouraging words of the drunken

patrons as he passed them and agreed to join in with their festivities as he sat down opposite Bork and lowered his hood to reveal a handsome face, oceanic blue eyes and short hair as pure and white as snow.

"Well now, don't you look strong!" laughed Bork as he guzzled from his tankard again, the spills pouring through his thick, bushy beard. "Bork's the name and I'm undefeated, bahahaha!" he laughed as he gargled vast amounts of mead.

But beneath the drunkenness and arrogance, Bork could indeed feel something awry from this scrawny young man. He noticed the black fingernails tainted not by colour or style, but by the everlasting residue of a deep and dark black magic.

"Give it all you've got now, son. If you win, I'll buy your bloody drinks for the rest of the night! Tankards at that, too!" finished Bork as he placed his burly right arm on the table, squeezing and preparing his hand for the challenge.

"I'll give it my best then," said the young man politely, accepting. They locked hands and prepared themselves.

"And you young'en? What's the name of my opponent?" asked Bork through gritted teeth.

"Nex," said the young man. "My name is Nex."

"Well then Nex, let's find out how much of a man you are! Ready? GO!" roared Bork to initiate the arm wrestle as everyone gathered around to watch Bork, the village hero, best yet another helpless adventurer. Both arms tensed firmly, pushing their opponent against them, the thick oak table beneath trembling in fear.

"Well you can hold me, can you?" asked Bork rhetorically as he gave it more, pushing Nex's hand down toward the table. "Have you got any more than that though, boy? Can you give it back?" he taunted.

Nex applied more power and brought Bork's hand back to the centre as a gasp escaped from all the audience in awe of the sight.

"Bah! You're strong!" roared Bork over the jeering crowd as his trained senses allowed him to detect Nex's potential. "But have you got enough to stop all my might?!" Bork could feel the strength welling in Nex's arm. Without realising he poured every fibre of his power into his effort and pushed the young man to the precipice of defeat.

'Such brute strength!' thought Nex to himself, looking past the huge man and at the chanting patrons. "Bork! Bork! Bork!" they screamed.

Nex, however, despite the enormity of the bulging, veiny muscles exploding from Bork's bicep, brought his opponent back to the centre again. The crowd stopped their cheers in pure amazement.

"What!? ARHHGGG!" shouted Bork in disbelief, unsure of just how long he could exert this force. With all his might, his will alone stopped him from passing out from exhaustion.
Nex's hand began to creep backwards in defeat once more as he took in all the jeers and celebration around him. The warmth of life and its embrace. Finally, his hand crashed against the table. The cheering erupted and the stamping of feet shook the wooden beams of the tavern, rattling the hanging lights vigorously to the point where they could fall upon them all.

"Not bad!" jeered Bork over the cheering. "Not bad at all!" He raised himself up triumphantly and displayed his muscles, accepting the cheers of his friends. "You really made me work for that one!" He grabbed Nex's arm and raised it too, as if the victory was shared. Bork thought suspiciously with his small brain as to how he almost lost against the slight, young man. 'This guy is strong,' he concluded. "For your effort you can drink yourself to sleep here tonight boy!" celebrated Bork as he rose, his revealing leather armour glimmering in the admiration of all his village folk, the wolf fur presenting him as a beast among men. "Can't do anything about the rooms though, they're all full! Although I bet there are plenty of people who wouldn't mind shacking up with you!" he stated as many of the patrons found themselves attracted to Nex's handsome face and his impressive performance.

"Thank you," said Nex honestly as he nodded towards the congratulating patrons, acknowledging them. Now welcomed into the festivities and given a new tankard every few seconds by a drunken patron.

"Another great day to have lived! If we are so lucky to live another, we shall celebrate even more gloriously until we are united with the Gods! We will stop the advances of anyone, even if it is the Sentinels or the Mantle!!" declared Bork as he and the rest of the townsfolk guzzled their tankards.

Bork saw fit not to challenge anyone else that evening. Whilst he may be able to best just about anyone in the local area with his immense strength, the force he had exerted against the slender Nex had made his arm heavy with ache. It was about all he could muster just to bring his tankard to his mouth.

The Tavern erupted with cheers and celebration. The mead ran thick and the wine flowed as they jeered and danced and drank and fell all over. Nex stood near the table, bashed around accidently by the celebrations, gradually moulding back into the crowd and swallowed by it.
He conversed with a few patrons who congratulated him on his performance against Bork. Men, women and children all, on their passing, said hello and smiled, offering to buy the young mage a drink for his efforts. The waitresses began to change their routes so they could catch a glimpse of his oceanic eyes as they delivered their orders hoping that he would find

just as much attraction in them as they did in him and accompany them in a night of bliss. Even some men looked at him with eyes of passion and lust. But the young man kept to himself and smiled and nodded modestly to passers by. Their attention meant he was able to avoid conversation as when one approached another was soon to follow to make some form of idle chatter. Eventually, when the mead began to run dry and the night threatened to become morning, he filtered outside to be alone in the warm darkness.

"Another war?" he asked himself as he found an old wooden bench to hold him. He looked upwards to the stars for the answers he sought, their tiny sparkles fighting a timeless battle to reach him across the everlasting night. "How unsightly."

After five or so minutes of deep thought the great champion himself joined Nex outside. "What a splendid night, eh?" said Bork.

"It sure is," replied Nex.

"You almost had me back there!" admitted Bork as he laughed, scratching the back of his head in embarrassment. Nex was, after all, like a stick in comparison and perhaps a whole pace shorter.

Nex, a man of few words, remained silent. Bork spoke again through the pause, sensing the young man wanted to be alone.

"Ember won't be a good place for those who aren't looking for a fight. You're strong, boy, that much I can tell. Even so, I hate to ask this of you, but your help would be invaluable to this town. There's gonna be a battle tomorrow and there's not much chance any of us will survive," Bork stated to the young man as he sensed something deep in Nex's eyes that no one else had. Beneath the oceanic blue there was something only a seasoned veteran could sense. He could see that Nex was no stranger to hardship and battle and that he had seen so much death it would be indescribable for him to recant such tales.

"Why will there be a battle?" asked Nex simply. In his mind he pondered the possibilities of wild beasts, evil spirits or at the very worst, demons. But even with all this conjecture he knew deep down who the true foe was.

"Surely you know?" asked Bork in surprise. "The Holy Church is conquering all four Kingdoms for the Great Reclamation. The Mantle is coming south for Myphos and we are all that stands between them and entry into our home."

Nex exhaled loudly at the tediousness of it all. Humans… again…why would it not end?

"I have a family. A wife, a son, a daughter, a brother. I want to protect them all," said Bork.

"I am happy to help. Although it has been quite some time since I used any magic. I'm bound to be a little…rusty," said Nex.
"I admire your bravery ,but I cannot lie to you," began Bork. "It is no simple fee I ask. The Mantle have got super-powers of their own. It's more than likely we will fail to stop their advance. It will be all we can do to thin out their forces, if only by a little."

"Have you not evacuated?" asked Nex turning to face Bork, his mind now in a strategic, battle preparation mode.

"A lot of them, yes. But you know what people are like. They can live their entire lives in just one village. They would rather die in their home than flee. There are those who will not leave," finished Bork.

"I see. Then I will help you however I can," said Nex as he smiled in comfort at their bravery.

"Thank you, Nex!" said Bork as he patted the young mage

on the back, turned, and headed back into the cavern yelling "Don't forget to celebrate like it's your last night on this world!"

Nex looked up at the stars in ponder before his eyes caught sight of the beckoning straw heap between the tavern and the wall. He hoisted himself up into the wooden dispenser and slumped down onto it. "Were the stars always this Dim? They were much brighter when we all looked upon them together, weren't they?"

Nex realised he was alone. His questions fell on only his ears. He closed his eyes and the stars disappeared into his mind.

Elsewhere, in a town not too far to the west, the silhouette of an assassin atop the pile of bloodied bodies of those who dared make enemies of the wrong people. Slashed and severed by a mystical katana, the assassin skillfully removed the blade of any sinful or murderous taints with a simple but abrupt motion. Covered in blood from head to toe the walls of the small room were canvas to the splatters of blood that had elegantly been drawn. Slipping away into the shadows once more and remaining undetected they began for their next hunt.

CHAPTER SIX: THE MANTLE

The sun rose again the next day. The dust between oaken planks illuminated and danced at the dawn of a new day. Nex found himself awoken not by the intruding sunlight creeping beneath his lids, but by the presence of unwanted travellers. With his keen senses he had indeed picked up the approach of four powerful auras.

In the night, under the guise of patrons and masked by the black sky drawn by the Dragon God himself, four elite Mantle soldiers had infiltrated the town in hopes to dismantle any rebellion before the true battle could begin. But no such plan would work against someone like Nex. Even with their talents and abilities they could not hope to conceal themselves against his keen senses.

In the early hours of the morning he approached them, locating them as if they were screaming his name at the top of their lungs. The town was only small, there were not many places they could remain concealed now that the sun shone bright and the people stirred. He found them plotting down an alley not too far from the straw heap he had occupied for the night.

"Hello," he spoke quietly to alert them all. The four soldiers were robed in dark cloaks to conceal their beautiful, silver armour. Startled, the captain spoke.

"Who are you?!" he questioned in a fright. The four elite soldiers were alarmed. They all possessed a very strong presence, equal to that of Bork, and surely had the combat prowess and magical ability to best most adventures, after all they were high ranking Mantle soldiers. And yet, as keen and trained as their senses were, they could sense no presence from Nex in the slightest. It was almost as if he did not exist.

"Naughty," declared Nex in acknowledgement of their underhanded infiltration technique. "I gave my word. Such a thing means a lot, where I come from."

There was no time for them to falter. Their plan would begin now before Nex could alert the town of their presence. The mere result of their presence being revealed would cause unrest and disarray amongst the rebellion stationed here, and so to that end, their mission was bound to be a success. But Nex was an unpredictable anomaly.

"You are too late. It has already begun," said the captain.

In mere moments Nex dispatched them all and re-emerged from the alley with barely a hair out of place. Comparing the power of those Mantle elites to that of Bork's, Nex concluded the rebellion army would be decimated by the Mantle's might. From his back, Nex began to unfasten the ancient, frayed rope from his chest and unwrap the cloth surrounding the concealed sword to reveal a jet black Shirasaya. He proceeded forth to the north of the town to await the army.

"Bork!" shouted a villager frantically, "Bork!" The two heavy oak doors flew open as the giant poured out clambering in his half-equipped armour, his wolf pelts trailing behind him after a successful night bedding multiple women.

"What is it lad?" he shouted across the village to the approaching man.

"The scouts have returned! The Mantle is here! They're here!" he shouted in horror.

Bork's eyes widened. He gasped at the words that clashed

against his ears. He looked down to the floor for a moment before raising his head to meet the men who began to emerge from the woodwork. They all looked to their Leader.

"Men! To the Northern battlements! We must protect the village!" he roared as another man threw him his great axe.

They began pouring forward and gathering at the northern side of the village. All the capable men flooded forth, faces young and old. They grabbed at what weapons they could find and held strong to their faith in their village chief.

The village of Ember was located at the most Northern point of the Southern Kingdom, Myphos. All trade from the North would pass through this town, but first, via the large stone bridge around one hundred paces long constructed over the fierce river. A perfectly formed defence from any Northern invasion.

The warriors, mages, fathers, smiths, and shop owners gathered in Ember's defence. Sons and daughters who did not look old enough to have even experienced their first kiss held their weapons in hand. Everything from fine steel longswords to rusty pitchforks and farming equipment would make all the difference in holding the bridge.

Bork paced ahead of them before turning, organising the frantic rabble into a makeshift defensive position. Horror had come in the form of an army. The ground trembled at the footsteps of thousands of intruding soldiers from the Mantle. They came, row after row after row, over the hills and down to the river, spanning as far as the landscape would let them.

There's...too many!" stated one.
"Would we even slow them down...?" said another.

Bork raised himself, looking outwards to the hopeless odds but his body did not tremble. The bones shook inside the leather skin of the farmers and warriors rattled before Bork began to speak.

"Steel yourselves!" he shouted over them all. "As long as we hold this bridge, their numbers will mean nothing. Just like before, we will use the battlements for ranged and magic attacks and if they begin to breach we will destroy the bridge ourselves. If we cannot repel them then we will die to stop them moving forward!"

The men mumbled at Bork's words and looked to one another in hopes of further words of encouragement. Bork looked at each face in the rabble, his eyes combing from one to the next as his spirit began to break at knowing the truth of this battle. This force was larger than any they had previously repelled. It was only a matter of time before the bridge was taken.

But above them, without warning or delay, a giant magic circle appeared. This large ring was a representation of a magic spell, it's presence daunting enough to infer something would rain down upon them with great power. The magic circle itself was made up of hundreds of runic characters that represented the written 'instructions' one would read and learn to be able to cast such a masterful spell.

Above them, it began to turn, rotating readily to disperse its magical effects and surely explode like hellfire to destroy them all. If there was any soul spared to recant this tale they would surely tell of how a magic akin to a second sun appeared above them.

But, discreetly raising his hand to the sky without worry, Nex dispelled the magic with the same effort a child would blow out a candle. A huge, unanimous sigh of disbelief spread across them all as the faux sun cancelled and collapsed into the wind.

"What the?!" the souls muttered.

From amidst the thousands of men before them, a man strode

from within their ranks responsible for the magic circle test. His cunning, initial attack was for two reasons: To conduct a split-second evaluation as to whether there was anyone powerful amongst the rebellious ranks and also, if successful, to decide the battle with one attack. This latter method is also known in military terms as 'Anti-Army'. A man sealed in white armour with beautiful, golden intricacies looked down upon them all like insects. Atop his head was a simple, yet furiously daunting military cap that matched the glorious white of his armour but peaked with a deep black. This attire, finished with his long, heavy, military overcoat indicated one thing about him. He was the highest ranking soldier within the Mantle beneath the Pontifex. Wrapped tightly around his pristine fingers were soft-hide gloves in pure white that protected his hands from soiling on the filth in which he had been sent to purify.

"This rebellion, against your church, your holy divine, is unforgivable," declared the man powerfully to the ransack group of farmers as if the meaning of the words themselves had no substance, as if he believed they were merely said out of courtesy to ensure the Maker's blessing. He paced forward with a few elite guards before coming to a final stop as he removed his spotless white leather gloves.

"Your names have no meaning. Your lives do not matter. A troublesome band of rebels to be absent from any of the pages of history," he said finally.

They all looked upon an army of mortal men through the low battlements to their leader. It was almost as if he was a monster. The power that emanated from him was grand and strong. It was not sinister like that of the corrupted Sentinel's but one could feel there was no hoping to best him in battle. Even those closest to him were brimming with power, Bork's huge size and strength meant nothing before these gifted mages. They were hopeless to even defend from his gaze.

"G-General Henrys!" shouted a man from atop the stone battlement.

"That's General Henrys! The Hymn of Faith!" screamed an archer from atop the bridge's battlements upon analysing the signature overcoat and cap. Doom was already in the air but the overwhelming sense of hopelessness soon flooded over them as they began to realise their efforts would barely result in slowing down this great army even with their advantageous defensive position.

"The Hymn of Faith?! The Flaming General?! W-why would he come this far south?!" shouted one of Bork's right-hand men.

"General Henrys..." said Bork in frustration at his luck.

"Ah, Bork, is it?" said the man in the white armour addressing the figure through the open gates. "It seems I've struck out in coming South. Vereoris must be having all the fun quelling the Northern Kingdom."

"You're a fool if you think Erba will submit to you without a fuss," snapped Bork at the general.

"They say the Erbian Prince is an Arcane master. He was the one thing that gave even the Sentinels pause when it came to discussion."

Henrys laughed at the empty words Bork drove at him in desperation. "*You* must truly be the fool if you think he could defy The Three Hymns of the Mantle. I am sure Vereoris will make short work of him. In the meantime, it seems I must educate your kingdom as to why it is exactly that I serve directly beneath his holiness. To think it was you that had caused such a ruckus for our army's previous advancements... Oh, my latest reports said that Kleese received word of surrender from your brother, Burk, in the Eastern Kingdom. Of course, he dribbled them out onto his boots as he was killed..." stated the general confidently.

"You lie!" roared Bork over the wide river beneath them. "He would never fall to the likes of you!"

"Something about going East to help aid fleeing farmers into Haraura through the Myphos trade routes? You cannot expect me to remember every report I receive, after all," said Henrys.

His words were true. Whilst there may be many monsters among men in Ares, Bork and Burk were by no means weak. They ranked well in their guilds of adventurers and in these times their assistance would be invaluable. But in this world, there are always monsters among monsters and such a creature was now among them. Henrys appeared to be a very composed, well-educated and a well-kept middle-aged man. He was well respected and feared throughout all of Ares for his incredible strategic abilities and his potent magic power. This earned him the title of one of the Three Hymns, those who lead the Mantle's military might and serve directly beneath the Pontifex himself. He wore a full set of golden armour donned with silver intricacies and a gold cloak, easily identifiable as one at the top of the hierarchy of the Mantle.

A moment passed as the silent army stood firm, the bracing farmers panting in readiness with their weapons already hoisted.

"We are not without mercy. We are all the Maker's children, after all, and we will treat you as such. If you surrender peacefully and let us pass, no harm will come to this town or its villagers. Be grateful that it is I, the Hymn of Faith, that has come and not the Hymn of Mercy or Wrath. If they had come south you would be afforded no such luxury."

"And me?" asked Bork as he pondered the possibility of surrender to save his hometown and its people.

"You will be executed right here, of course," said Henrys

plainly. "Treason is punishable by death."

"But no harm will come to this village or it's people?" he clarified.

"Depending on how long it takes you to answer, possibly..." said Henrys as Bork contemplated.

Bork laughed, regaining his momentum as a strong warrior, "You will spare none!"

"Hahaha of course I won't. Your faith has been corrupted. My duty is to banish you from this world!" laughed Henrys as the village folk. "I will burn you all to ash!

"FIRE!!" roared Bork as he ordered the archers to release their arrows from atop and behind the battlements. Tens of arrows launched into the air and began their descent upon the first few lines of the army. This attack, combined with the hefty magical spells that shot into the air, should do more than tickle the advancing army. Repetition of this simple tactic would affect the advancing army as they bottlenecked over the bridge in both morale and function.

Henrys simply raised his hand and gently swatted the projectiles away, releasing a blazing wave of fire. The arrows fell to earth as no more than ash and the magic spells burned away.

"I hoped that you would resist. Now there is no reason for this world to not be rid of you. You should curse yourselves for defying The Maker and his holiness," declared Henrys in disinterest as he gestured four of his elite guards to proceed across the bridge to prevent unnecessary casualty amongst the lower ranks.

"WHA-" said Bork.

Nex emerged from the men and began forward, his black cloak concealing his appearance with only his Shirasaya to identify him. The large portcullis grinded upwards on its rails to allow him through with ease.

"The gates! Seal them now!" roared Bork as he looked to the operators.

"It's not us!" they protested as they tried to stop the chains. The small stone battlements stood only at the bridge and some few meters outwards. All could witness Nex pass through the gates and challenge the undefeatable enemy.

"I'll take a look," said Nex calmly as the gates began to close behind him.

"And yet another hindrance?" asked Henrys. "Destroy him."

These other four elite guards were fast and capable of breaching the wall and dispensing the rebellion that had gathered there themselves. Their silver armour seemed as though it was weightless and malleable allowing them to conduct swordplay no regular man could achieve. There was no doubt it had been imbued with magical properties. The blades of their swords were true and unwavering, cutting through the air with the precision of years of training.

But although they were clearly of a standard much higher than that of Bork's village folk, the man donned in the black cloak seemed to be barely moving at all, and yet he was evading their attacks. He parried and blocked and sent each opponent flying back to their general defeated and unconscious.

"Incredible!" shouted the village folk in awe.

The general approached calmly, a crude smile spreading across his face.

"Ah, a mage. It was surely you who cancelled my spell. I imagine the infiltration force I sent was also thwarted by you?" he spoke before coming to a halt some ten feet away on the bridge. "A true talent at that. But I do not sense any magic from you, quite unusual... My elites are not easily bested. You know who

I am and yet you have dared defy us?" He spoke loudly, hungering to silence those who stood before him and challenge the Pontifex's rule.

"I bring fire and death to all those who dare oppose his holiness."

"Then I suppose you bring fire and death to me," said Nex, plainly looking elsewhere and reaching into his ear with his forefinger as if searching for the name physically.

"Such insolence! Your arrogance will learn its place," roared Henrys as he began to immerse himself in self-praise. "You have no idea how small you are compared to me. How insignificant you are a mage to those who stand so high above you. In this world, where magic is everything, you will learn that you are nothing but dirt that serves underneath us as gods!" He began to loosen his hands, rotating his cuffs and warming his muscles for a light exertion.

"What are you doing, boy!?" coughed Bork at the young mage from behind the safety of the battlements. "Get back here! We'll fight him together!"

Nex remained unphased and awaited the great Generals next move.

"I'll burn your world to ash!" shouted Henrys as he began to exert his magic power.

The air became thin and the wind was still. Life veered away from this destination in fear. The village folk felt the hair on their necks stand like spikes, intruding into their armour in an unwelcome fashion. His power continued to escalate vastly until it seemed like he stood twenty paces tall. The farmers looked upon the menacing general as if he were a Titan amongst men.

With his presence alone he held them there, frozen to the ground on which they stood. Nature reacted to his power, a human this powerful made the earth crawl in fear. This man was a monster.

Henrys opened his mouth and released a menacing grin. Red flames, layered in orange and deep yellow erupted from his hands as he conjured his fire magic, the immense heat began to melt away any hope of survival. With his hands now shaped like claws, he prepared to annihilate his foe and all that stood before him.

The wind flushed past him as he felt himself relieved of all his magic power.

Nex, without fear, waved his free arm and, in an instant, the thunderous aftershock sent every man in the vicinity to fall backwards against the tremendous force. Henrys' fierce fire became extinguished as he tried with all his might to remain standing against Nex's simple action.

"Arghhhh!" shouted Henrys as he battled the wind, shielding his face with his arm. "What?" he blurted as he squinted at his foe painfully. He knew he had underestimated the magicless opponent. He swiftly summoned all his power into a single attack.

"Towering Inferno!" he roared as he unleashed his most powerful attack. It whirled upwards like a tornado, the heat melting the very steel and iron weapons the soldiers held. "Burn!" he roared.
After seconds passed, the spiraling inferno around Nex ceased and the smoke cleared. The young man was unscathed from the immense flames.

"Brisk," stated Nex factually as he stepped closer brushing off his shoulder.

"Impossible!" stuttered Henrys in panic.

The young man found himself unable to contain his excitement." I see. And you're rather powerful too."

Henrys had lost all of his arrogance. He knew, better than anyone, just how powerful his magic was and how effective his flames were against humans.

But there is a feeling that creeps over a mage during battle like a fever. This is an encroachment of fear. When they realise they are truly no match for their opponent it is a feeling akin to instant death. For in these times there are few who spare those against whom they spar. This trembling feeling is enough to consume the strongest and most arrogant of men and beasts. This young mage was someone powerful, someone whom he had underestimated and was about to pay the price for doing so.

"Now, let's see if I can remember…" trailed Nex.

"General!?" shouted the elite guards at their commander desperate for an order.

"I…" spurted Henrys.

Nex focused, and raised his arm to the sky, hand opened as if to pluck the sun itself from the heavens.

"Infinity magic…"

"What?!" gasped Henrys as the young mage whispered the words.

"Eye of Oblivion," spoke the young mage softly and as he said those simple words, the world shifted.

He had torn a hole in the very fabric of reality. A giant, golden eye appeared in front of him as though a creature gazed in from another pocket of folded time and space. It opened wide and blazed at them all and released its menacing glare. The golden light was too bright and like nothing they had ever seen. They could not see a moment past themselves. They were nothing in the light. And then, just like that, the spell vanished.

The entire army had fallen prey to the incredible spell, the true effects of which were unknown but had left every opponent of it drained of all magic and energy with barely enough life force for them to stagger and crawl.

CHAPTER SEVEN: DAMSEL IN DISTRESS

The sun shone heavily down on the green landscape, the rolling hills stretched far before running into civilization, their green grass soft to the touch, warm from their bright sunlight sustenance. Without word or worry Nex had swiftly left the previous battle. He did not care for conversation or thanks nor did he wish to divulge the burdens of his magic.

A tall tree stretched off the hillside, cloaking all its offspring in its green shade. At the foot of the tree Nex finished exercises of his body and mind and thought deeply to himself as he rested against its base, running his fingers through the lushess grass beneath him. In the days that had passed since Nex had stood atop the mountain pass, it seemed much had transpired as he had journeyed across the vast countryside. He reached upwards underneath the tree, stretching his shoulders to embrace a full-bodied yawn that would hypnotise any viewer into re-enacting. There was something disturbing about the nature of this young mage's presence. All life emits an energy, an aura, a magic power, and yet, he emitted none. This, combined with his skill to hide his physical presence, gave him no visibility whatsoever. The only way to see Nex was with the naked eye.

Nex, on the side of the grassy hill, could hear voices down the valley on the common path toward the next town. It sounded like the usual rabble of uneasy conversation but something about the group appeared to be what he was waiting for. With a speed and guile that surpassed human movement as we know it, he darted down quickly to the source of the ruckus.

"Oh hello, young lady," said a low voice from ahead. "Look lads, we've found ourselves a little gem here!" he finished as he beckoned to his five thuggish looking friends, more than half of whom were demi-humans. Out here in the country demi-humans were even more popular than in the cities due to the presence of discrimination and, in some harsh cases, even slavery. A demi-human retains the same characteristics as a human and can possess numerous traits from almost any other species in all of Reath. Anything as minor as altered ears for heightened hearing or a tail for improved balance or possibly a set of wings in some rare cases. The origins of this human sub-species is unknown. Some say the first Demi-humans came from a curse from the Gods whilst others say it was simply human experiments that sought to enhance physical attributes like strength and stamina. In any case, the fact they are not completely human and are therefore 'slightly' different leads them to strong injustice and conscious prejudice despite their evolutionary advantage over the traditional human. To all other races of creature, beast and myth, humans are all the same.

The farm boys were dressed in a cross between common clothing and light leather armour, holding poor daggers and farming sickles as weaponry. "Oh aye, she's hot!" gleaned another as he leant sideways to appreciate the young woman, his lack of formal education apparent through his vocabulary as his furry ears atop his head twitched in interest.

The young girl spoke without hesitation softly interrupting their advance, her cold eyes cutting them deep with a glare. "Idiots threatening young girls with a sickle and your mother's kitchen knife will end up hurting themselves with all those pointy edges."

The young men were taken aback by her factual insults and cool, calm composure. She was not intimidated by their advancements or forward, threatening behaviour. Perhaps from the city that she was from, she had grown accustomed to such things. One could easily tell from her expensive, quality clothing and her unusual attire that she should not be tested. Anyone who possessed an above average potency for magic could detect she was strong. Being at the standard that they were, they could not see the whole, thick, dense aura that surrounded the young girl.

"You...what?" said the ringleader as he hoisted his hands onto his hips in interest.

"I don't have time to spar with your culinary utensils," she stated swiftly with her katana in hand. Nex stood fifty paces behind her on the path's turn, remaining unseen by the group, his presence completely concealed. He looked closely at the young man amidst the centre of the group, his expression evidently showing signs of cautious thought as his comrades' patience ran dry at the young girl's words.

"You what, love?" said one of the rabble rousers. "You 'fink we're scared of you? I don't fink you kwite understand da sitchu-a-shon" He stated with his country accent.

"Ross? What are ya doing?" asked one of the more freckly ones.

"Nothing!" snapped Ross as he regained his thoughts and found the young girl's gaze. "You wanna spend some time with us then, little lady?" he coerced as he stepped in with poor suavity.

"Cor blimey! Look at that sword!" realised the rearmost lackey as he took in the highest quality katana she had sheathed. But it was already too late. The beautiful young lady had been exhausted of her patience. It began to ooze from her, her bloodlust, her anger, her sinister intent. She reached outwards with her hand as if to break them all as she spoke. "You just can't take a hint when someone's having a bad day..." she muttered.

"Baby!?" shouted a voice from behind her, taking them all in surprise, Nex appeared to be jogging towards her slowly as he waved his arm in the air bashfully with a slight sense of awkwardness. "Baby! I told you not to go on so far ahead!" he shouted as he closed the distance between them.

"Hm?" she asked as she turned further at the approaching young man who she had worryingly not sensed at all.

"Jheeze. You're always so eager to beat me. Hm? What's this?" Nex turned to the young boys playing the ignorant lover, "you alright there, boys? What's going on?" he finished as he closed into the girl's side and gently placed his right arm over her shoulders to convince them he was indeed romantically involved with the girl. With their unusual attires and handsome young visages, they did make a convincing match. The now unified two, faced the six rabble rousers together.

"We-" started the leader, Ross, before the young lady began.

"They just took an interest in me travelling alone down this dangerous road," interjected the young girl with an immediate understanding of Nex's plan and concealing her bloodlust. "They just asked to see if I was alright."

This young lady was extremely quick witted. She had detected Nex's plan as a way to leave the area without her being forced to beat the young highwaymen senselessly. But there was also another reason for the young lady's cooperation. She was a very talented mage and yet she had not sensed the presence of the young man who sprang out to her aid. Nex was completely concealed until she caught sight of him with the naked eye. This was a troubling thought, even for someone like her.

Nex quickly processed the information and invented a response, smiling generously at the thoughtful young men. "Oh, it's okay! We're dragon hunters! We're used to bringing down all manner of creatures."

The young men were taken back by the legendary statement. "D-Dragon hunters? You mean you slay dragons?! That's imposs-" exclaimed Ross in disbelief.

"We're tracking one now actually," added Nex as he gestured to the air but in multiple directions indecisively as if he was still deciding where the fictional dragon would be. It appears he had not come up with the whole story beforehand. The young lady soon began to realise he came to her aid half equipped. "We've been hunting it for a few weeks now. The last battle we had destroyed the two nearest towns, we were hoping to catch it before it gets too close to another."

"But you...But Dragons are...*You're* Dragon Slayers?!" exclaimed Ross, sharing his thoughts aloud, his brain whirring.

"On a good day," said Nex, "but we'd better get going, don't want any more townsfolk getting eaten or mountains getting destroyed before we can bring it down once and for all." he said, each word layering on top of the deceit.

"Uhh...right," agreed the farmer boys, aghast.

"We'll be seeing you!" said Nex as he grabbed the young woman's arm, and pulled her through the six men. Normally she would object, catch the arm on approach and destroy it, but she was intrigued as to who had the courage to grab at her and tell her what to do.

"You mean you've actually seen a real, live dragon!?" shouted Ross as the rest stood bewildered in fear and awe.

"Yup!" replied Nex as he pulled the young girl away from them westwards. They gained a few paces before Nex turned back to them, this time his friendly, ignorant visage was absent as he spoke these stern words, an aura of menace seeping out of him. "You should stay off the roads boys. People out here can be dangerous."

As they rounded the corner some two hundred paces ahead Nex released the young girl's arm in preparation to explain himself.

"What the hell are you doing!? How dare you touch me?!" she scolded.

"I was-" started Nex.

"I don't need protection from some hormonal, country hicks," she stated as she stared at him. Although a brief exchange, Nex understood that this young woman had not only a troubled past but a troubled future too. She was not one to rely or trust anyone other than herself. She was not accustomed to acts on her behalf. Still, she was not impressed.

Nex paused as he waited for a chance to speak without interruption, "I wasn't protecting you from them. I was protecting them from you. I could feel the bloodlust pouring out of you like a maniac."

"MANIAC?! Did you just call me a maniac? Who do you think you are?" she shouted at him with volume and outrage but not so loud so that the recent gang would hear their quarrel. She may very well have been one, but he had no such right to call her one.

"I get you might be having a bad day, but you looked like you were about to start murdering those poor boys on the side of the road," he added in his defence. "You have quite the short fuse, don't you?"

She pouted as she looked away from him. "I wasn't in the mood to be dealing with country idiots. And what were you doing waiting in the bushes? Were you spying on me?! What are you, some kind of pervert?" she interrogated defensively after his barrage of insults, flipping the matter of the interrogation to Nex's character demanding an answer with her eyes.

With her fixed and still, staring into him, Nex noticed the young girl for the beauty she was. Her golden hair falling naturally down her like a waterfall of silk. He noticed her petite frame and young face, the deep green eyes that challenged the beauty of fine gems. Her rose red lips ignited the contrast of her flustered face that analysed Nex's handsome one. She wore an armour he did not recognise. It was dark in colour and grand in design. It was a combination of robe and armour, a common hybrid of clothing for a mage who finds themselves in battle frequently. The lightness of robes and their magical threads combined with the defence of armour in all the right places. It bore a similar resemblance to the grand armour Henrys wore and even bore the same emblem, but its makeup was somewhat different. Another internal faction perhaps? There was a subtle acknowledgement that the two shared the same theme. Her armour, however, was a revealing, feminine version. It oozed appeal and dominance and power and invited the eye to look upon the revealed skin and haunched waist. The bearer of such armour was clearly very confident in their appearance. Subtle boots elevated her slightly before falling into a long, dark sleeve that covered her left leg before breaking at her skirt whilst her right leg housed a bandage from her ankle up to her thigh in what appeared to be some form of fashion or unique style as opposed to being structurally supportive. Whilst under investigation from Nex's stare she too searched his simple design examining his plain, dark attire and catching sight of the sealed sword he carried before returning her gaze to his handsome young face. She caught his eyesight before looking away, her cheeks erupting into redness.

"Well!?" she demanded, averting his gaze entirely and then snapping back once she had controlled herself. "Why were you hiding in the bushes like some weird predator waiting for girls?"

"I, uhh…" began Nex. He had exhausted all his brain power on the young boys to come up with anything in a second round with the beautiful young girl before him, "was just researching up the mountain there…".

The young girl thought for a moment while she processed his story. When he took her arm she felt his warmth, his hidden power. This magicless man was a mystery. "Oh, if you touch me again, I'll kill you." she stated calmly as she assessed the arm he had grabbed.

Nex apologized with his expression before he spoke. "I'm sorry. I was trying to be convincing." He stood up straight with formality and spoke clearly, "my Name is Nex, it's a pleasure to meet you."

"I don't care," she snapped back at him. "If you knew what was good for you, you'd stay away from me," she said as she turned and began out of sight. Nex was taken aback. He stood there stunned, like he had just been slapped in the face. 'Had things changed over the last few years or am I just useless with people?' he thought to himself as he looked around the trees for an answer. Probably both, he surmised. 'I guess I did get quite good at concealing my magic' he trailed as he continued in the girl's wake but much, much slower so as to not catch her up.
'Hmph! I didn't want to be friends anyway…'

Nex found his mind wandering back to his first years of gruelling and unimaginable training where he learned the technique to suppress his magic power as a necessity.

"Magic is the source of all life. Magic is wisdom, wisdom is power, and power is magic, and that is humanities salvation. The Maker used magic to create this world and everything in it.

'Magic' was kept from us by The Maker, but given to his Lesser children as one of many tests when time began. Rightfully earned and inherited, all in his grace 'magic', the force that is purely incomprehensible to the creatures of this world, is alive. It flows and breathes, it reacts, and it flees in this world. It is much more than a tool. Magic can grow and it can die. It can be enchanted and imbued into objects to give them life and soul. Against time, its presence will always live on and with each spell cast it leaves a signature by the caster as clear as a name scribed on parchment. Why do I remember this text over the others? The Elder really ingrained this into us..."

Nex continued onwards long after the sun retreated behind the enormous trees of the forest path and brought night to the campsites for the travelling traders. He knew why he had indeed been drawn to this woman and how she was also being drawn to him without her knowing.
'A town? That must be it' thought Nex as he caught sight of the next village by its enormous cathedral spire. 'Hmm, fancy that' he thought as he began to admire it.
"It would be nice to not have to sleep under a tree tonight..." he said aloud as he rubbed at his back in discomfort of the thought.

This village was not unlike Ember. The same, basic structure of stone and wood, and similar in size too. Again, a central trade route through to the coast that was one of many to connect the kingdoms. A main road pathway leading all carts and wagons loaded with goods. Nex traipsed down the side of the hill and re-joined the path from which he had diverted.

The night sky was full of tiny lights. Nex looked up at the infinite expanse and smiled at the reality of how small he really was. He entered the town and turned to see the stables, with the night over him and the tiredness in his eyes, the penniless young man thought nothing could be more inviting than the fresh straw. And before he knew it, he had crashed down and fallen fast asleep on the warm stack outside the stables.

CHAPTER EIGHT: THE ASSASSIN

Nex hadn't dreamed for longer than he could remember. When he slept there was only tragedy to be replayed. He found himself revisiting a memory he had wished to forget. In the mountains far, far away across the reaches of the sea of Ares there was a small village embedded into the side of the land. This village was like every other in this western world, rich with agriculture and trade, but this one specifically held a true connection to one of the first Immortals of Reath.

The God Amaterasu lived in her kingdom above the mountain's summit and their dedication to her was rewarded in the form of pure, unrivalled magic. In a prison-like building made of cold stone three separate cells housed three young children beneath the age of ten. Of these prisoners there was a young girl with long silver, moon-dust hair that reached beyond her waist. The second, a boy with a balded head from the rigorous torture, meditated in the centre of his cell. Finally, the oldest of the three was a dark-haired boy who sat with his knees to his chest on the little straw that constituted his bed. The three showed signs of malnutrition and were very slender, their only clothing was a combination of rags and sheets which did nothing to keep them warm. But what unified them more than anything was the markings on their skin. The meditating boy in the middle cell was skinny and pale, with only a ragged vest and small shorts to keep him warm. This revealed two black bands circling each of his upper biceps on each arm. Another single band on the upper section of each forearm, just beneath the elbow. On his legs, two bands around each lower part of the thigh and one band around each ankle. Each of the children had twelve tattoo-like black bands on their bodies. These were their Clan marks, markings they were born with, that symbolised some very important.

These three podigies were subject to torture in the form of magical experiments, which were more rigorous and painful than any other members of the clan had ever endured before. Whilst painful ceremonies and traditions took place here as per the norm, these three children endured a pain others could not live through.

"It won't be long now, I'm sure," stated the bald boy in the middle of his meditation. "We will be free of this place, once and for all." he declared.

"B-but…" whispered the girl with hair as lush as moondust, "they cannot awaken my magic. No matter how hard they try or what rituals they enact…I cannot do it as you two have. I am a failure. They will never let me leave this place"

"It is because your magic is greater than any of ours! The day it births will be a day none shall ever forget!" said the balded boy.

"I just want this to be over," she said.

"Magic is not meant for this…" trailed the meditating boy, "magic is life. It is love. It gives us warmth and hope. It is a gift from the Maker." The young boy, wise despite his age, could sense his words had little effect to comfort his young friends. "The first thing we will do once we are back in the village is get some Jelly from old man Vidic, how does that sound?" he said through a cheeky eye open to the young girl in the dark corner. A small smile seeped across her face.

"I'd like that," she said.

"W-w-why can't we just escape?" asked the third boy, finally entering the conversation.

The meditating boy let out a sigh of exhaustion as he gave up on his focus and climbed onto his bed to address his other friend. "Thirteen times so far. That is how many times we have made it out of these cells and yet we are powerless against the Elders..."

"But we should keep trying! Until we are free..." trailed the boy with the dark hair. "Whatever it takes..."

"I truly admire your relentless determination but the only way out of this place is after we Awaken, you know this. The Elders said that once we pass through these rituals we can be free..." as the wise young boy said it he found himself doubting his own words ,but for the sake of his little friends he had to believe them. He knew escape was impossible and the crippling punishments he received when he took credit for the mischief still bore scars on his pale, bony back. "For now, we just need to get through this together," he said with a smile.

But their momentary happiness was short-lived. The cold steel bars, reinforced with tremendous magic, slid across their rusted hinges with an unbearable screech that reminded all three children only of pain and suffering. "Eren, it is time for your training," said the elder beneath his robe. Eren, the eldest boy with jet black hair rose slowly and dared not defy the elders request. But they could all feel something was off. It was too late in the cold night for the gruelling rituals to take place. A sharp, cold feeling pierced at the two remaining prisoners as they watched their friend leave. An unbearable feeling of horror and grief struck them both as they looked upon their friend for the very last time.

"Oh, get off!" complained Nex as he waved his hands to dislodge the teigu's tongue from his face. The cart drawing beast blocked out the sun with its broad shoulders like that of a bear while it pawed with its dire-wolf-like legs at the intruder. The sun kissed him abruptly as he was forced to adjust rapidly. "Fine, fine I'm going, I'm going," he said as he sat upwards, his bed hair unkempt and covered in straw.

He rose squinting at the bright sun, pleading for mercy with his forehead. He walked and turned onto the main street to head to the plaza of the market town where he had seen the Mantle's cathedral.

"That spire really is huge!" he said to himself as he approached it. The small fountain in the courtyard in front of it invited him to wash his face. He surveyed the area, canvassing the men and women as they went about their early morning business, before the area became busy during the morning rush.

He approached the stone water fountain and looked upon the statue that rose from its centre.
'The twin goddesses?' he thought as he looked upon their angelic stone form. "Which town is this?" he asked himself as he looked around thinking of the all too familiar tale of the twin goddess.

He put his hand to his face in frustration as he racked his brain deciding that the issue with his thought process was that he hadn't woken properly. He reached down with his free hand and cupped at the fresh, clear clean water and threw it over his face, dragging his grasp down over his skin slowly so as to soak as much as possible. He repeated this three times before putting a final scoop of water into his mouth to drink. He felt his brain relax. Thousands of complex notions coming to a halt to give him clarity, slowly organising themselves in his vast, mental library.

Meanwhile, four hundred paces above him, a young girl sat poised atop the great spire, swinging her leg gayfully in wait whilst her golden hair blew in the hurtling high wind. She was unquestionably graceful. Her intent however was not so kind. She stood slowly and looked to the blue sky for clarity, her face concealed by a black mask that bore white tusks through a sinister smile, as though the moment she had waited for had finally come. Without word or warning she stepped forward and off the great height to fall to the earth. She fell silently, her gleaming green eyes narrowed and focused on the unsuspecting young man below splashing his face with the cold water. Her speed increased as she fell effortlessly from the considerable height, the pressure around her increasing so that the impact of her fall would be tremendous. In her soft hands she held what looked to be a western sword of great craftsmanship, so sharp the air fled at its touch. As she poised and pointed the blade at her prey her heart began to race and soon enough, she was upon him.

The air was still and the village quiet as the moments converged into one short pause and in an instant the blade collided with its intended target. The stone water fountain, and everything else within an immediate radius, shattered, the debris flying in each and every direction towards the buildings and people destroying the town with the might of its weight. The dust spread and hung in the air creating a thick cloud that blew through the streets and alleyways.

In the crater, the girl rose, her long blonde hair glistening in the sunlight, blowing across her from the gust to reveal her sinister mask. She tightened her grip around the handle of her sword as she sensed a change in the atmosphere.

"Impressive…" said the girl in a soft voice, staying still and maintaining her intimidating composure. "I would not have thought you would sense me coming."

"Hello again" said Nex as he emerged from some rubble, dusty and dirty wafting the air away from his mouth, recognising the beauty by her mesmerizing emerald eyes that he had seen only a day before. "I Like your Oni mask," complemented Nex.

The girl immediately changed her stance and sprang for Nex, using the poor atmosphere to her advantage. She darted to Nex like lightning swinging her sword across his torso. The strike failed to cut his skin but ravaged through his over-robes and the force sent him flying backwards into a previously unharmed building. The young girl again braced for the challenge she had not anticipated from the seemingly powerless man, her sword clean of blood.

"I knew there was something amiss when we met," she stated as Nex emerged from the rubble dustily and dirty, but still unscathed. "I cannot sense your magic nor your presence. At first, perhaps I would have concluded you were just an ordinary man. But watching over you I can tell you are different. Your skill must be tremendous to conceal that much power in one go. But it is too suspicious…" she trailed.

"Your speed is extraordinary," he stated with a smile as he examined the blade in her hands, the reason the two of them had met. "You are indeed right. It is all concealed. But it was not commonplace for everyone to be surging with magic in my day. It seems the world has changed a lot since then."

"You released Infinity Magic against General Henrys. The highest tier of magic in the known world. I wouldn't say that was doing a 'good job' at concealing," she added.

"Yeah, but I have trouble remembering what I can and can't do at the moment," admitted Nex. "I'm still a little rusty. But I had spent nearly all my life concealing my magic power, it is something I do as consciously as breathing."

She paused before she questioned him again, to ensure he would not attack. "With my speed you would find it difficult to summon a top tier spell in the instant it takes for me to close the gap between us. But seeing how you went out of your way to protect those boys from me shows you are at least a little concerned about the citizens, so I can't imagine you would release such a powerful attack in this area."

Nex was impressed. The beautiful young lady showed serious intellect and combat experience. Not to mention she was extraordinarily powerful. However, she could not comprehend just how precise Nex could be with his magic. She lowered her guard slightly as she examined her blade in both hands, admitting a truth she told few. "If you beat Henrys, you are surely powerful, and powerful opponents are what I must overcome if I am to be the strongest," she said as she threatened him with her sword.

Nex examined her carefully with more than just his eyes. He reached into her with his senses to see what lay beneath.

"Let us begin!" said the girl with an eager smile and without any hesitation, she sprang forward with another attack. She released her power. The green aura began to seep out of her like a thick, dense fog. Nex could feel her true power release as she held nothing back against her formidable foe. She sprang towards Nex, with speed faster than before. Her sword striking at him in a flurry of attacks so fast the normal eye would barely catch sight of them. But her sword was of a power that even he could not defend against unarmed. With his sheathed sword he defended, but in her viridian eyes he could see the fire of passion and battle. With each strike she poured more and more of her power so that when her blow did finally land it would be devastating. He began to defend harsher and evaded more elaborately as he was forced to do so by her intuitive attacks before finally having to commit his entire skillset to evasion and defence. He ran and ducked, flipped and spun using the walls and building as tools as her blade destroyed everything he touched an instant after he left it.

Finally, after evading over a thousand strikes of her sword she broke away. Nex could feel it coming. "GODSPEED: TITAN RIPPER!" shouted the assassin as she vanished, closing the distance between them faster than the blink of an eye, slashing Nex with one tremendous strike that, without the aid of magic he could not defend. For some reason Nex used his forearms to take the brunt of the blow. He hurtled through the air smashing through the town's perimeter, wall after wall until he finally lost momentum and rolled into a field some three hundred paces away.

He took a moment to think whilst he was face down in the crater his body had made. 'That hurt…' he trailed as he pushed himself up to stand. He rose slowly, his black over-robes now completely trashed and concealing little of his appearance from the aftermath of the battle. Casting it aside into the wind, Nex revealed a simple set of black robes that looked old and outdated. But more peculiarly he wore white bandages from his ankles to his thighs and on his arms from his wrists all the way up to beneath his shoulders, with a black tabard with white trim placed over him with another white bandage around his waist and finally donned with a simple black cloak that ran down his back. Aside from this bland and boring appearance, the young assassin caught sight of a small ring housing a jet-black gem on the smallest finger of his right hand that matched that of his black fingernails. The pain was a lot more than he had anticipated. He found the young girl standing before him once more, this time in a less threatening stance.

"That spell should have gone through your arms and separated your body from your legs," she stated, "and you survived with only that? What are the bandages for? Are you already injured?" she asked rhetorically as she gestured to the two small, smoking, black burn patches on his white bandages.

"No, but I'll take that as a compliment," he smiled at her as the damage to the bandages repaired themselves. "I can feel the bones shaking around in there," he gestured laughably.

"I will keep coming at you until you take this seriously," she threatened him again.

"You are indeed strong. I can sense a superb amount of power beneath the surface. Out of respect and admiration for your great ability, I will face you seriously. But first…" trailed Nex as he brought his attention to her blade, "your legendary katana is cursed. It is draining your power rapidly. Unless the curse of the blade takes effect soon, you may be the one to run out of magic first."

She quickly assessed his words before she spoke. "So, you know about my blade. You know of its power and of its curse. Then you will also know that the blade must draw blood for the curse to take effect. Unless you wish to tell me that beneath those bandages you are indeed bleeding."

"I also know that it takes an enormous amount of magic power to wield it and with every moment it sucks the life out of you at an exponential rate. Right now, I would say the sword is more of a hindrance than help to you. It truly is an abomination and an insult to master craftsmen throughout this world."

"Choose your words more carefully," she threatened as Nex stepped closer.

"But I know the runes on that blade and…" he spoke softly as he reached out his hand and activated the magic within the sword, so it glowed a deep red, "I can remove them."

She had no idea what he was thinking. He was coming closer and closer, right into a place where she could easily lunge and kill him. Nex referred to the inscription of runes that coated the legendary blade, imbuing it with its mighty magical properties.

"There," he said as he poked the tip with his finger right in the reach of death. As the sword's glow ceased the assassin immediately felt the difference. The blade was fathoms lighter in her hand. She could feel her power welling up like nothing ever before.

"W-what have you done?" she asked in complete bafflement.

"I removed the curse that drains your life," he said simply. "Now you can use the magic draining effect on your opponents without detriment. Think of it as an upgrade."

The overwhelming surge of power erupted through the assassin. "I can feel the power welling up inside of me!" she declared as she tensed her body, her muscle fibres stretching past their limits like never-before. She stood upright and straight bringing her black katana true to her chest. She concentrated her magic into the sword, and her green aura began to glow deep within the metal.

"How are you able to do that? This blade is..." she began, still baffled.

"An abomination," reiterated Nex coldly. "It never should have been made..."

"Why would you do this? Willingly make me stronger?" she asked with sincerity.

"So that we can battle seriously. Like you, I cannot help but deny my nature." He said. But this was a turning point. Nex stood straight and took his opponent seriously. He breathed in and gathered himself in preparation to release not his magic power but simply his presence. This was the turning point. It came from him, a smog of aura that told the whole world that he existed here, in this moment. It rose up and up and up and engulfed him easily doubling that of the assassins. The world fled from him. The rubble shook and became weightless as the essence of his presence rose into the air. This was a release for Nex. He could not remember the last time he relaxed his body and unburdened himself. His magic power however, remained suppressed.

'He's...a monster!' gulped the assassin as her skin turned to ice and her lungs froze inhaling the thin air. 'He'll...kill me. There's no way I can win!'

Cursed from birth and resentful of magic and its power, he looked upon the girl before him not as an evil assassin, but a soul that resonated with him. But now, with his glorious presence on display and odds pitted insurmountably against her, a maniacal sneer spread across her face not only from fear and denial, but from excitement. She, too, resonated with him. Who was stronger? They both wished to know this truth.

"Will you unsheathe your sword?" she asked.

Nex looked down to his sword in comfort, "I said I would fight you seriously. I did not say I wished the world to end. But, if we are to battle, I wish to know your name." stated Nex.

"My name is Lily, "she smiled at his cheeky remark, "here I come." She stepped forward and exerted her power, the ground shattering beneath her foot as she propelled forwards to destroy her target. The force was terrific. The wind from their movements was enough to make the buildings rumble in their wake hundreds of paces away. The clashing of their swords caused the windows to shatter and force the village folk to cover their ears as the sounds ripped their eardrums.

Amidst the fury of their heated battle, Lily slowed her breathing to null and calmed her soul. "TITAN'S LIGHT: PHOBOS!" With this, she released her signature attack that allowed her to strike once in this world, and once in another. Through a convergence of time and space, the two attacks became a reality and where Nex defended from one the second materialised from the air, drawn from another dimension. But Nex was no easy target. Even with this masterful move, he defended fully. Using this as a decoy, high up above him, as high as the roofs of the houses would have reached, Lily spun and launched to deliver a fatal blow. But as she flew down towards him and her blade mere inches from severing his head, he was not there.

On her flank, Nex released a grin of victory as he brought his sheathed shirasaya down upon her vulnerable body as if to sever her head. It came with unstoppable power. Even sheathed she knew the force alone was enough to separate head from torso. She knew too late that this was more than defeat, it was death. With the end in sight, everything ceased as the sheathed shirasaya tapped lightly on the top of her head signalling his victory. This tap undid the seals of her Oni mask, allowing it to fall to the floor and reveal her beautiful face to him once more. There was no feeling like this. The threat of imminent death made the skin seep sweat and air hard to control in your lungs.

"I had to get a little serious at the end there," said Nex as he removed himself from her flank and began a normal, frontal conversation. Lily looked up at him rubbing the wound she had sustained. Of course, it did not hurt, she was just a sore loser.

"To be able to wield that katana as you do, is truly something magnificent. The soul within the blade has chosen you. That is how I know we were destined to meet and you and I are fated to be."

Lily's face erupted into a red flare. "Won me over?! F-f-fated to be? What are you saying?" She was indeed facing defeat, but now, less so from their battle and more so from his forward words.

"That smug smile humiliates me. I am hopelessly defeated," she declared.

Nex sealed away his presence once more with masterful technique and the environment returned to normal. Now, with the tensions of battle out of the way they both felt as if they knew a great deal about one another.
In this world to battle another is to tell them all your secrets, to share with them your past and your deepest and darkest desires. Lily looked at Nex properly for the first time. She noticed the frame of his face closely and began to appreciate him for the dashing young man that he was.

"You're far too young to be an assassin," stated Nex.

"Are you not going to kill me?" she asked, ignoring his observation, "even though my attack was intended to cut off your head?"

"I couldn't have killed you, you mean more to me than you know," he replied.

"How can you talk to me with such fullness? We have only just met. You know nothing about me," she declared.

"Do I not?" asked Nex as he moved a step closer. "You favour your left hand far too much. The only thing your right hand does is balance out your strikes. I doubt you can even swing a sword in your off hand. Let's see, whilst your magic is exceedingly powerful and incredibly beautiful, you only know one spell, although I was impressed with your Soul Clarity. You wanted to fight outside the town as much as possible even though you work best when there are tighter surroundings that could compliment your speed and change of direction. The initial blow was necessary for the surprise attack and was loud and big enough to warn people to stay away, and you also struck early before the streets got too busy to avoid civilian casualty. Your fingernails are pristine, your skin is flawless and you smell like summer, but the faint sign of calluses on your palms show an immense level of determination and focused training toward your sword mastery. Hmmm, what else?"

"Enough! How were you able to take all that in during our battle?" she asked in amazement but with a frustrated tone.

"A warrior who watches only the sword will know only defeat. I learned that from my time in training with a master swordsman," said Nex. "W-what's wrong?"
She looked at him with a faint smile, her eyes glistening a dark green as the light reflected off a small tear that escaped her control. "No one has ever called my magic beautiful before," she said.

"O-oh! I'm sorry! I didn't mean to upset you," he protested.

Lily quickly wiped it away before she composed herself, "but don't think you can get off lightly with the rest of those insults!"

"I apologize. It was constructive criticism," he amended.

"But If you aren't going to kill me, then I won't be afforded the luxury of standing around idle. I am not yet ready to die and so I must escape the sight of the Mantle," said Lily.

"How do you mean?" asked Nex.

"Those of us who fail our missions are expected to atone. When I return to the capital a punishment awaits me, or possibly even worse. If I turn and run I will become the prey," she said.

"Do not worry," Nex assured her with a wink and a soft smile. "I wouldn't let anyone interrupt us. You will remain under my protection forever, I promise."

This was not just a mere speech to her. She was perplexed by this inexplicable behaviour. He had indulged her request, defeated her, and now gives his word to protect her? In their brief exchanges he has done more for her than any other in this world. What was this aching in her heart that she began to feel?

"O-okay," she muttered through her soft lips, the weight of defeat seemingly weakening all her senses. "I don't really have many options right now. But if I am not to return to the Mantle, there is somewhere I must go."

"Okay then, it's a date!" snapped Nex and he smiled glibly ignoring her hopelessness and turned and headed back towards the town.

"Wait, what?!" she exclaimed as she chased after him in objection, her magical katana disappearing into nothingness as she placed it into her private magical space.

"I did lift the runes on your katana, after all! You can treat me," concluded Nex.

She jogged lightly as she caught up with him and walked by his side. It was impossible to predict that the two who were locked in a deadly battle moments ago were now awkwardly and uncomfortably returning to the town they just demolished part of.

CHAPTER NINE: THE STRONGEST

Nex was finally able to look at Lily without objectivity. He could see through the warrior to the person behind. He saw a young girl, her beauty far greater than anything he had seen in his travels. Her face was young and soft, her green eyes eternal and magnificent. Her lips, small and untouched and pink like soft fruit. She had waist length golden hair that fell untethered down her back effortlessly to blow in the wind. She was very light and compact, with narrow shoulders and a small chest. From the way she carried herself Nex could tell she was a seasoned fighter. Although she was young it was clear that she had years of experience, hundreds of successful battles and a significant death count. She had been taught discipline at a young age, perhaps forced to by events not of her choosing. The way she crafted her sword with magic, the concentration in battle, the steadiness and accuracy of her strokes, her immense raw talent told him much.

She stood at a moderate height. She was a fair way off Nex, but she was no more than a full pace. Her armour was tight and clung to her with grace and truly exaggerated her figure to a point where her beauty could be acknowledged by all.

"Lily? What a beautiful name," complimented Nex with a smile.

"T-thank you…" she trailed.

"Beautiful and delicate as the flower implies…" trailed Nex gleefully as he pointed out with his index finger.

Lily's face began to increase in temperature again at Nex's compliment. Her inexperience got the better of her immediately before she even had time to react.

"Nex…was it? That is not a good name" she mumbled bluntly in retaliation.

"I know! I've never heard it anywhere else," said Nex.

"No. no. It is good. I mean, it is an unusual name!" she exclaimed as she tried to repair the damage.

Nex laughed as he felt the looseness of their conversation relax him, "haha. That's okay. You're actually quite cute when you're annoyed. It's actually a very old name" he said.

"Mhmm" replied Lily as she accepted his kind words despite her aggression.
"I don't think we-" she began before she was interrupted by a group of men running towards them as they re-entered the town.

"Hey! You, there! Stop!" shouted the men as they approached them in a fuss. As they drew closer it became clear that they were the town guard, probably coming to address the issue of the half-destroyed buildings…

"You two! Stop!" they ordered Lily and Nex as they poised their swords toward them, "you two are in big trouble!"

"Your little tussle destroyed half the town! You're both under arrest!" ordered one.

"Stand down, you idiots," said Lily calmly, dealing with the casual guards. "You're all a little late to the party. Don't you recognise my armour?"

"We-I, We didn't see the crest," they protested.

"Enough with the excuses. This man is wanted for high treason," she stated as she gestured to Nex. "The Mantle has issued his arrest."

"M'lady…" they trailed as they realised their blunder, recognising the Mantle's insignia on her uniform and bowing apologetically. "We're so sorry! We did not mean to-"

"It is of no importance to you. Send those whose homes were destroyed to the cathedral for refuge, whilst their homes are rebuilt by the Mantle. Give this coin to your head priest." said Lily as she passed a special golden coin to the guard. She grabbed Nex's arm and wrenched him forward like a prisoner. "Now, out of my way."

They walked through the gasping guards and deeper into the town.

"Hey!" said Nex. "That was quick thinking!"

Lily relaxed as she found herself speaking before she could monitor her words. "How did you like that, hm? You're not the only one who can invent stories under pressure," she said as she attempted to claw back some of her previous defeat.

Nex replied with a sincere smile. "Well, It's probably true anyway. If that Hymn guy was important or what not."

"You mean General Henrys?" she clarified. "He is one of three generals of The Mantle and serves beneath the Pontifex himself. That would make him one of the five most important people in all of Ares if you included the Sentinel Arcon. So, yes, high treason would be a simple bounty for you. Your warrant also states that you're a western spy."
"A SPY?!" asked Nex in outrage. "How dare they?!"

"You seem…foreign" she defended as she examined his western complexion.

"I'll have you know I lived in Ares for a very long time! Some might even have regarded me rather highly back in the day, thank you very much," pouted Nex at the gall of people he did not even know.

Lily found herself chuckling at his childish behaviour. "Well," she began awkwardly, "you're not from Ares…" she stated as she took in his western ethnicity.

Nex replied with an awkward and shocked nod as he tried to protest the obvious, "I…might be!" Lily laughed again at his behaviour coyly, satisfyingly entertained. "Well…no, I'm not originally from Ares."

"You don't say…" she said as she rolledher eyes. Her speech was so much more relaxed now that she was not fixated on battle. She had almost completely let her guard down. "Very important, powerful people want you dead," she clarified with neat hand gestures to him as they walked, "and you're more concerned that I don't call you Aresian…"

"Well it's no different from the last time…" trailed Nex awkwardly. I have actually spent a long time in Ares on this visit. I haven't invaded anywhere in a long time"

"The last time?! In a long time?!" Lily exclaimed as she grabbed at his arm to pull him to attention, losing ground against his words, "you know, I'm starting to regret that you didn't cut my head off."

.

Nex pulled a face that she had not seen before on another human being. It was as if his face shrank into itself with awkwardness and bewilderment coated with sarcasm and jest.

"It's a big deal that you put a stop to Henrys, but it's more alarming to the Mantle that some nobody was able to stand up and defy them and slip away without almost any trace. People of that kind of ability do not go unnoticed. Even one of the Ten Kings would not remain unnotic-"

"Should we just forget about The Mantle and the Pontyflex and focus on the fate that has brought us together?" asked Nex.

"It's Pontifex and what 'fate' are you talking about?" replied lily. "There is no fate here. They could have sent any number of us for you."

"But they sent only you," stated Nex, "with one of my swords no less."

"What do you mean 'your sword'?" she asked in confusion.

"N-no, I meant that I know the sword from…t-the legend" he scrambled. "I'm a scholar. A historian. A librarian of magic," he protested in haste.

"I was going to ask what it was that you profess to do. You are a scholar?" she trailed in curiosity.

"Indeed, I am" he said smugly as if to impress her with his profession, the crisp air surrounding them and passers by mumbling to one another as they became interested in the unusual conversation.

"Okay. Where?" asked Lily.

"Excuse me?" replied Nex in a stun with a snap.

"For whom do you research and gather?" she specified.

"Oh um…I do it for a lot of places actually. You know, all over the place and mostly here and there," trailed Nex as he softly pointed to his left, then to his right before turning to look behind himself as if the answer was on one of the simple shop signs behind him, and by some miracle of a chance, it was! A small shop that cured and repaired leather boots and armour hung their sign from an iron post. "Leather care and oil treatment" it read.

"Leather-acre Oiling Company for magical research," he said confidently. If he wore glasses he would surely have adjusted the rim to portray his accomplishment.

"Leather-acre…" trailed Lily as she looked upon the genius who had come up with such a name on the spot and was so sure it would be believed.

"Yes they're a very renowned company who supply oil to various other companies for lanterns and…" he had run out of things to support his lie "…other stuff" he finished.

"Really?" replied Lily in a flat tone. "Do you take me for a fool?" as she struggled to decide whether to draw her sword and strike him again without mercy.

"Uhh…" trailed Nex as he realised his tale had not caught on.

"You have clearly taken the text from that sign and rearranged it. You would have to be an idiot to believe it, or more so to believe that someone could come up with it and then believe that they had fooled another person with it." said Lily. "That was so obvious it actually hurt my brain to even understand why on Reath why you thought it would work!"

"I thought it was really good!" defended Nex through sulking lips as he pondered on where his mistake lay. "Perhaps I pointed in too many directions-"

"Lucky for you, There is something I wish to ask of a knowledgeable scholar. Seeing as one has fallen right into my lap it would be a waste not to exploit your expertise. You did also lift one of the curses on my Katana, I guess I do owe you for that. Let's go in here," gestured Lily to the tavern they had reached. Lily thought for a moment at the strange circumstances that had befallen them before pulling at the iron handle of the heavy oak door of the bustling building.

The old wood creaked and groaned as their powerful prints

strode across them to an aged maple table meant for more than two in the corner of the room. They sat facing each other, Lily's back to the other patrons. Nex surveyed the room. He found that almost all eyes had followed them across the bar. Lily's beauty was breath-taking. The eyes that followed her were of pure longing and lust whilst snapping onto Nex full of envy and hate.

"Is it always this busy at this time of the day…?" asked Nex curiously as he sat, attempting to begin a casual conversation with the young woman.

"Well there's a lot going on right now. All sorts of people come here to drink away their troubles, especially during these times. In the early mornings it is popular for people who have come back from travelling or from the city or even those who have completed quests or mercenary jobs that require celebration. But yes, even the common folk are here early in the morning."

"You sound slightly hostile…" detected Nex.

"Ordinary people always seem so weak. They act as if they require protection from the strong. Magic does not reward the ungrateful or lazy. They expect others to protect them," said Lily.

"But aren't the strong supposed to protect the weak?" asked Nex.

"Perhaps in an ideal world, but not here, not in Ares," said Lily bluntly. "The weak are trampled by the strong. The gap between the powerful and the poor is greater than ever before. The Barons and Nobles cast the net of The Mantle throughout the lands, and all the people are subservient to it."

"So that's where people like you come in?" asked Nex.

"What?" responded Lily in confusion.

"People like you," he stated. "Powerful people willing to make a change. To protect the weak. To protect those you hold most dear."

"Protect them? I-" began Lily before Nex spoke again.

"You fight for more than yourself. I can feel it. Our battle told me much. It reminded me of something I have not felt for aeons. A pure drive. A desire for a strength more powerful than that of any other. The strength to protect, the strength to change. A destiny of your own choosing, crafted and woven by your own hands. A destiny to ensure that you can never lose."

"You speak as if you know me. As if you understand what it is that I want and what I must do. But you have no idea. You do not know what I have been through, what horrors I have endured and what atrocities I have committed to get where I am, to become stronger," said Lily.

"I may not know the details," admitted Nex, "but I know your darkness. I had lived in it myself for a very long time, and even with a power that I cursed and resented, I could not save those dearest to me. There is something that I was offered that was truly a gift, but I was blinded by power and revenge. I can offer you what was once offered to me, but the choice is yours as to whether to accept it."

"Perhaps you know something of my destiny. Perhaps there is much you know, and much you still do not wish to tell me," said Lily. "I will do anything to gain the strength I need, but I fear I will never be strong enough for the destiny I must face."

"Hmmm," pondered Nex.

"What?" she asked..

"You're lying," he concluded.

"Wha-" she began before he spoke again.

"You seek strength, but you dread your destiny still. You avoid fate and chance even when it pains you to do so. 'I am still too weak to embrace my destiny', or something like that, is your conclusion," said Nex. "But, one must know the reality. Fate and Destiny are but forms of magic. You will merely bend to their will. But my magic is my own. My magic cannot be contained by destiny or fate. My magic carves my own destiny and will deliver all that I love to the stars above. Until that day, I merely flow as my fingers follow the threads of fate. It was destiny that brought us together: My Destiny."

"How could you possibly…" asked Lily. Had he hit home with his words? He held nothing back as he pinpointed her failings with words sharper than her sword. "I was right in thinking you know much more than you let on," said Lily. "How-how could you know all this? Are you reading my thoughts?"

"Nothing quite so magical, I assure you, " smiled Nex in an attempt to comfort her. This was only a half truth, however. Nex did possess something, a trait perhaps, a personality, an essence. Something resided inside him, like a beacon, perhaps of hope or guidance that drew people to him. The strong and powerful inspire and those weaker seek to be sheltered by their strength. This was a feeling that Nex did indeed emanate. Unbeknownst to her, Lily was being drawn in at an exponential rate.

"Buuuuuuuuuuuuuuuut, on the plus side," he added in a more pleasant tone, "You and I are together from this moment forth. What burdens lay ahead for you are now my burdens. What battles and struggles lay ahead of you are also my battles."

Lily's eyes widened in outrage. This mysterious young man whom she barely knew, had tried to murder and had then spared her life, now offered himself wholly to her. "You can't be serious? We have only just met! I just tried to kill you! How can you offer me such aid? I am a stranger! A murderer who relies on only herself. How can you trust me? How can you expect me to trust you?"

"I have already told you, Lily," he began, "the fact you have that katana is more than enough for me. Our fates are intertwined forever. You can choose to accept it, to accept me, or you can fight it with all your might."

Lily thought for a moment with her mouth aghast. Nex lay it all out on the table for her, exposing himself honestly and without agenda.

"What about you?" she asked.

"What about me?" replied Nex.

"You are a monster. Your aura, it was like a disaster. Just being there in that moment, standing as your enemy, my heart almost stopped from the fear. I have only felt strength like that once before, from the most powerful mage in Ares. What could you possibly gain from helping me? You want my katana for yourself?"

"Oh no, nothing of the sort. That katana is yours and yours alone," assured Nex.

"You neither unsheathed your sword nor released your magic power. All I felt was the aura of your presence. I was not even an adversary worthy of your Infinity Magic. The gap in our abilities is incomprehensible. There is no logical reason as to why you would choose to help me," surmised Lily.

Nex pulled a face that implied he did not know the answer, "Is wanting to help another person out of the kindness of one's heart really that unheard of?"

Lily did not know how to respond to his grand gesture. With her life, with her experience, there was not one person in this world who wanted something in exchange for nothing. But before her mind could dive to the fathoms of suspicion and distrust,Nex spoke again.

"So, what do you do to relax?" asked Nex, placing both his hands behind his head as the waitress finally made an attempt to come over.

Lily was caught off guard as she readjusted her body to better to ignore the question, "you've landed more attacks on me from unsolicited questions than you have from physical blows," she stated lily as she canvased the room with her eyes, acting disinterested.

"I am merely a vessel. Words are my tools" said Nex humbly.

"I don't think I have ever met anyone who talks as much nonsense as you," she stated honestly.

"Well maybe if you spoke to people instead of slashing at them with your sword, they'd have a lot more to say," said Nex jokingly with a rather large smile.

"Haha. Very funny," replied Lily, unamused, smirking in retaliation.

"Oh, so you do have a sense of humour?" Nex continued to laugh at his joke as Lily thought of her next words.

"First you defeat me and now you attempt to humiliate me in public. Just how sick are you?" she asked.

"You're definitely a sore loser. But I guess I would be the same in your position. That's another thing we have in common!" admitted Nex.

"General Henrys is very strong. As one of the Three Hymns, he is not easily beaten. On the few occasions we have met I have felt his monstrous presence. In terms of battle, he is utterly boring with his fight plans and strategies, but even I must admit I do not think I could defeat him. For you to defeat me without using magic and to defeat him with Infinity Magic just makes me feel even worse."

"Please don't look into it too much. It was definitely overkill to use that spell on Benrys. Besides, he had like ten thousand men with him and I wanted to see if the spell would work. Having fought you both I definitely think you'd be able to beat him. I also know a little trick that could help you become even more powerful in a short space of time, but I'll save that for later. I actually quite like being wanted by such a big organisation," said Nex.

"What do you mean?" asked Lily.

"Sorry, talking about the Mantle general just makes me laugh. Bending him over and giving him the bottom smacking of a spoiled child seemed the right thing to do," said Nex.

"You spanked him?!" she said in complete disbelief. "There's no way!"

"Figuratively speaking..." trailed Nex. "I guess mages these days struggle against someone of my calibre," trailed Nex as he blew himself up, raising his chin and examining his black fingernails.

"Oh no," replied Lily with a laugh. "There are plenty of people I could think of who would have no issue in putting you down."

"Oh? Do tell," said Nex, disheartened but with intrigue, inviting her to continue.

"The Mantle doesn't get to just strut around with the Sentinels because of some half-baked power," said Lily. "They have some Mages that would put even you to shame. General Henrys is known as a dragon among men, yes, but General Kleese of the Faith is a league above him entirely. Kleese protected his holiness personally with his Vault of Infinite War magic when the eastern tribes invaded a few years ago. Lucky for you, he and his army set off to reclaim Haraura. Then there is General

Veroeris, the Hymn of Wrath and, quite possibly, the most terrifying creature in all of Ares. Not once has the General has ever been seen to use magic. Like you, there has been no need. No worthy challenge has presented itself as of yet, apparently. And this is just the mantle we are talking about here, not the Sentinels or the Sisters of Silence or independent champions and mages. Even without the previous Sentinel Arcon and his council there are still plenty of powerful people in Ares who are not to be reckoned with."

"Okay, okay, I get it!" said Nex in disappointment as the young girl educated him. He secretly hoped that in showing Lily his power she would be more impressed. Apparently, this just made him fodder for laughter. "But why have such powerful figures in the church? Surely it is a place meant for worship, not war."

"Practicing faith divides people. To canvas a continent in a belief is merely a dictatorship under the facade of freedom. Those who cannot see how war follows are either fools, or those who desire such ends. The Mantle commands an army far greater in size and power than any other entity in Ares. It is surprising they took this long to reclaim the three kingdoms," said Lily as the barmaid finally brought over a tray with some standard ales.

"They're fine, thank you," said Lily, happy to accept anything at this point.

"Thank you" said Nex as the waitress looked the two over thoroughly, admiring Nex's glow and Despising Lily's beauty. Nex replied with a kind smile, one the attractive barmaid may take the wrong way. But in comparison with Lily's beauty she dulled like candle light in the blazing midday sun.

"Do the other kingdoms really need conquering?" queried Nex with a trailed thought.

"The Sentinels are the Gods of Ares now. Their coup ignited the underlying corruption of the capital overnight. Treasonous plots and regimes that had been in the works for years suddenly sprang into effect. None of the kings, barons, nobles and dukes are safe from the new rules. They must show favour to the right people if they wish to remain in their seats of power. The Sentinels are truly powerful, yes, but The Mantle controls the entire infrastructure of the continent. Taxes, imports, laws, economy, all tie to the upper echelons of The Mantle, and they will do anything that will deliver them closer to the Maker. The combined might of the Sentinels and the Mantle is supreme. This influence will reach far past the coasts of Ares and spread across the rest of the world like wildfire. 'Where one leads the other will soon follow in pursuit of power' or so they say. This continent is getting darker, and so will the rest of the world."

"Ah," said Nex finally. "So, you *do* feel it?"

"Feel...what?" she asked in return.

"The flow of Magic," stated Nex.

"The flow of Magic...?" she replied.

"Magic is life. It is all around us. It connects us through a stream of infinity. At its core, your magic and my magic are the same. Whilst your soul resonates with your one, true magic, at its fundamental routes are the secrets and foundations to other magic. This is a truth few ever learn and fewer still come to believe. But what you can feel, on the ends of the flow of magic that exist in Reath, are those who will consume it. Your power allows you to feel this wavelength through your senses as if we held a length of string between us that I pinched and pulled from the other end. What reverberates down the flow of magic is darkness. You and I are hopeless to ignore it."

"This unease, this creeping beneath my skin. This is what you mean?"

"The Sentinels have not helped. They have added to the infection. The flow of magic is darker and more powerful than before." Nex looked deep into her eyes, the sun kissing the cobbled road and bustling streets behind him. "This is only the beginning. If it was just the Sentinels, I am certain I would still be contained on that mountain top."

"Hmm?" asked Lily in curiosity.

"Oh! That reminds me?" said Nex, his mind snapped back to the town. "Does the Mantle pay for all that destruction?"

"As I'm sure you will point out to me, I did destroy more than was necessary. With that coin, the town can use the Mantle's infinite wealth to reconstruct everything that was damaged. The run-down, neglected homes will be rebuilt as new," said Lily.

"So you are quite the thoughtful person," concluded Nex whilst considering Lily's lack of decorum when crashing and smashing through the town like the stone houses were crafted with parchment.

"Hmph! So, what is your plan from here, anyway?" she asked.

"I suppose…" he began pressing his fingers together nervously "I'll be going to Eos to stop the Sentinels."

"Uh, what?!" she exclaimed as she slapped both hands down onto the table in a dramatic contest. "What do you mean?"

"I'm going to head to the Capital, take a look around at the Sentinel temple, maybe pop in the Mantle's church to see the Pontyflex, and grab something that I left there a while ago. That's basically my to-do list for the moment but I feel like I am forgetting something…"

The Sentinel corruption has infected the world. They don't

realise the severity of what they have done. Otherwise, they clearly would not have done it…Or, would they?" he then asked himself, raising an eyebrow.

"I still don't understand?" she asked. "The Sentinels…they enacted some sort of ritual to enhance their powers. The capital was in disarray for days. But it was an old magic, Lost Magic. I think they used some type of ancient totem or something."

"Hmm…" thought Nex as he cast thought into his vast mind, the synapses igniting from one route to another as he searched his infinite collection of knowledge. "I thought as much. I should make haste then in retrieving my belongings."

"Talking to you is more exhausting than fighting," said Lily.

"It was not always Humanity which ruled this world. In fact, to this day, I would doubt that Humanity truly holds the power they think they do. Humans have the potential to grow and that's what makes them supreme. But, we are thousands of years too early to fulfil that criteria. It is our folly to believe we are the rightful rulers of this world. After the great war the Gods, Demons and Titans returned to their kingdoms to rebuild and repopulate. Whilst it has been nigh on five thousand years, time is nothing to these immortal creatures. Humanity has been fooled. Human history is simply whatever the most convenient story of the time was."

"So humans rule this world only because the other races are in hiding? But what does that have to do with the Sentinels?" she asked.

"It is a misconception that only humans can become Sentinels. Sentinel magic flows through all living creatures. The Sentinels of this age have found something that doesn't belong to them and borrowed its power," said Nex.

"The ancient totem?" she asked.

"Goodness, when you say 'ancient' with eyes like that it really feels like you're insulting me," Nex stated with a pain on his face.

"You must be older than you look to possess so much knowledge. But if it was received as an insult then good. But the ancient totem is what I meant...mostly."

"Sentinel magic is very powerful. For the kind of magic that corrupted the order you would need a near bottomless source of magic power. Blood magic, as we know it, is an ancient form of magic from the First Age that requires a substantial sacrifice in lieu of exponential power. But, to sacrifice human lives alone wouldn't be enough...No. If the spell was indeed amplified by this 'totem' it must have been something alive with its own source of magic and power. There are few such items that could accomplish this but it is known that one such item does indeed reside in the Sentinel's ancient catacombs. The Heart of Asashima," concluded Nex.

"The Heart of...Asashima?" asked Lily. "I have never heard of it."

"Ashashima was a Demon God from before the first Age. But like all creatures, regardless of their power and race, they were susceptible to the Kursed infection. Even when defeated, his heart could not be destroyed. Primordial deities of Reath, some of the first creatures to ever exist, are bound by the Magic of the Maker. No human can undo such craft. His heart was then encased in a specially designed artifact. Which, conveniently enough, would have been in the ancient Sentinel library which is far below the Nexus created thousands of years ago. It wouldn't surprise me if, as its seal weakened, its whispers grew louder and fell on the ears of someone...lustful." said Nex.

Lily listened carefully to the story Nex told with such accuracy despite his speculation and lack of knowledge of the current, modern world. Nex's words carried with it some emotion that Lily could not ignore. "This must have been quite some time ago..." she added.

"Probably" agreed Nex with a smile, lifting the atmosphere.

"I've never found anything like this in the Mantles Library - the biggest collection of historic material in Ares," said Lily.

"They have no need for such factual tales. Myth and legend are more appropriate in seeking salvation with the Maker."

So,"clarified Lily as she summarised aloud, "you're going to the Capital to reclaim the heart of Asashima, which will involve large scale battles with the Sentinels, and then you're going to knock on the Pontifex's door and give him a telling off for being useless and letting the Sentinels run amok and starting a civil war, or something along those lines?"

"WOW! I thought I was being rather cryptic and indecisive but, not that you say it out loud, it sounds like a great plan!" said Nex glibly in declaration.

"You can't be serious!" said Lily in outrage, again as she smashed the table with both hands again and rose!

"We'd better get going, then!" he said as he downed the rest of his tankard and stood up heading for the door.

"Wha-" said Lily with her mouth wide open in disbelief. "WE?! Wait!" I can't just let you go and do that!" she exclaimed as her confusion clouded all sources of rational reasoning, her hands preparing to summon her sword, "and you need to pay for the drinks!"

Nex turned with a friendly smile! "Don't worry, we'll be fine. After all, I am the strongest," he declared with a nod as he turned and left. He exited the tavern with purpose, ignoring the door as it hurled open and Lily rushed out.

"I never said I would help you!" she shouted as he continued onwards to leave the town.
"Hey!"

"Well we'll do your thing and then go and do my thing!" Nex had it all planned out as he laughed on the beginning of his journey to walk east to the west coast of the Kingdom of Eos. His logic was sound. And for some indescribable reason, she yearned to follow this completely mysterious man. She quickly threw some aur on the bar and chased Nex down.

CHAPTER TEN: A BLOSSOMING FLOWER

The day had gone by rather quickly, or so Nex thought. The warm sun had begun to disappear over the horizon, the rolling green fields invited the moonlight and the visit of frost. The young girl had eventually decided that the best way to converse was to stand alongside him and not trail behind like she had for the first few hours of their companionship. Nex and Lily talked about trivial things for hours as they walked throughout the day, their childishness easily passing between the two new friends. Nex regaled her with ancient stories of myth and legend from long before her time that hopelessly took her breath away. Their destination remained unspoken but they both knew where and what they were aiming for.

Finally, as the sun crept over the hilltop, they approached the last village between them and their destination, and exited the mountain walkways to join the village entry. "You can't just say things like that when a girl isn't expecting them!" roared Lily as the two covered the ground between them and the village slowly.

"Why not? You have extraordinary colour in your hair. It's been hard not to look at it in today's sunlight," stated Nex as Lily began to act coy and bashful.

"Out of the blue like that when they're off guard? A lot of people would think you're trying something!" said Lily with suspicion.

"Can you ever be 'on guard' to receive a spontaneous compliment? Where I am from it is normal to compliment people on their admirable features," admitted Nex.

"And where exactly is it that you're from?" asked Lily.

"Far from here it would seem!" he replied.

"Oh yeah? What a beautifully vague answer. I would expect nothing less from you," she added.

"It's a small village over the western sea in the Acheron province. As you so eloquently pointed out this morning, I am not originally from Ares," stated Nex as the mood became heavier.

"The Acheron province?" began Lily. "That would be the realm of Amaterasu?"
"So you know of the seven realms of the world? Amatersau was the goddess of all the people in my land. It was to the moon we offered our prayers, not to war and conflict like the people who worshipped the God of War, Ares. Anyway, my clan of people no longer exist. My entire village was destroyed by a monster," said Nex.

"That's a shame, it would have been nice to go there someday and see if everyone is as strange as you." said Lily, pulling the mood back up. I wonder what it must be like to worship the Goddess of beauty."

"Unfortunately, there was no one there as weird as me. Still, you wouldn't have been safe from compliments to your hair from my people," laughed Nex triumphantly.

"Oh 'har har'" said Lily sarcastically. They drew closer to the town as Lily related to Nex with her soft words. "For a long time, I have not had a home either."

"No family?" asked Nex, unaware of the intrusion of the statement.

"Where I come from, we don't really have family. If we did, we wouldn't have ended up doing what we do for the Mantle. Any family I may have had before that I can't really remember. Either that or I chose to forget them," finished Lily.

"Our answers lay ahead of us," said Nex.

"You know, I've always wanted to go on an adventure," said Lily. Nex's eyes lit up as her words brought him an untold happiness.

"But, don't you get to go on adventures all the time on missions?" he asked.

"That's different," said Lily. "I want to actually go on an adventure of my choosing. I want to be free to choose my own destinations. I want to see places I can't imagine and witness the creatures of this world devoid of the stench of death. I want to try the different things the world has to offer and be free. There is so much beauty in this world, I just want to see it all with my own eyes."

"It is the truth," agreed Nex, "and if that's how you truly feel, it should become reality."

"W-would...you come with me?" asked Lily bashfully.

"Me?" replied Nex in surprise.

"Forget it. It was a silly question," she altered quickly.

"If you would be so kind to invite me, I would be honoured to join you."

Lily did not know why she had asked if he would accompany her. She was free of the Mantle, and under his care, free from any harm. It was her destiny to choose from this point, and she asked if he could accompany her. "Knowing my whole life that I would be alone to endure what lies ahead of me, it would be nice if you could stay by my side. Just for a little bit, at least," she said.

"Deal."

"Do you know of any other stories?" she asked, trying to move on from this awkwardness.

"Long ago," he began, "there was a blacksmith who forged a collection of weapons with a metal that he plucked from the stars. From the mysterious ore he made four unique blades. He placed a curse on each blade, sealing them, to prevent them from being used by others. The curses on the blades were so potent they would prove too troublesome for anyone other than the blacksmith to use, and therefore render them useless. It was a failsafe of sorts. One blade, so sharp, it could sever the very magic inside a person's soul, but the cost of wielding such a powerful and dreadful weapon drains the wielder of their life force. This katana was given a special name, and eventually, became the very katana which you own. The second blade, named Akuma: The Soul Eater, can absorb the magic out of any living creature. By absorbing magic it becomes a vessel to all the parts of the souls it has absorbed, releasing them on command. But the cost of wielding Akuma casts one mind into the abyss. The souls within the blade seek vengeance and haunt the wielder snapping away their sanity. The third blade, Pynagol, the Will Breaker. This blade infects the mind. Itss possibilities are endless and its destruction unfathomable. These three blades are the ultimate calamity between magic, soul and will."

"And...what of the fourth blade?" asked Lily, enthralled by the story.

Something about Nex's blade resembled Lily's but, although sinister and dark, it did not carry with it the burden of curses that these legendary blades did. The sealed Shirasaya that Nex carried was burdened with something much, much heavier. Its darkness was not something natural. Like the cosmos itself, it swallowed the light whole. It would be inconceivable for his jet black sword to be crafted of the same star metal as Lily's for it would be impossible to taint a blade with such darkness.

"The fourth blade, which was given no name, was simply destruction. It was jet black, and encompassed the end of the world. It is power incarnate," finished Nex.

"Then that means...you know the name of my blade," said Lily. "It speaks to me, it whispers to me through magic, and yet it has not revealed its name."

"It will awaken," began Nex, "the phantasmal bond between you and that katana. I will show you."

"And so...you are in search of the other blades?" she asked.

"Precisely!" said Nex with a wink. "I will show you a truth that proves our destinies are intertwined! If you wish for the cosmos to speak, it will tell you the truth."

"I..." began Lily in bewilderment, "I think I'm starting to trust you even less than before..."

"Hey! That's good!" shouted Nex with a great smile.

"No, it's *not* good!" snapped Lily back. "It's the opposite! You should be building my confidence, not shattering it."

"Oh, I am so very excited for you to see what's in store!" said Nex. "I bet you're glad you tagged along with my insanity now, aren't you?"

"Quite frankly I am more intrigued by you than anything or anyone I have ever met. If half of what you say is true it will surely lead to something spectacular! Can't you tell me more about what is going on?!"

"Of course not. You would never believe me AND some things you just need to witness for yourself! Mwuhahaha" laughed

Nex. "Would you care to tell me how you obtained that katana?"

Nex raised both eyebrows as he pried the doors of Lily's mind open.

"I'm not sure who held this before me. I'm not even sure how The Mantle came upon it, but it is not surprising that they would gather this treasure. As you say, this sword is rather useless in the hands of most. But all who tried to hold it were sucked dry of their magic power in an instant as the blade hungered. When I was put forward, it reacted differently, and I was able to use it somewhat. I was accepted as its new master."

"I see..." said Nex.

"Okay! so I have some questions," she added. "You removed the runes from my sword and even after that, I couldn't damage you when I went all out!

"Aha! so you did go all out?" asked Nex glibly.

"Well, obviously not all out but I did hit you pretty hard!" defended Lily.

"Yes, you did." Said Nex as he grabbed his forearms and rubbed the bandages, "I still ache."

"So, my question is, what's your deal?" she asked. They were much more relaxed around one another now. There was no animosity in the air anymore or tension or suspicion. They spoke like friends, joking and laughing at each other's company. They had nothing to lose from accompanying one another and neither benefited from silence or withheld information. The area around them was warm and settling. So much so, that the other travellers they passed began to take little notice of their strange presences and behaviours and conversations as they plodded along the track.

"I never liked magic very much. It was always more of a burden than a gift, contrary to what most people who seek power say. But I do find some elements of it very interesting. Eventually I grew to accept magic and in time I grew to love it. Limitless possibilities awaited, just waiting to be discovered through research and teachings. The answers are all out there, it just takes a keen mind to find them. I loved studying all magic from that microscopic ounce that humans possess all the way to the divine magic of the Immortals. I love it all!"

"But Infinity Magic is the highest tier of magic in the known world. The Magic of Gods. But the runes on my katana are something else. Even so, you did not release any magic power. Perhaps that is because you do not have any. Perhaps you know more than one type of magic. Perhaps you are quite the knowledgeable, powerful scholar. Or perhaps, and this is a much more plausible explanation, you possess a very rare form of magic - copy magic," she surmised.

"Oh like this?" said Nex as he swiftly summoned an icicle into his palm. "I can copy magic that I have seen being used."

"So it is true? You use a form of capy magic. That way you would be able to enact top tier spells, but only at the power of your own level. Therefore an Infinity Magic spell would be catastrophic, but it is limited to your magic power. So, in the grand scheme of things, it would not be as effective as if someone with more magic power cast the same spell?"

"That's exactly right! Well done!" applauded Nex.

"So you're a copy mage?" she asked.

"You could say that, yes," confirmed Nex. "All magic is fundamentally the same. So a copy is a very good example of proving how similar magic is because one person is using the magic attribute connected to their soul and replicating the magic in someone else's. For that to be possible it would require immense similarity between the core of that magic."

"I see."

"But, alas, I am not at all fond of what magic is capable of. It was 'magic' that the Maker used to create everything we know. Albeit a stripped back, simplified version of his omnipotence, even the smallest of creatures are capable of such indescribable things. Both Gods and Humans have brought untold death and destruction with the power they wield. I can say for certain that there can be no justification for the terrible things creatures do in order to obtain power. Magic is evil. It corrupts even the purest of things. Like the cosmos, the soul of magic is pitch black."

"You really seem to know a lot," she said. "When you speak of the Gods, do you mean the Immortals, the Maker's first children?"

"Those he created to inherit this world after the Titan's shaped it, yes," clarified Nex. "Those same Immortals who condemned humanity when the Maker loved us. Children of perfect imperfection. Children not worthy of his divine love. The Immortals ruled over humanity in the ages before men, but it was their fatal mistake to whisper the first sins to us."

"How do you mean? I thought humans learnt magic from the Maker himself. Through devotion and praise," asked Lily.

"In their envy the Immortals whispered secrets of magic to humanity. They loved the Maker more than anything, but when he forbade them from interfering with humanity their jealousy and spite was too much for his perfect children to bear. Humanity was but a weak child, they needed guidance and order if they were to be the Maker's true children. Humanity was an eyesore,an infection. The Immortal Gods thought we were not fit to even exist as specs of dust in the Maker's gaze, and so they sought to corrupt us beyond repair. The Maker, in neverending disappointment, abandoned us all."

"The Mantle teaches us something completely different. It was the Maker who gave us magic to rise up against the other races and become the pinnacle of all life. His chosen children," said Lily.

"I am not surprised that the story the Mantle teaches is an alternative. I commend them for weaving such fabrication," said Nex as he acknowledged their influence and sway of history. "Humanity was never supposed to have magic."

"Immortals…The Maker's first children," began Lily.

"The Titans came first. The Maker made them in order to shape the land and the skies and the seas. The term 'Titan' covers all manner of creatures from the giant, bipedal, elemental, primordial deities to the Dragons and Demons who equal them in power and gifts of creation. The spirits and animals and fairies and beasts are descendants of their creation. Once the world was ready, the Maker hand crafted the first Immortals, the seven Gods in which the provinces of Reath were named. But with their everlasting life and immeasurable power there was much they could not understand. Suffering and pain and growth and mortality were things they could not comprehend. Their devotion to the Maker was fanatic and obsessive, and stripped them of their freedom and purpose. Long after their trial the Maker crafted Humanity. Infantile, weak and pathetic, we looked to the immortals as Gods, to rule and to guide our civilisations. We learned much from them, but their parenthood was too…coercive. The Maker fawned over the insects that we were and cared for us deeper than he had for any creation before. His guidance and love aided the humans and evolved them, but it was the corruption and whispers from the Gods that turned us bitter and evil. When the maker saw the darkness of our hearts he declared that only he would influence us when he saw fit. Any other interference would be met with harsh punishment. Stealing their father's love from them, the Gods began to resent humanity and envy them. It would be fair to state that humanity is equally responsible for corrupting the gods too. And thus, after thousands of years as primitive, undeserving creatures, humans gained magic, and the first age of men began."

"Some of this…sounds familiar," said Lily. "I think I read once, in an old text in the Mantle, that the second a god reaches the moment of their greatest beauty, they will never age another second. It sounded like a fairy tale."

"Oh, very impressive," said Nex as he clapped somewhat. "That is indeed true."

"Wouldn't that be nice, eh?" laughed Lily. "But I suppose they have the power to do just about anything they want?"

"Magic of the Gods works in a different way to humans. They are unique in their own way. Immortality, shapeshifting, mind reading, flight, Divine Rights, are just some of the attributes a god possesses. But they are so very similar to humans. Just like us, they are bound by their souls. Even they are susceptible to the Kursed taint."

"The Kursed…?" began Lily, "the ancient foe of all life, the reason the Sentinels exist."

"You don't say that with much certainty," said Nex through narrowed eyes. "Does the Mantle not teach the people about the Kursed anymore?"

"Well, not really," she said. "The Sentinel order was formed thousands of years ago to fight an evil known as 'The Kused'. They were monsters, an evil that corrupted everything and anything it touched. But having been defeated by the first Aresian King and the Ankou, the Kursed have not been seen since. All that remains of them are the tales used as stories to scare children to keep them from misbehaving."

"It's comforting to know you got most of that right," said Nex.

"It is not taught," said Lily, "It is just something I read once."

"The path ahead will be a difficult one indeed. It will not come without hardship, but it will lead us to places that you could never have imagined," assured Nex.

"Hey! How long do you think I'm going to be following you around for!?" asked Lily.

"Forever!" said Nex quickly.

"Bah!" she replied with a scoff. "You're not all that great! A weird name, shabby old clothes and the manners of a pig!"
"Whoa whoa, easy there," said Nex defensively as he felt the full brunt of her mockery as he examined his unusual attire. Lily paused to allow Nex to recover from the bombardment of her attacks before she inquired to learn more about her companion.

"So, being a scholar, that's how you learnt about all the ancient history? And you know about my katana?" she asked inquisitively.

"I have studied lots of different things for a long time. There's too much to learn in one lifetime. Magic is infinite." said Nex.

"I see," she replied in thought "Is it possible you know something that can defeat the Sentinels? Or is it, perhaps, that the collecting of these swords will help you against them?" she asked.

Nex gathered his information, and began to educate the young girl. "Hmmm how very perceptive. Perhaps I need the swords to help me. Their curses, after all, are very powerful. But these Sentinels are not the Sentinels that defeated the Kursed. This order appears to be nothing more than powerful mages who know nothing of true darkness."

"But the Sentinel Magic, their glow, it is a true force to be reckoned with. How will you fight against their divine magic?" she asked.

"Divine magic? What…do you mean?" asked Nex suspiciously.

"The Sentinels' power was a gift from the Maker himself. Just as the gods use Infinity Magic, Sentinel Magic was magic crafted by the Maker. A clash between the two would be deadly."

"No God or divine being gave the Sentinels that power. The source of their power, the Sentinel drive, the glow in their eyes, it is from a ritual undertaken when one is recruited. It, quite simply, amplifies their power and provides a soul destroying attribute for the purpose of being able to shatter and destroy the collected flesh and soul energy inside a Kursed creature. It is essentially a glorified God-slaying magic. But these Sentinels, devoid of any Kursed presence, would know it only as an amplifying technique. I fear that even if the order were to face the Kursed they would do little more than add to their ranks."

"Well it's only recently that the Sentinels have become insufferable. A change in leadership has steered them in a whole new direction. But no-one really knows why the sudden change," said Lily. "One thing is for certain, though, they are much stronger than they were before."

"Nothing ever changes. No matter what the species, they cannot resist the draw of power. These humans have forgotten what it is they were tasked to do," stated Nex.

"The Mantle teaches us that the Sentinels destroyed the Kursed with power gifted to them by the Maker. He gave it to humanity and humanity alone as they were his chosen children. But after they were destroyed by the Mantle and the Sentinels, which were once one in the same thing, the Kursed just became a story. Things like 'you better close that window before you go to sleep or the undead creatures of the night will snatch you up and take you to the nearest brood mother'," she finished.

Nex weighed up her story in his head before commenting "the bit about the open windows is definitely true. That story used to scare me to death when I was little...but then again I didn't have any windows so..." he trailed. "That's beside the point. I am unsure if the Mantle and the Sentinels have a collected History. Most of my studies predate Ares' more recent generations. But with your logic, why would the Maker Gift humanity the power to destroy them? Wouldn't he just not have made them in the first place? There seems to be a collaboration between the histories of the two organisations which has now unified them again in the present."

"In the beginning, I think the Sentinels and the Mantle were the same thing, but at some point after the great war, they seperated," said Lily.

"One of Faith and one of Power..." trailed Nex.

"How is it you know more about ancient history than you do of more recent years?" asked Lily, noticing that Nex possessed little knowledge of recent events. "You know nothing of the current day and age, but know, in explicit detail I might add, what happened in the first ages of man."

"Recent history simply does not interest me" he laughed as he gestured with his index finger to make the point. "Gods and demons and myths and legends! THAT is where true fantasy lies. It would be too mundane to learn about the affairs of humans when they are so insignificant."

"You seem to not really like us humans. Perhaps you're hiding your true divinity from me to prevent me from shattering into dust at the gloriousness of your brilliance," said Lily.

"That's not true either. When a human sees a God they don't just explode. They kind of just stand in awe."

"Regardless, that is what the Mantle teaches us," she said. "Thus, it was the combined effort of the Sentinels AND the Mantle that defeated them."

"WRONG!" shouted Nex, "not even close."

"And how would you know?" she asked as she laughed at his outrage.

"From books, Lily. BOOKS!" stated Nex. "It doesn't matter anyway," he said as he gestured her nonsense away from him with his hand as if to physically remove it from his area. "I take no interest in the affairs of men. So boring and futile. Our tale is only just beginning, however," he said with a smile. "We have much to do, together" he said as Lily looked away angrily so that he could not see her soft cheeks go a plum red.

"It should only take us a few days for me to prove to you our destinies are one! And then, we can be together forever."

"Then a good night's rest will work wonders for us. You must be rather fatigued sleeping on a haystack," said Lily as she watched her surroundings.

"Oh, I'm quite used to it. I was thinking we would just find a nice big tree and... camp there?" said Nex awkwardly.

"You don't have any money, do you?" said Lily, easily concluding he had not a penny to his name.

"I have none!" he said with no shame, almost proud of the fact.

"Well I'm not spending any of mine on you," she stated.

"Aw, that's okay. I do not expect you to. I doubt I'd be missing much anyway, I've not slept indoors for quite some time, after all!. You know, they say you don't miss what you don't-"

"FINE!" she agreed in desperation. "What's the point in even arguing..." she trailed.

"No! I cannot accept it. If you wish to do something like that for me then first I must offer something to you. For tonight you should try it my way! After All, what is an adventure if you do not sleep in the great outdoors?!" said Nex, and with that they headed onwards.

The two continued down the cobbled route, occasionally passing a traveller or two, the occasional patrol of guard and a couple of land workers. Most of the road's traffic had not altered. The road-side camps remained and bustled with all manner of people who needed to break from their journey. Perhaps it was the discomfort of being around too many people that prompted Nex to pick a tall tree away from the congregation. For whatever reason, he preferred to rest beneath a great tree on a hillside out in the open air and so that is what he aimed for.

Darkness had crept upon them gradually. The two moons of Reath shone brightly down upon the world's surroundings beautifully. It was not long before they could see a village in the distance, lit up with warmth and vibrance.

"It looks warm down there," said Lily as they turned off the path and headed to a great tree that Nex had pointed out as they approached.

"There's always warmth in community, but it comes with a heavy burden," said Nex as he turned to walk backwards to continue their conversation face to face.

"So, what was it that you did before you became an assassin?"

"Nothing," she stated. "It is all I have ever done."

"Your skill is incredible. It must have taken many years of concentration to hone your talent. You probably started quite young and had magic etched into your bones," said Nex with sadness in his voice.

Lily couldn't explain the aura that he gave off. Inviting and ambient, warm and gentle glow, offering a hand of friendship that she had never experienced before. His words caressed her ears and eased her breathing, his eyes elevated the tension in her body and his touch freed her of fatigue from their journey. She felt comfortable around him, relaxed even, and the more she tried to resist, the more her brain whizzed and whirred to align with him.

"I was very young when the Mantle took me off the streets," she began. "It was not long after that my magic began to show itself and I was selected for an internal program. As I made it through their tests, they only pulled me through more and more. It's a tale with little content," she finished as they neared the top of the hill where the trees began to gather.

"And the tale before the Mantle? How does that go?" he asked gently.

"That story, either I chose to forget, or I decided it was not worth remembering" she finished.

"I see," said Nex thoughtfully as they approached the great trunk of the largest tree in the small wood. "You know, I could probably reach into your mind and-" began Nex before he was abruptly halted by a firm NO! The two slumped down alongside one another on the dry grass neighbouring the bark.

"What about you? You have certainly got a lot to explain to help me understand," she probed, turning to gaze into his deep blue eyes.

He thought for a moment before breaking away from her beady green eyes, "it's uneventful, but I can relate. Most of my memories of training are splintered with resentment and hate," he assured her.

"Magic really is everything to us," concluded Lily with a painful sigh.

Nex laughed. "Your magic is rather impressive. And your Aura…how spectacular! I haven't felt such animosity in quite some time!"

"Okay, okay. That's enough now," she snapped as she got rather moody and refused to look at the young mage., mistaking his lauchs for a mocking tone.

"That would explain your unusual aura," said Nex as he revisited the viridian glow of Lily's sinister presence.

"How do you mean? What is unusual about it?" she asked.

"Well whilst you did well to conceal your overflowing bloodlust to slice me in half I could feel your magic power a mile off. Your presence, your aura if you like, you had suppressed somewhat to mask your intent. But unless you suppress that mighty, overbearing tornado of magic power that gushes out of you, you're going to struggle to sneak up on people as strong, if not stronger, than you are. What you would describe as my presence, was what I exhumed when we fought. It is something that comes with age and experience and each and every battle moulds it. It is something you come to recognise with age and expertise. Maybe when you are my age, you'll be the same!"

"Well you don't look that much older than me now!" she stuttered as she became overloaded with too much information and grabbed at the only thing in her mind that she could.

"I suppose," he said with a glib smile.

"How old are you, anyway?" she asked with sinister intent.

"About twenty one, I think," trailed Nex as he looked up catching the moonlight through the thick green leaves.

Lily thought for a moment before she spoke, "I would be more than happy to be at that power in three years."

"Oh? So, you're only eighteen?" asked Nex surprisingly, slightly embarrassed, but also relieved. "I'm surprised you are not married."

"You don't have to marry young if you are a soldier. Wait, how old did you think I was and how do you know I'm not married," spurted Lily in response.

"Well, you look younger than eighteen and at your power levels...I would have said sixteen..." he began to trail as he saw the fury build in her face.

"I Look older than sixteen!" she roared in anger.

"So maybe five years!" laughed Nex. Lily punched him at the expense of his joke, right in the forearm.

"Ouch! And you have no ring on your wedding finger. Haha," he laughed in pain as he saw a smile creep onto her face, pointing to his own marriage finger absent from a ring.

"You're an idiot," she stated directly with a smile as they both chuckled softly, their happiness warming the cold night around them. It was hard to believe that no more than a day ago, she hunted him in cold blood.

"We should set off as the sun rises," said Nex to the young girl, "let's get some rest."

"And you trust me not to kill you in your sleep?" she asked.

"Well If I'm the one who snores I'd be surprised if you didn't," he replied with a smile.

They remained in silence for maybe two minutes as they both looked up to the golden stars in the night sky.

"Beautiful, aren't they?" said Nex.

"They are so small and tiny I feel like I could just pick one from the sky!" she replied.

"Each one of those little lights has worlds around it just like ours. Out there, far, far away are creatures just like us share their own tales beneath the stars," said Nex.

"Do you think we could ever go there?" she asked quietly.

"With magic anything is possible," said Nex. "Goodnight."

Lily watched the sky for a few more minutes as she wondered if the man beside her was indeed, not crazy. However, she began to realise that he was just as much of a menace as she had surmised but that he also meant her no harm. It was her first night away from the life that she knew and it marked the beginning of a new one. This experience was sure to be an adventure she would never forget. One that would see her growing greatly more than she ever could have if it were not for Nex. Before she could fall asleep she noticed that Nex's dreams caused him some unrest. But as she thought to soothe his dreams with her hand, she turned away and slept leaving the trusting young mage to be at one with his dreams.

CHAPTER ELEVEN: INVITATION OF DOOM

There had been many orbits by the two moons since Thusien's dreams had come to fruition. He had drawn the council from far and wide together to usurp their power for his own purpose and reinvent the Sentinels for his new purpose. While his duty to protect against the Kursed may remain, it would always second to his search for power. But it seemed there was still hope for the Sentinel Order. For far from the Nexus' heart in the Capital, beneath a towering mountain hollowed out millennia ago, three Sentinels sent away by the previous Arcon himself in utter secrecy, stood uncorrupted and pure.

As far as Ares stretched, to the eastern coast of Ibis in the Kingdom of Horaura, these three Sentinel's finally neared their destination.

"Vosk," spoke in a soft voice, "surely we should return to the Nexus."

"The Arcon trusted only us with this mission," said Vosk with authority. "He ordered our return only after the investigation of the hollow mountain. If you could have only felt the terror in his voice. "Even if the moons come crashing down upon us, it will pale in significance to the threat beneath these mountains. We gave our word we would not return. ourselves and seen it with our own eyes."

"But surely you can feel what has happened!" she urged. "We

have been away from the Nexus for weeks now. The Arcon's presence is no more. The order will be in disarray without your guidance. Surely we must go back?"

Vosk continued onwards not deeming it a strong enough argument for him to stop. "Galatea," he said firmly, "we are Sentinels. There is no greater purpose for those of us who have taken this oath. The politics and opinions of the Capital are not for us to worry about. The Arcon was no fool. For him to send us away...it was not pure coincidence. If we are to rot beneath this mountain we can ask him in the afterlife."

"What do you think, Daisy?" asked Galatea to the third Sentinel who wandered at the back of the troupe carefree.

"Hmm?" she asked as she entered the discussion. "What now?"

"You haven't been listening at all, have you?" said Galatea.

Daisy was lost in a world of her own. She trailed behind them due to an abundance of company. She was slight in frame but no less daunting than her larger comrades and despite being demi-human she was welcomed by them as a sister. With her two, pale, furry rabbit-like ears protruding through the white hair on her head she took in all the marvellous sounds of the world around her. The local wildlife, drawn by her spectacular magic, found themselves caught in her grace by the droves. Where she stepped, flowers blossomed in her wake.

"You're so cute!" she weaned at the little mouse in her hands that she had carried for a few days now. Deer, foxes, mice, birds and even fairy whisps followed her. She was like the daughter of mother nature. Her slighter figure resembled the nimbleness she held for swift movements and above human agility. These traits, combined with her enormous affinity for magic and her induction into the Sentinels, did indeed create a strong force, one not to be taken lightly.

"I don't think we should go back," she said. "I think Vosk is right."

"What!?" exclaimed Galatea in disbelief.

"The three of us have been sent here for an important reason. Kalus would not have wanted us to return to him halfway through."

"The Arcon..." said Vosk, correcting her of her informality of rank, resentful and exhausted of this duty.

"Besides," added Daisy, "the animals are scared and troubled. They tell me that they fear the mountain above all else. That is reason enough for me to want to investigate."

"Fine, fine!" said Galatea, defeated.

"We have faced and fought all manner of creatures on this journey. The Arcon would not have entrusted just anyone with his task. He chose us because we are the Vanguard," said Vosk.

"Mhmm!" agreed Daisy with a nod. "Go on now, it's dangerous around here," she urged her adopted animal children back into the wild. They did not wish for it, but they could not resist the command. "Vosk will surely earn himself new acclaim with the order. There should be an open spot to replace Kalus."

"Arcon..." corrected Vosk again.

"Oh, yes!" added Galatea. "Whatever this disturbance is, it will surely result in a new appointment for you."

"I have no interest in promotions or praise," said Vosk. "If I am to be the next Arcon then it will be because I am ready. But I cannot ever hope to approach the great wisdom of Kalus, I am simply not worthy of the position."

Vosk stood at just over six paces tall. He was strong and muscular, his dark skin sweet like the taste of chocolate finery. He was aged somewhere in his fifties, but his physique argued that he was still in his prime. He held the title of the twelfth heleic and served the Arcon personally. Whilst he knew in his bones that the order was now broken, the best way for him to direct his grief and sorrow was to carry out his mission. With thick, short hair atop his head and face he often rubbed through it with the tips of his fingers when he showed discomfort in his thoughts. This was a trait that his two companions had picked up on over their many years together. Galatea shared his ancestry, but her skin was of a much lighter shade of brown. She stacked out further than Daisy in all the right places causing her to be very appealing to the eye. Whilst they all wore the magically imbued, star metal Sentinel armour they differed somewhat due to gender. Vosk's was hefty and impregnable and coated him like a traditional knight or adventurer so that he could take the full force of any blow. The female equivalent was akin to the Mantle's exaggeration of the female form. Their thighs and waists were revealed to show the wandering eye their beauty whilst the armour and trim wrapped around their curvaceous bones eloquently causing the heart to skip a beat with its pleasure to the eye. All donned in marvellous cloaks they walked forward with purpose. It was rarely spoken of during expeditions, but through the way Vosk and Galatea's eyes canvassed and stared at one another it was obvious to tell they held a fondness that expanded further than their professional relationship. As dainty and as oblivious as Daisy was, she could sense that the two were romantically involved. However she would always protest that she had picked up on the hints before she accidentally caught the two in suspicious circumstances herself.

"But you're getting really old now," stated Daisy with no thought. The words stung Vosk like that of the tip of a hydra's poisonous tail. "If you don't make Arcon now then- "

"That's enough, thank you," said Vosk.

"Still" began Galatea seriously, "we are the Sentinel Vanguard. A Heleic and two Primus'...we truly did come prepared."

"Well I'm glad he didn't pick Raiku…" slurred Daisy. "He gives me the creeps. That, and he is insanely boring."

"Loyalty to one's superior is not boring, Daisy," said Vosk with disapproval. "But yes, he is a weird one. You can feel it, can you not? Darkness is already upon us. The trees turn away at guests, the animals flee the land and the cold breathes on the grass with its icy whispers. Evil is preparing. Preparing for the Kursed."

"And so, Ibis…?" trailed Galatea.

"Do you know why the Domashu carved the innards of the mountains away?" he asked.

"For all those pretty Gems." stated Daisy with surety.

"To house the most powerful and feared Kursed creatures," said Galatea.

"They are tombs. Before the first Sentinels defeated Chakravartin in the second age of men, the Domashu were ordered to dig deep into the mountains. If they could not be destroyed, they would be buried deep beneath the surface. It is said they even made one for Chakravartin himself, but no one knows if they ever did. The Sentinels are yet to ever find his resting place. Each mountain became a tomb for the Kursed generals so that if their seals were ever to weaken the Sentinel order could collapse down upon them before they were released onto the world. That is why we have existed since then, to watch over the seals and ensure they are never broken. That is our true purpose. Our true power." Vosk's wise words carried well through the thick air with grandeur and gravitas only to rebound off against the dull drums of his companions.

Galatea and Daisy looked back at him in confusion, complexity and boredom. "Oh, right…" they both said simultaneously.

"And here it is," said Vosk. "Ibis." They had journeyed far. All across Ares itself to reach the eastern coast. The power of magic was strong here and it loomed above them in the sky like an unwavering storm. At the base of the hollowed mountain the path broke away to lead up through the trees to the enormous sealed doors that had remained shut for centuries. The three Sentinels prepared themselves for their mission and began. However, their perilous journey had only just begun.

CHAPTER TWELVE: CONFIDING IN LOST MAGIC

The hills were quiet to the south. The fields and the forests were still and the breeze had yet to awaken. As the golden sun grew through the gaps in the leaves it caused the two companions to stir. They awoke slowly, quietly familiarising themselves with their surroundings and preparing themselves for their journey.

They groaned and yawned and stretched without saying so much as a word to the other. They felt refreshed, but they could find no avenue to advance their conversation.

"So, it wasn't a dream…" said Lily.

Nex chuckled in response, "There was no way it could have been!" and the tension between them was gone. They began once more, converging onto the main pathway that would lead them to the coast. One more town stood ahead of them before the final stretch. The sun made short work of the light given by the two dwindling moons and it lit the land far and wide and basked Nex and his companion in its warmth.

"How did you learn infinity magic?" asked Lily.

"Like all magic humans bare, mine was already chosen at birth by my soul," said Nex

"But I chose mine. One book from thousands in the Mantle's Grand Library," contested Lily.

Nex prepared, "before we even come into physical existence there is already a magic our soul is entwined with. To find yours is merely fate. Each and every person is unique. People are drawn to their magic subconsciously through acts of nature and choices of their own doing. The freedom of a choice is merely an illusion."

"I'm not sure whether that is true or not," protested Lily.

"Magic is a force that is far more powerful than humanity. To encapsulate one form of magic in the human soul is the very limit of our physical and spiritual nature. There are few cases of this fact proven to be wrong, but, as a paradox can dictate, magic is limitless and therefore can accomplish anything. It takes an entire mortal lifetime for one to master their magical attribute, and that's if they are highly skilled and naturally talented. You, Lily, would fall into that category. There is neither the time nor capacity for one's soul to house a second attribute."

"I find it hard to believe that there are those who know more than one magic, but I do not doubt that it is possible. There are indeed some true monsters in this world. And as you have said before, If the strings of magic connect, then it does make it possible for people to use weaker, subsidiary magics," she said.

"Correct," said Nex. "It appears my teachings do not fall on deaf ears."

"It would be a waste to ignore *everything* you waffled…" trailed Lily.

"Do…do you have more than one attribute?" she asked cautiously.

Nex studied his hands for a moment whilst he pondered a reasonable answer. "Perhaps. Perhap not. The way I learnt my magic was unconventional. My powers revealed themselves when I was only three years old. Almost immediately I was trained and developed in my tribe's ways of magic. To say I use copy magic would not be a lie, but it would also be construed to the truth. It seems you also have an effect on me. I could not have predicted I would be this candid with you, Lily, but you truly are special to me. 'Born from the void, rumbling clouds and shattering skies, the cracks in the fabric of our realm strike hotter than the surface of the sun.' That is the first description in a tome of Lightning Magic. 'Born from the void, in a world where the Maker's warm gaze does not reach, the power of the air between the stars above. One kiss turns all to a frozen waste - Ice Magic. If I am to cast my mind back as far as I can remember those would be the first two tombs I recall."

"What!? Ice AND lightning? As well as infinity magic?! That's impossible!" shouted Lily over to him despite their closeness.

"It's all a blur! My mind was not my own back then! Who even knows!" shouted Nex sarcastically, matching Lily's volume. He spoke as though he did not know the answers himself. He did. He simply skipped around the truth gayfully to taunt his new friend.

"Prove it," snapped Lily with narrow eyes.

"You don't take me at my word?!" said Nex, insulted and with a gasp.

"Not a chance," she stated coldly.

"Well I don't want to show you. How about that?!" snapped Nex back as he increased his pace in a tantrum.

"Nex?! Nex?!" she shouted as she hurried along behind him. It appeared she had indeed hurt his feelings. But after spending only a little time together, she knew how she would be able to make things up to him.

"I guess I could tell you more about my magic…" she began.

Nex slowed completely, allowing them to realign on the cobbled path. Lily sniggers and winked with her tongue through her teeth in victory of her successful ploy. "My teachers insisted I learn from the tattered scrolls they gave me. No one else was really able to bond with it."

"Hmm," began Nex, "they must have been more intelligent than they let on."

"Believe it or not the Mantle has the best Magical minds focused on magical research. I wonder if it's them you would truly like to meet..." her words stung but they were indeed true. As much as Nex loathed them he would thoroughly enjoy hearing every little morsel of research they had ever obtained. Lily was beginning to understand him well.

"Incredible!" said Nex with excitement.

"What?" said Lily in surprise as Nex's excitement overflowed.

"You weren't taught by someone to use your magic?" he asked in astonishment. "Was anyone else able to learn from the same scrolls?"

"I'm not sure. They were just taken from a discarded pile," she replied.

"AMAZING!" said Nex. "And the runes, how did they appear to you, did they rearrange themselves or was it like they were written in a language you inexplicably understand?! Lily was amazed by the accuracy of the questions he asked. She thought it to be impossible to know these things but it was as if he were there, with her himself when it all transpired.

"They gave me old scrolls and they were barely readable, but I could make out some of the runes..." she said. Nex smiled like he never had before. He had unearthed a true gem that outshone any other he could see.

"But no one else could read it, could they?!" he added with his hands gesturing excitedly.

"...Everyone else just saw old hieroglyphics scribbled down on parchment..." she trailed, her eyes wide and weirded by Nex enthusiasm.

"NO WAY!" he said as he was brought to the climax. "That is marvellous!" he declared loudly, unable to contain his movements.

"That is the true reason I know only one spell and a limited version of it, at that. It's a little embarrassing to admit it out loud," she began awkwardly, completely averting Nex's gaze.

"That matters not!" he summoned quickly and loudly, "there are many many more ahead of you on your path. Oh! I am so envious. What I wouldn't do to be able to learn new spells again! The taste of knowledge in insaciable. The tingling at your fingertips when your body activates a spell for the first time! You are truly special beyond all comparison!"

"Wow..." trailed Lily, "No one has ever said that to me. There aren't many people who know about my lack of spells, but from those who do know I have only felt embarrassment and belittlement." A fleeting thought shot across her mind in epiphany! Perhaps, along the vast strings of magic in the known world, Nex possesses the knowledge of more spells for her magic!

"How much do you know about magic, exactly?" she asked.

"Too much..." he trailed, "but hearing stories like that make it all worth-while for me"

"It's not that great, is it?" she asked.

"Uhhhh," said Nex in a dull tone, his tongue pressed against his bottom teeth dumbstruck by the young girl's coolness on the matter, "a human girl learns Battle God Magic, not from a God or an exceptional human teacher, but from an old scroll that's barely legible? That's about as 'great' as it could ever get. It would be nigh on impossible for a God to teach that magic to a human for so many reasons that it would be inconceivable, but you taught yourself the magic…!" Nex was lost. He was no longer walking like a normal person along the long, busy roads. He was stumbling around like a drunkard, his brain overheating from the star before him shining brighter and brighter. He skipped and he hopped as he mumbled things to himself about all the possibilities of magic.

"Battle God Magic…?" trailed Lily as she examined her hands and the power she wielded still unsure of what he had previously informed her.

Nex calmed down before he poured more knowledge upon her "Ares, the God of War, one of the first Immortals, had seven chosen children who he made Gods of battle and war. One of these Immortal children was the hero, Himeros. With a katana formed from the crashing of clouds and the hurling of winds he could cleave a Titan in two before the creature could even blink! Himeros stood above all but one of his brothers and sisters as the ultimate God of War. His legend is said to have inspired the very katana in your hands. It is no coincidence that you have both his magic and the sword crafted by his legend. You see Lily, everything intertwines." Nex was buzzing with excitement. He was vibrating so subtly as energy poured from every morsel of his body. He was incredibly pleased with his new choice of companion.

"I do not know the name of my Magic. The scribes in the Mantle could understand very little of the ancient scrolls they collected. All that they read were a few, barely legible runes. It just so happened to be a speed amplification magic that would fit an assassin well."

"Hm?" replied Nex. "No, It's the Magic of the Battle God Hemeros, the eldest Son of Ares, the God of War," he corrected.

"Uhm no. Its amplification magic," corrected Lily, further.

"Hang on." Nex prepared his mind. "Are you being serious with me now or are you joking around with me?"

"I just told you-" she began before Nex exploded in her face.

"You're not, are you!? I WONDERED WHY YOU WERE SO QUIET AFTER YOU MENTIONED LOST MAGIC! You didn't even know you had it!!" exclaimed Nex overflowing with excitement and anger.

"No, I'm not messing you around! It's amplification magic from an old scroll!" pouted Lily.

"The incredible tier of speed amplification, the force and power and knowledge to carve up a Titan. Your magic is one of the highest forms of magic in this world. I'm surprised a human can even withstand its effect."

"You're...joking," said Lily as she listened to the words. "I just read it off some of the old scrolls I was given..."

"Wait, wait wait," he began again, "No one at the Mantle even knew what the magic was?! They thought it was some form of amplification magic!?"

"NO ONE KNEW ANYTHING ABOUT IT!" she snapped back, having lost her composure. "I was the only-"

"ENHANCEMENT MAGIC? HAHAHAHAHA" roared Nex in a fit laughter he had not experienced.

"H-hey! It's not that funny!" declared Lily as she traded anger for embarrassment. "H-hey!"

"You truly are a specimen, young lady," laughed Nex as he wiped the tear away from his eye. Remind me to come to you when I need a good laugh, okay?"

"Hmph" she pouted, folding her arms and looking away. "For someone who has no magical presence, you really are quite condescending. You must think you know everything," she concluded.

He thought deeply for a moment, "It's a curse... to know the things that I do."

"A curse?" asked Lily with a slight worry.

"It's nothing! Magic is a gift!" he said through a forced smile. "Everyone has a feeling deep down that they want to become stronger for so many different reasons. I'm ashamed to say that it was a feeling I, too, was unable to rid myself of when I was young."

"That's nothing to be ashamed about," said Lily. "Everyone craves more and more power so they can become stronger. Everyone is always racing for the top. If you're a scholar and you live in an age where magic rules over the world, the easiest and most rewarding way to stand amidst the higher echelons of society can be attained through magic." She continued to look at Nex, "power was the only way for me to survive," she stated with darkness in her eyes, one Nex did not like to see. "Magic is the only reason I have been allowed to live."

"Magic is life itself," stated Nex in argument, "the fact it resides in you with such potency is proof that you can truly be free. Your destiny could not be contained by the selfish desires of the Mantle."

Lily took in the words like an epiphany. Never had it been possible for her to comprehend such a truth. Always at the mercy of others she had more in common with Nex than she would ever know.

"There is a truth to magic that once you learn, you will be unable to resist its darkness," said Nex

"Darkness…" trailed Lily in light horror, "have you-" she began before Nex interrupted her abruptly.

"Do you feel that?" he asked as he raised his hand in front of her chest to halt her advance.

Lily looked out to the village they had approached as the day had dawned on them and the travellers and traders thinned along the main route. Taking a moment to pause, analysing Nex's stance as she focused herself. She could feel it. The hair on her skin rose and her eyes narrowed in assault. It was as if in the centre of the town there was a giant beast, easy to see with the eyes but easier yet to feel with your senses. Like the call of a siren loud enough to shatter your eardrums it beckoned them closer.

CHAPTER THIRTEEN: THE BLYTHEWOOD

"It's coming from the town," stated Nex as he gestured with a nod of his head.

"What is this evil presence?!" asked Lily.

"Well there's only one way to find out. We should take a lookS" Said Nex as he began. Lily threw her arm out to grab him and hold him back.

"What?!" she stated in confusion. Lily knew the boundaries of her power had increased dramatically, and yet, the unknown terror that awaited was enough for her to decline the invitation of despair.

Nex looked back to her and spoke softly. "What use is power if the one who wields it lives in fear?" and he turned and broke away from her, heading for the town with haste.

"You don't have time for this!" she shouted as he moved further and further away. 'They are just his words. What do I care if he runs in there alone? Hnnnn'. Unable to convince herself by her own words, she reluctantly followed.

The two headed to the town, running over the green pastures towards the pathway that led to the main gates. But as their feet traversed the lush, green grass the soil began to harden and the countryside began to rot beneath them.

Their feet left the unwavering soil and found the cold stone. They walked through the large wooden gates that usually kept the unwanted from causing trouble. It was clear to both Nex and Lily, that this trouble had somehow found its way in.

"This is the work of the Blythewood," began Lily. "Stretching far and wide over the south western plains of Myphos lies the Bythewood, the enormous forest coated in magic and mystery. It is not uncommon for its inhabitants to wander from its fringes to the nearby towns. The tales of enticing nymphs and dryads are whispered aloud by the adventurers and traders who journey deep into its heart in search of rich materials for trade and wares and the rich treasures guarded by beasts. It is an area of awe and mystery that, through its dense and maze-like structure, cannot be mapped efficiently. For the Blythe Trees cut and felled for use all across the land as strong, sturdy wood, foresters adopt an outward-in approach so that their backs are always open to the air and not barricaded in by the mystical lures of the heart of the forest."

"Then it does not surprise me that a creature of the Blythewood has left its oozing home. The magic of that forest is tremendous, but there is no doubt it is ominous and sinister. Darkness looms on the horizon and it breeds in the air inviting all those who have tasted its taint to emerge from their dormant slumber and quench their thirst for despair. From the Blythewood danger creeps out," said Nex.

"This is the village of Wick, the timber town that lies to the very north of the Blythewood," said Lily, knowing that Nex was enthralled at her description.

The town was empty. Further and further they stepped down the barren streets. Stall wares and shop stock were strewn and ravaged. The blacksmith's anvils showed signs of weapons frantically forged in desperation. The town had been abandoned in a frenzy and none had been left behind.

"No guards? No people around whatsoever," said Lily nervously as she crept through the unfamiliar town, her suspicion rising exponentially by the second. "Something's not right..." she trailed, "where is everyone?"

Nex remained silent as he pondered before finally concluding his thoughts. "It doesn't look like they evacuated. Provisions and belongings are still here...the weapons were taken from their racks. There must have been some form of battle. But there are no signs of bloodshed..." finished Nex as he examined a battle-axe that had been left on the floor.

"This feeling...I've never felt anything like it before" said Lily. "It's like..."

"Evil," Finished Nex.

"Look!" said Lily loudly as she pointed towards the town centre. "A child? Over there!"

She began forward as Nex grabbed her arm and stopped her. "An apparition," he stated, "this place is shrouded in a veil of magic."

"A magic veil?" she asked. "Impossible. A veil of this size would take an immense amount of magic."

"Look past the walls of this village," gestured Nex as he took her gaze. "There is nothing here but this town."

Lily looked around frantically in perplexed confusion. "Where on Reath...are we?" she asked Nex.

"I don't think we are on Reath anymore. When we entered the town, we passed through a veil that coated Wick. Where we are now, is a fabricated dimension based upon the town. And this veil is immensely powerful and skillfully concealed. That would explain why we could not sense such powerful magic here until we were almost upon it. It is incredible," he said in awe.

"I- I...I feel like I'm being drained," said Lily as she brought her hand to her bowed head.

"This place...it feeds off life," said Nex as he finished surveying the area. "Lily!" he snapped for her attention as the situation worsened.

"Remember my eyes, Lily. Trust nothing," he demanded. "Remember our last night and how we sat beneath the stars."

"What?! she asked in confusion. And in an instant, she found herself alone, the fog around her consuming Nex.

Lily was now trapped and alone inside the cold village. The air had become thick and murky with a fog like poison to the body. Slowly, Lily could feel her magic being sapped from her pores

"Nex!? Where are you?!" she shouted loudly. There was no echo. The wind did not carry her voice to his ears. "Nex!" she shouted again as fear began to spread through her body, the fog sealing her away from the rest of the world. 'Remember our last night under the stars?' she thought to herself puzzlingly as she tried to align her thoughts. 'If I head back, I might be able to leave the same way we entered. How does such a veil work?" she thought to herself. "It's no use! With all this fog I can barely make out the walls of the buildings in front of me. Which way did we even come from?!"

"This is...this is not where I lost Nex," she said to herself as she turned. But the moment she had thought of Nex, she could hear footsteps coming towards her.

"Nex?" she asked cautiously as the footsteps stopped just out of sight.

"Lily!? Is that you?! said a familiar voice.

"Is that..." trailed Lily in disbelief and confusion.

A young boy and girl held hands as they cried and asked for Lily's help with their tears. "Lily?" They spoke as if they knew her and she recognised their soft faces somehow.

"Are you two okay?" she asked as she hurried towards them. They both continued to cry loudly, cold and scared of this nightmare.

"Have you two lost your mother?" asked Lily rhetorically trying to soothe them, bending down to their height. "It's okay, you're safe now." Lily began to show a thoughtful, loving motherly side of herself she had yet to show Nex. It only amplified her beauty even in this dark place.

"Lily?" they asked again.

"Where on Reath did Nex go?!" thought Lily as she was stopped by the feel of cold steel slipping between her ribs.

"Arg!" she gasped as her eyes widened, looking upon the faces of the two fiends smiling back at her with sinister eyes.

Lily waved her arm across herself defensively, releasing an enormous amount of force that crashed into the ghostly summons.

"What...are you?!" she asked as she rose to her feet, her right hand clutching at her wound.

Their faces were horrifying. Like a nightmare. They looked at her like no human could, their soulless eyes filled with evil with a crescent moon sinister smile. 'How could I have let my guard down so easily?' she thought frustratingly. She summoned her sword to her hand and prepared to slay the apparitions. They darted towards her menacingly, their hands poised like the claws of a rabid bear. But Lily's speed was leagues above theirs, and in one swipe, she extinguished them and they wailed as they returned to nothingness.

Lily fell to her knee from the exhaustion of the attack and the damage of her wound. She grimaced in pain as she looked at the deep wound pouring with blood.

"I was too careless. What has Nex done to me?" Her eyes widened as the epiphany consumed her. "Was it all a lie? He drew me here on purpose. Did he lure me in here so he could lose me? How did I not see this coming…? He betrayed me…He left me. Just like everyone else…" she said softly in defeat and yet she longed to see him again. For his face to appear and smile as he did.

"Nex…" she exhaled softly as she saw his smile in her memory. She saw her past self in her mind as she laughed at his weird words looking into the night sky with him beneath the green trees. The hand she rested upon him to soothe his nightmares. These were not her thoughts. She did not doubt her new companion. Something in the air was poisoning her, twisting her most cherished thoughts.

"Who's there?!" she asked the darkness. She could feel someone around her again.

"Nex?" she raised her head to see the man before her with an outstretched hand. She couldn't believe it. The hopelessness and fear evaporated as she reached out her hand to meet his. "Nex…" she breathed as he raised her to an embrace. Lily plunged her sword through him in a flash. She knew that the embrace was a façade. Whatever was at work here sought to lower her guard even further. To recreate his warmth and his affection would be impossible, no matter how great the deception.
The apparition stepped back with a wounded stagger before looking back at her and becoming nothing but mist beneath this shrouded veil where nothing could be real.

"Not once did I feel a cold touch from him," she declared as the apparition fell into the fog as dust. But the threat had not yet ceased. Whatever was at work here possessed a great strength. Something beyond human. Two more apparitions appeared, but this time they surged with power. Each individually was more than a fully functional Lily could handle. However, if she could just strike their being with her blade the curse would still take effect on these ethereal beings.

Like mutated humanoid parasites they sprang toward her with immense speed. It took everything Lily had just to prevent their claws from ripping her in half. But the loss of blood from her initial wound was taking its toll. She could tell she was losing consciousness. This was like nothing she had sustained before. It was draining her of her power as she bled. The creatures toyed with her in their one sided battle, leaping and phasing and slashing and slicing at the girl who could barely defend The words of the spell she knew could not be found in her mind. As the two creatures prepared to rip her apart, they slipped away into a crashing mist.

Lily fell to her knees and her face went pale. This was the end.

"Oh, that's bad!" she heard as she felt a hand on her shoulder. A warm voice spoke to her through the cold air.

"Nex...?" she replied as she began to lose consciousness.

He had found her. His presence alone allowed her to rest easily. He hurried to her and held her petite frame before she could collapse completely. She could feel it, slipping away from consciousness, Nex's true warmth.

Nex lowered her gently after a few moments and placed her on the ground delicately as if she were a precious flower. He raised himself from her body and stood up straight, focusing on where the two apparitions had disappeared. Nex had already begun his magical spell that emitted a beautiful green glow from his hand and encased Lily's wound.

He could already hear it, the approach of his true enemy.

"Nex…? Is that you?!" It spoke in a wayward tone. "It's m-" spoke the young, frail girl battered and torn in her little night gown.

"Your illusions will have no effect on me, Demon!" said Nex calmly as the apparition froze.

"Ohhhh? Is that so?!" it spoke again, but with a sinister tone, the poisonous evil expression upon its visage once more. "This one is not like them. Different to them. Hmm, not like the others…" said the apparition as its mouth and eyes widened greatly to create a deformed head, the features vanishing into the abyss.

"You devoured all the people in this town?" said Nex in a serious tone.

"These ones have been consumed, yes," it said, "different creatures must see a different façade as they approach. Something that appeals to them. Otherwise the others will not come."

Nex, for the first time, was showing signs of frustration and anger.. He had taken a young mage into his care and acted recklessly. Her wound was a result of his arrogance. His blood began to boil slowly. He looked back at the demon with a stare more menacing than that the creature had ever seen.

"You look into our mind to find our nightmares and our fears," he said.

"Hahahahaha," roared the demon. "This one is humorous. Humans are all the same with their arrogance and ignorance. The Blythewood has been my home since before the ages of men," said the Demon as it looked into the distance. "Now the darkness covers all this land. We are welcomed from the shadows," said the apparition as it grew in size. In this domain, where the world slips through the veil into the spirit realm, there was no opposing this presence.

"You do not fear it? What lies on the horizon?" asked Nex. "This one fears the taint! Fear not, young human, the taint will destroy us all," began the demon, "and in the darkness we will all become one."

"I see," stated Nex with clarity, "It is your obsession with your maker that drives all you children to such insanity. Even after all the years you have lived you cannot deny your nature."

"Neither can you, human. Now," began the demon, "this one's little friend here is quite the prize. I've been in search of a strong vessel to permanently bind me to the physical world for quite some time. When I sensed her approach, it was difficult to contain my excitement, hehe. But here she is. Now, what to do with the unwanted vermin. Would this one like to sit and watch whilst I fuse with her? It will be a beautiful spectacle to behold. I will charge this one no fee. No...yes! This one's audience will be payment enough. Oh, and the despair. I will feast on it! Devouring a magicless worm like you will be no good! You must be shown despair."

The demon laughed at him loudly, reaching out into his mind to corrupt and destroy Nex's will and drive him into despair. But as it lunged forward with all its might. It found itself frozen in fear. It retracted its aura and retreated back into the form of the tiny young girl it had first assumed.

"What is it that you fear?" Nex asked the demon.

"This one, his mind..." began the demon. "It's...it's...."

Nex looked unlike he ever had in our eyes. It was good that Lily had not yet regained consciousness to witness the monster awaken from inside him. "You fear me," he stated.

"W-wait" stuttered the demon as it began to stagger backwards. "This one is…This one is…"

"You have one too many sins to bear. I shall ease the suffering of your soul," stated Nex. He closed his eyes and released his aura, and with a tremendous whirlwind and updraft it rose. The fabric of the demon's reality began to tear at the force he emanated alone. This Demon, this powerful creature, had challenged a being it could not possibly ever hope to comprehend. Its chance of survival was zero. This was Nex's true presence!

He reached outward with his right hand and spoke the last words the demon would hear. "A human, no less. Not a God or Titan. But what is this one? How can it instil such fear inside me? ME? What is this feeling? Is it darkness? Am I about to die? Is this despair?!" quivered the Demon.

"I will show you…what It is that I am burdened with," began Nex as he revelled in the feeling of release. The Demon could not defend against the power. In this dimensional pocket Nex was safe from prying eyes as the demon, a substantial one at that, did all it could to remain intact at the vying forces that began to tear it apart.

"Bu-" it sputtered. "I am no lowly demon! This one must stop!"

"It is your turn to be devoured," said Nex as he consumed the demon, vanishing it into nothingness before concealing his power once more.

CHAPTER FOURTEEN: CORRUPTION

The thick fog lifted instantaneously into the air as the warmth of the sun poured in and lit the dark corners of the town that had been swallowed by the demon's curse. Nex turned his attention to the young girl at his feet as she groaned, slowly regaining consciousness. He leant down to her to help her to her feet.

"Ow, ow, ow," said Lily as Nex raised the disorientated girl to her feet, the warm glow of his healing spell calming her body and soul.

"What happened? Am I not dead?!" she asked in disbelief.

Nex smiled at her, "don't be so foolish. I promised I would protect you forever. You did almost die, though," he admitted.

"Whaaaaat!?" she said as she broke from him and began touching herself to make sure her form was physical.

"The demon had cast its veil over the entire town, a curse that separates us from the real world. But if you were to die there it is incredibly difficult to get your soul back to your body in this world."

"So that was Demon? I have never seen one before," she trailed in utter amazement.

"Demons use curses to devour their victims. Whilst it is different to magic, fundamentally it is an unexplainable force derived from it. Demons will reach into our minds to find the memories that will make you most vulnerable. They consume people for sustenance and power. This one, sought a suitable, powerful vessel. You would have been that person," said Nex

"Possessed me as a vessel..." trailed Lily, somewhat subconsciously familiar with the concept. "But wait, 'looks into my mind'? Isn't that something you said you could do for me?"

"I remember no such thing!" said Nex swiftly in denial and going back to the subject at hand. "A creature that powerful fused with a human as like you would have created something truly terrible!" assured Nex.

"Wow," said Lily, "but what of the townsfolk?"

"There was nothing left. I am not sure how long the demon had been there. A few weeks, perhaps?" said Nex.

"Those poor souls..." trailed Lily as she remembered her wound. "It wasn't real."

"What great timing," said Nex as he turned away from the village to look North.

Lily turned with him, sensing the presence he had sensed moments before her. "This pressure..." she trailed as the fear struck her like lightning

"Oh?" said Nex as they approached over the hill.

"Sentinels!" said Lily in awe.

Lily was astonished. She could not fathom its power. Despite being as powerful as she was, she had never been looked upon by a Sentinel as its prey. This was truly a rare sight. The pressure it gave off was amazing, the malice in its eyes and its hostility was no longer human. A Sentinel approached accompanied by two masked warriors from the Mantle. Its Silver, Star Metal armour, blackened by dark magic. His skin discoloured and tainted. It came to a stop before the two companions. Its presence was overwhelming, taking an effect on the soldiers it led.

Nex remained silent, wholly unimpressed by the Sentinel's display of power and fear.

"You know of death. I can feel it radiating off you, despite your lack of magic and aura," said the Sentinel. "As the strong do, they seek others in which to test their power. You may just satisfy my desire. Henrys is weak. Know that to face me is to face total and utter despair. Please, allow me the honour to acquaint you with true terror."

"They are like me. Assassins," said Lily as she gestured to the two cloaked soldiers that accompanied the Sentinel.

"Ah" began the Sentinel. "An assassin who, not only failed their mission, but out of fear of discipline chose to side with her target? Tell me, do you align yourself with this man or are you playing some type of elaborate game with him?" Lily was now given a choice. Was she to side with the man, her previous target, that she had only known through a few moons? Or was she to return to her previous life and fight her new companion. This was her test.

"Do not feel like you are constrained, Lily," spoke Nex without taking his eyes off the threat. "I will bear you no ill will if you choose to return to your previous life. I will cherish the time you shared with me, no matter the outcome."

This did not help Lily decide. She wanted to stay with him. She wanted his warmth. She wanted to hear his ludicrous stories of the distant past and laugh and joke with him. She wanted to suffer his compliments so she could retort with hurtful comments. There was no decision to be made.

"No," she stated. "I do not fight for the Mantle any more. My loyalty is with this man, and him alone. I have begun my own adventure and I am in control of my own destiny."

"Ugh. To think I would be re-assigned from my team to dispatch lowly creatures like the two of you. Timoleon, my love, oh how I miss you. Very well. Kill her" ordered the Sentinel.

Lily launched at the two advancing assassins to intercept. It was unclear if she knew them. The assassins rarely met each other and, in one of their conversations on the road, Lily had expressed that they all held a distaste for one another. She crashed into them displaying her immense skill, completely revitalised by Nex's healing spell. These assassins were truly formidable. They must have accomplished as many missions as Lily. But against her, their efforts were for naught, even outnumbering her two to one. Something inside had been ignited by Nex. Her new drive to live her life had granted her a strength she previously lacked, combined with her unhindering blade, Lily defeated them with relative ease before pointing her sword at the Sentinel in defence.

"Oh?" asked the Sentinel with intrigue. "The curse on your blade has been lifted…by this one no less," he concluded as his senses informed him. He looked at Nex with interest. "This must mean your abilities have increased exponentially. Perhaps I will see more stimulation than I first anticipated…"

"Come if you will," warned Lily as she poised herself and focused her power in Nex's defence, "but I will not let you have him."

Nex watched his beautiful new companion challenge the tainted foe with awe and admiration. He found her performance inspiring and brave and his heart became warm at the thought of her.

"I would not have it any other way, Mantle assassin."

Lily accepted the Sentinel's advance and greeted him in battle. She launched onto the Sentinel with a strike of her sword akin to what she used on Nex when they first met, but with her new, enhanced power. The force of the blow staggered the Sentinel and created an incredible amount of dust to inhibit their vision, but the Sentinel's gauntlet reached through and grabbed at her collar, wrenching her out of the air and throwing her to the ground behind him with a tremendous crash. She rolled and recovered quickly, striking again. This time, it collided with the Sentinels open hand and her katana shattered as if it were made of glass. The Sentinel quickly snapped his hand around her neck and began to strangle her as he lifted her above his head.

"Pathetic," he said beneath his helmet.

Lily stopped struggling and raised her legs up and around his arm, gripping him and rolling to throw him on his own weight. He, too, rolled out of the attack and recovered.

The Sentinel became frustrated by Lily's adaptability and her strength. Being thrown down was almost as insulting as being defeated. The Sentinel, as he rose to his feet, accepted her challenge formally as a worthy opponent for his mighty power.
Nex was excited. He watched the young girl improve with every action against the formidable foe. But his excitement was beginning to reveal a malice inhibited with sinister intent that he had previously hidden extremely well. His distaste towards the Sentinel was beginning to emerge. Lily continued to battle the sentinel hand to hand for hundreds of blows before, after one tiny mistake, the Sentinel landed a sweep kick to her legs that sent her crashing to the floor. He quickly raised his leg to bring it down on her head with a skull shattering force, but Nex came between them in a flash and sent him some one hundred paces down the hill.

"He's on a whole other level!" exclaimed Lily as she accepted Nex hand.

"Have you never fought one before?" he asked.

"Thanks. And no, I haven't," said Lily as regained herself. "This would be the first time I've fought a Sentinel. I can do this," she assured Nex. He smiled at her with comfort as he put his belief into her words so she may begin her second attempt.

"Believe in yourself. Remember you have a new sword now, and you truly know the magic that is in your soul."

Lily honed her breathing. She widened her stance and summoned her sword back to her, the air cracking and whining with the snarl of the magic that brought the katana to her from a pocket of unknown, magical space. She now knew the true form of her Magic. A magnificent and powerful 'lost magic' used by a God. This understanding, this truth, connected her fathoms deeper to the power. "Godspeed: Titan Ripper!" she shouted from her busted lung as she released herself towards the Sentinel. With only one swing one hundred cuts shredded the landscape. The Sentinel was unprepared. The spell packed much more power than he had anticipated and his lack of defense made his body suffer. He had underestimated her greatly.

'He is both fast and strong' thought Lily. 'But compared to Nex, there is no contest. I can beat him!'

"Fall!" shouted Lily as an emerald magic circle appeared above the Sentinels head which released a charge of emerald shock at him. "Banishing Star!" This was a spell Lily had never learnt. It was not taught or read from a magical scroll but bellowed from her mouth as if she had known it forever. This was a gift from the magic itself, bestowed upon its user from their soul in times of desperation or growth. An enormous blast of magic beamed down upon the Sentinel whilst he roared in pain. Once the smoke cleared and the dust settled, the Sentinel emerged, reinforced and with only minor damage. Nex was in awe.

"To think I must use my magic to defeat someone like you," muttered the Sentinel in disgust. "This is *my* power!" He opened himself up, channelling all of his tremendous Sentinel powers unto him. The wind and the air poured in and the trees pulled toward him like he was a vortex demanding the consumption of all that surrounded him.

"So...powerful..." exclaimed Lily as she felt herself being crushed by his overwhelming magic power, protecting her face desperately at the cataclysm of power.

"I commend you. You have stimulated me more than you could ever know. You have raised my hopes. I pray you do not die before I have had my fill!" roared the Sentinel. He summoned his power to himself in a fury "Enchantment, Iron hide of the Elder Dragon! Strength of the Domashu, speed of the Rakusha."

Magic erupted from the Sentinel as his body was enhanced with the tremendous traits of legendary creatures. "Re-enforcement magic?" questioned Lily. Lily released herself again, only to find his armour akin to that of a great dragon, impenetrable and ultimate. Her legendary, cursed blade could not even scratch it. Her movements felt heavier and slower under the Sentinel's colossal pressure whilst his enhanced body was faster and stronger.

"Come now, you do not think your Legendary sword can pierce the hide of a dragon!?" scolded the Sentinel. Nex scoffed at the ridiculous question as Lily re-examined her approach. She launched, the ground crashing at her might, but this time, the Sentinel employed his speed and evaded her attacks before bringing his strength down upon her. She crashed into the ground once more and looked up at the victor.

The Sentinel did not proceed. His senses would not allow him to take his eyes off Nex as the last time he did, the magicless mage was upon him faster than he could comprehend. The concealed aura that began to creep from Nex like smoke was something he could not deny. His eyes found the black sword Nex carried.

"Another cursed blade of the master smith?" asked the Sentinel. Nex smiled at the challenge and invited the Sentinel to approach.

"Superb, Lily! Your performance was spectacular. You were much closer to beating him than you might think!" said Nex.

The Sentinel lowered his head and aimed at Nex, death and despair in his eyes as they began to glow a deep crimson. "You fool! I'll show you just how great the gap in our power is! This is the true power of a Sentinel: Sentinel Drive!"

This spell was the activation of the Sentinel power. Through the glowing of the eyes, the Sentinel employed his full abilities and prepared to decimate his opponent. Like a swooping dragon, he launched, and posed a blow unlike that of any power he had previously demonstrated, the likes of which could possibly even dent the great walls of the Nexus Temple. The punch collided with Nex creating an avalanche of devastation to cover them in dust and debris.

"NEEEEX!" shouted Lily. The raw surge of power from the blow spelled only destruction and loss. In an instant, anything Lily had to begin to feel for her new friend was shattered by the all powerful, unopposable Sentinel. With all her might she stabbed the ground with her blade just to prevent herself from being blown away.

The dust settled slowly, but it was too late for the Sentinel. He had realised that his attack would have no effect. In order to fight against a foe of this calibre, Nex was forced to get a little serious. His aura was immense. The world itself became hollow. Energy swarmed Nex as if extinction was at hand. Nature yearned for the apocalypse so as to not suffer exposure to his power further. Simply, it was if a God stood among mortals.

"Nex..." trailed Lily, too amazed to shield herself from his power.

"Impossible!" said the Sentinel in complete disbelief.

"That was pretty good," said Nex, "but your Sentinel powers don't seem to be like the ones I remember. Now, let me put on a good show for my dear friend who did oh so well against you," he said to the amazed Sentinel who had frozen.

"Wha-"

Nex returned with a punch of his own that crashed into the Sentinels abdomen piercing the dragon-scale enchantment like glass, the force of which could be felt far and wide as the shockwave spread. Nex threw the Sentinel away and allowed him to recover.

"What a blow…" muttered the Sentinel through blood and gritted teeth, the internal bleeding apparent.

"That's the spirit!" shouted Nex, all excited. "Come, give stimulation to my existence!"

The Sentinel roared and re-enchanted himself with his enhancements in a last-ditch effort to destroy Nex. "I WILL NOT LOSE!" as he sprang. With his sword still sheathed and held weightlessly in his left hand Nex evaded the Sentinel and defended with ease. After a few attacks, he found himself tiring unnaturally. He received a blow to his own abdomen and staggered back.

"You are only human, after all" said the Sentinel.

"Impressive. You can not only enhance yourself, but enchant others with negative attributes. You didn't even need to say the spell." He turned to Lily for his next statement, "these Sentinels truly are terrifying. He straightened himself and recovered fully knowing his next move would finish the fight.

"Come!" roared the Sentinel, "You have yet to release your magic power. Am I not worthy of your magic?!"

"Not even close, corrupted filth" stated Nex coldly through dark eyes.

"RAAAARRRG!" roared the Sentinel as he rampaged towards Nex, his magic power destroying the ground beneath him with its intensity. But Nex was already around him and caught his back with a soft chop. The Sentinel could do nothing. The earth absorbed him from the force akin to that of a meteorite crashing from the skies.

"You weren't half bad, you know," said Nex as he turned away from the defeated Sentinel and looked for his comrade as she rose to her feet.

"That power…" she trailed still in complete awe and amazement.

"ILook how far you have come already! You even learned a new spell through your own connection to your magic!" said Nex enthusiastically and with pride. "You are completely different!"

Lily found it impossible to comprehend Nex's overwhelming power. In this world, where magic was everything, he had used not even a morsel to defy the strongest order of warriors in the world. Was he truly human and was defeating the Sentinels and destroying the Kursed really something this man could achieve. It seemed, with his power, it was possible.

Lily began to stutter as her words danced around on the end of her tongue, "N-Nex…"

"Your power will only increase exponentially. Come, Lily. Our destinies await us."

"But-" began Lily as she thought to protest accompanying him further. "I…"

"It's okay. We are already great friends," assured Nex with a smile as they began off to the final village before the coast.

CHAPTER FIFTEEN THE HOLLOW MOUNTAIN

Far from the intertwining fates of Lily and Nex, in the mountain kingdoms to the North, horror and despair lies on the horizon for all those who dare take for granted the warmth of peace. Beneath the peak that pierces the sky, the mountain of Eayr has been hollowed out for milenia by the ancient Titans under the influence of men. Enormous creatures built for shaping the land by the maker.

This great city erupts with wealth and flourishes on the trade of its valuable jewels found deep below, buried and formed before humanity's existence. This kingdom was never meant to be a dwelling for any living creature, but over time, humanity's greed and ambition has led them to ignore the legends of old. But the civil unrest has the trade in tatters. Production and distribution suffer at the hands of power and lust. Dark times gather within the sanctuary of this mountain and beneath them is a darkness they are too ignorant to learn. This negative emotion, this cold atmosphere, is the first arrow to pierce humanity in the great chaos that is to come.

Three Sentinels, dispatched personally by Raiku, have been sent to investigate the disturbing reports from beneath the mountain. As in all places of Ares, the Sentinels and the Mantle hold great influence and respect in the mountain kingdoms, but it is fear that concedes to them now. Children flee from the streets as mothers and merchants cower away from their presence. But on this dark night, where the black skies are so bold they creep beneath the mountain, an ancient manifestation of evil claws its way to the surface...

"Tomlin?" said a mother in beckon of her young son.

"Yes, mother," he replied from the safety of his bed.

"Ah," she said softly, "you are already in bed," she stated as she walked over to him to perch by his feet.

"I am very tired," he lied.

"I see," pondered the mother, "and Martha?" she asked as she turned her attention to the other bed in the room.

"I'm ready for bed, too," replied the young girl.

"Very good you two. You are both so well behaved," said the mother gently as she kissed Tomlin and Martha on the forehead, wishing them a goodnight with her bedtime demeanour. "Mother?" asked Tomlin before she could leave, "could you close the window," he asked in fear.

"Of course, my dear," she replied as she walked slowly over to the window smiling back at him in comfort. "But we must not forget our 'please' and 'thank you'. There," she said as she sealed it shut. "Now there's no need to worry. You two get a good night's sleep now! Remember, you both promised to help me with your father's shop tomorrow, didn't you?"

"Yes, mother," they replied in synchronicity as she blew out the candle-light and left the room. The children's senses had not yet been dulled by time and experience. Their young age allowed them to feel more of the world around them. The pulsing life of the ore in the rocks and the crashing of the streams from within the walls. But tonight they could feel something else.

The air was cold and sharp in their lungs despite the great

heat of the forges far below them. The turning of the wooden structures diverting their eyes from the oncoming horror. The crying screams of the stones that fall far from the walls in suicide. The inescapable feeling that something watched them sleep and waited for them to be alone, but for them to be so brimming with fear that their flesh becomes delectable and tender.

"Tomlin?" asked Martha from her bed, almost completely covered by her bedding, "are you asleep?" she asked.

"No," he replied softly, staring hard at the ceiling.

"Could I sleep in your bed tonight?" she asked in hopefulness.

"Mhmm" he agreed as he readied himself to receive his younger sister. "But you have to be quick!" he ordered.

"Okay!" acknowledged Martha as she drew up the courage to move. She threw back her covers and jumped out of her bed and ran over to her brother, her little feet scurrying across the cold floorboards like mice. As she came upon him Tomlin threw his covers open just long enough for her to jump in. He sealed them both shut beneath the sheets as they took their time to breathe after their desperate endeavour. A few moments passed as they both regained themselves, the worry seemingly passing by.

"Tomlin?" asked Martha in a whisper.

"Mhmm?" he replied.

"I saw a monster," stated Martha as she clung to him, only now did Tomlin notice she was squeezing her eyes shut. He took a moment as he waited for the right words to find him. "It's okay, Martha," he assured her with brave words. "Mother closed the window," he stated, "nothing can get in."

Martha recovered her breathing and opened her eyes, the two of them sealed in their impregnable sheet fortress. "It wasn't out the window," she said softly.

Tomlin kept his composure for his little sister as he processed the tone of her voice for truth. He knew what her words meant. With all his braveness and chivalry, he could not stop the heat as it rose from within him and the sweat that erupted from his pores. It was his duty to protect his family in his father's absence. His duty to protect his little sister and ease her mind of any pain or worry. He would face any enemy with unwavering courage in order to defend his family. He had to peel back the covers slowly and canvas the room with his own eyes for the 'monster' his sister spoke of. He had to check that they were both safe. He took a deep breath and pulled the duvet down slowly past his head just so he could reveal one, little eye to survey the room.

It was dark. Against the cold wood he could see that there was nothing there. The room was empty. He exhaled softly and slowly in relief as his heart slowed in his chest as his eyes caught a glimpse of one particular spot against the wall, where no light could possibly reach. He couldn't see anything, but his senses were screaming. His eyes studied the sight, glaring harder and harder to search for an inkling of shape. His heart and soul begged him to look away but his eyes could not move. They kept searching and searching for something to be there. What could have been a shadow or a mouse or anything other than what it was would have eased their fears. But it was none of those things. With all his honourable might gathered, Tomlin pulled himself back under the covers and sealed them shut, this time for good.

"Did you see it?" asked Martha as she looked at him. Was it courage and will that finally allowed Tomlin to pull away from search, or was it the sinister smile that broke through the black canvas and bore rotten teeth towards him as it crept from the shadows with insatiable hunger, devoid of mercy and feeling?

"We're safe under here," he assured her quietly, his voice rattled and desperate. "No matter what, nothing can get into our fortress."

The screams could be heard all through the mountain town. It was not just Tomlin and Martha who had fallen victim to the attack but the entire town beneath the mountain. It was impossible to identify the menace. It was as if the darkness of night itself was ripping people apart, searching for their souls from within their bodies, spilling their blood to quench the thirst of the cold stone and gathering their flesh for a mighty feast. But the Sentinels could feel it. A darkness so black and twisted it put even their armour to shame. A threat so ancient and so evil it could not exist. A feeling so terrifying it was not meant for mortal men to endure.

These 'new' Sentinels were elite. Their already unrivalled power heightened by Thusien's new reign. But they were not the Sentinels of legend. Would their power be enough to stop the ancient foe for which they were created to combat?

"Raiku was right," said the Sentinel Captain to his two men, "the seals have been broken. Beneath us, they have come," he roared as he summoned his magical, star metal forged greatsword to his aid.

But this hallowed town beneath the mountain was already lost. The Kursed had erupted like a wildfire burning and destroying anything that was left after they took the lives of everything they could find. Was it possible for these three Sentinels to make a difference?

"Captain!" shouted one of the Sentinels. The Captain swung around to his subordinate to find there was a Sentinel missing. They exchanged a look of despair and hopelessness.

"Kayne!" they shouted in desperation for their companion over the sounds of screams and fires and death.

"Stay sharp!" ordered the captain as he canvassed the destruction, his stomach turning at the stench of the evil that surrounded them.

"Rey?!" he exclaimed as he found his second soldier had disappeared.

The Captain found himself alone, his companions snatched or defeated. But *he* was a Sentinel Captain, after all. He released his full power. The crimson magic erupted from him and the Sentinel glow of the eyes prepared for what could be his final battle. But that is when he felt it. The hair on his neck pierced his skin as it attempted to crawl from his very body. The weight of the hollow mountain above his shoulders and the doom of the dark sky enveloping his entire being. Something stood behind him, tall and powerful. He turned slowly to witness it in all its disgusting glory with his very own eyes, for it would be the last thing they would ever see.

CHAPTER SIXTEEN: THE TWIN MOONS

The two had continued their journey towards the coast since their battle against the Sentinel. They travelled well together, engaging in interesting conversation and learning more and more about themselves, magic, and the wonders of this mystical world. Off the central path they had ventured into the thick woods to rest near the river. But from their travels Nex had learned that Lily bored rather quickly. She often probed on less personal matters and sought Nex's thoughts and feelings on a variety of ethical questions. However, it soon became apparent that she loved to hear one thing above all else.

"Nex?" she asked with a pestering tone, "tell me a story!" she demanded childishly.

"Hmm…" thought Nex as he pondered which tale to weave. They had spoken of Lost Magic and how it earned its name from being lost to humanity in the second age. They had spoken of the legend of the first King of Ares who rose to power with his might and journeyed across half the world to recruit the Ankou in humanity's darkest hour. He had even told her of how the night sky came to be. For a world ever bathed in sunlight was tedious for the Titan of the sun and offered him no rest, giving little duty to the twinkling moon. And so, the brother of sun god, Anoctis the black, would travel across the sky and cloak the world in darkness with his immeasurable wings.

"Long ago there was only one moon in the skies above Reath?" he began.

"No! I thought there had always been two!?" exclaimed Lily in surprise, believing his words undoubtedly.

"Well it's true. There was only one moon. One of the Maker's first immortal children, Amaterasu, was born as the Goddess of the moon. Before her, the seas of Reath were still and silent. It was only when Amaterasu was born that the tide began to push and to pull."

"Oh!" said Lily in excitement, "I think I will like this one!" she assured as she brought her hands together quite excitedly.

"The second, smaller moon was born when the goddess took pity on a small, human child. Living a life of only suffering and misery she met an untimely death by those sworn to protect her. But this child, from birth, was always destined to become the moon. Her hair was long and beautiful and held the sparkling glow of flawless moon dust, a feat of beauty unobtainable for mortals. In her prison, all she ever did was reach up and out to the moon as if she could almost seize it. She was mesmerized by it, truly. She wanted to search the entire world to look for the best places to see it. High on mountains or on islands over the sea, she dreamed of witnessing it wherever she could. But, failed by those whom she loved, she died before she could even walk in the moonlight. Her life was so sad and the tale of her innocent wanting touched the heart of the moon Goddess. And so, she reached down and lifted up the spirit of the little girl and placed her by her side. She became the daughter to the moon. Since then, they have travelled the entire world together on an eternal adventure. Even now, the young girl looks down upon us all."

"Wow!" gasped Lily in awe, the twinkling of the light catching the water gathering in her eyes. "What a magnificent story! Do you think it's true?" she asked.

"Hmm. Well the young girl who became the daughter of the moon belonged to my tribe, so the story was learned as gospel. This was thousands and thousands of years ago, of course."

"WOW! How beautiful…." trailed Lily. "Oh, I also wanted to ask about that power of yours."

Nex raised his hand and wiped at his eyes and cheeks in regret, "I know I should have mentioned it earlier…I didn't intend to keep it from you but I had to wait for the right time-" he explained.

"To defeat that Sentinel you did not even release your power. You won just as you were," she stated.

Nex exhaled heavily, "I suppose it is time I revealed the truth. There were a few reasons why I chose to keep my presence hidden. It bears a heavy burden on those around me and it also attracts the attention of creatures drawn to darkness. When I met you, you would have been too weak to withstand the full aura of my presence. It would have strained your body and collapsed your mind. I suppose there is no need to conceal it any further. The forces of Ares will have already felt it. As you are now, you could bear it. But you must accept that my aura bears you no hostility. You are my ally, my friend. I would never turn on you."

"When I was younger I first learned to suppress my aura and then my magic power. Being an assassin, you will have learned some stealthier techniques," he said. "It took some time to get the hang of it, but I do it without even thinking about it now," said Nex as he examined his hand, thinking back to the harshness of his magic training.

"I trust you Nex. I am ready. Can you show me please?" asked Lily with a smile as she came right up to him.

"How can I refuse when you ask me like that?" said Nex.

Nex sighed with a smile and accepted her request. He closed his eyes and revealed his presence, releasing his aura. His eyes cut through Lily like a sword through flesh as the pressure became weight around Lily's neck. The wind began to gnarl and the trees began to creek wayward out of his path. This was his true presence. He had become something else. Lily was frozen. She could not move. Terror had consumed her entire body down to the depths of her soul. Her eyes did not look to the man she had already made so many memories with, but to a being that could kill her before she could even blink. This was true despair. Lily had underestimated him. There was no chance she could even approach his power. Her lip shuddered as a voice somewhere deep down wished to ask him to stop but could not carry itself to her tongue.

Although terrifying and destructive it lacked the animosity and anger that it had before. It was a display of pure power yes, but ultimately it was not directed at her.

"This is my presence, Lily!" said Nex with glory.

"I..." breathed Lily, "You give off the same aura as the Pontifex, maybe even the Sentinel Arcon himself!"

"Pretty intense, eh?" said Nex.

"I think I'll need a break before you show me any magic power. I don't think my body could withstand it," she stated.

The world could not return to normal as Nex's presence became known across all the land. The various mages across the continent felt the tingling of his dark presence, but he sealed it nonetheless to spare Lily from harm.

"I am worried to see you release your magic power. But perhaps you could tell me your most powerful spell?" she asked him an intimate question reserved for only the closest of bonds.

"Hmm…" Nex thought for a moment before he brought his sheathed sword in front of him for her to witness, its small parchment note blowing in the wind on its piece of string.

"Your shirasaya?" she asked as he cemented her suspicions of a legendary blade. Nex thought for a moment as he weighed the heavy words in his mind. "This sword is my most powerful weapon. But to unseal it would cause more destruction than any threat to unseal it could ever pose," he stated.

She thought for a moment. His sword was indeed sealed. but it did not release the sinister magic aura that hers did. But even sealed within its casing and magically enchanted by the simple white parchment and bandages there was something awry and alluring about the blade.

"This isn't just some writing," added Nex. "The bandage seals are the same as the ones I have on my body," he gestured, "and the note is an Infinity Seal. The Maker himself would have to take a moment to break it."

"Incredible," said Lily in awe. "So the bandages on your body also seal your magic power. There's so much to process…."
Lily slumped to the floor with her legs crossed, in defeat of an overflow of information. Nex scratched his head with his whole hand as he thought of the right thing to say.

"It's a lot to take in and even more of a task to understand. The technique to conceal my aura is different to the suppression of my magic. Both are something I can teach you in time. First, we will move on to something more suited to your offensive abilities."

Lily smiled up at him as his gentle words met her ears with kindness and friendship. Words had never danced to her before in the way they did when Nex spoke to her. She felt as though she had made a true friend.

"Tomorrow, I'll show you a surprise!" said Nex as he looked for a soft spot of ground near the base of a tree.

"Mhmm" smiled Lily as she clambered back doing the same, the silver moons wishing them goodnight. Her cheeks reddened slightly as her mind began to think of the more romantic things he could show her before she slapped her cheeks in disapproval.

CHAPTER SEVENTEEN - POWER

Nex and Lily had woken early the next morning. Between them they managed to gather some fruit from a nearby tree for breakfast. The warmth of the sun invited them to train and practice to hone their magic skills.

"Something as simple as eating wild fruit from a tree is another step along my adventure," claimed Lily.

"With a little bit of magic in the soil these fruit trees can produce the sweetest fruit. There's nothing like the replenishing sugar rush in the morning," he concluded as they finished some body training exercises per Nex's instructions.

"So you even keep your bandages on for this?" asked Lily, examining the topless man with his four magical bandages on him.

Nex was wearing his base layer of robes on his bottom half and was barefoot, his shimmering, chiselled torso glistening in the sunlight but his arms and legs were still concealed beneath the mysterious bandages, the remainder of his attire hanging from a low branch whilst his sealed shirasaya rested against the tree.

Lily was wearing a minimal amount of clothing. Her short shorts and a low-cut top protected her from prying eyes but did not prevent the wandering of lust.

"Should I not be wearing all my armour for this?" she asked in embarrassment as she knew Nex would be looking upon her revealed body.

"But you are training your body, not your armour?" asked Nex.

"But my body will be stronger if I train with the armour on," stated Lily. "I wear my armour while I train so my body is used to my movements and its limitations."

"I understand what you are saying," said Nex, "but it's quite the myth."

"How do you mean?" asked Lily.

"Your body, your skin is the strongest armour that exists in this world. Your magic power exists in abundance within your body, you can project it outwards to reinforce the metal in your armour but it can never compare to the strength of your living flesh" said Nex.

"I see…" she trailed.

"What is the strongest most impenetrable thing in this world?" asked Nex to further his point. Lily thought for a moment before answering.

"The scales of a Dragon," she concluded with enlightenment.

"Exactly," said Nex. "One will waste an incredible amount of energy with your armour on, energy that could pour and surge through the fibres of your body."

"Hmm, okay," said Lily.

"Look, let me show you." Nex put his hand out and summoned a steel gauntlet from thin air. "Typically, a mage will imbue five to ten percent of their power into their armour to reinforce their defence. I have reinforced this with five percent of my power. Now, summon your sword and cut through it," said Nex.

"O-okay," said Lily uneasily, as she reached out and summoned her blade, the green lightning of her summon cracking the quiet landscape with its power. She assumed her pose, her sword sheathed, her power increasing. "Godspeed; Titan Ripper!"

In a flash Lily had sliced cleanly through the gauntlet and it fell to the floor in two pieces.

"You see, and that was with five percent of my power. Now, with my magic power concealed, cut off my arm," he Nex as he offered her his arm.

"Um, what?" asked Lily.

"Cut it off," he said calmly.

"But-" she began.

"Trust me, it's fine. Just do it," said Nex.

"I am not going to cut off your arm!" she defied.

"You were willing to chop my head off a few days ago, it is not that big of a deal. Besides, I have no intention of losing an arm, just yet. Please, trust me."

"Ugh, you know what? Fine," said Lily, giving in to his stupidity. She focused her power once more and repeated her strike on Nex's arm.

"Argh!" cried Nex as he grabbed at his arm in pain and agony. "Nex!" she shouted as she began toward him as the dust settled.
"Just kidding!" he grinned as he showed her his arm, unscathed.

"You! Absolute! Arse!" she said as she ignored his arm and shoved him backwards in a strop. Nex laughed loudly at her and he tried to show her his arm again. She grabbed at it and pretended to look at his uninjured forearm.

"Wow! Great, no scratch, good for you!" she said moodily as she dropped his arm.

"So, you see my point?" asked Nex, "your skin can be pretty damn tough"

"I get it," said Lily in a pout.

"Okay. That's a very important lesson!" began Nex, "now to move onto what I actually wanted to show you."

"Okay…" replied Lily, retrieving her interest.

"You are fast. Very fast. But you can be so much faster. Combined with your incredible attack power and you'll be a little menace!" said Nex

"Less of the Little!" she shouted back at him. "You definitely woke up on the 'piss Lily off' side of the bed, didn't you?!"

Nex laughed at her furious expression. "Okay, okay."

"So, what is it you want to show me?" asked Lily.

"Himeros was said to be so fast in the drawing of his blade, he could strike and re-sheathe his fabled katana before his opponent could even witness the strike. Mastering this led to all sorts of possibilities. He then progressed to the 'Ten thousand Lightless Flash' which was, basically, exactly what it sounds like. An incredible magical attack that will strike a thousand times in the blink of an eye," said Nex as he summoned a steel sword, his sealed Katana still leaning against the tree.

"So you do know of spells for my magic?" she learned through his words. "And where do you keep summoning all this stuff from?" she asked.

"It's just a little pocket of space where I keep handy stuff," replied Nex.

"And I bet you have got money in there, don't you?" she asked.

"I…uhhhh," trailed Nex. Lily tutted as she looked around in disappointment. "Ready?" asked Nex.

"Ready for what?" asked Lily suspiciously. Nex smiled and pulled the sheathed sword to his left side, entering an attacking stance. He withdrew the sword slowly to reveal around two inches. The blade rang out, Its steel echoing all around. He then sheathed the sword once more, with speed and delicacy to stop the ringing immediately. The surrounding trees, so enormous that they could hold up the skies themselves, had been cut through, cleaved with one simple slice. All of the surrounding trees fell.

Lily's eyes fixated on Nex as he returned to an upright posture and released the sword into nothingness. "Did you see the blade leave its sheath at all?" he asked.

"I...didn't..." she said.

"It was fast," said Nex. "That was just the single strike, not the one thousand. But once you get that down, you can start to add other swings, too."

"But...how do I know you didn't just use a different spell to crack the trees...?" said Lily.

"Aha! Wonderful!" said Nex. "You are a great student!"

"Since when did I become your student!?" bellowed Lily, her face blooming red with embarrassment.

"Most people who claim to have mastered techniques similar to this, do exactly that!" said Nex as he walked up to Lily using his index finger to demonstrate his point. "The technique is simply too difficult to learn and so they spend years devising and mastering a technique which is a false 'hidden blade'. They remove the blade from the sheathe, and when re-sheathing, they then, with the most minimal of movements, release a separate magic attack to cut like a blade."

"That seems believable, actually," trailed Lily in thought.

"And it does in fact take years to master this false technique," said Nex.

"But…" began Lily, knowing there was more to what he said.

"Yes…" encouraged Nex with both hands as he knew what she was going to say and was too excited to hear it.

"With the false technique, the attack would be after the sword is sheathed, but with the original technique, the strike would have already been made."

"EXACTLY! Absolutely right!" he said in excitement to his student with pride and warmth.

"So, if the two were to face each other the true technique would win," concluded Lily. Nex nodded in agreement. And a pause emerged between them.
"So, are you going to show me the false technique?" asked Lily.

Nex looked at her in horror. "What? What? Why would I do that after everything you just said?" he said in total bewilderment.

"I assumed the reason you were telling me all this is because I wouldn't be able to learn the actual technique of a hidden blade strike?" said Lily.

Nex slapped his head in amazement. "It's the exact opposite, dummy!" he said.

"Huh?" said Lily.

"I have absolutely no doubt in my mind that you can do it!" Nex assured her. Lily was taken aback completely by his words and the faith he had in her potential. She was not used to such tutorship. The only reasons for her to learn any magic was that she would be worthless if she did not, and that without use, she would be disposed of.

"This will be a piece of cake for you. Your katana will show you the way," he added.

Lily was lost deep in thought.

"The name of this spell is Iaido-no-shinken. Once mastered, you will open a path within your magic that will cause your enemies calamity. But before that, there is one more thing you must know." said Nex.

Lily looked up at him with admiration and hope. "Okay!" she said with a smile. For the first time she was learning a spell of her own free will under the tutorship of a master and a friend.

"You katana has not truly accepted you yet. You hear its whispers and iots calls, but the connection between you is not complete. The soul of the blade and your own soul, are not yet entwined," said Nex.

"I can hear…the voices in the blade, but I cannot understand the name…" said Lily as she clenched her katana tightly with frustration.

"Once you know the name, there will be no turning back. The sword's soul will pour into you and your compatibility will truly be tested. If you do not overcome it, your soul will be corrupted and destroyed."

"Destroyed…?" gasped Lily lightly. It took her a few moments of pondering, but Nex's faith was not misplaced. Lily's resolve was strong and she had come to accept her destiny, so long as it resonated with Nex's.

"I…will overcome," she declared.
"Of that, I have no doubt in my mind, Lily. Forged from a star plucked from the cosmos, the master smith imbued the powers of a primordial Titan with the power to bestow magic upon other living creatures. It is his soul that lives within the blade. This Titan was known as Tsumikiri!"

As soon as the name was spoken and Lily learned of the great mythical creature she became engulfed in an emerald cyclone of magic power, everything around them snapping and snarling away. The very trees Nex had severed became weightless in the light air around her. The shade of magic of the sinister Tsumikiri and Lily's was a perfect match, and in harmony with the fierceness of Lily's will, courage and determination, the souls began to infuse and entwine.

After thirty seconds of immense focus, the power subsided, and flowed deep into Lily's body. When the atmosphere settled once more, she was fatigued and sweating under the immense strain of the transaction, but the power that welled up inside of her was undeniable.

"There was not a doubt in my mind you would not overcome," said Nex. "But the trial is not over. Tsumikiri will always challenge your control. You will be tested through magic. This is only the beginning of your connection."

"I understand," said Lily, still clutching at the blade tightly.

"Now that that is out of the way, we can move onto the spell!" said Nex with a clap. "It's actually quite simple. Do it with me now, slowly. Withdraw the sword from your sheath, and bring it across you to strike, in the same movement, remove any imperfection on the blade and simply return it to its home."

Lily mirrored his movement exactly and completed the technique with an incredible amount of precision. "Now let's just repeat that a few times…" he said softly so as to not disturb her concentration. Her movements were splendid. There was no muscle waste or waiver during her movement. Her skills were already at that of a master. Together, they repeated this movement over one thousand times as the sun rose through the sky.

"Marvelous…" he said softly. Now, close your eyes and empty your mind. Picture the strike in the future. How it will strike and how it will cut everything you wish it to. The secret to this technique is that you know, deep down, that you have already executed the strike and therefore the action is now in the past. Magic is instantaneous. It is the limits of human flesh which cause the delay. Lily began to draw her sword slightly and prepared to strike. She trusted in Nex and his faith in her, she used this feeling to her strength. She pictured the blade cutting its target with perfection and then realised the thought she focused on was now an action of the past, her magic spiking around her with immense focus, channelling energy to all the right follicles and atoms inside her.

"Yes…" whispered Nex softly, "it has already been done."

"GodSpeed: Iaido-no-Shinken!"

The air pulsated like a shockwave from the devastation of Lily's strike. Like a blade of air the emerald magic cut through the trees and in the same moment, the katana returned to her and slid masterfully back into its housing.

"Magnificent!" said Nex. "You did it first bloody time!" he said.

Lily relaxed and stood up in amazement of her accomplishment. "I…did it?" she said in disbelief.

"Yes, you did," said Nex.

"Ouch!" grimaced Lily as she looked at her right hand. "Apparently not quite there," she said as she looked at the deep cut in her hand that had occurred from the sharp blade.

"I would be lying if I said I didn't cut myself dozens of times whilst I was trying to learn," he said. "What you have just accomplished is a truly spectacular feat."

Nex took Lily's injured hand and placed it between his and expelled a small green light onto it. Lily felt its warmth and radiance and the pain disappeared. 'A healing spell?' she thought as she became lost in his eyes. An unknown length of time passed as they were lost within one another before they returned to reality.

"Healing magic is so rare…" she stuttered in more amazement of her master.

"Uh-amazing!" said Nex as he broke away and serenaded her in compliments whilst tapping her head. "It will take some more practice, but you've done the impossible part! See? I told you, you would do it!"

Lily examined her hand which was now completely free of any wounds. "You're just a good teacher," she admitted bashfully. Nex became coy himself and reached to the back of his head.

"Oh, I don't know about that!" he said in embarrassment. "It's been too long since I have done any of this."

"You must have had a great teacher," she said.

Nex had a sudden thought of the time he was educated with magic and the pain it brought him swept across his face for a brief moment, a moment long enough for Lily to witness. "Only certain magic was part of my curriculum when I was young," he smiled deceitfully. You and I are a lot alike, Lily. We are not hindered by the magic of those around us. Instead, we learn from our own power," laughed Nex at her accomplishment.

"So, who taught you my magic?" she exclaimed. Nex did an empty gesture to the young girl.

"No one," he said.

"Wow…that's…unbelievable." she said as she thought of all the little pointers Nex had given her that surely were the key to her success.

"I know, right?" he said awkwardly. "But you are far more skilled with a blade than I was when I tried to learn the secrets of Himeros. There is no doubt you will master his techniques in the times to come, I wish only that you had a better teacher."

"You are a superb teacher!" assured Lily enthusiastically and with a smile.

"Oh, thank you," he began, "Iaido-no-Shinken actually incorporates a type of Foresight Magic. It's a kind of a Demon thing. Once you know that little secret the technique becomes a whole lot easier to learn. Of course, you must have incredible talent to begin with. So with this you have technically branched your magic into a completely different area. But that is enough for today. You can use any free time just to practice what you have learnt today but it never hurts to go over the movements in your mind when you cannot hold a sword in hand physically. This is another secret of mine for mastering things. Most of the day is already gone, we should probably head out soon" said Nex. "I'm just going to wash in the river first. I am SOAKED!" he finished as he gestured to his sweat.

"O-okay" replied Lily as she realised again that they were both half naked and revealed to one another. was common for a reserved woman to reveal herself only on their first bedding as a couple. Trying, with even more focus she had employed learning the techniques of a god, she attempted to suppress the adolescent heat rising within her.

"I'll head down river a little to give you some privacy," he said as he grabbed his clothes off the tree branch and his resting shirasaya. "Come down to me when you're done!" he waved as he followed the river down and out of sight.

CHAPTER EIGHTEEN: THE VANGUARD

Ares was indeed vast. An island once believed to house the entire world within its shores and, during the war of the races, the largest and most important battles transpired here. When the Kursed were finally vanquished, their leader, Chakravartin, was slain in the very place Eos stands now. Across this vast continent, far to the eastern reaches where the land ends, Vosk, Galatea and Daisy find themselves on the cusp of despair.

Roving fields lay strewn across the landscape as far as the eyes could see. Strategic stops had been built by the farmers who tended the land to rest in the sun on a hot working day. Three Sentinel's emerged from beneath the mountains of Ibis alive, but with something invisible to the eye missing. All around them was an unwelcoming environment. Across the cobbled path with the large landscape behind them, the green farmland withered into harsh shrubbery as little light was left on the meadow as they retreated from beneath the hollow mountain. The sharp, cold air pierced their lungs as they put distance between themselves and the great magical doors of Ibis. They were alive but they were not unharmed. Vosk was coated in cuts and bruises, bandages wrapped all around him with Galatea's rare, ambient magenta magic healing him slowly, with her own arm in a sling, bombarded by bandages of her own. But it was Daisy who had sustained the most severe injuries. Both arms were wrapped and stored against her stomach so that they could not be disturbed. It was incredibly rare for there to be a healer amongst a party of three, but due to their nature as the vanguard, they required a huge amount of recovery after their legendary battles and so a support was imperative. All three of them limped in defeat.

"Galatea," said Vosk, "you should heal yourself first"

"And then you can heal us faster," said Daisy as she gestured to both of her arms, unable, both through immense pain and suffering and the complete lack of her own magic power, to heal herself.

"I'm sorry," said Galatea. "I'm almost completely drained, too. I gave everything I had back there and more."

"It is by your will alone that you are still standing, Galatea," said Vosk.

"I can keep going," she protested.

"I am fine," winced Vosk to ensure his juniors did not worry about him. "Heal yourself when you can and then see to Daisy. We must recover as soon as possible," said Vosk in worry as he prepared to draw the magic circle and incite the spell that allows a Sentinel's immediate return to the Nexus via teleportation.

"Vosk!" said Galatea swiftly as she felt an unwelcoming presence. They stopped and peered cautiously to find five figures approaching the gate in the same direction from which they had come only a day before. The Primus raised his arm in order to bring his companions to a stop. The five figures halted in perfect synchronisation in a strategic figure of V only ten paces before them. But unlike the traditional party of three which was sacred to the Sentinels to display their immense power even when battling the most fearsome of foes, a group of five had come for Vosk, Galatea and Daisy. This was no mistake. This confrontation was between Sentinels.

The new corrupted and dark Order of Sentinels had come.

"Heleic Vosk InBarba," spoke the Sentinel Primus, "you have orders to return to the capital."

"Eumenes…" said Vosk as he recognised his fellow Sentinel. Even the seriousness of the situation was almost not enough for Daisy to retort 'we were just about to.' This Sentinel who had been stationed this far east with his two comrades was conversing with members of his own order whom he almost did not recognise due to his corruption.

"Galatea, Daisy, be on guard," he warned his companions as they stopped at his support. "We are the Vanguard!" said Vosk with authority, "we take our commands from the Arcon himself."

"As do we," replied Eumenes. Vosk, Galatea and Daisy looked upon their corrupted brethren with unease and confusion.

"What has become of you?" asked Vosk with worry.

"Quite the costume change?" whispered Daisy to Galatea as she secretly unhinged her arms from inside her slings.

"The seals on the Mountain Kingdoms require investigation, we are to relieve you of your duty," stated the corrupted Eumenes. Vosk glared back at him.

"The seal of Ibis has already been broken. Perhaps you would have some idea about that?" asked Vosk as he came to understand their situation. "It is not to be discussed here," stated Eumenes. "Return to the Nexus at once via Recall."

Vosk understood their corruption, their taint. What awaited them at the Nexus was a purging. The Sentinel order they knew was no more. "And if we refuse?" said Vosk, concealing the fact the Nexus would not answer him.

"You should know that to defy the Arcon is punishable by

death, even if you are a Heleic," said Eumenes.

"Since when was such a penalty introduced?" asked Vosk. "Besides, we do not heed the call of a usurper."

"You will heed the call of our new Arcon, Thusien," said Eumenes. It was not difficult for them to understand. They were Sentinels after all. And they understood the corruption of power all too well.

"If we are to understand that Thusien has transformed our order, then you, too, should understand that a coup of this nature shall not escape our justice," said Vosk.

"Hahaha" laughed Eumenes in response. "The vanguard is indeed powerful with these misfits among your ranks. And you are a Heleic, you hold the title of any prospective Arcon. We were under-appreciated amongst our old ranks. But you know not of the power Thusien has gifted us. Even you fall short of the stature we all now hold."

"Hmph," scoffed Vosk. "One who must proclaim power must lack the means of demonstration. If that is what you truly believe, then come, and test your mettle against ours."

"What is your answer, Vosk InBarba. Galatea Destoria and Daisy Iminates. You too, are free to choose," wanted Eumenes one last time.

Nothing needed to be said. Amongst the great ranks of the Sentinels the Vanguard held a hope in their hearts akin to the founder of their order.

"Then I guess we have no need for these," said Vosk as he, Galatea and Daisy stripped themselves of the sacred, draconic symbol of the Sentinels off their armour.

"We will have no part of this 'corrupted' Sentinel order," said Vosk. "The Arcon was right in suspecting Thusien. His loyalty and belief in others had always been his greatest weakness," said Vosk with regret at the death of his leader.

"You should understand that not even you cannot defeat us, Vosk," said the Primus. "We need not even mention the substantial wounds you have already sustained."

"Compared to what lies beneath this mountain, we will take our chances with you fools," said Vosk confidently, eager to forget the trauma they had just faced.

"Death it is then," ruled Eumenes quickly. They somewhat recognised the opponents standing before them. Alistar, Timoleon, Gelon and Margos were the four supporting Sentinels. They were all captains, a rank below Primus. A sinister and evil aura seeping from them like death, the stench of their presence caused the stomach to wretch, armour black as night, their presence bringing a chill to the setting sun's warmth. Their pale visages struck a small glimpse of their recent past into them but did not falter their step. Vosk exhaled slowly before acknowledging his Sentinel gifts and began forward to the threat. Galatea and Daisy completely freed themselves of their slings and followed in suit, withdrawing the hilts of their unique swords given only to the Vanguard triumvirate.

From the mantles on their right thighs each housed on their armour three hilts of star metal whose blades emerged like starlight from the heavens. Vosk, Galatea and Daisy's advance evolved into a battle charge, gaining momentum with every step. Bringing their swords upright to their chests, leading with their left shoulders, their eyes erupted in the cobalt-blue glow filling them with immense power. The smoulder soon ended as the surge began to spread like the fuse on an explosive through their bodies.

The Fallen Sentinels retaliated, blinking their eyes into their Scarlet red, corrupted power. The smoke seeped out of their eyes and poured out of their souls before evaporating into the cold air. Galatea and Daisy took up their respective flanks,

Daisy charging past Vosk, bracing to engage their enemy. The level of magic was fierce. Blows from the swords toppled the trees and carved into the mountainside with no remorse. The level of skill was also immense. Vosk, Galatea and Daisy were indeed incredible Sentinels competing efficiently with their enhanced counterparts. They were the Sentinel Vanguard, after all.

Whilst they used their signature swords the corrupted Sentinels summoned their own unique weapons. Alistar wielded a two handed great-sword that even the strongest of men found difficult to lift yet, he swung it as if it were weightless. Timoloen had two Eastern Cutlasses that he spun around with tremendous skill. His mastery of dual wielding blades was top tier, even amongst the Sentinel ranks. Gelon and Margos shared more than a similarity to one another. They both bore the same great-axe and struck together. They had trained since a young age with the same tutor and even employed the same magic. They shared a deep connection that presented itself incredibly in battle.

The blows were immense. An elite Heleic and his two trusted Primus' had fought a myriad of creatures in their time, but these corrupted Sentinels were something else. They were like evil itself. The feeling they experienced was all too similar to their battle beneath the mountain. The combat ensued as they each exchanged countless blows before Vosk ordered them back in retreat, just as they had taken the upper hand from their betrayers despite being outnumbered. Vosk tilted his head up slightly, raising his chin to cut the air, staring in wisdom at his opponents.

Even with their substantial injuries the Vanguard was not to be underestimated. The fallen Sentinels would lose this battle against some of the strongest Sentinels that were in the order. They would not journey all this way only to be defeated. Vosk knew they had something with them that would be enough to put them all down, permanently.

The footsteps echoed through the wind, getting louder and heavier, forcing the ground to shake under its immense power. Emerging from the distance between the fallen Sentinels was a supreme figure. Standing at eighteen paces tall was the Goliath. It walked through its masters and came to halt at the front of the pack. This Goliath was identical to that of the Sentinels once pure design, its shimmering armour was recognisable as being Illyrium, the famed and indestructible star metal. The Goliath was not human. An ethereal being housed in a suit of armour, created by the Sentinels as a weapon possessing no mercy, no emotion and no pain to combat an enemy which fed on flesh and soul. Its head was like a heavily armoured helmet that was blank of expression revealing no anger or discrimination to its opponents, it merely stared openly at the three Sentinels. The Goliath stood without the need of a cloak, revealing its broad shoulders and hugely built upper body. Designed in the image of an Immortal, used to deliver devastating power in battle.

It began, sprinting into an advance, the ground shaking and shuddering under its tremendous weight as the Sentinel's bones vibrated painfully within their sockets.

"DAISY!" roared Vosk as he commanded her into action as he himself brought his left hand to his shoulder, charging up an attack. "Chaos Light: Reproduce!" roared Vosk as cobalt blue light erupted from his hands and created two perfect versions of himself out of magic which charged toward the Goliath to meet its advance.

"Whispering Nature: Guardian!" roared Daisy over the noise, sending an echo of sound throughout the valley.

"Titan Soul: Dryad!" summoned Galatea as she activated her own immense magic. She began to morph, both her body and her essence as she grew upwards, transforming into the Titan whose form she had assumed.

Vosk and his two Solid Light apparitions engaged the Goliath and held it back before it could reach the others. But the Goliath was overwhelmingly powerful, shattering a solid light Vosk with one swipe and adjusting to strike the other. With both now destroyed it released a thunderous attack at Vosk who caught the enormous fist with both hands and his entire body of strength. It pushed him, his feet planted firmly in the ground, further and further back as it charged. It drew closer to a conjuring Galatea and Daisy before the ground began to shake once more at the mercy of a different creature. Something leapt from the treeline and tackled the Goliath away from Vosk, who's injuries had now worsened drastically.

Daisy's magic allowed her to commune with all creatures. Without enslaving them to her command, she communed with them like a mother in need of protection. Her call had summoned a myriad of creatures to her aid, but the largest, and fastest of them all had come first. A legendary creature that had fled the hollow mountain in fear of consumption of an ancient evil. A two-legged, four-armed colossal beast that galloped through the trees on all six limbs crushing them with its immenseness. A Domashu. Vying far above the Goliath at almost thirty paces, with skin of onyx and eyes sharper than the gems it mines. The expansive shoulders stretching wide, housed the two, heavily muscularly defined, onyx stoned sets of arms. The four-armed giant possessed the normal two, accompanied by the bonus set just underneath, emitting from the sides of the chest. The giant stood indisputably to defend its mother against the threat of the Goliath. With its stocky, muscular build it roared upwards into the sky, challenging it and sentencing it to death.

Galatea's transformation was complete. Her Lost Magic was superb. The soul of a Titan, a Dryad. From her many battles she had indeed defeated one, albeit weakened from a previous fight, her magic then allowed her to synchronise with its soul. This was a rare form of transformation magic. She stood almost as tall as the Goliath. A slender humanoid figure with fingers long like claws and a thick, dark brown skin with green veining impervious to blades. With long green hair and dark oak roots caressing and shrouding her figure. She had become a Dryad, a Daughter of Titans, Mother of the Forest. Naturally, she commanded the lifeless trees into action, spurring them with her commands into taking heed at her orders.

The landscape began to shift. The huge Goliath and Domashu wrestled and rolled across the land, destroying everything beneath them. Galatea began to bind them with the roots of her magic whilst Vosk began another spell. "Chaos Light: Goliath!" he roared as he summoned his hard light once more, forming into the shape of his very own Goliath that joined the fray. Meanwhile, the Corrupted Sentinels remained un-phased, watching one of the ultimate Sentinel weapons combat three incredibly powerful Sentinels.

Their confidence was well placed. The combined might of all the opponents that faced the Goliath was not enough to defeat it. Galatea's Dryad roots snared the Goliath momentarily while she released a powerful spore-like spell at it. The Domashu quickly followed up by smashing it into the ground once more. Vosk's Hard Light Goliath Pulled, as hard as Vosk's remaining magic power would let him, at the Goliaths left arm and Galatea aided it with her Titaness form, and by the pure, brute strength, the combined effort of the three giants ripped the Goliaths arm away from its shoulder.

However, this was only a momentary victory. A Goliath feels neither pain nor fear. It grappled at Vosk's weak replica and shattered it. Before swinging to Galatea who barely defended against it, sending her backwards towards her comrades. Without enough magic to sustain her Dryad form, she reverted back, the injuries from their previous battle taking a toll on her. The Goliath rose and as the legendary Domashu charged forwards it used its remaining arm to hold it at bay before quickly and gracefully slipping through and repositioning behind the giant creature and breaking its neck of onyx with its remaining arm. The death of the creature's energy reverberated back to Daisy and knocked her to the ground. In a flash the Goliath had slain all its opponents. It turned and began again towards Vosk he raised himself battered and broken against the impending doom. He would defend his subordinates until the very end.

"Run!" he roared. "I will hold them here without fail!" he declared. With that Timoleon and Gelon had darted past him in an attempt to take advantage of his weakened state but they were met only by Vosk's impressive strength and speed. Despite his injuries, his will would not break. But as they flew back towards Eumenes, Margos and Alistar had vanished to take advantage of the now vulnerable Vosk. But they too, met an untimely end. Galatea had landed a kick on Margos which sent him flying backwards into the trees. Alistar, however, was not so lucky. With Daisy's soft fingers enveloping his face he found nothing but the cold, hard dirt as she smashed him into the ground in defeat.

"We will not leave you behind!" assured Daisy as they regained themselves.

"We are the Sentinel Vanguard!" roared Galatea. "Come, brothers! Let us see if your corrupted power is truly greater than the Sentinels who vanquished the Kursed!"

This was a war cry. Galatea had re-invigorated their minds and bodies with her words. Vosk smiled through the blood accumulating in his mouth as he raised his blade at Eumenes. Daisy stepped forwards and took centre stage of the battlefield with an aura that was fathoms different than before.

"O soulless creature of Star Metal that knows no fear, you will wish you could...."

The Goliath squared up to her as both Vosk and Galatea engaged the five Sentinels. Vosk held Eumenes whilst Galatea held Timoleon, Gelon and Margos at bay. The Goliath straightened and took little notice of both its missing arm and the insignificant scurrying around it whilst it focused on the true threat, Daisy.

"Aphrixian Black Magic: Hela!" roared Daisy as she enchanted herself, flames of black darkness erupting from her palms.

"Two attributes?!" said a stunned Eumenes before Vosk regained his attention.

"My magic is one of contradictions. One preserves life, the other destroys it. Tell me, creature, can you be cursed?" asked Daisy.

The Goliath began forward towards her as she engulfed the area between them in darkness, her hidden power only seen before by members of the triumvirate. It was formidable, but Daisy had already been severely weakened and not much of her power remained. This form required an absurd amount of energy and concentration that she was depleting rapidly. She would need to finish the Goliath quickly if there was any hope for their survival. However, she was not even sure if the true form of her magic would affect the soulless creature who is said to be impervious to magic. The Goliath pushed through the inferno of darkness with difficulty as Daisy grimaced, pushing more and more of her strength into it. Finally, it broke through and it released a phenomenal strike with its remaining fist to have Daisy block it with two hands and be pushed back, but not as far as Vosk previously was. When she halted, ancient, jet black runes began to appear and creep up the Goliath's arm magically like a swarm of scurrying insects. She was imbuing the creature with a curse of black magic. It returned its limb to itself as it noticed its armoured skin began to flake slowly. Daisy let out a 'Ts' as she kissed her teeth in disappointment as she learned the curse was a failure. Either its immunity was too great, or she was weakened to a state where it could not take effect. She leapt forward and struck the Goliath with a mighty physical blow, forcing it to stagger backwards, she then became nothing but black smoke taken away by the wind. When the Goliath regained itself, she was above, crashing down with both fists clamped together. The Goliath took the blow to the top of its helmet and crashed. As soon as Daisy's feet met the ground she was met by Gelon, who had broken away from Galatea. His kick clashed with Daisy's right side and the bone snapping sound indicated several broken ribs. By her strong will alone she managed to become smoke again and vanish.

Vosk was almost immediately pummeled by both Eumenes's swings and Gelon's battleaxe. He crashed into the ground using all his remaining power just to stay conscious. Galatea had already lost her sword to the floor, which now appeared as just a shimmering hilt beneath the moon in the tall, green grass. She defended as best she could but found her body moving sluggishly. Timoleon and Margos soon overpowered her and she crashed backwards against a great tree, her back breaking with a snap. When the black smoke re-emerged it was grappled in less than a moment by the Goliath's colossal grip. The soulless creature hoisted Daisy up as it crushed her, briefly loosening to allow her to slip through so he could hang her by one arm. The Vanguard had been defeated. The Goliath, showing no mercy or repent, crashed Daisy into the ground with tremendous energy. It straightened in triumph after its titanic attack as it reached for the air once more with an open hand, it readied itself for its killing blow.

In their defeat, the Vanguard looked up at the cosmos, the vast darkness that had given them all a splendid and plentiful life. But the feelings of regret and of pain filled their minds and their hearts became heavy with sadness as their prayers of survival ascended to the stars. But, far above them, the cosmos answered.

Jet black, darker than the night the infinite expanse of the universe reached out to embrace them. Slowly, it descended, a span that covered almost the width of the mountain. With their last moments of consciousness, they saw a creature that could destroy kingdoms simply with the beat of its wings.

CHAPTER NINETEEN: THE WOUNDED COAST

Nex and Lily continued onwards to the next town: the last signs of civilization before they would reach the coast. The cold night was now upon them and their bodies were tired, ready for rest and nourishment.

"I'm looking forward to sleeping in an actual bed tonight!" admitted Lily as she wore off today's training. "But I think I'm open to sleeping outside again sometime."

"Ooh," gleamed Nex as he understood her words, "does this mean you're buying us a room?" he asked in hopefulness.

She looked at him with a baffled expression. How could he be so bold? "With two separate beds," she specified.

"Anything is fine!" he said with a large smile alien to any implicit meanings.

"I don't suppose you're going to pull out any money from that pocket, are you?" she asked, knowing the answer.

"FOR THE LAST TIME, I DON'T HAVE ANY IN THERE!" he protested her sharp statements.

"Tss" she hissed at his deceit. Nex turned his gaze from his beautiful companion and looked at the coastal village of Fallow that was now in sight as he brought his hand to his stomach hungrily.

"Food first?" asked Lily.

"Definitely," said Nex.

The two entered the small food establishment. It was surprisingly full. Most of the tables in the centre of the room were filled and so they chose one in the corner next to the small, panelled window. Couples occupied the majority of the tables. Villagers, soldiers, tradesmen and craftsmen all dotted around the room, while a few families sat around and engaged in squabble or domestic chit chat while singletons rested on the bar drunk and drained. Lily's entrance stirred the room, the cold, outside air washing in her scent to all the nostrils it could find. Men and women alike with varying ages turned their heads subtly to gaze at the blonde beauty as she stepped inside. The female eyes soon drifted to the man that followed her, his handsome face and enticing eyes, luring them into his slight, toned body. The room grew dramatically warmer as if someone had tripled the amount of wood on the log fire at the end of the room. Partners of the affected yanked at their other halves in anger and embarrassment, whilst trying to hide their own attractions to the stranger of their preference.

Nex remained mysterious in his peculiar robes, his black cloak trailing easily behind him as he passed through the room. Lily's armour was rather ostentatious so she could not help but look death defyingly beautiful in the well-fitting clothes, her figure easily analysed by all as the audience who gazed lustfully and with jealous rage leaving only the greatest parts of her to the imagination. The ultimate tease.

Polite facial expressions were worn by almost everyone as they passed through, finding their seats by the humble window. Lily sat confidently on the chair with knees crossed in the very corner so she could face the rest of the room, her high-class etiquette too hard to conceal. An assassin must have many skills. Nex pulled out the chair and sat opposite her, sitting slightly, awkwardly, diagonal to face outwards. Lily stared out the small window and admired the beauty of the incoming night sky before looking back to Nex.

"That's quite the reception you got there," stated Nex as he acknowledged all the watching eyes glaring down the beautiful Lily with his keen senses. He immediately realised what had just slipped out of his mouth and he turned his head to the right to look at the bar in embarrassment.

Lily turned her head back to the window as her face went bright red. Nex switched his focus and emptied his mind of mortal thoughts, focusing on the woman in front of him.

"Should I pull her over?" asked Nex as he tilted his head towards the young demi-human waitress.

"What?" said Lily awkwardly as she thought he had just said his thoughts out loud.

"We won't know what they have unless we ask the lady" he specified.

"Oh, right. One second" said Lily as she struggled to regain herself from Nex's previous complement of her beauty. She was used to the attention, the glares, and the admiration of her beauty. But never had she felt as she did now, on the other end of the spectrum.

"Hey there!" said the waitress enthusiastically with what looked to be the ears and tail of a magnificent, slinky fox. Her hair was a rosy ginger tipped with white as one would expect. She was truly a specimen of the demi-human race. She was young and slender and had an appealing face, you could hear the cute, coyness in her voice. "We have steak, lamb and fish, and a few vegetable stews this evening, plenty of mead and wine too'.

"Just a meat free stew and some mead!" said Nex with a smile.

"The fish please and some wine," said Lily.

"Okay!" said the waitress as she jotted down on some parchment with a magic quill. She hung around awkwardly staring at Nex, waiting for him to ask her the age-old question 'what time do you finish?' before coming to her senses and backing away.

"What was that about?" said Lily under her breath as she leaned in to Nex.

"What do you mean?" asked Nex ignorantly.

"She was all over you! She couldn't even look into your eyes!" spurted Lily for reasons unbeknown to her.

"But there's nothing special about my eyes…" muttered Nex as he brought his attention to her.

"'T-That's not the point!" she stuttered as she concealed her true opinions of his eyes to herself.

"Haha" he chuckled once more. "Your words seem to be fumbling out more frequently" he said glibly, completely oblivious to her behaviour and her feelings. Lily flew back in her seat and brought her hands together in a clap.

"You're such an idiot!" she said as she closed her eyes and smiled in retaliation.

He laughed again, "I'm sorry, I'll try and be more sensitive in future," he apologized.

"When did chivalry die? You should be buying *me* a drink!" 'oh my goodness! Did I just ask him out? What the bloody hell am I saying?!' she thought to herself frantically. She quickly spoke to avoid an awkward silence, "You don't eat meat?" she asked.

"I try not to," he replied. "I am only allowed it on really special occasions."

"Oh," said Lily. "I see."

"I need to get myself some gold," concluded Nex after Lily's previous remark.

Lily questioned his words, wondering how one could exist without any concept of money. "Gold? Unless you're buying a house you won't be needing that much money," asked Lily. "Most transactions in Ares require Aur now," she stated.

"Aur?" asked Nex, confused.

"O – R – E" she highlighted the pronunciation for him. That's the currency here," said Lily. "It has been for centuries."

"I see…" said Nex with eyes wide as he cast his mind back to Ember, where he had used his only gold coin with little thought.

"You know, I'm not surprised in the slightest that you didn't know that. I imagine you have always been a freeloader?!" she said.
"Always!" he snapped back in joy.

"It's named after the metal from which it is made. It's worth much less than gold, but does have some fragments in it. Gold is hardly used in the everyday," said Lily in amazement. "You really have no concept of money, do you?"

"What can be more entrancing than the rays of the stars and their glimmering rays that travel to our eyes amongst the overwhelming cosmos, inviting us to ascend on their infinite eternity," said Nex with wise words, swiftly changing the subject.

Lily looked up with a confused, weirded expression on her face she had yet to equip, "what on Reath are you talking about!?" she asked.

"It's from a poem…" trailed Nex with intense awkwardness.

"It's very befitting for you. Irrelevant nonsense" said Lily through an enormous smile.

In the silence that followed she could see the clarity in his eyes. In their depths they could feel each other's substance. Their souls were in a place where only they were able to understand. She felt comforted by the thought of their connection, in their acceptance of one another and their flaws. The redness spread across their faces gradually as they held each other's gaze, slowly becoming more awkward with each passing moment.

"Excuse me?" spoke a sultry male voice. Nex could hear the oncoming footsteps heavily homing in on their position. Nex and Lily looked up to the caller. It was a good looking, young man, one who surpassed Nex's looks easily, and with his entourage in tow, he approached the table.

"Hello there, miss," he smiled persuasively as he clicked his fingers discreetly. The handsome young man's four goons quickly leaned in to Nex and whispered loudly to him.

"There's something pretty sketchy going on outside! You look pretty tough, they could use your help," said one of the handsome henchmen as Nex looked to Lily. The room had fallen silent as the local gang had come across the room, their reputation preceding them. Nex awaited Lily's response.

"It's okay," assured Nex with a smile. "I won't be long," he finished to his young lady friend. Nex couldn't help but release a smile as he agreed to go with them to whatever awaited him outside…

"You'd best hop along now like a good little boy," said one of the men as they left the tavern and entered the empty street, the ruse ending.

"Well then, now that it's just you and me, let's say we make this evening more eventful," said the handsome young man suavely back inside the tavern. "But where are my manners? My name is Eric, and I would just love to know the name of the young lady who caught my eye from this little window here."

"Shouldn't you have gone out to help them?" asked Lily in his companion's wake.

"Oh, I am a true gentleman. Brawling in the street is beneath me," he stated elegantly with his posh accent.

"I could tell you my name, but where would be the fun in that?" smiled Lily innocently.

"Oh, I like you!" admitted Eric as he clicked the cute waitress back over.

"Y-yes?" she said with fear.

"Two glasses of your finest wine, Elinor" he snapped disrespectfully.

"Yes, of course, Eric!" she replied, backing away in a fearful bow.

"My father is the Baron of these parts. This town is but a number of the ones within his domain," he boasted. "We are related to the Pontifex, after all."

Lily pretended to act impressed as she gave him the smile and attention he desired. Although she did so for the benefit of this ruse, she found it somewhat exciting to see what reaction it would provoke from Nex if he saw her acting this way with another man. She could not help the thoughts sweep across her mind as she smiled invitingly back at him with her beautiful soft cheeks, allowing him to bring his hand in and brush her hair.

"You know, I very rarely approach a lady myself and compliment her. You should feel honoured," said Eric as he leant back in his chair like he owned the place, where in this instance, he actually did. The young waitress brought two tall glasses of clear wine back to the small table and the additional order that Nex and Lily had placed and laid them down softly, retreating backwards when finished. Eric grabbed his wine slowly as he awaited her answer as she pulled hers towards her slowly, in thought. Eric positioned his free hand on the table for her to accept, and she replied positively, warming his hand with her soft touch.

"I'm surprised," said Lily.

"Oh?" said Eric. "Why's that?" he asked.

"That you would use the word 'lady' to describe me," added Lily.

"Well of course I would!" replied Eric. "With your beauty and delightful figure you truly are the most magnificent girl I have ever seen!" Although he was clearly scum, Lily acknowledged his incredible, good looks. It was a shame that this was all a façade and that once he got what he wanted he would probably dispose of the naïve young women and girls he captured. Her interest was rapidly decreasing. She would much rather be spending this time conversing with Nex and laughing and learning of his weirdness and ancient tales. Company other than his was…disappointing.

"So, what do you say?" asked Eric. It seems he had been talking this whole time. "Would you care to accompany me back to my estate?"

"Oh, I'm sorry," said Lily. "I wasn't listening."

"Excuse me?" said Eric.

"Hm? Yes, of course. You are excused," said Lily, disinterested.

A small vein popped up on Eric's forehead. He was clearly losing his patience with the girl who was not besotted with him. "You should be grateful that I am offering you such kindness!"

he snapped as he reached out to touch her face. In the blink of an eye her hand left the glass and grappled at the laid-out cutlery on their table and she brought it down into his hand and through the solid oak table.

"If you try to touch me again, I'll make sure you'll never be able to take a girl on a 'real' date."

To further add insult to injury she then threw his glass of expensive wine over him. "You're foul, and I wouldn't touch you if you were the last man alive!" she snapped as she grabbed her glass and downed the expensive wine, threw some Aur down on the table and took her and Nex's meals outside. "Thanks for the drink" she said as she left him.

"You bitch!" he screamed in pain as she exited. "Ahhh!" he screamed again as he writhed like the spoiled brat he was.

Lily left the building to inform Nex of her situation and see how he was getting along with Eric's goons. But, as expected, she stepped down the small oak beam steps to find the four young men strewn across the floor unconscious with Nex leaning against the post of the building opposite.

"For a minute there I thought you were going to take him up on his offer…" said Nex smugly as he pushed his shoulder against the post, allowing himself to straighten up to greet her.

"Hmph, I had to make you sweat, didn't I?" said Lily with equal smugness, flirtatiously. Nex smiled back at her, his feelings adapting softly under his skin without his permission.

"YOU STUPID BITCH!!" screamed a voice from behind Lily as the door to the tavern flew open again with Eric standing bloodied in the doorway, the knife in his uninjured hand. "DO YOU KNOW WHO I AM?!" he screamed desperately again as he began down the steps for her. Lily took little time to deliberate her actions. She swiftly landed a precise, very low powered kick to the side of Eric's head sending him crashing into the steps.

Without mercy she quickly raised her right leg and placed it down on his chest whilst he lost consciousness. "Stay!" she commanded. "Maybe, next time, he'll think twice before treating girls like playthings?" she asked without awaiting a response.

Nex reached out his hand and erupted the green magical energy from it, healing Eric's hand. Lily glared back at him fiercely, her eyes cutting through the still air.

"It looked nasty! Oh lovely! Is that my stew?!" said Nex as the waitress came out of the tavern with their food.

"Why am I not surprised that this is what you are focused on?" she sighed heavily as she walked over to him. "Thank you, we will take it with us."

"Good idea," said Nex. Lily paused in thought for a moment as she weighed up their options.

"Let's just eat this on our way to the inn" she thought aloud.

"Perfect!". replied Nex in agreement. "Lead on to the warm, comfy bed!" encouraged Nex.

"I don't think I have ever met anyone as weird as you, and I mean that in many ways," trailed Lily as she turned down the street for the Inn.

They continued some few paces before Lily spoke again. "The Kraken," said Lily, "I've stayed here before,"

"So, no skulking through dark alleys to find a safe place to rest?" asked Nex jokily.

"I think people will think twice before hunting us. After what you did to that Sentinel they will have to think more carefully about their next move," said Lily.

"But, sleeping in luxury can ruin an adventure," said Nex.

"Okay. I'll remember that when *I'm* in a warm bed and you're sleeping in the nearest hay-stack," said Lily with a smile, irritation building.

"The Kraken it is then," said Nex quickly in agreement.

"Villages like this one are right on the edge of trade routes. They rely on tourism and adventurers. Seaside towns like Fallow will have multiple inns but I do have a favorite," said Lily with insight.

"I'm surprised the pretty boy back there hasn't had his ass handed to him already by an adventurer then," said Nex as they continued through the evening life of the quaint seaside village.

"He probably has some sway in the guilds. And if his family truly was related to the Pontifex there would be serious repercussions to the factioned that infringed upon his interests," said Lily.

"But you're not worried?" asked Nex.

"My only affiliation is with you; A wanted criminal, so no, I'm not bothered," she confirmed.

"Fair enough. Have you ever thought about joining a guild?" asked Nex.

"A guild for adventurers?" Lily did not take much time to answer. "Once. It is something that all children dream to do," she said as she pictured the smiling faces of a young girl and a young boy, "but I don't think I ever could now."

"How come?" asked Nex, intrigued. "You could just go on adventures yourself if you didn't like any of the people there? It would be a perfect opportunity to-"

"I promised I would join a guild one day," she began, "but I'm not sure it would be right for me to fulfill that promise alone. It's painful to explain."

"I see…" said Nex as he knew he had touched on something sore and painful.

"Plus," she added, "if I stayed in Ares, I would always have the Mantle on my back. I'm not sure I would be able to escape them as an adventurer either."

"I'm sure if you became one of them, the guild would stick up for you, somehow…" said Nex.

"True. Guilds are independent factions in Ares," she replied. "There are some truly powerful adventurers at the Illyrium rank. But the Mantle would definitely try to throw their weight around."

"Illyrium?" asked Nex. Something he had not heard of.

"Illyrium is the name of Star Metal, the rarest metal in Reath," she stated. "My katana is made from Illyrium."

"I see…" said Nex as he looked at his own blade. "It must have been named after…"

"After?" she asked as she dismembered her fish and ate.

"Oh, nothing," said Nex quickly. "This Illyrium rank, is it impressive?"

"It's above bronze, silver, gold and platinum ranks in terms of adventurers. I think there are only three Illyrium adventurers in all of Ares. I think Meleager is currently the strongest Illyrium adventurer. He spends his time doing requests like dragon slaying and demon quelling and so he is often not seen for years during his quests."

"Hmm," sighed Nex as he ate another mouthful of stew..

"Now who's being childish? Perk up! It's depressing." said Lily with a cheeky smile.

"Ooh," said Nex, "all this talk of ranked adventurers really piques my interest. That was something I, too, dreamed of ever since I was little. To be free to go on adventures all over the world," he began as the two became like minded.

"It is a common dream for all. I wonder where we would rank…" said Lily curiously. Would they still be monsters of power amongst the ranks of adventurers?

"It is decided, then!" shouted Nex enthusiastically. "Once we get the chance, we are going to take a look at a guild and see what they offer!"

"I think there's one in Rook that would be worth having a look at, a town to the North in Eos, But you'll have to live through the Sentinels first…" said Lily.

"Dawh!" said Nex in disappointment. "Ah, you know you're immature when an eighteen year-old assassin has to cheer you up."

"Haha!" she laughed as she winked at him in triumph.

"Mhmm," concluded Nex. "We have both got a lot going on inside these heads of ours. It'll be nice for us to empty them to one another on the long journey to the Capital."

"Don't get ahead of yourself, I feel like I have already told you far too much! About myself" she lied.

"Maybe. But I am certain we will learn much, much more about each other before then."

"You're so narrow minded!" blurted Lily in a spout of frustration at Nex's prizing of her mind.

"Haha!" he laughed triumphantly.

They continued until they reached the village's main cobbled road, passing drunkards and merchants running the night life. As the street-lamps hung low with their numbing, ambient flames, it led the two companions into the arms of Lily's favourite Inn, The Kraken.

"Here it is," she stated. Nex looked back at her in obvious sarcasm observing the large, cast iron sign of a two armed, four legged, eight tentacled sea monster destroying a ship with its might.

Having finished their meals on the walk Lily placed them in the cleaning barrel commonly placed outside of taverns.

"What's this?" asked Nex.

"A boy will come first thing and empty the barrel, returning the cutlery and bowls to the right tavern for a small sum of Aur. Now, let me do the talking, he has a soft spot for me," said Lily as she led up the stone steps with her small frame.

They entered the small, comfortable Inn. Its character was overwhelming, encroaching every inch into their personal space with its charm.

"Lily!" shouted the average looking man crammed behind a small greeting desk. "Lily! It is you! It has been far too long! Here for a room, yeah?" he finished.

"Calm down Geraint. It has not been that long since you last saw me. You know the drill. What have you got for me?" she said swiftly.

"Oh, course course-" he cut himself off as his eyes caught the handsome young man behind her.

"Can I help you, mate?" he said as he gave him a disapproving once over.

"I don't think so," Nex replied, brushing the awkwardness back onto Geraint.

"Relax Ger, he's with me," added Lily.

"But you...you work alone?" said Geraint as he looked back at Nex, catching a glimpse of his awkward smile. "You once said to me you'd rather be strung up in the town square and beaten by poles than have a partner-"

"That's enough, Geraint!" laughed Lily awkwardly, reaching over the desk to shut him up physically. "It's nothing Ger, He is just some foreigner that carries my stuff back and forth, that's all. His name is Nex."

Geraint's face lit up once more as his body language exploded in a sultry manner. He flew his arms onto the desk and leaned into the blossoming young girl. "Of course, of course. There's no way you'd be travelling with someone else unless you HAD to."

"So, Geraint," she began, her voice ringing like velvet through the air catching her unexpecting prey like a fish on a hook, "I've come all this way just to see you, is there anything you can do for me whilst I'm here?"

Geraint's pale, spotty skin grew into a scarlet red as his boyish charm began to overload. "Of course!" he said as he scrambled around for his last key, "I've only got one room left though!"

"Two beds?" asked Lily as she tilted her head.

"Oh yes! Two beds. Yes. indeed. There's two," he repeated, glancing back and forth.

"Here," said Lily, handing over three Aur coins as payment. "Now, what else is it that you have for me?"

"umm..." he trailed before catching a fleeting thought, "what is it that you need to know?"

Lily turned to Nex. "Geraint is quite the information hoarder.

He gets his sweaty eyes and ears all over this town to learn about the goings on." With every word Geraint nodded to Nex as Lily praised him.

"So, has anything out of the ordinary been going on here, then?" she asked, hoping for a slither of information to connect Nex's quest and her own.

"Eric's father has been running into lots of trouble with the Mantle. I think the Pontifex has threatened to remove him unless he hikes up the taxes. Obviously, no one is happy about it, so tensions have been higher than usual around here" said Geraint.

"Anything else?" asked Lily inquisitively.

"Hmm…" he thought. "Some Sentinels came through a few weeks ago but they didn't stick around for long. They were as cheerful and talkative as they normally are," he added.

"Did they say what they were after?" she probed.

"No, they didn't, but I think they were worried about some strange creatures. They mentioned something about a tomb as well."

"I see" said Lily as she looked to Nex to see if any of this information triggered anything. "Is there anything unusual about the town itself? You've not seen someone with a sword like mine by any chance?"

"A sword like yours" he clarified. "No, I don't think so."

"Nex?" she asked, hoping he could add to the conversation.

"I am looking for something mysterious and great, Geraint. I'm looking for an ancient artefact that I know to be around here but there is a distortion that prevents me from locating its exact position. It is, without question, unfathomably dangerous and likely to cause the environment around it to become unstable and hostile. I'm looking for something like that."

The way Nex engaged the conversation was unlike any tone Geraint had ever heard. He was captivated by the way Nex phrased and posed his words, each syllable as beautiful as the last. Perhaps there was some form of magic behind it…

"Hmm…Oh," snapped Geraint quickly, "a large group of adventurers came through here a few weeks ago to try and sort out the keep at the top of the Heath cliffs. A place called the Reach. They looked seriously strong too, but they never came back."

"The Reach?" asked Lily with confused air. "I've walked all across the paths over the Heath and I've never seen a keep."

"No," said Geraint. "The Reach itself is built into the cliffs of the Heath and it's so old that it's mostly in ruin now. Only the catacombs beneath it remain. That is where those adventurers went. You wouldn't see what's left of the Reach from atop the Heath Cliffs, you would have to go down the cliffside paths. It's only in the last few weeks that some really weird stuff has been going on up there, though. That place gives me the creeps!"

"That sounds like the kind of place an ancient artefact might be," said Nex.

"It does sound like the right place," said Lily with a satisfied smile.

"I wouldn't go down there!" warned Geraint. "Those adventurers were packing some serious firepower. They had members ranking from gold all the way up. I think they even had two platinum ranks and NO ONE saw them come back out. In the night sometimes, over the sounds of the waves crashing against the cliffs," began Geraint as he leaned towards them with his story "we can hear the wails of the creatures below. We think it's some sort of sea dragon that uses the catacombs as a nest. Its presence has brought an eerie cold darkness into Fallow."

"It's definitely worth checking out," declared Nex, feeling the presence from afar.

"I agree," said Lily. "Plus, I've never seen a sea dragon so that would be exciting."

Geraint was astonished. The tale of woe he had recanted petrified his usual patrons. Lily and Nex were excited to journey into the unknown abyss, Lily took the iron key from Geraint's hand whilst he was still stunned by his own words. "Goodnight Geraint. This way Nex."

"Did you not just listen to a word I said?!" shouted Geraint as they walked away.

They continued through the hallway and up the cosy, carpeted stairs, "so that's why you chose this place?" asked Nex as they ascended.

"I know him, he hears a lot, and the rooms here are so incredibly cute it would be a crime to not stay here," said Lily, attempting to control her excitement.

"Expensive?"

"Not at all. You may think me cheap to only give him three Aur a night for a room, but I place a large down payment at the beginning of the year. That more than covers multiple stints here. Plus, Geraint is a gem and I like to try and support small businesses etcetera"

"Ah," said Nex in discovery. "

Hm?" asked Lily swiftly, turning her head back.

"It's nothing. It's just nice to see the softer side of you come out every once and a while " he smiled.

"Oh, shut up. I'm too tired to argue." She reached down to the small thick door and put the key in, turning the lock and entering the small room. "I will wash quickly and you can go in after while I get ready for bed," as she headed for the en-suite bathroom.

"One must always be spotless before they go to bed, for if they were to pass away in their sleep they must be sure that they are pristine when they meet their Maker!" recanted Nex.

"What?" asked Lily in confusion.

"That's…that's why it's customary to wash before one sleeps in a bed," he stated with obviousness.

"What? No way! I thought it was just for cleanliness."

"Everything comes from something, my dear student," assured Nex.

"Ugh. Shut up. You're so condescending sometimes."

Nex examined the small room, taking in the small, unique characteristics that made this place 'cute'. It felt like only a moment had passed before Lily emerged from the bathroom drying her face.

"All done," she said. "Make sure you knock before you come back in."

"Sure thing," replied Nex as he passed by her.

Lily began undressing, glancing over her shoulder to make sure Nex hadn't left the bathroom without notifying her. She folded her clothes and only her underwear remained, revealing her soft curves and luscious skin, the body and shape of a goddess. She launched herself quickly into the warm sheets and covered herself entirely. She froze there for what felt like minutes until two stern knocks hit the bathroom door.

"Are you respectable?" asked Nex through the door cautiously.

"Yes…" muttered Lily as she prepared herself.

He had undressed into his small clothes but remained bandaged on his arms and legs, his tabard and undershirt in his hands folded with his cloak and boots. Laying it all down neatly, he placed his Shirasaya atop it all.

His incredible physique caught Lily off guard as she awed in his masculinity. She was a human woman, after all, and therefore not immune to his well trained body. Being young and slim it was almost impossible to identify that Nex possessed such a physique. A body moulded by years of intense training. She gazed in awe at the muscles of his torso while his white hair caught the candle-light and reflected back into the dark corners of the room with elegance.

"You wear the bandages to bed?" she asked.

"The scars beneath them are...unpleasant. It is best to leave them on for now."

Without the shroud of Nex's magically enhanced robes, Lily found it harder than usual to take her eyes off bandages. Although his magic was sealed into his body, she could almost feel a flow beneath them like a gentle stream of water that trickled through the crack of hard stone. She was drawn to these above all else.

"Are you okay?" asked Nex normally, catching her gaze. "Mhmm, yup goodnight!" said Lily frantically as she turned away. "Goodnight." Said Nex softly as he blew the candle-light out and climbed into his bed. "Lily?" asked Nex through the quiet night. "Yes?" she replied softly, clinging to the sheets firmly. "Thank you." said Nex. Lily tried to grab the words from her vocabulary to respond, but she was hopeless to defend against his sincerity. Years of isolation and now I'm surrounded by warmth' though Nex guiltily as he stared up at the ceiling. Lily remained turned away as she relaxed her body and closed her eyes.

CHAPTER TWENTY: THE REACH

The morning came swiftly, too fast for Nex to enjoy the luxury of the indoor sleeping that he had not experienced in such a long time. The beds were so forgiving and welcoming to his hardened body he thought he would dream free and feel refreshed, but not long after Lily had drifted off, he sought refuge on the floor. Something about the soft, welcoming down contained within the mattress violated his hardened body and so he had retreated to the floor. Nothing in this world could be so inviting without consequence…

As euphoric as the experience of sharing a room with a beautiful girl was, what awaited them was unrivalled. Nex rose, forgetful that he had a companion in the same room. He absentmindedly headed for the washroom to splash some water over his face. After making a few noises, he turned around to see Lily free of her underclothes, quickly trying to get something over her before he returned to the bedroom. The two exchanged a long, awkward glance.

"LOOK AWAY!" she howled.

"Ahh!" screamed Nex as he attempted to turn around with haste only to find the door frame first. He brought his hand to his head as he turned back around to Lily, who had revealed herself again in an attempt to get some clothes on.

"GET OUT!" she shouted as she grabbed at the crockery from her bedside table and launched a wooden ornament at him which connected with his face.

"Ahh!" he shouted again as he looked down at the floor to return to the washroom.

"DON'T TURN AROUND!" ordered Lily as she frantically tried to get some clothes on her. Despite his pain, Nex had the image burnt into his mind and held a sinister smile across his face as he cowered in the bathroom.

"Hello?" asked a voice at the door.

Lily had only enough time to don her underclothes and was absent of her armor, whilst Nex was still in his small trunks and bandages. The two exchanged a look of readiness. Nex reached out his hand towards his sealed sword and it flew to him. The threat was unlike what they had faced so far. Their new foe was employing the master technique akin to Nex 's of sealing their presence.

"It's me, Geraint. I've brought some warm bread rolls."

Lily exhaled heavily as she knew the custom. Geraint had always done this, but her time at Nex's side made her more skittish.

"You see?" she said to Nex. "This is what you have done to me. You've made me paranoid. Come in."

Geraint entered with a small basket of bread rolls inside and a large jug of fruit juice. He quickly assessed the beauty in her unkempt clothes and the shredded young man in just his undergarments. He thought their tension of imminent battle was of deeds interrupted, and Geraint became annoyed with himself for not being as impressive as Nex and not seducing Lily sooner.

"I-uhh," began Geraint as he placed them down. Lily went bright red as she caught on to the thoughts that flooded Geraint's mind. After All, she had forgotten that she was only wearing very little. Her face erupted with red as she began to emit a sinister aura to the two men watching her.

"I'll kill you both!" she declared as she stood there and prepared to summon her sword. Geraint quickly turned and hurried away whilst Nex flew into the washroom to await further instruction.

Lily quickly put the majority of her gear on before speaking to Nex. "When we go downstairs we go as fast as we can. No dawdling!"

"Yes, Ma'am," replied Nex.

"You can come out now." she said.

He crept out slowly with his head bowed so that he could not make the same mistake. Lily was now fully clothed and buckling up her greaves whilst sitting on the edge of the bed. "Eat up." She gestured to the basket of bread with a nod "you get the brown ones." Nex looked broken, the white ones were his favourite above all else!

"I'll meet you outside" she finished. Nex swiftly proceeded to cover himself with his gear. Of the four rolls left, he quickly grabbed two of them and hurried out of the room. The immediate threat of an unpleasant Lily was the only thing on his mind, and he did not wish to anger her any further. Nex descended the stairs to catch sight of her already out of the door and beckoning back to him to hurry. Swiftly, without Geraint noticing, they slipped away to avoid any awkward conversations and began off towards the Reach.

Closer to the deep sea they found the air colder and rich with salt. The wind was stronger and more unwelcoming as if to tell them to return from where they had come. They continued onwards for around two hours until they came across the ruins of the ancient keep buried into the cliffside.

"This must be it," said Lily to her companion, breaking the

awkward silence.

"I-"

"It's nothing. Just keep it in mind next time," she said, banishing the redness from her cheeks.

"Next time…" trailed Nex as he caught on to her indication of sharing a room again. Lily was unable to contain the rosiness in her face as she filled both with embarrassment and anger preparing to lash out. Nex skipped forward in anticipation as to not receive a blow to his arm from one of her relentless strikes.

"Well, there's definitely *something* down there," confirmed Nex as he looked down to the remains of the great keep embedded into the cliff-side.

"It feels so dark," said Lily, focusing her mind. "Perhaps it really is a sea dragon?"

"Akuma is definitely down there," he clarified.

"Do you suppose the dragon was drawn to the darkness of the blade and now protects it?" she asked.

"I can hear the fear in your voice. Below us, is where our destinies intertwine. It is the reason you have kept yourself living all this time. My words were not mere jest. Come, Lily. Embrace your destiny." Nex reached out, and with his magic, searched the catacombs for answers.

"It feels almost like…?" trailed Lily in thought of their previous experiences.

"A demon…" he concluded. "But this place is not a trap. It's a tomb."

Nex could sense a powerful, dark power emanating from the keep's catacombs, but there was something else uneasy about the situation. The only thing he was certain of, was that the path before them led to their goal.

"Such a dark atmosphere," trailed Lily. "All this darkness and evil is surfacing throughout Ares."

"As the light fades, creatures are lured to the call from beneath Ares. It is only a matter of time. Are you ready?"

"With you here, I think I finally am. Let's get going, then" she said as he began forward down the jagged rock path that led down to the keep.

"O-okay, Just be careful not to get too close to the edge!" warned Nex.

"I have fallen further. Plus that's the sea, down there, we would be fine if we fell."

"I'd rather fall onto land!" he mumbled as he looked at the vast expanse.

Lily could not help but laugh at him. "You don't like the sea? I didn't expect that from you."

"It's not that I don't like it, it just freaks me out, that's all." he stated.

"But surely you would have had to cross the sea to get to Ares originally?" she said..

"Oh, goodness. Don't remind me!" he winced, "that was the worst journey of my life!"

The Reach had been reduced to almost nothing over the centuries. The only steps to pass through here in a decade belonged to that of the adventurers Geraint mentioned. There were many battles in which it had not won against the harsh weather and cruel seas. The once high standing walls that looked far out over the ocean had collapsed down the cliffside and into the sea. The ruins revealed a large hole that would have been in the central hall of this once great castle.

"Do you think they survived? The adventurers?" asked Lily.

"No. I don't think they did. I am unsure as to how powerful a Platinum adventurer is."

"How would this demon fare against the one at the Blythewood?" she asked.

"It would win," stated Nex firmly as he listened to the call of darkness with his own senses "Here."

They stopped at the top of the abyss. "Down here?" asked Lily.

"This hole was made by magic, maybe a decade ago," said Nex as he examined it with his fingers.

"How deep do you think it goes?"

"There is only one way to find out," he said as he stepped forwards and dropped down into the bottomless pit. Lily did not hesitate to follow. With their skills, they would likely not come to any harm even if the distance was somewhat considerable. They fell for around ten seconds before they landed onto the hard rock at the bottom, crashing with an immense impression, but unphased.

"These must be the catacombs?" said Lily as she rose up and looked around in the dark. "A handy shortcut!"

"These catacombs are thousands of years old. Hm?" He ran his hands over the jagged walls as blue flames erupted from the torches mounted on the rocks ahead of them. One after another, hundreds of them, lighting the pitch-black cavern with the deep blue flame. They had dropped through a magic made shortcut into the depths of the catacombs and into a passageway that led from one area to another. At this time it was uncertain as to whether the adventurers before them dared plummet straight into the abyss.

"It knows we are here," said Lily.

"Look…" gestured Nex with his head. The tunnel led forwards for a hundred or so paces where it was then cleared into an opening. "There," he said as they began forward.

The suspense built as they approached the unknown. The pitter patter of the drops of salt-water leaking into the bedrock and dribbling under their feet in the dank, subterranean cave added to the tension. They came upon the end of the tunnel where the bedrock had been annihilated to create a large opening. The room was like a great hall, jagged rocks outlining the perimeter that was once a large armoury or perhaps a place that built ships. At their feet, they began to notice the corpses of the grand adventurers that came before them. As they entered the clearing they saw the rest of them pierced by the stalactite of the cave itself. In front of them the rocks began to climb, almost like a set of unnatural steps towards a central feature where a throne made of stone held a dark figure. They were not alone.

"So you are the Demon here?" said Nex casually as he looked around the dwelling. "Nice place."

Lily refrained from talking, not knowing how she could add to the conversation.

"Something feels…off, don't you think?" claimed Lily.

"I think you're right," agreed Nex.

"This one identifies us without thought to its remark," said a hollow voice back to him, "and yet we reserve ourselves for such a question. Perhaps our manners are not yet all lost."

"Oh?" said Nex back to the demon intrigued by his knowledge.

"This one reeks of the blood of our ilk," it said in its hollow voice. "Has it come to rid this dank cavern of our existence, too?"

"We are looking for something, demon. It would not be wise for you to withhold any information from us," said Lily.

"We have no desire to fight. If it is only knowledge you seek then there can be an arrangement," spoke the demon defensively. "The creatures before could not let us be, and so we destroyed them." The Demon gestured to the bodies strewn around the room slowly decaying In the moist arena. "I wished for them to bathe in their despair but this one would not allow it. He killed them before I could enjoy my feast."

"Why...is it talking like that?" asked Lily with an uncomfortable demeanor.

"You have not fully taken control of your host," highlighted Nex.

"Ah!" it snapped quickly, "this one knows more of Demons than the others. Tell us, of *what* do you speak?"

Nex turned to Lily too as he explained the situation. "It refers to itself as 'we' because it has not taken full control of the vessel. The two souls are vying for control. A demon, to be held back by a lowly human? How very rare."

"Silence! This one knows nothing of my host. He is weak, yes, he is troublesome, true, but he is mine and his power is one worthy of my demonic power." The demon brought its own hand down the side of its hidden face, "it is only a matter of time before we are one. Perhaps with more death, he will submit."

Nex stepped forward. "O creature of the abyss, your voice trembles when you talk. We both know why it is that you cannot take control of this host. In his soul, is something far more powerful than you could hope to overcome. Even in all your greatness you have been defeated."

"This one is knowledgeable, indeed. Perhaps you will offer a new vessel?" spoke the hollow demon.

"I am afraid I am not compatible with your soul, and you would find the same issue with this one here as you do with your current host," stated Nex. "The information we require from you is more...physical."

"No!" shrieked the demon, now in a different, almost human, voice. "Please, leave this place! The Demon will kill you both!"

"That voice!" gasped Lily.

"You see, demon? Your grasp on this vessel is weak. He takes your consciousness from you with ease," said Nex.

To the Demon, Lily was an impressive flame of burning green aura that was calm and innocent. But Nex was something else. Incomparable in size and presence the Demon saw him as a gulf of eternal blackness. There was only one monster here.

"You know much, human, and your aura howls danger. But if it is this human you wish to reclaim, know that he will not be as whole as he once was. And if you seek his treasure, know that that too has consumed him. If you care for this vessel his highest chance of survival is to fuse with me."

"I think we both know I'm here for the sword," admitted Nex honestly. The demon paused for a moment as it thought.

"Yes..." it said slowly, "we can *feel* it. Even here, where the air is rank and the skin boils at the touch of moisture, we can feel Akuma. We can feel Tsumikiri. To think, from across all this world, you would bring us the Life Drinker. We thank you for delivering us power." It aimed at Lily, finally addressing them as beings of interest and not objectifying them as mortal maggots.

"No, no," interjected Nex for clarity. "It is I who cannot thank you enough. You have given me something more valuable than you could ever perceive. You have proven destiny exists and that my fate, intertwined in the fabric of magic and space, delivers me to the stars I have chosen. Look upon this demon, Lily. Know that in your heart, this is where you were destined to be. Here, in an abyss of death and fear you and I will truly start an adventure. Your soul had fed off the hope that one day you would come here and save this man from extinction."

"I-" Lily was dumbfounded. Everything was happening too fast for her senses to follow.

"It will give us the Life Drinker!" roared the Demon as its sprang.

"Below!!" Nex darted and thrusted Lily out of the way.

Beneath them, its presence masked by the overwhelming aura of sinister, murderous intent was indeed the Sea Dragon which revelled in this environment. It ruptured through the floor between them and swallowed Nex whole, slithering with its reptilian body through the corridors of the catacombs as easily as a rat-worm through mud.

Lily had no time to avert her eyes from the demon that stood before her and she knew that it would take more than a little sea snake to defeat Nex. She only cursed herself for being too slow to sense such a creature and forcing Nex to cover for her. The demon welled up with a deep green emerald aura that mirrored Lily's that flooded the cavern like a dense fog. A green magic power glowed dangerously around the Demon's hands as it prepared to unleash an attack.

Lily evaded the incoming impact spell with difficulty. It was larger than expected with more force and speed than she had anticipated. It blew through the wall behind her with immense force. The demon lowered itself down from its self-proclaimed throne to reveal a tall, slim and muscular young man with long, black, matted hair down to its waist. As it lowered, Lily could see that deep underneath the tattered hair was ancient bandages covering its eyes.

The battle in the other cavern raged as Nex wrestled the colossal Sea Dragon. But Lily could not let herself be distracted from her own fight. Her opponent was stronger than anything she had faced so far and she would not let her guard down again. She readied her katana.

"Let us…free you," said the Demon softly as he unleashed waves of green magic from his hands towards Lily relentlessly. She dodged skilfully, flipping side to side, horizontally and vertically in each and every direction with such finesse it was majestic to the eye. Cutting the last spell in half with her sword, she gathered herself again.

"Oh?" said the demon as it came to a halt. "Interesting." It poised its hand at her and prepared. Slowly, the magic gathered, and the demon summoned a great Katana to him, cracking the air more violently than that of Lily's. It stretched on and on until finally, at a length of nine full paces, it stopped.

"Akuma!" gasped Lily as she recognised the brother to her blade.

Lily launched, her sword heading straight for a killing blow only to find herself blocked by his humongous sword. She flipped backwards out of her attack and began another, swinging her sword furiously and skilfully faster than the eye could see, quicker and deadlier than her battle with Nex. The demon swung hard and fast, the aftermath of its strokes devastating the walls of the cavern making the ground shake. But Lily did not falter. She poured more and more strength into each blow, increasing in power more than she ever had before until they locked swords and she gazed upon the demon's scarred face.

It hit her. The feeling of wretched pain and horror as she saw the strip of cloth that covered its eyes. "Flowen!" she screamed.

The lapse of concentration was a fatal mistake. The demon exploded with a magical spell, and sliced at Lily to take her head. Barely evading in time with all her skill and flexibility, the katana slashed at her beautiful face, whilst the following blow flew her backwards into the unforgiving rocks.

"Delicious…" drooled the Demon. "Your soul will be a bountiful meal. Your companion is sure to be consumed by my little pet. Submit to us now and your death will be…slow."

"Give…" roared Lily lowly as she rose, "my brother back!"

The demon paused as it conferred silently with the soul inside of itself. "This one…a relation?"

"I have waited my whole life to be strong enough to save you, brother. I did not know for certain but in my heart, I knew it to be true. You were alive. This demon, I recognise its stench. I remember the precious things it stole from me. With all my strength, brother, I will set you free!"

They engaged once more in an intensive battle. The demon swung its great sword at nothing as Lily evaded with great skill and athleticism. It was her will alone that kept her going against the curse of Akuma. With her movements slowed, Lily felt an immense amount of magical pain in her right thigh. She looked down to see that during the barrage of attacks the demon's blade had cut her velvet skin. It was not a physical pain. It did not send signals to the brain that screamed of the gauging of flesh, no. It was a spiritual pain. A phantasmal energy that is said to be akin to the material of the soul. That is exactly what it felt like. It was not her body that had been pierced, but her soul. It was the most unbearable pain she had ever experienced.

"Akuma!" said the Demon. "The Soul Eater! A blade so sharp no seathe can withstand it!"

Lily fell to one knee. The Demon poised as it faced her hateful glare and it was struck with horror and revelation. The wall to the cavern shuddered as it collapsed through, the head of the Sea Dragon crashing down, its eyes rolling in their sockets with Nex emerging triumphant. "I think we are all lucky that it was only a young one."

He walked over to Lily, his hand already outstretched and emitting the healing glow of magic. But the sight of a victorious Nex was not what stunned the demon. Flashing at the forefront of its mind were the memories of the human it once was. A barrage of anything and everything held within the demon's heart was crashing and collapsing causing immeasurable pain. The demon stumbled back, cowering at the thoughts that flooded its mind, the internal conflict of its being tearing it apart.

"Lily?!" it shouted.

Lily breathed deeply, Nex's magic refreshing her of her wounds, healing her body and soul. "Flowen?! Flowen! It's me!" she roared over the crumbling of the cavern.

"The two of you resonate as one. This is the destiny I wished to show you!" said Nex.

"Nex, please! I beg of you! Help me save my brother!" Lily urged her words with the strong will of her soul to Nex's ears. He did not like this tone. Lily was supposed to be happy and carefree and bring light into his life. But now, her voice carried pain and anger to him. Her suffering caused him great anguish.

"Silence!" snapped the demon to its alter ego. "Akuma is in my hands! We will consume you both!"

"I am sorry Lily, but his blade is designed to take considerable effect on the soul. My magic will take time to heal you. As I promised, your struggles are my struggles! You will not regret the faith you have placed in me!"

"I am not strong enough! Please! Save him!"

"Bah!" The demon lurched as it released a defensive blow to gain some distance between the powerful Nex. Its green, viridian magic surrounded it in a deadly aura before it sprang towards Nex faster than anticipated and slashed across his torso with ease, drawing a deep canal of blood. However, Nex had no intention of defending. He was too enraged to control his body fully as he looked down upon the demon.

"It doesn't matter what move I make, for you can see our futures. Your magic of Future Sight is truly something to behold. I will simply show you a future in which you cannot win," said Nex.

"ENOUGH!" roared the demon as, with a wave of its arm, the cavern erupted with stalactites from all around, piercing through the air truer and sharper than any arrow. Nex dodged them all with a speed greater than Lily had ever seen him use before and, when the barrage was over, he clenched his fists tightly in preparation and clicked his old bones, the bedrock crunching and rumbling at his power.

"Here I come," he warned. The demon prepared, and saw it. Nex was upon it in an instant, a trail of blue light in his wake. But the demon had already seen Nex's attack with his Foresight Magic and took the blow into its guarding hand.

"USELESS!" he said as he felt the emptiness of the strike. "Wha-" it spoke as it felt the true blow collide with its face. The demon flew with unrelenting force diagonally down into the rock-solid stone.

"My afterimage doesn't do much damage, eh?" said Nex as he

circled the recovering demon.

"Our eyes…cannot see?" questioned the demon as it rose. It retaliated in full force, releasing huge magic attacks with its sword towards Nex. From the solid ground beneath them, huge grey stalactite skewers erupted from every surface and surrounded Nex, only to instantly shatter and fall. He continued to bombard the Demon with a speed faster than it could see with its magic. Hand to hand, it did not stand a chance. Nex did not even need to use his sealed sword.

"Horror Demon's Soulless Lance!" it shouted with yet another high-level spell. An enormous black spike emerged from thin air and flew like a javelin from a ballista towards Nex, only for him to slash straight through it with his sheathed sword.

"Horror Demon's Phantasmal guillotine!" summoned the demon as it unleashed its most devastating spell. A giant stalactite that came from behind him filled the cavern almost completely before it shattered.

"I can see that you're going to keep shooting things at me," stated Nex as he summoned a fight-finishing move. "This will set you free!" roared Nex as he manipulated his body in a form of martial art.

"Infinity Magic: "said Nex. As the demon stood aghast at its awe, with defeat imminent "PURGATORY RAY!"

An eruption of gold magic beamed into the demon faster than the light of a folding star clashing with it indefinitely. There was not a chance the demon could withstand such a spell. Nex walked over to the demon, his god-like presence sealed once more and the air calming down around them as if the un-natural existence had been exorcised.

"Flowen!" screamed Lily as she hurried over in a frenzy. "Brother, are you okay?" She slid down beside him and hoisted his head onto her soft lap.

"He is okay, Lily," assured Nex as the peace returned. "It was the demon I was aiming for. I only hit him with a little one."

CHAPTER TWENTY ONE: FLOWEN

The Demon stood up quickly, ignoring any pain from the injuries it had sustained, and grappled at Lily's face with his damp hands. He held her head firmly and gazed through his bloodied bandaged face.

"IT CANNOT BE! Lily…" he sobbed as the overwhelming traces of the demon subsided within him. Lily could not explain it. The foe that held her with its cold, damp hands radiated only his passionate warmth. This was a feeling she had not felt since long, long ago. A feeling she had all but forgotten.

"Flowen?! Brother?! Can it be?!" she sobbed, the tears falling like raindrops upon his face.

The demon remained silent as it continued to glare at her through its magical senses. "L…Lily? Is it really you…?". Beneath it all, the years of neglect and turmoil, the malnourishment and exile, Lily could see the face of the young boy who watched over his little sister all those years ago. The demon held his younger sister in his hands. "This…this is impossible."

Flowen raised himself to look upon the young woman. If he were not so unruly and unkempt one could recognise their shared heritage. How long had they been apart? What could drive these two souls to separate into lives of such desolation? The two looked upon each other from a perspective they had attained through the years of their suffering.

"How can this be?" said Flowen, taking Lily's hand from her side.

"I...don't believe it!" she mumbled as he pressed her into his cold, damp chest.

"Little sister...you were dead! I felt it with my own senses!" he pleaded as if asking for forgiveness. "I am so sorry, Lily. I felt your heart stop as I held you in my arms. Your body grew cold no matter how desperately I tried to warm you. The days passed..."

"It's okay, Flowen!" she assured him. "When I awoke, there was no one there. I was all alone. But somehow, all this time later, I knew you were here. It is my fault for not coming sooner." The two continued to exchange back and forth, begging the other to forgive them only for it to be accepted, and then repeated.

Nex thought now would be a good time to intervene. "Perhaps you can forgive each other and call it even? Moving forward is what's important."

They exchanged a long stare with one another as they accepted Nex's words and began their movements forward.

"I am a Demon," said Flowen sharply. "As much as I wish to be with my sister, I fear I would only put you in danger! I cannot control this power."
"I dont care!" protested Lily, taking Flowen's hands.

"Flowen," began Nex, "I can help you become one with your power."

"What?!" he exclaimed. "It cannot be done. Do you not feel it within me? This darkness, this malice, this anger. This hunger to destroy everything!"

"Your demonification must have been something truly gruesome, and the forging of your soul with the Horror Demon cannot be reversed. But when you obtained Akuma, you unbeknowingly obtained a power far greater than the demon could control. In short, Akuma, the Soul Eater, has devoured the demon's soul, and you have accomplished something impossible for any human. You are a Human-Demon Hybrid."

"A hybrid!?" they both exclaimed.

"If the demonification occured around the time you thought Lily to be dead, that could be why you did not sense anything from her. There are unfathomable complexities between the senses of a demon and a human."

Flowen dropped to his knees in complete and utter defeat. "So, all this time…you were alive?"

"That is not something you need to be sorry for, brother. In my soul I could feel your presence sometime after we were separated. But I was too weak in body and soul to come and face you," said Lily.

"No, no. Do not be sorry. You can never be sorry for such a thing!" He comforted her as they embraced.

"If it were not for Nex, I wouldn't have come. It was through his power that I was able to face this journey. He brought me here to face my destiny," she said.

The half-demon, half-human, Flowen, looked to the mage that had delivered him his little sister. Through his gnarly appearance and knotted, long, black hair, he poured all of his happiness and thanks through one of the most beautiful and sincere smiles Nex had ever witnessed.

"It was my pleasure," said Nex, accepting his thanks.

Flowen comprehended the formidable man before him who, to his magical eyes, was a black volcano of surging power in aura.

"I'm Nex. It's a pleasure to meet you," he said with a smile.

"Why did you help my sister? Do you seek…me, or is it the blade you truly want?"

"I have come for you both," replied Nex.

"Did you know that there was another blade here?" Lily asked as she wiped away the last of her tears.

"I had my suspicions," replied Nex, holding her gaze trustfully. "Along the stream of magic *everything* is connected."

"The power of Akuma is something that cannot truly be understood. It is not just magic and metal forged in fire. It has a mind and a heart and a soul. It whispers dark and disturbing thoughts…" added Flowen, his magical gaze fixed on the blade.

"Flowen…" began Lily, reaching down and placing a hand on his shoulder in comfort, "Nex understands it all."

"I have freed Tsumikiri from its curse. Akuma devours souls, even that of the wielder." Nex raised his hand and smiled ,"here." A glowing green light erupted from his hand and filled the subterranean cavern with its glow before vanishing.

Flowen could feel the effects immediately. "I'm…"

"I was not overly keen on lifting the curse before our battle," admitted Nex, insulting Lily's power indirectly.

Flowen could feel the blade's curse vanish and its effects withdraw from his very being. The talons it had dug into his white soul withered out and left in the moist air, the corruption on his face surfaced completely before disappearing.

"Removing the curse is actually a very complicated procedure. In the state you were in, with the Horror Demon in control, it was possible that I could have destroyed you in the process. Akuma will still activate its power, but the hindrance placed on you has now been nullified. You have become stronger," explained Nex.

Flowen's demonic and human power erupted from within him into a new height. His dense aura of magic erupted beautifully and freely. He had been cured of his demons and his new purpose had reinvigorated him.

"Those curses were a little…excessive," admitted Nex, "the toll Akuma takes on its user is a heavy one, indeed. As your soul is devoured, your humanity is drained and your soul becomes infested with demonification. But it seems you were already powerful enough to become one with Akuma. Though incomplete, your fusion has begun."

"Thank…you" breathed Flowen, still short on breath.

"I have so much to ask! So much to tell!" began Lily, "I have been alone…for so long. But you have had it so much worse for all these years. I don't know what else to say."

"Hush now, little sister," began Flowen as he smiled, his face wrinkling with an expression that had not been displayed on his face in a lifetime. "We are together now and that is all that matters."

The two held each other in an embrace for quite some time, pouring in the unsaid feelings of a lifetime apart. Their very souls began to connect once more.

"So, how about it?" said Nex as they finally pulled away from one another, "are you coming?"

Flowen placed his hands on Nex and Lily's shoulders. "I owe you my life. Wherever you go, wherever my sister goes, I will follow."

"To the Capital, then!" said Nex as he turned gleefully and walked through the destroyed cavern towards one of the massive openings that had been made from their ferocious battle. They left the cliffside and began North east to the nearest town.

CHAPTER TWENTY TWO: DESTINY

The walk was not silent or awkward. The sun set warmly on the reunited siblings as Flowen probed Lily for information

"You've grown so beautiful!" he said. "You look just like mother."

"Do I…?" replied Lily, blushing uncomfortably, "I don't remember her face."

"You really do! You're the spitting image of her! From what little I can remember of her, looking at you is like looking into the past."

"She was no doubt a beautiful and splendid woman, I'm sure," added Nex.

"Thank you, Flowen," said Lily. "And thank you again, Nex, for bringing me here."

"I hope you're at least a little convinced that there is some merit behind the nonsense I spout. The three of us were destined to be!"

There was a long pause. No one dared say anything at this point. To agree would be almost as awkward as rejecting the notion.

"You two will have a lot to catch up on, no doubt," began Nex, "but let's not overload your reunion too hastily. We should get you cleaned up and get you some new clothes. You can trust me when I say that it's hard to reincorporate oneself into society.You'll scare too many people walking around like the God of Death."

Lily chuckled, looking upon Flowen holding his enormous blade with his unkempt hair and jet-black robes shredded and draped over him. Despite this gnarly appearance she looked upon her brother with a feeling of heart-warming kindness and affection. From Flowen to Nex her eyes wandered as she examined their unusual attire before speaking, "I'll definitely be the one picking out his clothes."

"What?! You have a problem with my style?" said Nex defensively as he turned from the lead to walk backwards to protest whilst both he and Lily chuckled. Flowen faced out toward the open sea, feeling the sun rays for the first time in a long time before turning his attention back to Lily,

"I haven't been to the surface in over ten years...I've forgotten how to be human."

"Don't worry, I'm pretty good at it," assured Lily in comfort to her brother. "Plus, I'm sure you won't be the one who sticks out the most…" she trailed.

"Is that another insult!?" gasped Nex from the wounding comment.
Lily looked at him seriously knowing he knew exactly what she meant. There was no reason for her to explain further any element of his weirdness,

"It was most definitely an insult," Nex mumbled back to her whilst facing only the wind. "Well I suppose we all have our downfalls. *You're* not all that good at making friends either!"

"What!?" Lily snapped.

"Nothing!" he declared quickly as they continued onwards.

The early night was soon to be upon them. The three travelled in soft conversation North along the Heath Cliffs where the paths became more usable and friendly towards the adventurer's town of Rook. Despite their differences and their previous battles, they laughed and joked as Lily educated Flowen of the world whilst Nex took a keen interest. Flowen had an immense presence. He was easily identifiable as a powerful warrior and mage but with a sinister air around him. That, combined with Lily's beauty, power and status and Nex's inability to not fit in, made this party incredibly suspicious. Perhaps some expensive bodyguards to a very wealthy heir? Nex liked to think this would be a good cover story if they were ever to need one. At some point in time, he would like to bestow this idea upon them and it excited him to think that they may get to employ it on an occasion. Lily had gradually removed some of her brother's tattered robes and given them to Nex to burn so as to be rid of them, forever. Flowen was now down to his bare feet, some plain black trousers ripped immensely and a baggy top, covered in holes and tears.

"I think we have earned a stay in an Inn for tonight," concluded Nex, nodding immaturely to himself. "Then, I guess, Lily can take you to buy some new threads in the morning?"

"Threads?" asked Flowen in confusion.

"I think he means clothes," clarified Lily.

"All the popular people used to say it when I was young!" mumbled Nex in disappointment.

"YOU ARE YOUNG!" snapped Lily.

As suspected, their presence did not go unnoticed. The three companions entered the town of Rook with many estranged stares burning holes into their heads. Village folk walking grabbed at their better halves and pulled them closer to themselves to avoid unnecessary trouble from the trio whilst no attempts at conversations were made.

Rook was a bigger town than Fallow. It had many quays reaching out into the great blue sea, implying it was rich with import and export. Attached to the main trade route in the south it surely did have some wealth passing through it in both terms of commerce and tourism.

"Here?" asked Nex.

"I don't have the capacity to walk any further, I'm exhausted," declared Lily, "It has been a long day." She made for the door and pulled back on the cold, iron handle.

"Sorry..." muttered Flowen, responsible for the damage to her petite body.

"No,no. It's fine!" she smiled back at him warmly.

Flowen was clearly uncomfortable being surrounded by people. He had been isolated for quite some time and, any he had met since, he had surely killed whilst under the demon's influence. It did not help that he was carrying a 9 pace long katana and had a gruelling, bloodied bandage covering his eyes.

"Maybe you should put that away..." said Lily, nodding at his sword.

"But Nex still has-" began Flowen in protest as he pointed like a child to Nex's Shirasaya.

"Just put it away!" she snapped quickly and quietly as a mother would to a misbehaving boy.

"O-okay" said Flowen nervously as he tried to ignore the people looking and mumbling about him.

"Three rooms," said Lily to the little boy at the desk indicating with her fingers.

"MUUUM!" he shouted, scurrying away. A few moments later a startled woman emerged from a small room behind.

"H-hello," she said, looking between the Mantle assassin, the oddly dressed black mage holding a sealed sword and the blind, homeless man knocking over a large urn clumsily.

"I'm sorry, I'll pay for that!" Lily assured as she glared at her brother and gestured to Nex to pull him next to him and out of harm's way.

"Three rooms?" she asked in clarification with a nervous voice.

"She's paying," stated Nex as he walked beyond the desk further inside with Flowen as if to symbolise that the further from the desk he was the less likely it was for him to pay. Lily rolled her eyes and handed the innkeeper ten Aur as payment.

"I'm s-sorry, we are so busy at the moment with all the refugees. We only have t-two rooms," said the in-keeper nervously as she fumbled for two room keys attached to some small blocks of wood and handed them to Lily.
"That will be fine," smiled Lily, encouraging the innkeeper to retain the payment of three rooms.
"Oh, thank you kindly. I-it's just up the stairs and on your right…" said the innkeeper gesturing up the stairs and then pivoting her wrists to indicate the right so she would not need to escort them.

"Thank you," Lily bowed politely and respectfully in the dwelling of another, and turned to join the others. Lily handed a key

"Nex, we might be sharing again tonight," she said.

"It may be better for Flowen to be alone. I have a feeling he is going to sleep for a while and I don't want to disturb him," she admitted, considering the difficulty of him settling in.

"Don't let the bed freak you out, Flowen!" warned Nex loudly as he stopped by the door as Lily chivvied Flowen into a separate room, "don't trust it, it will betray you!"

"Nex!" snarled Lily furiously. She held Flowen's hand for a moment, "this is still so fresh, brother. I am sorry if I do not seem overjoyed at the moment. I truly am, but you see, there is so much going on in my head," she said as she put her hands across her face, "I'll be better in the morning after some rest, I promise."

Flowen smiled back at her and placed his hand on her head, "it's just so good to be with you again, Lily."

She spent a short time with him, comforting him and showing him the room. He had seen it all long ago, but his life in the cold, dank cave meant he had all but forgotten how humans lived. Lily helped settle him in with her smooth voice and showed him the intricate controls of the water in which he would use to wash himself. They were both exhausted, but for Flowen, whose demonic ways had led to his exile of human nature, had internal struggles more fatiguing than the usual wounds would incur.

With this, she planted him on the bed and left him. "If you need anything, just come and get me. I will only be next door. Goodnight"

"Good…night," he replied.

The rooms here were more lavish than expected. Flowen did not know where to start, he stared at the bed in suspicion but had no time to waste. He slowly stripped off his clothes and splashed a little water over himself to clean his body enough so that the bed he slept in would not reek after his departure. He knew not of any pre-bed customs. When this was done he remained naked and climbed upon the mysterious bed slowly. He wriggled uncomfortably on its soft down before standing back up again. He pulled off the covers and lowered himself to the floor and stared at the ceiling. Nex's wise words were indeed true, the bed was not to be trusted. Its soft and absorbing manner unsettled his muscles to a point where he felt like he was being eaten by the mattress. This was not a pleasant feeling. The floor would be far more comfortable than any bed at this point. Lily returned to the room which Nex had already entered to find one, large bed before her. She could not help but let out a sigh.

"It's okay, I'll take the floor," said Nex. He did not bother undressing into his small clothes. He placed his sword beside him and began for the floor before Lily came up to him.

She intercepted him, planting her head in his chest, her arms dangling hopelessly by her side, tears pouring down her face more beautiful than starlight.

"Hey…" he spoke softly as he wrapped his arms around her in comfort.

"Thank you," she sniffled through the tears, wrapping her arms around him. "Thank you for giving me your strength. Thank you for everything."

Nex placed a hand on her head and smiled whilst he assured her it was okay to cry. "There, there. It's okay. It was the least I could do after all you have done for me."

Nex, of course, spoke of the incredible experiences he had shared with Lily. The very privilege of being in her presence and sharing the beginnings of a friendship with him. No one would believe how long Nex had been alone and unable to share himself with another. After betrayal, even the greatest of magic cannot heal a broken heart. The room was quiet. The air around them was soft and warm and in his arms, there was a feeling of godly ambience and peace. It was truly a spectacular place to be. Lily pulled away and she started up at him and his warm smile. They need not say anything further. Their bond had cemented into one of great friendship and reliance and they began to resonate with one another, beginning to understand the signature of each other's souls.

"Let's get some rest," said Nex, understanding how tired Lily must be both physically and mentally.

"W-what are you doing?!" he asked in surprise. Lily was red in the face. She had indeed started undressing and revealed her immaculate skin. She did so coyly with a lack of confidence keeping her movements simple and close until she was finally in her revealing smallclothes.

"Y-you've seen it all before so what's the point in making things awkward..." she mumbled with embarrassment. This was Nex's most difficult battle yet! It took all of his strength, every piece of will he could muster to command the fibres of his muscles to lock down his body. Alas, he was triumphant. Lily climbed into bed whilst Nex removed his cloak and lowered himself onto the floor where he had already made his makeshift bed. The two remained silent for some time before Lily spoke again.

"How did you know?" she asked, "how did you know that all of this would happen?" Nex adjusted himself at the foot of the bed so he could face the ceiling for a better projection. "Destiny," he clarified.

CHAPTER TWENTY THREE: A CAPITAL DISPUTE

Nex rose with the sun. He was able to wash his body thoroughly in the bathroom, a rare extravagance for him. But he had learned his lesson. He was quiet and considerate this time so as to not wake the sleeping beauty. He dressed himself calmly before wrapping his mysterious, white bandages around his body absent of Lily's gaze. He exited the washroom just as he completed his last orbit, further sealing himself beneath them. Greeting him as he returned, Lily was also completing her armament clipping and fastening the various intricacies of her armour.

"There's more to those bandages than just covering up your skin. When you remove them, I can feel a change in the atmosphere. What exactly do those bandages do?" she asked, "I can sense a magic inside them that I could not feel before."

"They are indeed enchanted with magic. That you can feel the faint lingering of the spell is proof that you have grown in the time we have been together," he replied, examining them. "They are quite heavy."

"Somehow...they seem it," she trailed.

"How are you doing, anyway? Yesterday must have been quite difficult."

"I'm okay," she said with unease. "I still don't know whether to feel overwhelming joy or undeniable guilt," she furthered in disappointment with herself.

"Nothing can be done about the past. It is the future which lies ahead of you both, now," Nex stated wisely.

"I know him. I love him. I am so overjoyed with happiness…" she admitted, "but I cannot string together the memories. There is so much I cannot remember. I knew in my heart he was there. Even from my time in the Mantle I could feel a familiar magic in Ares. One that, no matter how far away I was, I could always sense. I have just never had the courage to come here. Not until I met you."

"It was not my strength that helped you find Flowen, it was your own," added Nex. "Come. A whole new journey awaits us all, together."

"Mhm," she agreed.

"He's not up yet?" asked Nex, casting his gaze to the next room.

"I checked on him twice in the night and he had brought up a small fever, tossing and turning in his sleep with nightmares. When I looked in on him earlier he seemed to have calmed down but he was still out cold. Have you been casting any magic on him?" she asked.

"A little, yes. But his injuries are more mental than physical and much more complex than anything my magic can conquer. It is a form of healing only he can accomplish. He will just need time to adjust," said Nex

"E-excuse me," said a voice with a knock on the door, "I've got your breakfast."

"Come in."

"H-here," she said as she placed down some steaming porridge and warm, newly baked bread with an accompaniment of freshly squeezed fruit juice, enough for three, on the closest set of drawers.

"Hey," began Nex, "Is that included in the price?" he asked.

"Cheapskate," muttered Lily under her breath.

"Y-yes," replied the innkeeper as she backed out of the room and left.

"Oh, he won't be needing anything next door. Thank you, though," said Lily as she gestured to the remaining portion on the tray for the innkeeper to retract.

Nex walked over and grabbed his bread roll from the breakfast tray, "I'll stay here for when he wakes up. We should try and check out the town for the moment if we are going to stay here for a few days. It is advantageous to know your surroundings. You could maybe get him some 'new clothes'," he said sarcastically with air quotations.

Lily agreed, "are you sure you don't mind? To be perfectly honest, getting out would help me align my thoughts."

"Not at all. You go on ahead. I will do my best to comfort him from here," replied Nex as Lily picked up a bread roll and left the inn. He thought it would be best to give the two siblings some space before they interact again.

"Lily," he said, "The turmoil and resentment you hold for yourself will not disappear overnight. You are not the only one whose duty it is to protect your family."

"Thank you, Nex," she said as she turned and left.

Lily and Flowen had discussed much with their words, but there is a limit to what one can say. An reveal of one's soul is how mages truly understand one another, as their magic *is* the very essence they are composed of. They reveal everything about themselves. With their actions, their movements, and their magic they clash and concile.

Nex was grateful for the peace as Lily left the room to go on her reconnaissance mission. He returned to the floor and sat in meditation. There was much that had happened in his past and even more that was to happen in his future. His mind needed to be clear and open. It also allowed him to pry on the demon next door and watch over him. Whilst Flowen was fast asleep, his mind was in turmoil. Nex could feel his thoughts burning inside his head with pain. He had entered a cold sweat of withdrawal from Akuma's curse but, as Nex once offered to Lily, he is able to reach into the minds of others with his magic. In the time he had, he sought to help Flowen through his struggles.

To the North the dark Sentinel Thusien blackened the halls of the Mantle's most holy temple as he sought audience with the Pontifex. Even Thusien, with all his tremendous might and knowledge, tread carefully around his Holy Eminence.

"Do not speak to me of sin, Thusien the Usurper. The turmoil and despair that you have caused this nation displeases us all," said the pontifex in discontent. "If it is not the Maker you seek to provoke then it is surely Odin's Ten kings who will look to you with their gaze. Even I, the Holy Priest of the Mantle of the known and unknown stretches of this world, abide by their law and wisdom."

"Oh, please!" replied Thusien as he paced disrespectfully around the Pontifex's grand throne room. "Let us not forget that while you may have the trust of the people and their beliefs, how you lied and conceited your way to your position, and who aided in such a despicable route to ascension, I wonder?"

"What I did to get here was for the good of our creator! To ensure humanity's survival through the coming ages, your little escapades included," replied the priest with unwavering conviction.

"Piaus," said the dark Thusien, his pale skin corrupted by his new power and capturing the fleeting candle-light, "whilst I do not underestimate your power or influence, it is the Sentinel legend that keeps foreign invaders at bay. It is the Sentinels who strike fear into all of the souls of this world with their might and power. My new order has grown to even greater heights. None will dare defy us, not even the fabled Kings of Odin. But to ensure Ares prospers *you* must reel in your influence and support us. We cannot hold authority in the courts of the other realms without your unyielding support. Together, we will restore the Sentinels and The Mantle to their former glory. Ares will once again stand atop the kingdoms of this world. We *must* be united in our aim."

The Pontifex was an aged man. He looked around forty to fifty years old physically. He stood short and plump in the traditional attire of head of the Mantle in white robes adorned with gold lace and gems of inconceivable wealth. He did, however, look astonishingly alike to many of his predecessors. He was not only wise, but he possessed a great amount of magic power. So much so that Arcon would do wisely so as to not make an enemy of him. Even so, there was a threat that superseded him in Thusien's mind.

"You are wrong, Thusien. The Sentinels do not command respect and authority. They only instill fear and violence. The Mantle is the Maker's will. We command faith, respect and humanity. Do not lump your kind in with those who truly seek to preserve humanity," spoke the Pontifex. "But, alas, I have not forgotten your aim. Whilst I may not walk this path alongside you, you and your order are all children of The Maker. I will pray to the Maker for your enlightenment."

"Spare me your religious drivel," said Thusien disrespectfully. "You cannot hide your greedy ambitions from me. My former master could not see past your façade, but you and I are alike. You and your general will prove paramount in the change that is to come to Ares. The power you both wield guaranteed our alliance, otherwise you would have been removed along with Kalus."

The Pontifex began to relax exhaled slowly releasing his true nature, "you are quite the cunning one yourself, Thusien. I must admit not even I saw that you would betray your own order and usurp the throne." The Pontifex sprang up and addressed Thusien more casually, taking little notice of the threats the new Arcon made. "What of those expeditions you were conducting within the mountain kingdoms? Do the fabled Sentinels still hold a purpose in this ever evolving world or is this simply another one of your expert deceptions?"

Thusien remained composed and spoke to the Pontifex, now, with a more diplomatic voice. "We have not yet heard from those that were dispatched. But regardless , there is nothing to fear from ancient tombs that hold only the dead."

"I see. And what of the anomalous issue?"

"The presence emanating from the south has not yet been identified. It is likely a slumbering creature of old that churns as it wakes. We felt for ourselves the sinister and menacing power from afar. If it is human and not one of Odin's Ten Kings, it would be of good use to align ourselves with them. We can allure any human with promises of power and authority to achieve our ends."

"Such a creature could not have been human," clarified the Pontifex.

"Does the Pontifex reject the belief that humans are not the most powerful children of Reath? The movements of Dragons, Titans and Demons alike are becoming more frequent than before. Their awakening is in response to something. Our scouts will soon ascertain the truth," finished Thusien.

"Hmph," grunted the Pontifex disrespectfully at Thusien's claim. "I cannot deny the Sentinels' unrivalled power. Even the Kings of Odin pause in their advance, but something of this magnitude cannot be overlooked. Dispatch a correct solution."

"Hmm, you dare order me?" raised Thusien. "Can you not send your little Hymn of Wrath on an errand?"

"Hmph! You should know better than to make such foolish suggestions. Vereoris does not take heed from any order I issue. If it takes the general's interest, we might be fortunate. We are simply grateful that the Hymn of Wrath shares in our interests. Upon the defeat of Erba, the Wrath of The Mantle will return and spell its fury South," said the Pontifex, revealing his trump card.

"Oh? The famed General struggling with a few Northmen? Perhaps the Hymns of the Mantle are not all they are spoken up to be? After all, I heard of Henrys' crippling defeat on the border of Myphos. Am I on guard against your generals for naught?" Thusien spoke with a condescending tone similar to that of a young child who sought to provoke something into action.

"General Kleese will be moving south after Henrys' grand failure. But rumours of the defeat are surfacing. Plebeians talk, and with it my eyes and ears learn new things. Perhaps this new anomaly may spell us more trouble than we can manage as independent factions."

"Hmm," trailed Thusien as he turned to look at the great detailed walls, "cooperation will benefit us both. Then, perhaps, when the Hymn of Wrath returns you could have them sent to the Nexus so I may bend their ear."

"You should not speak of the impossible. You know I could never allow such a thing. There would be no balance," stated Piaus as he returned to his throne. "If you are truly candid for your reasons of an alliance, you should put your famed Sentinel vault to use?"

"I do not wish to weaken my arsenal before the true battle begins. I will dispatch Raiku personally to the Tower of Gitterung. Have Kleese accompany him and I shall open the vault door once more. I will put faith in the fact that you are a reasonable man, and that above all else, you would rather die than lose your position. Commit Kleese's army to Vereoris and have an entire, united Mantle army under the Hymn of Wrath. Once the Eye has been used and the threat identified, you can conquer Myphos with ease with Vereoris at the helm. It is all done to my perfect calculation."

"Interesting," trailed Piaus, "we both are truly alike."

"Nothing can fail, not now. Not after all I have done," declared Thusien.

"That beast is unworldly. It makes us all uncomfortable," said Piaus as he felt the presence of another corrupted Sentinel. "These joint ventures are not something we should get into the habit of forming. But with Haraura already claimed and news of the Erbian prince's defeat, I can expect Vereoris's return. Kleese will not take kindly to the redistribution of his army but he will surrender them with little fuss. Myphos will be returned to the Mantle once more."

Thusien smiled at the admission and revelled in its representation. "Until next time," turning to leave. Raiku awaited him as he left the Pontfiex's grand hall.

"He is in agreement. I have already opened the vault. Kleese will surrender his army and accompany you. After you use the Eye of Gitterung you will be the spearhead of the Mantle's invasion of Myphos. Our Sentinel plans rest on your shoulders," implied Thusien with a strong faith in his subordinate, placing a hand on his shoulder.

"Yes, master. I have news of other matters," he began.

"Yes, I thought as much. I do have one Heleic unaccounted for, after all," sighed Thusien as they departed.

"We have lost all contact with the Eumenes. The Goliath under his command returned via Recall but had sustained substantial damage from a volley of attacks. Dragon-fire seems to be the greatest cause. It's Index is heavily damaged and thus we were unable to pull any information. We do not know if the Vanguard still lives," reported Raiku.

Thusien calculated and considered all the possibilities in his mind in only a few brief moments all whilst bringing his hand to his corrupted chin in thought.

"It is no coincidence a Dragon joined the fray and Vosk would certainly not allow for an easy death of his dear pupils. It appears I lacked sufficient knowledge of their abilities. Kalus did well to keep them distanced from me. One of them has a great secret, but it is no matter. One way or another, they will return to the Nexus. Oh, how I love when my plans come to fruition."

"Master?" asked Raiku, the young, corrupted dog.

"My predictions do not fail. They will return here and they will fulfill the purpose I have given them. But it is imperative that you and Kleese do not fail. You are the only one who I can truly trust."

"Yes, my master. And what of the Hymn of Wrath?" asked Raiku.

"Vereoris has not yet returned; I must watch the Pontifex closely. One wrong move could result in the Pontifex seizing all control," said Thusien. "Let the land yield to the strength of your march and ensure nothing comes to the capital. I know you will not fail me."

CHAPTER TWENTY FOUR:
THE FLOWER

"Our mother died shortly after Lily was born. Two years separated us all with Isla, our eldest sister, around nine. Magic, when it began to reveal itself to us, was our curse. We were driven away from our town as creatures of evil with monstrous power, blamed for the blight that took the lives of many in our village, including our mother's. We were stoned and beaten and hated by any who were once our friends or family and cast out into the wilderness. I do not remember much, and perhaps that is for the best, but with my curse of magic, I heard the whispers of the Demons that dwelled in the ruins outside our village. To protect my family from the wrath of those who sought to blame us for their misfortune, I would give the demon my body in return for power. In my frenzy to defend my village I killed my own sister."

"Flowen..." trailed Lily softly as she tried to comfort her brother, the sun setting through the glass of the tavern and casting night onto them.

"What I did only for the power to protect my family, was the thing that destroyed it. It was not the Demon who did this, it was me. I knew nothing of magic or Demons , only that the eyes were the gateway to the soul. In a desperate attempt to protect Lily from myself, I gouged out my eyes to break the seal of the Demon. But with the senses I had left I could feel Lily's lifeless body. I was too late."

Lily and Nex looked deep at the broken visage of the young man with a new, clean bandage placed around his eyes. Lily was frozen as the tale was told. Small tears glistened down her expressionless, soft skin.

"Then, there was nothing. I was alone. I had banished the Demon deep inside of me, but there was now no reason for me to live. There are no memories of our village or my sisters after that."

Nex exhaled at the sad story. It was a tragic tale indeed.

"Oh, Flowen!" cried Lily as she fell onto him crying. He stroked the back of his head while he looked at her golden threads "but, I never forgot you, little sister."

"So Does that differ very much from what you remember?" Nex asked Lily.

"I'm not sure… the priestess of the village took me in and brought me to the Mantle. She was the only person who ever helped us out after our mother died. She had me placed into the Mantle as an orphan with strong magic power. In hindsight, it is likely that I was a tool used to further her career."
"The church took you?" asked Flowen surprisingly.

"Yes. I was strewn not far from our home. I was found alone and half dead."

"I see," said Flowen as he turned to Nex, "then, are you with them, too?" he asked.

"Haha, no. I am not a part of the Mantle," laughed Nex. He knew he did not possess the affinity to have a place in such an organisation.

"Well, I was part of the Mantle up until a few days ago…then I met Nex," said Lily as she gestured.

"When you tried to assassinate me..." corrected Nex.

"I-" stuttered Lily in protest.

"Assassinate?" asked Flowen as he turned from his sister to Nex and back again.

"Well, technically, I am an assassin by trade," she admitted awkwardly to her brother.

"An assassin...?" questioned Flowen "For The Mantle? Isn't that just a tiny bit...confusing?"

"Just a little," added Nex.

"Shh, you." hushed Lilly to Nex with an attitude. "It's a long story," turning back to Flowen, "but it is true. But now, I think, I follow a new path. Those days are behind me."

"So, who are you, Nex, and why would Lily be sent to assassinate you?" asked Flowen.

Nex answered quickly with no sign of hesitation, "I am no one special!" he said with an honest smile. "Just someone lucky enough to be fated to Lily. I am merely a scholar who flows with the stream of magic. First, Tsumikiri, and then Akuma!" Nex was clearly chuffed with his decisions up to this point. "I should let you two catch up! There are some things that should be said to family and family alone without alien ears present," said Nex as he rose to leave, "we passed a nice little trinket shop earlier that looked interesting. I feel compelled to have a peek. I am a scholar, afterall!" he said with a smile as he left.

"I don't remember a trinket shop..." trailed Lily at his departure.

"What an odd man..." said Flowen to his sister.

"Oh, you have no idea," she said as the two laughed together like the innocent times when they were children.

Flowen's smile faded as he entered a deep thought. "What's wrong?" Lily asked her brother concerningly.

"It's just…" he began, "I cannot define his presence. It is almost as if sometimes he is there, and sometimes he is not. His aura wavers between light and dark, between physical and ethereal. It's as if he is human, but also as if he is not."

"How do you mean 'as if he is not human'?" asked Lily interestingly.

"It's hard to explain. I see things differently…" he trailed.

"Well," added Lily, "he is definitely unique. And no matter what he is, he is my friend. He says he researches magic and has the wisdom and knowledge, and power, to back it up."

"He is no doubt mysterious."

"I could not even sense a presence from him when we met. In battle, he is unquestionably strong. His etiquette is appalling and his common sense lacks greatly. He has no concept of money or value and he sticks out in every situation worse than anyone else. But his heart is true. His words may seem unbelievable and unlikely but his feelings pour from him and envelop me. He is kind and thoughtful and takes care of what I say. He values my opinion and treats me with respect. In his presence, I am warm and I am safe and there is little I care to do if it is not with him. It's as though I understand he tells the truth in earnest but also in part. It is as thou-" Lily stopped herself abruptly. Her tongue had run loose and rampant, drunk on the overflowing feelings she could not understand. In a flush, her soft cheeks reddened with embarrassment.

"I think I understand," stated Flowen with a smile.

"N-no! It's not like that!" protested Lily, jumping to her feet and blocking his magical gaze with both hands.

"He is very important to you," clarified Flowen.

Lily averted her gaze from Flowen. Although he did not have any eyes, it was as plain as day how he looked upon her. "Yeah…I guess so."

"You must have been through many battles together," concluded Flowen.

"My first meeting with him was reconnaissance. Shortly after we fought each other," stated Lily.

"So I suppose the part about an assassination was true?" said Flowen.

"Well, I tried. But he didn't take it very seriously," replied Lily. "Oh?" laughed Flowen.

"Flowen…" she said softly. "I'm sorry for not finding you sooner…I just…I…" she tried as her lips wobbled.

"We are together now and that is all that matters," he assured with a smile as they embraced one another, their warmth basking each other in love.

"Well!" said Lily in a more cheerful tone, "you really need a wash!" as she wafted his stink around.

"I already washed yesterday!" he laughed with his sister.

"Not enough! You must not have got it all out properly last time! I'll cut all that mingy hair off you and that beard, too! It's so mangy!" she stated. Even on the streets, Nex could feel the warmth of their radiance as they rekindled their love.

He did keep to his word and make way for the small trinket shop. He saw it upon passing into the town but there was indeed something about it he could not fathom. Perhaps a sense of mysteriousness or charm, magical allure or possibly the suspicious amount of an ancient and subtle magic that radiated from it. It was something that, on his travels, beckoned him to explore for reasons even he could not understand. Given this opportunity to be alone he could think of no better way to spend his time away from Lily and Flowen. As he approached with a wandering mind, he collided with the customer who had just exited the shop with a haste like that of a child who had received a present of immeasurable value.

"Oh my! I'm so sorry!" apologised Nex, snapping back to reality. He had, in his daydreaming, crashed into a young woman carrying a large basket of apples. With his might he had bounced her to the ground with such force she was sure to be injured and to be free of her apples. But, unharmed, she looked up to him with a bashful smile only slightly dishevelled from the collision.

"Please," he said, lowering himself down to aid her.

"Oh, it's alright," she spoke warmly as they raised together, her smile almost as blinding as the rays of the bright sun above them, but Nex's breath halted momentarily as his heart skipped a few beats. The woman whom he had collided with was slender and of average height and gave off a golden glow akin to that of a divine being that enveloped and surrounded her permanently so that even those lacking in senses could see it. She wore a simple, long, thick woollen dress that a farmer's wife would wear, strong and durable for manual labour but cheap and lacking any sort of grandeur. But this woman's face was unlike that Nex had ever seen. She was disastrously beautiful. So much so that Nex could not remove himself from her presence even if he summoned all of his legendary power. Her skin was soft and supple and showed no signs of aging or blemish and her lips looked like if one were to exchange a kiss their heart would immediately explode from an uncontainable bliss. Surely only the most magnificent and beautiful sounds could escape lips as supple and delicate as those. Her slight and magnificent figure was surely hidden beneath the drooping of the uncomplimentary dress that she wore. But this modest approach made her all-the-more beautiful. The bashful and underappreciated beauty of this woman made it impossible to believe she had not been wedded by a rich and wealthy baron or lord. To even exchange a glance with her was as if the Maker himself appeared before you and gave you his divine blessing. It was all of these features which captured Nex's very soul, but there was one last thing that flustered him beyond mortal comprehension. Her hair was long and majestic, falling down beneath her waist more magnificent than that of a prize-winning stallion or the breath-taking silkiness of a spirited water dragon. The colour matched that of the two moons, as if it were the sole vessel on this world capable of capturing the irresistible twinkle of light. This hair belonged to one and only one person ever to be born in this world. This woman was apparently the second. Her face held a modest cherry colour at the awkwardness of Nex's long examination of her.

Coyly, she spoke soft words, "thank you." She clenched both hands around the handle of her basket and bowed her head.

"No, no," began Nex, "It was completely my fault. My mind was far, far away. I was not paying attention." Nex had never been so flustered. Lily was indeed truly beautiful but the attraction for Nex here was completely different.

"I cannot let you take all the blame," admitted the young woman, "my thoughts were also in a far-away place."

What felt like an eternity had passed, but Nex felt as if it were nowhere near enough time to appreciate her. With every fibre of his body he willed himself to stand aside to let the young lady pass by him, probably for the last time ever. Nodding with a pure smile and brushing some strands of her silky hair behind her ear, she increased her speed and hastily walked on disappearing out of sight to surely return to the luckiest partner in the world. In her crimson eyes Nex saw many things. Love, hate, despair, destruction. If the questions to all of the cosmos had been derived, the answers surely would be found within that girl's eyes. But there was something else he found in her gaze that he yearned to understand. A sadness, a disappointment, an everlasting sense of soul shattering heart break. Such a thing should not exist in those scarlet eyes. With fatigue now on his brain Nex entered through the small wooden door into the warm, golden light of the shop. He could read on the delicate, wooden sign that the shop was soon to close. How very lucky.

"WOW!" he exclaimed loudly as he looked in awe at the hundreds of thousands of gold and treasures. Though he lacked the ability to value them he could tell they were impressive. The interior of the shop was possibly one hundred times bigger than it appeared from the outside, a common magic spell used for smaller shops on the highstreet that house large or many products. "Incredible," his eyes marvelled at the ornaments.

The trinkets were countless, the gems too! A sea of gold coins intermingled with gems of onyx, ruby, sapphire, jade, opal, and jet that overflowed from everywhere and anywhere all over the place like a sea of gold. His sharp eye also caught sight of a voluptuous, red apple on the front desk of the shop, prime for consumption.

"Oh? You like it?" asked a voice hidden behind the counter.

"It truly is incredible," said Nex, marvelling at perfection.

An old man rose from behind the counter and stood low, placing his hands on the desk, "well you know, even the smallest of things can be found. And even the darkest of things shine when the sun kisses them with its warmth," he said with a chuckle, his wooden glasses falling down his nose.

Nex agreed with the movement of his head as a smile crept across his face as he wandered through the labyrinth of trinkets. "You sure do have a way with words," smiled Nex.

"Words have their way with me, too!" assured the old man with a reciprocated smile.

"How can you hope to ever sell any of these?" asked Nex, "there's so many. No order. no organisation. They don't even have prices on them!" as he examined a golden cup laying atop a mountain of poorly displayed treasure.

"Oh, these are not for sale! You cannot truly value things such as these with something as fleeting as a number," said the shopkeeper as he sorted some of his recent findings.

Nex nodded as his smile began to fade.

"Are you looking for something in particular then, young man?" asked the shopkeeper, raising his head slightly as if to hear a response.

"I'm not sure," said Nex as he placed the golden cup back down, "perhaps," he admitted. "I just saw this place when I came through yesterday. I was curious as to what you classed as a 'trinket'."

"Oh?" It is only those who yearn for the unattainable to visit my shop," said the old man. "But even if there was something even you could not grasp, that would not stop you from reaching it, no?"

"I suppose not," replied Nex.

"I thought as much. What do you think?" asked the shopkeeper, gesturing to the sea of treasure.

"There must be a countless number here. This must have taken your lifetime to find this many?" asked Nex.

"Oh, my dear boy. A lifetime indeed. But these...these are only the precious few I was able to save," said the old man gesturing to the hundreds of thousands, possibly millions of trinkets.

Nex smiled as he laughed in realisation, "I see. You seem very wise. I bet you have seen some truly marvelous things in your lifetime."

The old shopkeeper fumbled through another purse of gems and coins, "Indeed, I have! Tremendous things. Spectacular things. But also, horrible things. Terrifying things. Things no creature was ever meant to see," his eyes not looking up to find Nex's. "And so, is that all?" he asked as he returned his attention to sorting the trinkets on his desk.

"I'm...not sure," replied Nex with a sense of unknowingness he had not felt for an eternity.

"I have seen that look before, young man."

"What look?" responded Nex.

"You are wayward. Incomplete. What it is you truly desire masks itself behind another feat. It is not that you have forgotten your destiny, but that you rejected it. I am afraid I have nothing here I can offer you," said the old shopkeeper. "But, perhaps you can help me?" suggested the old man.

"I-Uh, Sure. What do you need?" said Nex.

"Well, you see my predicament," said the old man as he gestured to the sea of trinkets. "These are just the few in my possession. There are many, many, many more that must be preserved and collected."

"I'm not sure how I can help with that," trailed Nex. "Would you like me to put up a sign outside of your shop or something?"

"My, my, are you always this slow? No. This is not what it was supposed to be," said the old man with a saddened heart. "It was supposed to be so much more marvellous! Every one, I was supposed to have them all! Do you think...you could help this old man with the order of things? These old eyes have seen everything and the twinkle in yours reminds me of a young boy whom I knew aeons ago. Even amongst these I do not have the trinket you have lost. But if you help me find a home for these trinkets perhaps you will remember what it is you search for!"

"I think I understand. It is not the first time I have begun this journey. Thank you," said Nex with satisfaction and a warm smile.

"Now, away with you please. I still have all this to organise and unfortunately for you, you neither have the time to spare nor the capacity in your current state. My shop is about to close. There is no time to dawdle," said the old man as he beckoned for Nex to leave, now disinterested in him.

Nex smiled at the thought of his new quest, "I better get to it then. See ya!" said Nex as he left, lifting his hand to gesture goodbye.

He left the shop and turned back onto the busy streets, he wandered with his mind deep in thought as he stared into the sky.

"See?" you look much better!" said Lily. "Going short was definitely the right choice."

Lily backed away from her brother, stepping in the pile of scraggly offcuts of his hair that looked like a bird's nest or a wild animal's den. She revealed a young man in his twenties. He was slender and tall but despite his slumber was incredibly well toned his muscles took a good form. His hair was a hazel brown and somewhat tidy, slicked back like that of an important baron or duke. His long, scraggly beard had been reduced to an almost clean-shaven face, just some stubble to maximise his appeal.

"You look fantastic!" she assured him as she placed the scissors down on the wooden chest of drawers next to a small, magical measure tape. The bandage around his eyes had been replaced with a newer, dark green piece of cloth, tied tightly in a simple Western knot at the back of his head leaving two long trails.

"Does the bandage unsettle you?" asked Flowen as he touched it.

"Not at all," said Lily, "it's perfect. Now all we need is to get you those new clothes. I found a great shop, but I didn't know your measurements at the time. I've picked most of it out. All I need to do is give the measurements. In the meantime, have another wash and get all that old hair off you. Oh, maybe I'll be able to get Nex some new 'threads' too," she pondered aloud, a sinister smile spreading from ear to ear. "You'll be okay by yourself, yes?"

"I'll be fine Lily…I just won't leave this room," assured Flowen. He laughed as he lowered himself to clean the mountain of hair off his body and begin to wash.

'Quite the young lady she turned out to be,' he thought to himself as he operated the taps.

Lily went downstairs. Catching sight of Nex who was leaning on the bar, she approached him slowly, unable to forget the rambling she had done to her brother. "Hey…" she said softly as she sat on the stool next to him.

"Hey," he replied, cradling a tumbler filled with a light brown liquid. "How is he doing?" asked Nex, avoiding eye contact.

"He's adjusting. I think it will take him some time to really be free of his…darkness," she trailed.

"Want a drink?" asked Nex, examining his own, "it's called a wizard's crash, apparently."

"No, it's okay," she said, "maybe later."

Nex replied with a warm smile. "So, do you want to come?" she asked again.

"Oh, to get some clothes?" he asked, uncertain if that was her original question.

"Hm? Have you stopped calling them 'threads' already? she asked.

"I think it's for the best," said Nex.

"I think so, too," agreed Lily with a hint of a smile. "I have already picked the fabric and style. Once I give the measurements it shouldn't take long to make it."

"Let's go then!" he said.

"Great!" replied Lily as they began outward.

"Maybe he would like–" began Nex as they walked.

"Nothing too loud!" she said, "he's not a Dragon Slayer. There's no need to fit him with some super expensive armour with a high resistance to fire."

"Well, you never know…" trailed Nex as he canvassed the shops.

"Oh? I assume you'll be paying for this then?" grilled Lily.

"Oh yeah," said Nex as he remembered, "that drink went on a tab."

"Of course it did."

"He must have a cape though, right?" said Nex as he examined his own, incredible cloak that trailed behind him.

"Must he?" laughed Lily as they journeyed on.

"You know," began Nex, his heart opening wider than it had for an eternity. "I always wanted to be an adventurer, too. I wanted to fight, to travel and become famous. In my village, the mundane and normal things that I aspired to be were frowned upon by everyone else. but it is all I ever really wanted to do."

"Did you not have any guilds where you are from?" she asked.

"Guilds aren't a thing back home. Ares is a lot more modern. It is the centre of the world, after all. But, I hope that one day we can go on a real adventure together. One that doesn't involve such perilous conditions."

"I think I'd like that," said Lily, fully converted into Nex's companion. They had soon reached the shop where she had placed Flowen's order and the tailor there revealed the plans for Flowen's new attire to Nex.

The night fell calmly onto the small village where Nex, Flowen and Lily resided. Neither death nor fear had crept its way into the innocent midst of the bustling townsfolk and all was peaceful and warm. Most had gathered on the town's famous roof-top bar, upon the premium tavern they had chosen. Many came to look upon the stars as they listened to their friends converse with the charms of ale and wine. Nex and Flowen cradled large, wooden tankards whilst Lily cherished a small wine glass.

"I still can't get over that get-up, Flowen," exclaimed Nex loudly. "You really are a Demon!" he said with rasp and sass.

Flowen donned his new, impressive set of robed armour. Strangely, despite all her protests, it appeared to be rather similar in style to Nex's, though Lily would never admit where the inspiration came from. He had a simple, dark green pair of robe trousers that concealed elegant, silver greaves that hugged his calves well before running to the floor and converging at a pointed toe. He had matching gauntlets that reached beyond his elbow that hid beneath the sleeved cloak that Lily had been 'convinced' to purchase. It, too, was deep green in colour with a black contrast. On its shoulders it held three stalactite spikes on each pauldron to compliment his signature, demonic abilities. Finally, he wore an enchanted mid-emerald bandage to permanently replace the bloodsoaked white one he had adorned for so long. This one was tied with Lily's special knowledge of a western knot around the back of his eyes before the long streaks reached down behind him towards his hips.

"Hic! This stuff is great! Hic," said Flowen merrily as he looked from his drink, the 'merry mage', to Nex, Lily, and then back to his merry mage.

"I knew this would be a bad idea," said Lily as she rolled her eyes at her male company.

"It's good for him!" Nex defended, "he has missed these things. What better a way to relax than to sip some fine ale!" he said merrily, gesturing to Flowen with his tankard and his index finger.

"Right!" shouted Flowen in agreement. "This is another Demon I must yet defeat!"

"HAHA!" roared Nex.

"Maker, save me," trailed Lily under her breath.

"Whoa! What are you, the party poopers?" attacked Nex jokingly, laughing at his impressive retort.

"Party...boopers?!" added Flowen, leaning in to support Nex's interrogation, unable to keep his head balanced like a normal human.

"Hey! Don't you two gang up on me!" protested Lily, "I cannot be the only one who acts like an adult here!" "More like... A-doofus!" roared Flowen at his childish insult.

Nex Laughed loudly too as his second tankard began to affect him, wiping away the tears from his eyes. "I have no idea what that means but it was definitely hilarious."

Lily remained un-entertained as she tried to conceal the effects that the terrible joke had on her, her cheeks erupting with a blossom red and inflating with air. "Haha," she laughed. "That was so bad!" She shook her head in disbelief, "I might have to do a Flowen and get rid of these ears!" she added.

Nex and Fowen stopped suddenly and looked at the young girl with horrified expressions.

"Was that… too far?" she asked at her mistake.

"BAHAHAHA" erupted Nex with another hysterical laugh, spurting the mead he had in his mouth over the railing and down onto the street.

"That's my little sister!" said Flowen as he swiped at the air trying to place his hand on her shoulder.

"Hey!" shouted an unhappy voice from the street down below.

"I did that for you!" said Flowen, roping her in, "just like I did this!" he shouted as he pointed his finger and placed it on her chest, forcing her to look down so he could flick her face and laugh hysterically. "Ahahha!" he roared.

"Hahaha" laughed Nex "This guy!" pointing at his new idol.

"You two are a pair of idiots," stated Lily unamused. "For someone with your fortitude, you get drunk far too easily. And you-" she turned to scold Nex.
"If he has been underground for the last ten years he is going to have missed out on all of this growing up. There's never too early a time to start doing the things you may have missed. And, he's falling…." said Nex.

Flowen collapsed backwards with a merry smile on his face, crashing into the wooden decking.

Lily knelt down to check on her brother, "Flowen!"

"I'm okay, I'm okay" he assured them both as he rose and waved, "I think the Demon took the hit on that one. I," he hiccuped, "I think I should go to bed," he admitted in defeat.

"I think so," agreed Lily and Nex simultaneously.

"Go! Get on out of here!" followed Nex drunkenly, shooing him with all manner of actions.

"Okay, okay, I'm going!" declared the drunk Demon as he began off to return to his room, grabbing at the railings and walls as if any faith in his legs to carry him was misplaced.

"Should we…?" began Lily as she prepared to follow him.

"He'll be fine!" assured Nex as he waved it off. "It's important that you put some faith in him. If he is coddled too tightly now it may come back to bite you."

"How very wise of you," she concluded. Lily watched as Flowen left her sight. She smiled as any proud family or friend would smile when they are truly happy. She turned and joined Nex in leaning on the railing to look out to the North. They remained silent as they arranged their thoughts, their resting arms almost touching, the warm flames of the torches ambient in the corner of their eyes.

"See? Over there," said Lily as she pointed outwards, "if you look carefully enough. You can see Gitterung's tower."

"Who's tower?!" asked Nex, his drunken brain attempting to straighten itself to the question. His eyes found the torches atop the tower in the far distance over the mountain, "that's a tower? I thought it was a star. T-that's a stupid name."

"Coming from you? Hmph. It's just behind that mountain," said Lily, gesturing to the nearest protrusion of the sky. "It was built a few decades ago by a mysterious mage named Gitterung. It's almost as tall as the Sentinel Temple. It reaches to the highest skies where dragons still fly and even the Gods look upon it. Words struggle to do it justice."

"Whoa…" trailed Nex impressively. He turned his head to her. "Have you been there?" he asked.

"Yes, but only once," she replied. "The only reason it is so tall is so that the lens at the very top can look out upon all of Ares. The same principle as the Sentinel Nexus, really. It's called the Eye of Gitterung."

"Stupid name…" added Nex.

"Gitterung is a very powerful mage. He's so powerful, in fact, it is no surprise he has taken no sides in the war because if he did, whichever side he aligned with would win. Surely to be an unfortunate thing for us, on the rare occasions he has been seen it is always within the Mantle so some whisper a secret loyalty to them, but I don't think so. I believe him to be one of Odin's Ten Kings, the ten most powerful humans in all of Reath. He built a special lens at the top of the tower that can show the user anything in all of Ares."

Nex was suddenly filled with an idea, "oh really?" He trailed in thought.

"No!" began Lily as she anticipated his next words.

"Perhaps I could use it?" wondered Nex quietly.

"How did I know you'd say something as ludicrous as that?" sighed Lily.

"As I was with you and Flowen, I am drawn to things. It cannot be explained, but that is how I found my way. That is how I find my destiny."

"If that is truly your belief, then we will follow. Nex," began Lily all seriously, "I know I haven't been the easiest person to get along with, and I have been quite reserved, but Flowen and

I will follow you wherever you go, no matter where it is. You promised you would stay with me forever, after what you have done for me, it is the least I can do to return that gesture. It is thanks to you that we are reunited. I have never been so sure of something in my whole life. We have found each other through all the impossibilities of this world. You have shown us what it really is to be alive, and what it means to have friends…and to love," she finished, the warmness of her words uncombatable by even the darkest of hearts.

Nex looked back at her with a kind smile respecting her belief. The two remained silent, lost in each other's eyes, Lily drawing closer in the light of the two moons. Her lips pulled towards his like a natural force as powerful as gravity, and they embraced.

A small, soft gentle kiss was exchanged. Lily's young, inexperienced skin, so soft to the touch. Nex could not remember feeling anything so smooth in all his life. They were both transported to a time in the height of summer where the sun shone down upon them like they were the only ones in the world. Nex felt her soft, sensitive lips. They were like the petals of the flower that had the honour to share the same name. Nex pulled away abruptly. Leaving the young girl suspended in bliss.
"I think we should get some sleep," he stated. Lily was not red with embarrassment. She was warm and sure. Their exchange was a memory to never be forgotten. She began to return, too, and as she followed through the door she found Nex standing over an unconscious man.

"Who is fairest of them all?" muttered Flowen unconscious on the floor.

Lily gave Nex a scolded look.

"I've got him," Nex apologised as he hoisted Flowen up, "come on, let's get you to bed."

"I told you we shouldn't have left him!" berated Lily.

"I thought he could make it!" Nex defended with hand gestures that delivered him more glares from Lily. Nex hoisted him up and supported him to his room and laid him on his bed.

"I'll stay with Flowen in here tonight to make sure he is okay," said Lily as she helped her brother.

"I'll see you both in the morning, then," said Nex as he turned to leave.

Lily refrained from speaking or looking at the man she had just kissed, placing all of her focus on her brother.

"Goodnight," said Nex as he closed the door behind him and returned to his room.

"Goodnight."

CHAPTER TWENTY FIVE: TITANS

Meanwhile, under the same starry sky, to the far East, Vosk, Galatea and Daisy began to regain consciousness in an unfamiliar setting, absent of Sentinels and Goliaths and dark magic.

Vosk was the first to come around and take in his surroundings. He found himself atop the large, hollowed mountain where the battle had taken place. However, he knew that the danger had not yet passed.

He could feel the tremendous magic power, like the mountain itself was alive. He turned to see it, the Titan. A colossal figure moulded by the maker himself to weave the land for his creations.

"Do not fear, Human," it bellowed softly with its hurricane of a voice, "I mean you no harm," it spoke from its position of power.

Vosk was weary, tired and defeated. But if this Titan wished him and his comrades dead, it could have done so easily. Was this creature responsible for their rescue?

"I have healed you," said the Titan slowly, "but I have woken you and you alone."

"My name is Vosk InBarba, and these are my comrades, O great one," said the Sentinel.

"I know what you are," said the Titan as it turned its gigantic head to the sky. "The land whispers your tale into my ancient bones, over the brow and under the limitless skies so that I may know. Vosk...you may call me... Astraeus ..." it finished.

"Astraeus!?" asked Vosk in surprise, "I thought Titan's extinct?"

"We do remain," with an echoing voice through the mountain, cracking the trees with its force, "but I am one of the first of my brothers to awaken from our slumber. My primordial being bids it so."

"O Ancient One, why have you spared us?" asked Vosk as he raised himself clutching at his miraculously healed wounds.

"I am a Titan of creation and care, my duty is to nature and nurture. A call was answered. Alas, it was not my ears that headed your call, but a lesser Titan. The young son of Anoctis, in his juvenile ways, answered your prayers. We do not wish for the extinction of our father's most precious creation. It was our purpose to shape this world and continue to do so until our father's next words."

Vosk was in awe. Astraeus was a being of myth. A supreme, colossal Titan who's very stone flesh was shaped by the maker. He had existed since the beginning, in the era before time. The giant Titan made up of earth and soil and rock blinked slowly, "what is corrupted, cannot be repaired, even by our hands. But what is cared for and preserved can stand against the test you would call 'time'."

"You speak of The Kursed? The creatures to undo the very fabric of magic? The ones who will ruin this world forever." asked Vosk.

"Even with our power, granted to us by the Creator of all things himself, we cannot erase their taint, nor can we resist it," said Astraeus at the disappointment of his own failure. "That is why you must exist," he finished.

"You mean the Sentinels? We are not what we once were thousands of years ago. The order is chaos and ruin. We would need another thousand years to prepare for their return!" declared Vosk.

"There are few who know the stories of the war of the Fallen God, and even fewer believe it. Mortal human..." Astraeus began, "it is not the Sentinels who are key to salvation."

"But the Sentinels are the only ones who can destroy the taint. Our magic was created with the very purpose of doing so!" protested Vosk, becoming confused with the Titan's words.

"Long ago, when the light of the stars were young and warm, the Kursed rose from the depths with a God as their king. One of the Maker's first children, the first of Seven Elder Gods, of which the thousands that followed were bred from. His power was great even amongst his divine brothers and sisters. But, even he was defeated, and returned to the dirt. This feat, this impossibility, was accomplished by mere mortals, the weakest and lowest of our father's creations, but also his most powerful. It is not the Sentinels who are key to the gate ahead, but Humanity. Soon a new order is to begin. The fourth age of man has already begun to dawn and with it, the signalling of the rise of another child of our father. The Kursed are as much a child of this world as you and I, no matter how abhorrent their creation. We *all* yearn for his love, *that* is why we are susceptible to their corruption. Chakravartin was merely the first."

"Another Elder God?" asked Vosk in conclusion to the Titan's story. " If the Kursed have already discovered their new king, The Dawn is already here! We have seen their brood deep beneath these hollowed mountains."

"The wind carries more than just the wings of Dragons and birds..." said Astraeus. "There are those who know the secrets of old tales whispered millennia, even those who know the words Chakravartin himself whispered to humanity to corrupt them"

Galatea and Daisy began to regain consciousness at Astraeus' will, cautiously witnessing their captain converse with the mythological Titan.

"Is that…" said Daisy in disbelief.

"Impossible!" trailed Galatea.

"A Titan!" they exclaimed in synchronisation.

"We are not the only creatures who look upon the horizon with fear and dread… she will rise, and with this, she will seek only to claim this world…." said Astraeus.

"I do not understand, O Ancient One" said Vosk with respect at the marvellous sight. One could live aeons without looking upon such a creature. "If it is not the Sentinels who will defeat the Kursed, then who? It has been our duty since our order was created. We alone hold the power to destroy them."

"No Titan or Dragon or Demon or God can stand before the might of Humanity. For the might of Humanity is the might of the Maker, and his will inherited as theirs!" said the wise one. "An Elder God can only be destroyed by the Sentinel. No other power exists to accomplish this feat. Your gifts are short of the legend. It is you who will slay, but not you who will devour. The Kursed's hunger can only be…starved.".

"We are all that remains of the order. There are no others, and the Nexus has been corrupted and destroyed. No rituals can be incited," said Galatea.

"Ah…" said Astraeus. "In our slumber we had sensed its fate. But the flame of the Nexus is merely the embers left behind. We were weak and defeated and our numbers were few. But in his absence, we were not the only ones to recover as the magic flourished through the land."

Vosk, Galatea and Daisy leant in as the Titan spoke more of its ancient knowledge, "for five thousand years nature, wisdom and magic has been free like never before. But she, too, has feasted upon it. Her awakening was inevitable. We can all feel the taint beneath our feet but we are hopeless to stop it."

"Of what do you speak, Ancient One?" asked Vosk. "What can we do to save this world?"

The Titan looked to the sky slowly in search of his creator like a lost, forgotten child. "It has already begun. Mortal humans, you must return to your home and purge the source of your power from its naked flame. I cannot whisper to you anymore. Children of our father watch and listen at our exchange. Return, and the Sentinel will emerge."

The three Sentinels exchanged glances with each other. The Titan, supreme and overwhelming, held restraint in its voice. Even over its bellow they could feel the wavering of his words from a fear he could not share. In agreement they looked to each other to be on their way. They knew that, before all else, the Nexus must be restored."

"But, be careful," the Titan warned, "he also holds the power to extinguish it. We are all at the mercy of his awakening."
Vosk, Galatea and Daisy were not overly sure of what the Ancient Titan meant. But they did understand that the Nexus was their next destination.

"Our answers lie in Eos. That is where we must go," concluded Vosk.

"Now you understand," said Astraeus as he began to move his entire body like a rumbling mountain.

"WHOA!" screamed Galatea and Daisy at the colossal movement, the ground shaking as far as the eye could see.

"Another…answered your call, little mortal" said Astraeus as his gaze fell to Daisy. "Even Titans…are not immune from your charm. It would appear that your love for this world inspires even legend and that love is yet to truly awaken."

They could feel it. Another power akin to that of the great titan. The pressure of the creature could have pushed them down into the very earth. For above the clouds and below the vast skies lies the domain of the creatures who craft the very fabric of the world above the land. When their paths meet in disagreement, they release a roar of imminent battle that shatters the sky with their light, and as they engage, the beat of their wings makes the sky tremble and bellow. Human's later came to call this phenomenon 'Thunder and Lightning'. The creature most capable of natural calamity; A Dragon.

As large as a moon it swooped down from the skies, its wingbeat excited the sea into retreat and snapped the trees in its hurricane. Blacker than night and able to blot out the light from one whole moon these wings were vast, and yet, only those of a youngling. Its branches stretched far until the bones formed its destructive, grappling claws as its two legs absorbed its landing, its blackness consuming the moon dust.

"Ahhh!" screamed Galatea in horror and disbelief.

"A DRAGON!" roared Daisy in utter awe. "BEAUTIFUL!" she screamed as she jumped up and down on the spot, absent of fear.

"Impossible..." said Vosk with his jaw aghast.

"We must already be dead!" trailed Galatea in disbelief of witnessing the two impossible sights consecutively. Little did they know, it was not the only creature atop the clouds that watched them with prying eyes...

CHAPTER TWENTY SIX: A GUILD OF ADVENTURERS

The three companions rose late the next day, the alcohol still lingering in their system. Groggily, they obtained breakfast and re-dosed on vast amounts of water. Lily and Flowen were communicating well. They had successfully rekindled their loving nature towards one another with enough confidence to tease the past. They knew they owed Nex a lot.

"Well there was this one job where I had to take out a corrupt official in Erba. Your typical lord with no regard for his subjects. He had four bodyguards that claimed to be the 'strongest' in the country. He even hired adventurers from the town's guild to fight for him. It got quite messy in the end, actually..." finished Lily.

"And? What happened?" probed Flowen.

"I had to take them all down. It was one of my hardest missions," said Lily.

"So you've killed a fair few people too?" asked Flowen nonchalantly.

"I suppose I have..." said Lily. "It was the only way for me to survive."

"There is always sin in taking a life, Lily. You must be prepared to carry those souls with you for the rest of your life," said

Flowen wisely.

"Well said," added Nex. "Ending the life of another is just about the worst thing anyone can ever do. The least that can be done is to carry the hopes and dreams of the fallen on our own shoulders and make peace with them. We can strive for atonement along the way."

"Have you killed many?" Lily asked Nex as he revealed a slip of his past.

"More than I could ever atone for. Even those I have loved and cared for have met terrible ends by my own hands. My past is not one without grave sin. All I can do now is strive for a better end and to not forget those whose souls I now carry with me. That is why I tend not to kill my opponents. The weight of death is a heavy one."

"It seems we all bear the burden of killing another..." said Flowen.

"There's something you should see here in this town," said Lily to the others. "I think you'll both find it quite interesting in light of all this dark talk," she stated as she spooned in a mouthful of porridge.

"Oh, I think I remember you mentioning something before," said Nex in thought of the subject.

"So, we will head there next?" asked Flowen as he finished his breakfast.
"Right," confirmed Lily.

"Ready?" asked Nex as he and Flowen exchanged a look as the petite young girl with them finished her last mouthful of porridge and wiped away any trace of it from her lips with etiquette.

"Mhmm," she replied from behind her napkin.

It was bright outside. The sun was yet to reach its highest point in the blue sky. But the air was cold and unwelcoming to those who stepped outside into its brisk commute. The sun was trying its hardest to rid the world of the darkness that was to come, but even the great star itself could not stop it.

They trod lightly on the hard cobble, navigating their way through the town at Lily's directions, catching the eyes of those who passed by. They certainly stuck out.

"Here," said Lily as they stopped before a substantial building, crafted by stone and wood. Aside from the buildings that related to the Mantle, this was the most extravagant in the town.

"What is it?" asked Flowen as he looked up and down the large, tavern-like building.

"It's a Guild," stated Lily.

"A adventurers guild?" asked Nex.

"It's like an organisation, spread all across Ares with branches like this where people can submit requests and other people can accept them if they chose to. Yes, It's an adventurers Guild," she finished.

"Adventurers guild…" trailed Flowen as he came to understand. "So, those people who came for me…"

"What kind of requests?" asked Nex curiously.

"Well…" began Lily as three moderately armed individuals passed them by with a distasteful look and entered through the wooden double doors. "It would be easier to explain inside. But please, whatever you do, don't cause any trouble."

The three then entered the stone building. It was reasonably substantial. The air was filled with a pleasant aroma of wealth and enjoyment. Everything looked thick, heavy, and durable. The rugs were well crafted, the tables, chairs and ornaments were solid and sturdy, and the architecture was substantial and well thought out. They entered into a large room blessed with traits and treasures from the accomplishments of adventurers that called this guild home. The mighty bounties of quests and requests lathered the oaken framed stone building like trophies of triumph. A guild of adventurers was a place where both humans and demi humans existed almost free of discrimination and prejudice. A comrade in arms here was like family, and the guild was their home. At its reception it housed a counter-like bank booth on its side and an open hall on the other filled with tables, chairs, and an abundance of adventurers. Laid to the side on a sturdy, oaken table there lay an enormous leatherbound book entitled 'A Guide to Adventures', stuffed with notes and additions of any information adventurers had shared amongst their peers. This information was always found to be invaluable for those learning the ways of the adventurer. Needless to say, there were countless stories in here that could entertain the three companions for many hours.

Of the many occupants only a few had taken notice of the new entries and carried on with their daytime rituals of quest planning or party functions and manoeuvres. Of the few that did take notice they looked at Nex's party with suspicion and the strongest of the adventurers subtly took interest in the three formidable mages who entered and watched over them with an eager eye. For the strong react to the strong in ways the weak can not understand.

In front of them was a large board with the lettering 'Requests' printed at the top. Around two dozen pieces of parchment were nailed to it, each littered with an illustrated border, a large title, a description and finally a number.

"These must be the requests…" said Flowen thinking aloud.

"You can read those?" asked Lily.

"I can!" began Flowen, "I can see the dried parchment and then thick ink quilled onto it. I can see it all with my magic."

"Oh, I see!" said Nex excitedly as they analysed the types of jobs that could be undertaken.

"We could choose almost any of these if we wanted," confirmed Lily, the only one with an idea of society among them.

"Field ploughing, Dire wolf attacks, mysterious disappearances, Demon hunting…" trailed Nex as he read aloud just a few of the requests.

They all exchanged a quick and awkward glare as Lily reached out and ripped off the quest that rewarded the slaying of a demon at the Heath Cliffs and rammed it beneath her armour. "These are the kinds of jobs that anyone can request of the adventurers here and they can then choose whether or not to take them on. They will vary in difficulty and the reward will reflect that. Some of the harder, grander quests require renown or minimum group size to prevent unnecessary deaths on mission. This is the type of adventure I always thought I'd end up doing," she said awkwardly, scratching her face in embarrassment.

"I'm not going to lie," started Flowen as they both turned to the mage whose eyes were covered by a magical bandage, "I may be able to see the lettering, but I can't read it," he stated plainly. Nex thought for a moment as they realised one of their blunders. "Actually, seeing as you are wearing a blindfold you can probably get away with that quite easily," he said, attempting to make light of Flowen's confession.

"Or," said Lily sharply, "I can just teach you to read," she said as she scolded Nex with her eyes.

"Oh, right!" said Nex, "and I can probably teach you how to write lettering on the parchment with your magic."

"Oh really?" said Flowen happily.

"You can do that?!" asked Lily in surprise.

"I don't see why not," said Nex.

"Ah, fantastic!" said Flowen. "But there is no rush. I can rely on you two to do the reading for now."

During this time, the three clerks that undertook the administrative side of the Guild looked upon the three companions with a calming, normal gaze. Amongst adventurers, these three individuals were quite ordinary. "C-can we help, at all?" they said with a warm and welcoming voice. Lily peered around Nex to speak for them.

"Oh, no thank you. They just needed a bit of educating. I just wanted to show them what an adventurers guild was all about," she stated.

"Ohkay. Please just let us know if you need anything. We are glad to see anyone interested in joining, everyone is welcome. The jobs are flooding in at the moment!" said one of the clerks politely as she turned her attention back to her paperwork.

Lily then turned her attention back to Nex and Flowen, "though it's for profit, the purpose of places like this is so that anyone can submit a request. This means just about anyone can do something for someone else if they need the work. Most of the time the local towns guard will need some relief and will be grateful for the help. I think sometimes even the town pays the reward on certain quests."

"I like that idea," said Flowen.

"A somewhat honourable profession," added Nex.

"Hey, Allyn! Take a look at these guys!" spoke a male voice from their left with a large entourage of adventurers. Nex, Lily and Flowen turned to them to see they had drawn the attention of some of the more prominent inhabitants of the Guild who looked at them with unease and suspicion.

"A Mantle Assassin," he spoke with rigour and gusto clad in his thick, grey armour. He kept his distance at first as he continued to grill them. He looked strong. Perhaps the strongest adventurer this guild had to offer. A correct analysis of Nex's group, combined with the confidence to confront them *and* the aura to spur his comrades into action meant he was indeed strong. Whether he was intimidated by the three new adventurers or whether he just wanted to look impressive to his peers, he spoke loudly and clearly.

"And they are all super friendly," said Lily sarcastically to her companions, triggering a smirk from her brother.

"You two might be able to make it here," said the imposing adventurer, Allyn, "but I don't think your scrawny little friend here will do much."

Nex bashfully smiled and brought his hand to his head in embarrassment, "O-oh," he said nervously.

"But by the Maker, you will do just fine. You truly are beautiful! I suppose we could overlook the fact you're from the Mantle if you were willing to join us. We have quite the knowledge on how things work around here." Allyn gestured with his thumb to his comrades in an attempt of flattery.

"No…thanks," replied Lily with disinterest as she turned away from them and back to her comrades.

"He really freaks me out," said one of them.
"Yeah. What happened to his eyes?" asked another.
"Gross," said a third.

"You should ditch those guys and come with us," added Allyn. "We take on all the biggest jobs here. You'd make a good living."

"Mind how you speak to my friend. While she may have the

manners to rise above your retorts, I am afraid I do not," said Nex at Lily's defence.

"Oh? We have a yeper do we? We weren't talking to you boyo" said Allyn slowly. "What kind of mage are you, anyway? Oh, I see. You just carry her sword, don't you? Just the caddy for the road, eh?" said Allyn as he squared up to Nex, pushing his shoulder in threat.

Nex exhaled deeply and smiled back to them, "Yeah. Something like that."

"Listen chum, you get your magicless ass out of here before we throw you out," piped one of Allyn's retinue.

"Hey now, you shouldn't talk like that," said Lily, "you call yourselves adventurers?"
"That's rich coming from you!" snapped Allyn back at her. "We only exist here because the Mantle fails to do anything for the people that fill its coffers with gold," he said as he stopped before Lily. The adventurers examined Lily thoroughly with their dirty eyes and, at the numerous rebuttals of their advances, turned sour and resentful in their speech. "I'd bet you'd do anything to get into this Guild. Maybe we can come to some sort of arrangement and I'll help you pay the entry fees?" proposed Allyn.

Lily looked them all up and down distastefully, "you're alright, thanks."

"Tss," hissed Allyn, now completely rejected. "A slut like you should be grateful we're taking an int-" Allyn was indeed strong. But it seemed in the grand scheme of things, compared to Nex and his companions, he wasn't quite there yet.

Nex was upon him first, and slowly, containing himself as best he could by Lily's wishes, he found his hand on the collar of the bold adventurers chest plate, and hoisted him into the air above them like a child would hold a strand of grass, his Platinum plaque twinkling in the light.

Allyn grabbed at Nex's arm with his hands helplessly as he struggled in disbelief whilst Flowen also began to seep out his magic power. Between them, they would level the entire guild and all its occupants.

"Now, why would you go and say something like that?" asked Nex as he held the man there and moved him over slightly so that he could see the rest of the adventurers yet to move.

"Allyn!" one shouted as they prepared to come to his aid but weary to engage.

"Nex…" said Lily softly as she walked between them and placed her hand on his outstretched arm. Nex released the puny adventurer softly. They were all a lot more poised now, weary of Nex, Lily and Flowen. "Right then! We'll be going now!" smiled Lily knowing they had outstayed their welcome. She turned on her heels and span the other two, chivvying them through the doors.

The sun shone calmly from its cradle in the sky halfway through its daytime shift to illuminate Nex, Lily and Flowen's journey. The three comrades headed North from the guild at Rook.

"I thought I told you both not to make a scene?" asked Lily.

"But he-" they both began.

"I can handle myself!" she snapped, "I've been in far worse situations than that. I swear, you're both just big children."

"They didn't take kindly to the Mantle there," said Flowen, "are they really that bad?"

"For something that's foundation is based upon the people, not many seem to treat you with much fondness," added Nex.

"Some towns, ones like this one especially, suffer heavily on taxes and receive little aid in return. I haven't seen a single Mantle soldier stationed here. They therefore feel like they get very little from the high prices they pay and when the Mantle changes direction they expect everyone to follow. They definitely are not overly fond of Mantle 'enforcers' such as myself."

"Oh…" both Nex and Flowen trailed.

"So the best route is North, cut through the pass at the mountain and then we'll come out by Gitterung's tower. Simple," said Lily, gesturing the directions with her hands.

"Great!" clapped Nex as he ate a torpedo loaf of bread stuffed with some goat's cheese he had been hiding somewhere.

"I'm not quite sure I am on board with this plan of yours, Nex, but if we are to ultimately head North to the capital from here, it is the fastest way," added Lily.

"Sounds good to me," said Flowen as he nibbled on the last bread roll he had brought with him.

"How are you finding the food, Flowen, and how's your head?" asked Nex gesturing to the bun as it was scoffed down.

"Great!" he replied. "I never thought I'd eat this kind of food again," he trailed as he began to ogle Nex's loaf.

"What did you eat exactly…down there?" asked Lily.

"Not much really. Anything that just happened by. The occasional rat or sea snake."

"EW! Gross!" cringed Lily, as did anyone who overheard the conversation on the busy street. "I don't know why I asked."

"Maybe we shouldn't talk too loudly in public about the intricacies of my life?" said Flowen loudly.

"Haha! I love it!" laughed Nex at the atmosphere and the quabling between siblings.

"Yeah Nex, what's your background, huh?" asked Flowen confidently. "Lily tells me you are rather mysterious?"

"Flowen! I said no such thing!" snapped Lily in an attempt to defend herself before she returned to munch on her buttered slice of loafed bread.

"What?!" he jested defensively.

"There's not much to tell," expressed Nex, "I'm not as interesting as you two, that's for sure."

"Lily said you were a scholar?" probed Flowen.

"Well, I mean technically, that's true. Magic research has been my focus all my life, as far as I can remember, anyway," said Nex.

"Your knowledge is already greater than anyone I have ever known. Even after my demonification I met a wonderful and knowledgeable mage who took me in. Even she was immense in her power and wisdom. But you...you are something else.``

"I have been around for a long time, and before that, I was around for what felt like a very long lifetime. I had picked up many things before I left home. I remember my thirteenth birthday distinctly. The day I would leave my home behind forever," said Nex. There was an awkward silence as Lily and Flowen took in Nex's story. It was short and blunt but it carried with it a depth they could not comprehend. Lily had not yet been able to pry out such valuable information from Nex in their travels but she felt this natural unloading to be warming and one of trust. Nex soon realised he had shared the secrets of his past and brought his story to a swift close.

"But, it's very useful," added Lily. "Akuma and Tsumikiri have both been lifted of their curses. Tsumikiri is weightless in my hand and listens to my every command. Such a feat is truly remarkable, all thanks to your knowledge of enchantments."

"And is your sword a sister to ours?" asked Flowen.

Nex thought for a moment. "Not quite a sister, no. But I suppose they do share a heritage. They were forged by the same smith with the same magic and star metal, but the curse mine possesses is…different. It is sealed by a mage much more powerful than I, and therefore, it cannot be undone. I do know a great deal about them though. Pages and books have been published on all of them."

"All that knowledge and yet he didn't know the name of the metal was Illyrium. The rarest metal in the world," added Lily.

"Ah ah, that's just a made up name…" trailed Nex, "it doesn't count!"

"All names are made up!" snapped Lily.
Flowen leaned in with his head inquisitively,"do you have any other secrets to share?"

"Flowen! Don't pry! If he had anything else to share he would do so at a time of his choosing," said Lily at Nex's defence.

"I'm curious as to your magic. I am not sure what my innate magic was, it wasn't until after my demonization that I possessed Foresight and Horror demon magic. You used Infinity Magic against me in the caverns, but did not release your magic power. And Lily tells me you are also able to use healing spells with a different signature. Healing that can even repair a wounded soul…"

"FLOWEN!" snapped Lily again. "Shut up"!

"Haha I'm sorry," laughed Flowen.

Nex took a moment to find the right answer.The others could see the difficulty spread across his face whilst he thought of the right words.

"It is rather hard to explain. I-"

"I was just thinking out loud! You really don't have to answer. You could be the Maker himself and I wouldn't care. You reunited me with Lily!" said Flowen.

"Okay. So, what's the plan then?" asked Lily, swiftly moving onto the next matter as each stride he took on the surface paved a path forward for himself. "We are going to the capital to fight the Sentinels?"

"Hopefully," said Nex coyly.

"I think it will take more than just the three of us, though," said Flowen looking between his sister and Nex. "Even I remember the Sentinels being a supreme power."

"A Demon, an assassin and a scholar, " added Lily. "We have already defeated one, though."

"REALLY?! You have already fought a Sentinel?" gasped Flowen

"Mhmm. And he was much tougher than expected," said Lily.

"Oh. That's not good."

"I don't think we will quite cut it," said Lily.

"Oh, on the contrary, I think it is the perfect party for the job. And who knows, we have a long way to go yet, we might find others along the way," said Nex with a smile.

"Regardless, I'm in!" said Flowen enthusiastically, needing no more information. and oblivious to the task.

"I already told him we were…" said Lily

"Great!" said Flowen enthusiastically, "wherever my sister goes, I'll be right there with her, and she's got her sights set on-"

"Flowen!" interjected Lily.

Nex smiled in return to their optimistic cooperation, "Thank you. I really do admire the love you two share for one another. But this will not be like anything you have faced before. This will not be so much of an adventure or a journey. This is a battle to save the world. You both may truly lose everything."

Lily and Flowen looked at one another and then Flowen spoke again, "We have lost everything before. We are indebted to you. This time we have together now is a gift from you, Nex. From here, we will only move forward with you leading the way."

For the first time in a long time, Nex struggled for honest words. It was all he could do to smile back at the family he was beginning to feel a part of.

Lily and Flowen had learned much of each other already the short time they had been together. What they didn't say with words was understood by their family bond. They conversed much in their own ways and shared themselves to one another's habits, becoming more and more alike than they both had dreamed. After a long day of walking and talking they soon found themselves at the tall Eayr Mountains.

"There is only one more village after this," said Lily with her knowledge of the area. "These last two are actually quite close. Wait. Do you feel that?"

"Dark magic lingers here," said Flowen as they entered the small town.

Ahead of them, the bodies of the townsfolk lay strewn across the streets. The rancid smell in the air told only the story of burning flesh.

"What...has happened here?" asked Flowen.

"Bandits..." trailed Nex as he took in the people that began to emerge from all corners of shattered home and hearth.

"Adventurers! Kill them!" shouted an impressive bandit that had emerged from the town's main hall. With the order, the rabble poured from each and every crevice to attack the three adventurers in droves.

Flowen acted first. He already had three upon him that were dispatched with ease and comfort. An unfortunate opponent had charged at Lily only to receive a side kick to the chest which sent him flying backwards into a barely standing house which then collapsed onto him. She then continued forward to take on the rest. Nex remained at the rear, picking off those who had charged straight for him, sensing little threat in comparison to the other two. With barely any concentration at all, Nex dispatched them, but his mind had ventured elsewhere. The traces of dark magic that cloaked the town were troubling.

"Wha-!" shouted the leader as his entire operation was defeated. Before he could move any further, multiple stalactites pierced through his armour and pinned him to the wooden wall behind, free of any injury.

"What happened here?!" asked Lily swiftly as she approached in a fury. "Whisper one word of a lie and I'll punch a hole through your chest and leave you here for the wolves."

"W-w-wait!" he cried in horror.

"Hold on, Lily," said Nex as he placed his hand on her shoulder.

"W-w-we only just got here! The town had already been attacked! We came in after just to make the most of it! We didn't want all those deaths to go to-"

Lily hurled a punch to the side of the bandit's head, breaking through the wall with ease. "Then who?"

"Sentinels," said Nex.

"Y-yes it was Sentinels. We followed far behind knowing that it would be an easy target once they were gone. But we didn't know they were going to slaughter the entire village! It would have been a crime to let all these valuables go to waste! They were mad with power!" replied the bandit.

"But there are women and children! Why would they have killed everyone?!" asked Lily in confusion.

"I don't know, I don't know. I swear! They just went in, killed everyone and moved on to the next one!" pleaded the bandit.

"The next one?" asked Flowen.

"The next town up," clarified Lily.

Flowen and Lily looked to Nex for their next move who already held a displeased expression. "Let's go."
"What about him?" asked Lily.

Nex reached out his hand and a small, blue symbol appeared on the bandit's forehead, singing its way into his flesh. "Murder, steal or even whisper one word of a lie again and your head will explode."

"Ah-Wha?" stuttered the bandit as the stalactites fell from his armour.

"Now, run," ordered Nex.

Frantically the bandit fumbled and tumbled his way out of the town, looking back every few seconds to see if he was being hunted. Flowen and Lily looked at Nex in worry of the enchantment he had just cast.

"Wasn't that a bit...dark?" asked Lily.

"Don't worry," assured Nex, "His head won't explode. Just a few fingers will fall off."

"Nice," approved Flowen.

Lily looked concerned, But she had no time to worry about filth. "Let's go!" she said as they began for the next town along.

They had already started to climb the great mountain. The first town was a mountain village maybe just over half way up. The second was only a stone's throw away. They approached cautiously as they exchanged battle-ready expressions whilst their senses told of powerful auras ahead. This ravaged town had new occupants, clad in corrupted, silver, star-metal armour. Nex, Lily and Flowen could all sense the strong power of Sentinel warriors as they approached.

The houses had been struck and demolished. Only splintered wood remained, their fiery flames dwindled as they burned the last of their innocent fuel. Shops and stalls had been destroyed in the fray with ease as the Sentinels had wielded their powers fully. Only the stone endured, buried with the dirt. It was a massacre. It reminded each of them of a past where they, too, had committed unforgivable sins. Sentinels laying waste to townsfolk in mass is an inexcusable crime, one that these three adventurers must make them atone for.

"Women…and children, too?" asked Lily in disbelief, as if the first incident was a mirage.

"By the Maker. I can see it all!" added Flowen.

Nex remained silent. A seething rage began to boil inside of him, one his companions had not yet witnessed. Nex's expression turned hard and his composure unwelcoming and strained.

"Nex?" asked Lily softly, her rage like a calm sea compared to his tsunami.

"I can hear them. The souls crying out to me. Humanity…Sentinels…how could they have done this?" he whimpered as they came to a halt.

"Are you okay?" asked Lily with a follow up.

There was a rotting inside Nex. A truth he had known for

far too long. That humanity, the Maker's perfect imperfection, was a dark and cruel race. Two Sentinels began their approach, sensing the two new formidable presences. They walked slowly, their corrupted armour giving off a very unique, sickly steam.

"What's…that?" asked Flowen carefully.

"Star metal cannot be tainted. Nothing in this world can stain it," said Nex.

"Like Tsumikiri and Akuma, the blood burns off it." trailed Flowen.

"That means…we were already too late?" said Lily in horror as she brought her hand to her mouth with a sickly disbelief, her stomach turning and retching at the thought. Nex exhaled his anguish and prepared to converse with the Sentinels. It seemed that upon closer inspection these Sentinels belonged to a higher echelon in the order. Perhaps captains or even Primus.

However, the rule of three remained. The corrupted Sentinels approached them with one goal only: to kill. They could sense their formidable foe's power, and came to a halt before Nex, Lily and Flowen waiting for the first move to be made. As always, Nex broke the tense confrontation with little regard to his own safety. Nex already knew why these villagers had died. He could smell the stench of fear and unrest in the air the moment he left Rook. There were no words for him to say. His mind fluttered with various slurs and offensive words to direct at the scum he saw before him.

"What have you become?" he asked rhetorically without the expectation of an answer.

"They must die," stated Flowen plainly.

"This will be quick," assured Lily as the air cracked and

whipped at the summoning of Tsumikiri and Akuma. But it was in the corner of Nex's eye, between the ravaged buildings and smoke and flame, that he saw the third Sentinel, the Primus who led them. His armour released a ferocious steaming as he stood over something. His foot was perched onto the abdomen of a small villager, his star-metal sword slowly being withdrawn from its tiny chest, before turning his attention to the three witnesses.

Nex's mind was fragile and unstable. Although he did well to commonly suppress himself to others, deep down, there was a torment which he had buried. When triggered, it would surface like a hydra in the ocean. Now, stretched beyond its containment, a snap violently lashed inside Nex's mind. His true power could no longer be kept at bay. His magic, released.

He erupted like a hurricane that poured out of him. A dark cyclone of magic was beginning to surround Nex as he emitted a power of black magic. He opened his mouth slowly and, as he spoke his next words, it was as if one thousand voices could be heard from just one man. A bone chilling declaration rang through the air,

"Curse yourselves for being a scourge worse than Kursed, for you have damned yourselves to an eternity of despair, soulless and wayward." The One Thousand Voices spoke through Nex, their vessel.

The Sentinels were not estranged to insurmountable amounts of magic before them, but this power made even their bones tremble. Threatened with magic and death, they prepared to engage the monster. "Freeze," said One Thousand Voices. His arm was already outstretched. A blistering cold overcame them in an instant. Frozen in ice thats radiance could trap the light of a star shooting across the cosmos, the powerful Sentinels were completely incapacitated. As a moment passed, Nex waved to his right and the two Sentinels shattered. Defeated and destroyed, their life energy, their magic power, and their very souls left their bodies to be devoured by Nex and his One Thousand Voices.

The Sentinel leader approached calmly despite the destruction at Nex's fingertips. Flowen and Lily could barely move. The existence of his presence and the release of his magic power caused a natural disaster.They were pinned by fear to the ground. Their very souls felt as if Nex was absorbing them even now.

"Aaaaaaargh!" roared Nex in a fit of pain. He writhed and pulled at his head, as if to scrape the inside of his skull with his fingernails. It was almost as if the release of his true magic power pained him, causing internal turmoil within his soul. He roared outwards, crashing and clashing with anything around, falling to one knee with his head buried in his hands.

"N-Nex?" mustered Lily through the impossible as his movement stuttered and he became sealed once more. "Are you okay?"

"What's wrong?" asked Flowen as he placed his hand on Nex's shoulder inquisitively.

"He's...stopped?" said Lily, confused.

"That was an immense power. Maybe it did something to him? Is he losing control?!" asked Flowen.

"Let us deal with this one ourselves," said Lily as she poised and prepared to combat the Primus with Flowen in toe.

"Insolence," spoke the Sentinel Primus, assessing their power. He sprang, before they could react, and collided with Lily, the force devastating her and the area around her. Flowen, even with his magic of foresight, could not read the future as fast the Sentinel moved. With his hand grappled around his jaw, the Sentinel plunged Flowen down, cratering the floor with his body.

Lily sprang forth and intercepted, the wind whirring around her with her formidable speed, but the Sentinel was leagues above what they had fought before. Flowen backed up his little sister with stalactites from all around to pierce the Sentinel, interrupt his footing and give her the edge.

The skirmish continued as the two battled ferociously against the Sentinel with every spell they could muster. They lept and spun and sliced and chopped with every fibre of skill they possessed but the Sentinel was too great a foe. He collapsed a magic spell upon them, "Spirit Magic: Brabus, roar of the wild bear!" With his arms outstretched and his fingers interlocked, the Sentinel collapsed the powerful energy onto Flowen and Lily with devastating effect. Once the scene began to ease, they struggled to reach their feet.

"So this is the power of a Sentinel Primus?!" coughed Lily as she raised herself.

"I guess it's not just a calling card," added Flowen.

"I've never seen one this strong. Even together, we cannot beat him?!," surmised Lily.

"Nevertheless, little sister," began Flowen. "We have no other choice."

They readied themselves once more to combat the Sentinel. They could feel his magic power boiling inside him ready to pour out at any moment and scorch them to death. He came upon them, smashing and crashing them around. Their blades, although powerful and effective, found themselves deflected by the Sentinel's Illyrium armour and magic spells. The ground and buildings did not last long under the might of this battle. Soon, neither Flowen nor Lily had enough strength to stand.

"This one is...tainted," said the Sentinel as he walked past the two defeated mages to the still entranced Nex. "You reek of it!"

The Sentinel did not hold back. He battered Nex with a barrage of blows to which he barely defended. Even in trance, Nex's muscle memory raised his arms in defence and attempted to take the brunt of the blows.

"Nex!" cried Lily as she tried to raise herself.

"Bastard!" roared Flowen in frustration.

"It's no use," began the Sentinel. "My Spirit Magic drains people of their power. The longer you spend fighting me the weaker you become."

When Nex had finally been crushed into the ground, the Sentinel roared another spell into action."Disappear! Spirit Magic: Fenrir, Claw of the Dire Wolf!"
The spell was enormous in calamity and effect. The surge of power leveled the entire village in one fell swoop.

"I apologise," said Nex calmly, as if the light of the moons shone only on him. "It has been quite some time since I have felt like that. I let my emotions get the better of me."

The Sentinel did indeed look shocked. "You should not have survived that!"

Nex released his power once more. The air around him began to snap and crack as small, but disastrous, claps of lightning merged into the air with a static vibrance before disappearing into nothingness. This was the overflowing amount of magic power taking a physical form around him. .

"I-it cannot be!" stuttered the Sentinel. "Spirit Mag-"

One Thousand voices spoke, "Die." A brilliant white beam, surrounded by cobalt blue lightning ripped from his hands and ravished the ground between them, enveloping the Sentinel fully, disintegrating him to ash in the wind.

Nex released a sigh and sealed his power once more. It was now, as the wind whistled away and the dust darted, that both Flowen and Lily could just make out a glimpse of an ethereal figure that gently took hold of Nex's trembling hand to comfort him, her long, moon dust hair carried weightlessly by the air. His rage had passed, and his emotions subsided, allowing him to take control again, and the ethereal creature vanished like a mirage.

Lily and Flowen remained silent. A combination of awe and tremendous fear and disbelief was crashing against the fronts of their minds. The animosity of Nex's power brought even his companions to the verge of breaking. It seemed that he had kept his power hidden to prevent the destruction of his companions. His magic power was cataclysmic. Too great and too sinister for them to even move to their friend's aid. With their hearts racing and their breath short, they were forced to wait.

CHAPTER TWENTY SEVEN: A TOMB OF SEVEN

Nex looked around at the magnificent countryside. Rolling green fields and flourishing nature created such a beautiful atmosphere for them all. The mountainside was tickled with snow and ice, deterring the warmth of summer. The path contained magical enchantments that kept most of the wildlife away and prevented them from attacking those who traded and worked along these routes.

"The path will split up ahead," said Lily. "The main route that navigates around the mountain is far more dangerous and tedious than going straight through. The larger path is the one we will be taking. It cuts straight into the mountain and leads through, but it is under the control of The Mantle so I should be able to get us through it. The path around would take four days longer."

"Straight through we go then", said Flowen powering on, Nex and Lily following.

The path that led north was normally fairly popular. On their travels they had passed all manner of people from traders to refugees and farmers, soldiers and priests. But they had only seen very few people in the last stretches between the small town at the base of the mountain and the paths upwards. Lily had informed them both that it was commonplace for all the southerners to pass through the Eayr mountains if they wished to go North, via the town that was built within the hollowed-out earth. The other routes around, usually used by those who wished to remain undetected for a myriad of reasons, were far harsher and almost impossible to traverse for the ordinary man.

These well-maintained cobbled roads connected various parts of the country in an efficient network to allow the flowing of goods and trade. The main cobbled path that led to the entrance of the Eayr mountains was the easiest and fastest route, and so Nex and his companions aimed for the front doors of the Mantle occupied town.

"So, Flowen, how exactly do you see?" asked Lily.

"It's quite simple really," began Flowen, "I see the magic that comprises life itself. It's actually much more beautiful than seeing with my own two eyes." Flowen thought of the image of his younger sister which he could see with his magical gaze. Impossibly enough, she was more radiant and more pure with golden light than the human eye could normally capture.

"Wow!" said Lily in amazement. "That's incredible."

"Magic of the eyes and of the mind. I can see the magic itself, and I can also see into the mind," he added.

Lily thought for a moment. "That may have been the key to you defeating me then," she said quickly, trying to establish that she was more powerful than her older brother.
"Don't get too ahead of yourself, little sister. I feel completely different from when we fought. And absent of enslavement to Akuma's will, the blade and I have grown closer."

"You do seem stronger," she added.

"The clarity he has now will add to his strength tremendously. A reason to fight and a reason to protect, they can be the sources of great strength but also of great weakness," said Nex.

"WELL!" said Flowen loudly, looking to see if there was anyone within earshot, "Being a demon does have its privileges."

"I bet!" said Lily as they all laughed on.

"Nex?" asked Lily.

"Yes, yes. Can I tell you a story?" he replied.

"Please." She confirmed.

"Very well. Perhaps one of a truer history?" he asked.

"I don't mind," said Lily. "Something for Flowen, too."

"I have just the story…" began Nex

"Did you know, long before humanity ruled Reath, these lands were overflowing with Demons and Dragons and Titans?" said Piaus to one of the children under his guard. "The Dialect, the written scripture of humanity's history, tells us all we need to know."

The Mantle's magnificent temple had its doors flung wide on days like these to invite all and any seeking redemption into its halls. Piaus, as he often did, took the opportunity to lend a knee to a group of young children to teach them the words of the Maker. For what better way was there than to start a fanatics' obsession if not at a young and naïve, vulnerable age.

"The pages of the Dialect teach us that the Maker created Titans first. These Dragons, Demons and elemental deities would shape the whole world for his greatest creation. When he made the Old Gods, The Immortals, they were a complete and utter failure. They could not die, they could not age, and they could not live. This immortality made their lives everlasting and content. They would not know of suffering or hardship or of fear or death. They could, with their powers gifted by the Maker, accomplish anything. But without the drive to better their already perfect beings, they revered only their father, and cared not for the world he had made them. This was not the perfection he sought. Freedom, will, hope, endurance, evolution and growth were the key elements the Maker wished to witness as his children developed, but these immortals could not accomplish these feats. He was disappointed and saddened by his children. And so with his final creation, he bound the ethereal, elemental, phantasmal magical form known as the soul, to creatures not born of his flesh. Identical to that of our predecessors, we shared not their infinite life, their divine flesh or their contentment. He blessed us generously with the warmth of his gaze and breathed the freedom of his spirit into us. This tiny fragment of his soul is what gives humanity their will, their freedom to exist free of constraint and fear and free to fulfil our reason for creation. We were his imperfect perfection. And now there are those of us who revere him in our everyday lives as a small token of everlasting gratitude. I hope when you all grow up, you will praise him with all your heart and live good lives. For if you do not, you will surely find your souls not elevated to the Maker's kingdom high in the clouds, but on the plains of oblivion where he banished the most terrible of his first children."

"Is that true, your holiness?" asked the young boy. "Is humanity really the Maker's favourite child?"

"The Dialect tells us so, young one. The Dialect is the history of mankind, and it carries the word of the Maker," assured Piaus.

"But what if someone wrote down the wrong story?"

Piaus laughed at the child's naivety, "This is the word of God, there is no variation."

"Is that so?" asked a voice as a group of figures entered from the side door into the hall. "Perhaps the boy is right."

Piaus chuckled "Off you go now, children," he said to the young group as he chivvied him from his knee and to the attendee priestesses. Piaus smiled at them all until they disappeared out of sight before looking disgusted at his hands. "They are always so dirty! You would think the priests and priestesses would take the time to bathe them before bringing them to me!" he said in amazement as he invited a servant to clean his hands so that he could speak without interruption.. "You have returned sooner than expected, General."

With the shadows of the great hall upon them, the General and their personal troupe of gifted mages had come to the Pontifex himself. Where the light beamed through the intricate stained glass, the new attendees avoided it religiously as if it were to cause them grave harm.

"While the Northmen like to build high walls and sit in their castles of ice, they aren't much for war it seems," said the General. "Although I am grateful that you gave me the task of defeating the Erbian Prince. He was quite entertaining. But it would seem the true prize was far to the south where Henrys was deployed."

"I am amazed you returned before the rivers of blood of the northmen overflowed into the capital's waters. I have heard only tremendous tales of your prowess against the Northmen. It is good that you have concealed your return. Your presence must remain…silent," said Piaus in accomplishment of his Hymn. "I hope you do not have any trouble settling back into the Capital. Much has happened since your departure for Erba."

"Oh please," said the General, "You know as well as I do, I will not remain here for long. Whilst I thank you for giving me the opportunity to reclaim the Kingdom of Erba, you cannot understand how unfulfilled I feel still. The prince put up nothing more than a teenager's tantrum. Perhaps if you had not submitted to the Sentinel order with such ease I could have had my fun without leaving home."

"Mind your tongue, Vereoris. You know as well as I that our

whispers carry into their halls," snapped Piaus in a worried tone. "If not for my backing and that of the weight of the Mantle your actions would draw the attention of the Ten Kings which, even you, could not hope to defeat."

"I must admit, Piaus, I thought you were more intelligent than that. Perhaps drawing the Kings near is my true objective. I wonder, with my power as it is now, if I could defeat them all. It has been far too long since I have truly had a battle worthy of recollection, I have all but forgotten the stimulation. Warring and conquering for you is about as exciting as this province will get."

"Bold words, Vereoris. Odin's Ten Kings are the most powerful human mages in this world. They wield magic far greater than you or I. Only Odin himself can defeat them, the man who became a God. You may find that your reckless actions will result in your demise. Nevertheless, if you were to draw the attention of the Ten Kings here, it would be the final act of disobedience against me. You are *my* General, do not forget that, but it does bring me to why I summoned you here. Thusien keeps a watchful eye on us all. He is fearful that once we have reclaimed all the kingdoms of Ares we will overthrow him. His paranoia has even gained the attention of the Ten Kings…"

"So the Ten Kings have surfaced. How interesting," said Vereoris, shrouded in the presence of darkness.

Piaus let out a large, exhausted sigh, "I know I need not tell you of what has transpired. You, of course, will know far more than I, as you always seem to do."

"You have sent Kleese to accompany Raiku south to quell Myphos' 'monster'," stated Veroris.

"Henrys failed greatly when securing the kingdom of Myphos. Both he and his army were repelled and there is no ignoring his claim of Infinity Magic. You, despite your distance, will have felt the magic. Therefore, the Sentinels and I have come to an arrangement. They will see to the matter and be the spearhead of our invasion into Myphos. When your men are ready, you will take the armies of all the Hymns of the Mantle South. I will not ask you to stay here as I know you will not listen."

"They will not win," said Vereoris plainly.

"Thusien has gifted them two Goliaths for reassurance."

The General let out a large sigh of disappointment. "Such a waste. If they truly wished to succeed they would have taken a Dural."

"The creature the Goliath was based on?"

"The God Killer…" trailed the Hymn of Wrath.

"Thusien is far more powerful than any Sentinel has ever been," stated Piaus with worry. "Alone, even I would struggle to quell his power and that of his apprentice, not to mention that of the weapons he has at his command. And now, with the attention of the Ten Kings, I cannot afford to take any chances, or I will lose all I have worked so hard to achieve. While I cannot rely on your faith, integrity, or loyalty to me, I can rely on your unquenchable bloodlust and hunger for death and destruction. If such calamities were to converge, I would wager heavily that your heart's desire would be to participate. Thus, with Thusien alone there is no threat to me here. When Raiku and Kleese fail, you must be there to succeed. Only with your victory, will the Mantle be able to unite the people of Ares and the four kingdoms. The Victory must be ours and not the Sentinels'."

Veroris could not contain the sinister bloodlust that began to fill the great hall. "And so, you delay me here to become a swooping saviour and not a conqueror?" clarified Vereoris.

Piaus sat distastefully and he pondered the thought of threats.

"Only for a short time. You will remain here to deter any unwanted ideas, then you will go south. Kleese will temporarily surrender his forces to you and depart free of his army."

"Hmm" snapped Vereoris from their cloak, contained in mystery..

"You may allow your men to recover and keep your merry little band of psychopaths with you. But when you leave, they must stay here in case I have need of them in your absence," ordered Piaus.

"You would do well as to not order me around, Piaus. I gained some satisfaction from journeying North and I learned a great deal of what is to come, therefore I will do as you ask. But in two days, when their time is up, only the Maker himself would be able to prevent me from entering the fray," hissed Vereoris beneath their cloak from the darkness, the marvellous sparkle of the Mantle armour not able to catch any of the sunlight.

"To think there has been no enemy worthy of your magic. I am sure you will surprise us all when you reveal it. I only hope that this battle can calm the raging soul within you for some time. You would be of far more use to me if you actually listened."

"Be grateful I have allied myself with you at all. If only you knew the truth as to why the Ten Kings keep their distance, you would not dare speak to me in such a condescending tone. At any moment I could change my mind and destroy both the Mantle and the Sentinels."

"That…I do not doubt. You are my trump card, my ace. You are the Wrath of the Mantle. It is inconceivable that you would ever fail. Tell none of your departure to Myphos. Oh, and there is another thing. One of the assassins from your program has defected after a mission. It appears her target was the same creature that has caused this upset. She has turned her back on the Maker, but his gaze watches over her still. I think you would recall her by name more accurately than I. Wielder of an Illyrium sword, I think…"

"Lily…" mumbled Vereoris, picturing the talented young assassin. "Such a beautiful and talented young girl."

"Her defection cannot go unpunished and if she is aiding this heretic then only death will suffice as punishment," stated Piaus. "If Raiku and Kleese should fail as you claim, it can be another reward for you for your troubles."

A wide smile spread across Vereoris' face like none the Pontifex had ever seen. "She will bring me great satisfaction, in more ways than one. But even she pales in comparison to the true presence. You shall have two days. I will let my men rest and then I will deploy south at the head of the entire army. My assassins will stay here once I have left. Demand what you will of me until then, your holiness," finished Vereoris before turning and disappearing from whence they had come.

Piaus slumped his head onto one hand, "Such a troublesome child. To think the Maker could create such a creature…"

CHAPTER TWENTY EIGHT: A DYING FLAME

The day had passed as Nex, Lily and Flowen had set off. They had taken the faster route through the Eayr mountains and were soon to be at The Mantles doorstep.

"It feels like it's getting darker sooner…" said Lily as the sun escaped to the east.

"I wouldn't know," said Flowen sarcastically as he held his hand to catch the last of the sun's warmth.

Their footsteps became concealed in the shadow of the great mountains as they caught sight of the two large doors that housed the underground Mantle temple.

"Well, that's weird…" said Lily as they approached, "there's usually lights and guards and stalls open till late."

"Great…" trailed Nex

"Outside a temple?" asked Flowen. "We are in the middle of nowhere."

"The temple is merely the gateway. There is an entire kingdom within this mountain. One giant town. This is the smallest of the seven hollowed mountains and the only one that people live within. But priests aren't the only ones who live there, it is a whole metropolis filled with people."

"Like them?" said Nex as he gestured forwards with his head.

"Yeah…" said Lily

"Hello? Hello there!" shouted a woman from the foot of the doorway to the three travellers.

Lily took the lead "Are you okay?" she asked loudly as she closed the gap, "Is something wrong?"

"You-You're from the Mantle!" asked the woman as she recognised Lily's incredible attire.

"Yes," said Lily gesturing back to her friends, "We are," On the spot.

"Thank the Maker!" said the women in relief.

"We have been stuck here for days!" shouted a man as he came forward gesturing to his caravan of people. "We can't get in!"

"What do you mean?" asked Lily curiously. "They aren't letting you in?"
"They aren't letting *anyone* in," said another woman.

"Wait, What do you mean?" asked Lily again as Nex and Flowen Looked to one another as she tried to gather some sense of the situation as the people began to crown around her.

"We haven't had a response," said the man. "No one has answered our calls. The doors haven't even opened to let people out!"

Lily looked back at her comrades in worry. "Something must be wrong…" she said to Nex and Flowen. "They would never turn people away from here."

"Please, we really need to get through," said the first woman. "We need to get to the capital for sanctuary. You're from the Mantle, right? Surely you can do something to get us in?"

"We'll find out what's going on here." said Lily as she assured them trying to put them at ease. "Let's see if we can get them to answer."

Lily led Nex and Flowen to the great temple doors which sealed the mountain shut. "Hello?! Is anyone there? We need to get through! I am from the Mantle."

There was no response as they awaited an answer. The crowd behind them suppressed their noise whilst they waited in hope.

"I guess no one's home?" said Nex.

Lily replied in a fearful tone. "The doors are operated by an enchantment, I wouldn't be able to override such a complex spell without knowing the runes…"

Nex looked at the fifty or so people all huddled together in fear. Men, women, children and elders all worried for their lives. He could tell from their scars, that they had been through something terrible. These were the few who had survived the Sentinel cleansing at the foot of the mountain.

"Please, The Sentinels have destroyed everything we had. We cannot return home. We must have sanctuary here!" pleaded the woman.

Lily removed herself from the group and turned to her comrades in hopes of a solution. "Well? What do you think?" she asked. "We can't just leave them here."

Nex cleared his throat and made an announcement. "We have defeated the Sentinels that destroyed your village. They cannot harm you any more."

"What?!"

"Defeated them?!

Impossible!"

"There's no way!"

"I had a feeling that even if we told them that we killed the Sentinels back there, they wouldn't believe us," said Flowen.

"I just wanted to be sure," whispered Nex. "Even if they did return they wouldn't feel safe."

"We must take refuge within the Mantle. They are the only ones who can keep the Sentinels away!" shouted a woman.

Ne leaned in to whisper to Lily and Flowen, "This path is too dangerous for them. I fear we will not be able to protect them all. Perhaps they would be better off taking the route around."

"It's far too difficult a journey for them. Look at them, they won't last a day," replied Lily, knowing the path well.

"They may come to hate us more than the Sentinels," trailed Nex.

"What choice do we have? We can at least get them inside and work something out. Once we are inside, we can go from there," argued Lily.

"I'm not sure it's a good idea…" trailed Nex, knowing a truth that the others did not.

"I agree with Lily," confirmed Flowen. "If they want to be coddled by the Mantle, let them be."

"Our biggest issue is the doors…" trailed Lily.

Nex sighed heavily as he looked at the incredible, ancient stone doors. "I don't think they will be the problem."

"If no one is answering we should try to force them open, then," said Flowen.

"The doors are infused with powerful magic. If they can't be opened by a Cleric from the inside, then we will struggle. These doors are ancient and were built a long time ago."

"You can't open it?" asked Flowen to lily.

"I wasn't exactly customer facing in my role. You need to see the runes, and even then, I think we would struggle. It's in a written Titan language."

"I can give it a go," said Nex as he looked from them to the door.

"I don't even think you'd be able to open it" admitted Lily, mentally preparing to smash down the door. "The door is ancient."

"If this is the shortest route, then I will be going straight through," said Nex as he made it clear he was not faltering from this path. Something about him made him appear more serious than normal. He was being unusually stern and hard hearted to what Lily and Flowen had become used to. "But should it prove too dangerous, perhaps you should suggest they take another route."

"Okay," agreed Lily before turning to the crowd. "We will take you through, but we don't know how safe it is yet, so I'm going to need you all to get behind him."

They all mumbled and stumbled as they hustled, grabbing at their belongings, hope igniting their steps. Nex looked back to ensure they were behind his protection and that of his comrades.
He raised his hand to the door and focused. He concentrated deeply, sweeping his mind for the location of the magical runes, his fingers tracing the air as if he were caressing the ancient hieroglyphs that remained unseen. He exhaled, and with it, the great stone doors began to open.

"Wow!" gasped Lily...

"Amazing!" gawped a young boy from amidst the caravan.

"I am not actually that surprised," stated Flowen to his sister, poking her cheek with his index finger.

The doors grinded heavily until they opened in full swing, the atmosphere was tense and unsuspecting as the dust cleared for them to look into the opening. They all braced for the threat. But nothing came. As the dust settled, they began to see what had befallen the inhabitants of the mountain...

"What the..." said Lily as she scanned with her eyes.

It was a horrific site. Traces of blood and entrails stained the floors and walls. Sealed in, none could escape. Nex began forward to investigate closer, his nose tingling with the familiar smell. "It seems they are all dead."

They all began to analyse the scene. They could sense the anger and desperation of the malice lingering in the humid air.
"This feeling..." said Lily. "I've never felt anything like this," she said horrified. There was a blackness in the air. An unfamiliar, gut-wrenching stench heaved at the stomach. Like needles, their hairs stood on end and begged to be retracted within the skin.

"The magic here..." began Flowen, "It's like nothing I have ever sensed."

"This is not magic. This is evil itself," stated Nex

"It may not be the best idea to take these people through here after all," said Flowen.

"I agree," said Lily.

"But this is the only way!" shouted a woman, the self appointed leader of the caravan. "We cannot go on the main route. None of us could survive that journey! If you are going through, take us with you!"

"Rita!"

"She's right!"

"Please!"

"Take us with you!"

"Even if it means your death?" Nex asked her.

"Even then," said Rita on the whole caravan's behalf.

Nex understood their desperation. He could sense in their bones they could not be deterred. "Very well. I admire a strong will. If you can see it through to the end, you will survive."

Lily looked at the horrified caravan with sympathy as she declared to Nex. "I think this is the right thing to do. If whatever did this is still in here, we will have to face it ourselves. Besides, the three of us make quite an opposing team.." she admitted modestly.

"We will keep them between us at all times," said Flowen.

Nex thought for a moment as he sensed the lingering decay of power and flesh, the skin on his body beginning to crawl as he released the most subtle signs of discomfort. But this did not escape the notice of Lily or Flowen. 'Was this something that even he feared?' they thought.

Nex had hoped to go in alone, for he was almost certain he could protect his comrades. Not entirely sure of what lay ahead it would have been enough burden for his retinue to accompany him, but a caravan of powerless civilians spelled nothing but trouble. For these people to remain here would prove their greatest chance of survival.

"Flowen, you take point. Lily, support him, but keep an eye on the people. If they are to strike, it will be from the rear. I shall guard our escape. If I give the command, run for the gate and do not think to look back, even for me," said Nex.

"But-" she protested.

"These are my only orders," stated Nex. "No matter what happens, you both must escape."

"Okay," they agreed reluctantly. "We will put our faith in you."

"Everyone, stay between Flowen and Nex," instructed Lily with gestures between the powerless man and the blind demon. "Group together around me. We must move fast. Give aid to those who cannot keep up and dispose of anything that your life does not depend on."

They all bickered between them as they made their own minds up on whether the idea was a good one and dumped packs and wares that did not have as much worth as their lives before entering the unknown.

"Maybe we would be better off going around..." said one.
"I think I would rather try my luck on the other route than find out what's in here!" said another.

"If you wish to stay, you can. But if you are coming, we are moving now," roared Nex loudly as he made their decisions for them. He allowed them to enter, beckoning them past him as he examined their faces.

They all entered, Flowen taking the lead of the caravan. As they did, they each took in the sights of what looked to be a massacre. The innards and flesh that remained had filled the mountain with a terrible stench, but the air carried something to their sensitive and weary nostrils, something far more unpleasant. Then, the great doors began to close behind them.

"Ahh!" cried one
"It's closing!" screamed another.

It took them a moment to notice the young mage was in fact

sealing them shit as he had opened.

"What are you doing?!" they shouted at Nex.

"What is in here must be contained at all costs. We cannot allow it to reach the surface."

They all rumbled and fussed as Nex spoke again. "Come on guys! It's containment one-oh-one," he said, shrugging his shoulders, looking to his companions for support. Despite the tense situation, Flowen and Lily both found comfort in Nex's new lightness. He must have some idea what was down there, but there was no point in sharing it now, it would only worsen their shaky spirits.

The party wandered down from the gates into the underground city. It was magnificent. The mountain had been hollowed out almost entirely, incorporating the mountain's stone into grand walkways and chambers. An entire industry did in fact exist underneath its summit. All the buildings were made of huge stone. Lanterns and posts of light still burned, illuminating the expanse in a city where it was always night.

However, the magnificence of the city and its structures did not dull the overwhelming feeling of death. As they walked down the central path through the city, they found themselves looking at the empty streets.

"I really don't like being underground," said Lily, not taking in too much of her surroundings.

"Where…are the bodies?" asked Flowen

"Maybe most of the people made it out, and the survivors did exactly what we did: sealed the doors behind them." said Lily over to him. "From some of the armour left behind most of these look to be soldiers," she said gesturing at the pieces of armour strewn and torn across the streets, "maybe the citizens were given priority."

"Or maybe it was the citizens that did this…." trailed Flowen in suspicion.

"We should pick up the pace!" shouted Nex from the rear.

"Okay!" replied Flowen from the front, raising his hand in acknowledgement in worry that his voice did not carry.

The caravan began to move faster, to a fast paced walk. The elderly and the young kept up with the assistance of the more able as people gave up more of their luggage to the dirt. But Nex was different. He guarded the back but with discreet seriousness and worry. Lily was able to pick it up. His feelings and emotions carried to his companions subconsciously. He was tense and suspecting, he knew that something unspeakable, something only the darkest evil was capable of, happened here. Even he, with all his tremendously power and strength, had taken a demeanour more serious than any battle in which Lily had accompanied him through so far.

Flowen and Lily looked to one another in worry for their friend as they tried to figure out his thoughts.

"A Demon? No. This feels different," said Lily as she left from assuring the people and came to her brother.

"Could it be…?" they began to think, "The creatures that Nex spoke of?"

Flowen turned and nodded in the direction straight ahead, "Look!"

In the distance down the long road that stretched in a straight line between the two main entrances they could see the two great doors, embedded into the shell of the mountain. "There's our exit."

"We are making good ground," said Lily. "Just focus on moving forwards! I don't sense anything between us and the gate either."

They were now past halfway, currying like tiny insects through the vast, empty kingdom. The great ceiling above them had reached its highest point and the rocks had already come to slope back to them, reducing the empty space.

"You vile creatures…" said Nex under his breath as he sensed movement in the shadows.

"FLOWEN!" he signalled loudly, all noise drowned out by his supremacy.

"MOVE! RUN!" Flowen increased his pace again into a harsh run. The caravan poured through and attempted to match him in desperation. Lily increased too and allowed more of the caravan to pass by her whilst Nex slowed in preparation. The pressure around them began to build as the humid air went dry and thin as Lily and Flowen summoned their power to them in preparation. A great crack erupted from the summoning of both their legendary, cursed blades, the green lightning- like aura indicating battle was imminent. The exertion of Lily and Flowen's magic power enveloped the group in both a sense of danger, but also in comfort. No matter what horror they may face, their escorts held a power that would surely be enough to defend them. But beneath it all, both Lily and Flowen were scared. They could not comprehend even trying to hold back an ounce of their tremendous power.

"Above?" said Nex as he glanced upwards at the scrambling figures. Hundreds of them, clawing into the hard rock with their fingers prepared to ambush the caravan.

"This sickness…" wretched Flowen as movement approached him from the dark alleys and streetways.

"That stench…" said Lily as she looked to the roofs of the buildings.

They could not even describe what they saw. Humanoid figures, grotesque in appearance. Their smell, their presence, their aura was so sickening that to even look at them made even the most dedicated and holy believer of God conclude that no such omnipotent, benevolent Maker could exist. If these creatures were truly real, life itself was its mortal nemesis. There was no mistaking what these creatures were.

"Go!" roared Nex as the horde emerged, sprinting towards them like mindless beasts, clawing and grasping at everything, ripping it from their path as they hungered for their prey in a frenzy, dropping from above with no fear or mercy.

"Lily!" shouted Nex again as they hit the middle of the caravan, cutting and clawing at the petrified people. They had come from the darkness between them. Anywhere there could be a shadow the rotten creatures clawed and ravaged them. Lily and Flowen's large-scale attacks were able to keep the larger droves at bay, but for every one that flew back, another ten would emerge. Nex severed their numbers from the rear, defeating them with his power whilst Flowen used his magic to maintain their path, impaling and skewing them as they rose. But they just kept pouring in, more and more, from each and every direction, each injured or impaled creature clambering from the stalactite and rushing over to them free of impediment of their wounds.

Lily severed and sliced at them, protecting as many people as she could with all her skill and potent ability. Whilst they were by no means weak individually, Lily and Flowen had soon slain more than two hundred and fifty of the creatures each. But the exertion of their tremendous magic power had no effect on the creatures. They were unphased by such mortal might. The fear of death did not bind them nor did the threat of incapacitation or dismemberment. They did not waver in their drive to rip the people apart and consume them.

Lily and Flowen soon noticed their magic had little effect on the creatures. Even Lost Magic could not rip the flesh of the Kursed. But their swords, made from the bones of a fallen star plucked from the Maker's kingdom, could indeed inflict upon the beasts a mortal wound. If it was not for this aid, they would surely not have been able to survive this long.

"Hurry!" roared Flowen as he dealt tremendous blows with Akuma, sending them crushed and flying back into themselves. They continued to fend them off as best they could as the horde began to overwhelm them. They could see no end to a sea of yellow eyes in the darkness. They were trapped beneath the mountain with their power draining rapidly in their desperation. But the problem only worsened.

"What are these creatures? There's no end to them!" shouted Flowen over the crashes and clashes of sword on rotten flesh and broken armour.

The overwhelming, undying force was soon to be their end. Like insects that pour over prey one hundred times their strength and size, the Kursed continued to pour from every crevice, every splintered doorway and crack until, like a tsunami of rotten corpses, the tidal wave crashed upon them. They would all be consumed.

Lily and Flowen had not dared to bring up the topic of Nex's sealed power. They did not ask what spoke from within him like a sea of souls, or why such magic power forced him to lose control. Their souls were so scarred by the event that discussing the topic would require much more delicate circumstances. But Nex could no longer afford to keep his power a secret. He submitted, raising his fist in the air before crashing it into the solid rock beneath them with a mighty blow. The earth shook and shuddered and rumbled deep beneath them stunning the creatures and blasting them back, but only for a moment. The Mountain continued to roar as the innards began to break from their natural supports and man-made splints, falling through the air and crashing into the city below. But the activation of Nex's power seemed to hold another effect on the creatures. Not only did their animosity intensify tenfold, but they began to focus on Nex, and Nex alone.

Like a hostile virus within human blood, in unison, they focused themselves on the one who had released a cobalt blue smoke from his eyes. The cobalt blue smoke of a Sentinel. One Thousand Voices thundered over them and rebounded off the hollowed out mountain to strike fear into the Kursed creatures that had never felt such a thing. "Run!"

The great doors ahead of them began to grind open as Nex enchanted the runes with his power. Lily and Flowen rallied the caravan forward until they were away and only Nex stood between them and the horrid sea of the ever-growing plague.

"Neeeeex!" screamed Lily over it all.

Like moths to a flame, they were frenzied for him. Like the Kursed search for their fallen Immortal for aeons beneath the ground of Reath, they clawed for Nex in the same way. Were they drawn to his power that rivalled that of a God? Or was it, that with his might, their master willed his extinction in fear of its own life? None could know at this point, only that Nex would not let them leave this mountain alive.

The great stone grinded open as they managed to squeeze through, "Come on! Go, go!" shouted Flowen waving them through hurriedly, Lily covering the rear.

They could no longer see Nex. As the mountain crumbled from above and the horde of darkness engulfed the area where he was, it pained them to not look back. But they promised his trust. As the enchantment wore off the doors grinded shut and, as the last of them slipped through, they felt Nex's presence fade away beneath the collapse of the mountain. But, as they ran clear, despite the shuddering of the earth quaking and the sound of a disintegrating mountain, they could all hear a voice as if it was in their very minds.

"Nexus!" A soul shattering, splintering magical voice whispered to them in discovery, wrenching at their very beings.

They continued away, getting distance between them and the sealed doors witnessing the enormity of the collapse. "No!" they trailed peeling away from the caravan to watch in hopelessness. Lily and Flowen took in little of the devastating calamity before them as their hearts grew heavy with loss and sadness as their friend vanished from their lives.

The voice that had spoken inside them had scarred their very bones with its words but yet they could not bring themselves to discuss the phenomenon. Petrified and afraid. Even the demon with Flowen trembled at the magic.

Nex's sacrifice was too heavy a grief for them to bear. He had reunited them, and at the beginning of their quest, sacrificed himself for them.

"Did you hear it?" asked Flowen to his younger sister finally as the calamity subsided around them. "Did you feel it? That voice..." he said in horror.

"I could *feel* it, like it was coming from inside me" Lily replied.

"Yeah..." said Flowen as he looked at the door in hope.

It took many moments for them to notice. Lily and Flowen were too stricken with their own loss. Of the fifty villagers, perhaps only fifteen remained.

"Oh, my beloved!" screamed a woman as she cried hysterically in the arms of her daughter.

"My son! Where is my son!" cried a man as he searched among

them.

"They…" said Lily as she looked upon the horrified bunch.

They didn't know what to say to the caravan to appease them. In their loss they only bore resentment and hatred for their escorts.

"I'm so sorry" said Lily to the grieving woman. "We can-"

Rita, the leader of the caravan, spoke above the noise "You have done enough!" she snapped in a fit of rage.

"You were not the only ones to suffer loss. We help-" protested Lily.

"Helped!? We had braved and endured all manner of beasts. Dire wolves and ghouls and bandits brought us to the brink. But those creatures…You doomed us all by taking us in there! " she ranted.

"But- " began Lily before she was interrupted.

"Get away from us!" shouted Rita as she moved back to her people and began to funnel them away.
"You had a choice to follow us there. Do not wipe the blood of your lost on her hands. You shame yourselves with such words!" said Flowen to the caravan as they limped off in anger and sorrow.

"It's okay, Flowen!" said Lily. "They are right."

"It was as Nex said. It was of their choosing to enter the mountain. Their deaths are not on our hands," assured Flowen. "At least some of them survived."

"But at what cost?" said Lily frankly. "They didn't even get to say goodbye to their loved ones."

"That was pretty crazy, no?" said a voice from behind them both.

"Nex?!" exclaimed Lily and Flowen at the same time, their relief overwhelming and sincere.

"Phew…" whistled Nex with a smile. "That was something," he laughed.

"You crazy fool!" shouted Lily in a rage as she grabbed him and wrapped her arms around him. "What were you thinking?!"

"I'm glad you both made it out," declared Nex.

"Thanks to you," said Flowen.

"We saw your glow, Nex," began Lily, "We saw the Sentinel power pour from inside of you. The power that the old Sentinels had."

"Ah…" said Nex.

"Why did you not tell us?" urged Lily. "You could have told us sooner!"

Nex paused for a moment, admitting that even he himself did not know the current state of the Sentinel Order. It was because he was ashamed of being a Sentinel, but for another reason.

"I feared you would not follow me if you knew," said Nex. There was a silence as they all looked upon him with judging eyes. "I suppose, I truly am a coward," he declared.

"No." said Lily. "Not at all!"

"Hmm," surmised Flowen, "It was right of you to keep it from us. It was only through the actions that led us here that we would have been able to accept your truth. Had we known from the start, it would have only seeded unease and distrust. I think…we do not have the right to judge someone for what they are. A demon and an assassin have both been treated with an open heart by you, a man of the unknown.

"No matter your secrets, Nex. You have our trust and our eternal gratitude," said Lily.

"I…thank you." said Nex after a long pause and staring at his friends with admiration.

Lily understood his words. Both she and Flowen would likely do the same thing if they were in his position. They understood that he kept it to himself not only for his own benefit, but for theirs too. The already mysterious Nex had become slightly less secretive to them and this only strengthened their ties. They were all the same.

It seemed to be a mutual, unsaid understanding between the siblings as they accepted Nex for what he was. What they could not know was that this was merely one chapter from his never-ending book.

"Those creatures…were they what you spoke of before?" asked Lily, moving on from the Sentinel bombshell. "They were much worse than you let on. They were mindless and they attacked like a swarm. They moved with speed and cunning and yet they looked…dead" she stated in confusion. "My magic had no effect on them."

"Akuma was the only thing that worked against them. Do you mean to say that our blades also hold the power of the Sentinels? I could feel their hunger as they ripped those people apart and devoured them," said Flowen.

"Tsumikiri rang out to me as it sliced at their flesh. The blade longed to fight them," added Lily.

It was also, after these statements, that they both noticed something they had never seen before. On the blades of Tsumikiri and Akuma the blood of the Kursed remained. It had not steamed off and become one with the air. It's impure presence stained the blade, before being absorbed into the very soul of the legendary weapons.

"They are an infection: a blight," announced Nex. "They are the ancient enemy of all life in this world. There is but one way to kill these creatures."

"Don't tell me…" began Lily in disbelief.

"Sentinel power," said Nex.

"The Mantle teaches us the Sentinels destroyed the Kursed thousands of years ago. How can they still be alive now?" protested Lily in confusion.

"The Kursed were not completely defeated in the battle after the great war. The Fallen God was slain and his soul destroyed, but they were not wiped out. Some great Kursed creatures remained and were buried beneath these mountains. Thus, the Kursed could never be truly destroyed. They will always linger. As long as there is turmoil on Reath and blood is shed, the Kursed will feast on despair and destruction."

"But…why now?" asked Lily in an attempt to make sense of it. "Why are these ancient creatures only coming to light now?"

"The Dawn," said Flowen.

"The Dawn?" asked Lily.

"The Demon spoke of it. The last time the light of the world sets and then begins anew in darkness," said Flowen.

"The Kursed have fed on the magic and despair of this world whilst they lay dormant underground. Without the presence of powerful creatures to draw in the magic Reath's core into their souls, the Kursed have fed on the overflowing magical energy emitted by the world."

"Magic power?" asked Flowen.

"Magic power is drawn from the life and earth and air around us. But all magic power is emitted from Reath. The creatures and plants of this world channel it and release it for us to absorb," said Nex.

"Are you saying that the first Sentinels, these 'Ankou', the most powerful humans thousands of years ago, drew their power by bypassing this process? They drew magic power for the earth itself?"

"They became so powerful there was simply not enough on the surface for them to absorb. The source of magic itself was the only thing that could match their vessels," said Nex.

"And it is these Ankou who have vanished? The Kursed have feasted in their absence?" queried Flowen.

"It is not only them. Titans and Gods also draw their power from the Source. That is why they have slumbered. To replenish themselves.

"Then…" said Lily, her impressive train of thought catching fast, "Then the Sentinels are the key. They are the only ones who can slay the Kursed."

"This Sentinel Order," thought Nex in worry, "cannot even comprehend the threat beneath the mountain tombs."

"Tombs…?" asked Flowen.

"PLURAL?!" asked Lily in outrage.

"You said it yourself. Seven of these mountains remain, all hollowed out by Domashu and other Titans," said Nex, educating them of the world's true nature.

"Even in a world of Demons, Dragons, Titans and God's, The Kursed are to be feared above all else" added Flowen.

"But…" realised Lily, "Didn't the Gods and Titans help humanity defeat the Kursed? Will they not do the same again if all life on Reath is threatened?"

"It is true," said Nex. "Titans and Gods fought back against the Kursed, but there is more to it. Even with their divinity and their power they are not immune to the Kursed's taint. Titans and Gods who were consumed by the Kursed only ended up strengthening their ranks as corrupted creatures. Their power and divinity become slaves to the desires of the one who leads them. Additionally, there are those who, despite the Kursed's undeniable threat, believe Humanity to be the true curse upon Reath. They would rather see us destroyed than save the world. The old Gods want nothing other than to be with their father."

Lily and Flowen turned to each other to process it all. It was a difficult concept. There was much going on but they required more clarification.

"On the pages of the Dialect, which were destroyed long before the ones that existed now, history told of a Great War where the primordial Titans, the immortal Gods and Humanity battled for their own selfish desires. Each battle, each death, each drop of blood that leaked allowed evil to manifest itself in a putrid and horrifying form. This essence of magic, dark and umpire, drew closer to the God imprisoned in the earth below, and corrupted it. When the creatures rose from the ground deep beneath us all the races found themselves not only hopeless against their magicless strength but also unable to resist the call of their taint. Even the combined might of the three races were not enough to defeat the Kursed and the Immortal, fallen God who led them. The Kursed do not 'kill' in the traditional sense. They consume you. Your body, your flesh, your mind, and your soul all remain intact, but slave to the taint. They hunger eternally, souls unable to be released. It was the Ankou, a clan of humans who lived below the goddess Amaterasu who gave birth to a magic that could destroy the Kursed. Both the Sentinel magic of today and the magic in your cursed blades is a fragment of the pure, cosmic energy which destroyed the fallen God, one of the Maker's first immortal children. Their return was inevitable."

"Is this why you are here?" asked Lily to Nex "To tell the Sentinels that the Kursed have returned and help destroy them?!"

"They already know. But I cannot blame any other than myself. This is a destiny I cannot ignore again," stated Nex as he looked into the wind, accepting his truth.

"When is the Dawn? How much time do we have?" asked Lily. "We have time," said Nex. "If only a little."

"But what can we do against such a force" pleaded Lily "If even the Gods cannot defeat it how can it be done?"

"There is a way, be it only one," said Nex. "But for all my want to say it…I cannot share it with you. If you would trust me with this secret, then that is enough. But, from here on out, I can understand if you want no part in this. It is my burden to bear."

There was something about the way Nex said this. Something in his eyes, or perhaps in the tone of his voice. He opened himself to them with a sense of vulnerability that he had not previously shown. Both Lily and Flowen were free to choose how and if they were to trust him.

Unanimously and unaided, they spoke. "Of course, we will help you save the world!" said Lily.

"You have reunited our family, Nex, and you have also found a place in it," stated Flowen.

"Thank you both," said Nex. "It has been a long time since I have had any friends quite like you two. Flowen, we have only just met and yet I feel as though I truly know you. Thank you for this time you have given me so far. Lily, although you originally tried to kill me when we first met, I will never forget the girl I met in the woods. You have grown so much recently, and I thank you for sharing both your power, your thoughts and your kindness with me. Really and truly. Thank you both."

His heart-warming praise warmed them both. Even with the mountain still crumbling behind them and the threat of apocalyptic death buried beneath it they felt safe and loved in this trio of companions.

"Wait," said Lily in revelation. "Won't the Mantle use Gitterung's tower to try and find you?" said Lily in revelation.

Nex needed to quickly pretend he had not already thought of this. "I suppose it is possible."
Of course, Lily already knew of his deceit. She could see it as if the words were written all across his face.

"You had no intention of using the eye, did you?" she said. "I bet you can just use the magic anyway."

"They will be heading to the tower and anticipate that I will use it. It makes sense to meet them there. Although I must admit I am excited to see how someone has incorporated a form of Gravity Magic into an item," admitted Nex.

CHAPTER TWENTY NINE: THE TOWER OF GITTERUNG

The Tower was not far from the mountains in which they had emerged. It was the tallest building in all of Ares reaching higher even than the Temple of Nexus upon closer inspection. It was erected only two decades ago by the great mage, Gitterung. It was said he enlisted the help of Titans to build it with their knowledge of the earth and unrivalled strength. At the very top, where the sky split, the clouds sank to allow the great Eye to see clearly over all the continent. It was not an inviting structure. The height gave goose-bumps to those with the fear of falling and its constant guard by the Mantle made it unbreachable by unwelcome guests. But our heroes did not seek use of the great tower, it was only in Nex's interest to fall face first into the enemy plan. The fate of the world would come to rest on their shoulders.

"It's huge!" said Flowen through his magical gaze, the structure not moving a millimetre in the wind despite its towering size.

"Yeah," added Lily. "I think it's slightly taller than the Nexus Temple. Gitterung made it only slightly taller on purpose. Some say, when it was built, Anoctis himself approved the monument and changed his flight of darkness in respect."

"Who?" asked Flowen, unfamiliar of the myth.

"The primordial Dragon God, Anoctis. When the world was nothing but light, his wings brought darkness to the world," said Nex, recanting the legend.

"He sounds big," added Flowen, "and horribly fictional."

"He is pretty big, yes. But there is always only one way to find out if something truly exists."

"Gitterung did not seek to insult the Dragon God, and so the tower is slightly shy of the heavens. Just," said Lily. "Gitterung carved a passage of praise into the walls where the eye is: 'The Eye of God is purely borrowed. Do not think to claim it as your own'." They both looked to Nex as they came to understand this was his area of expertise.

"It means the eye is a magic spell and by 'God', he means divine magic, and there is only one form of divine magic. Infinity Magic."

"Then maybe he uses Infinity Magic? The same as you?" said Lily.

"If you have indeed told me the right inscription then by 'borrowed' he would mean that he does not know the spell of the Infinite Eye. Also, there is a zero percent chance that he knows infinity magic," stated Nex plainly, easily believing his own words. He clearly knew something about the true nature of his god-like magic that he was not willing to share just yet. "It is Gravity Magic."

"Wait. Hang on. Who on Reath is this Gitterung? Am I supposed to know?" asked Flowen in confusion, looking to both Nex and Lily, starting to get fed up with all these alien names.

"Beats me," shrugged Nex.

Lily sighed heavily at them both. She was starting to find this role of teacher rather tedious. "Gitterung is one of the greatest mages in all the world. Apparently, he is one of Odin's Ten Kings. He has no affiliation with the Mantle or the Sentinels," she informed them.

"Then why does the Mantle guard it?" asked Nex. "Apparently, Gitterung built the tower, used it once, and then abandoned it, never returning. He was a mage of mystery. The tower is super important and therefore the Mantle took it upon themselves to claim it."

"I wonder if it is stairs all the way up…" trailed Flowen unable to draw himself to Lily's story.

"I don't actually know how one would reach the top," said Lily.

The structure was huge. They were but insignificant specs compared to the enormous tower that pierced the night sky.

"Should we take a look?" asked Lily.

"I'm curious as to how it works," admitted Nex. "Would you care to knock, Flowen?"

"Well, there's absolutely no way they are going to open the doors for us…" said Lily using her expertise from within the mantle.

"So, we'll knock hard'. said Nex.

"I would bet an entire, full week's stay, all food and drink included, that there is a one hundred percent chance that they will attack us on sight," she stated.

"Well then we won't give them the chance!" laughed Nex as he approached it. Flowen began to summon himself, his sword snapping through the air as it appeared with its aura of green lightning, Lily's following soon after, their presence and sinister malice breaching those who resided behind the heavy, wooden doors.

Flowen released a powerful, but minimal blast of magic energy at the doors and prepared for the defenders of the tower to combat him. His attack had disabled over a dozen guards, all blasted around the great room, wooden beams and supports destroyed and strewn across the place. Lily and Nex joined him slowly, looking upon the remnants of the defence as it gathered itself.

The tower was circular and tall, but the interior looked to possess a flow of magic that streamed up the walls higher than the eye could follow, encasing it in a strong source of magic power.

"Who are you!?" shouted the Captain as he ordered his remaining men to take their place.

"We would like to know if anyone has used the eye recently," stated Nex plainly.

"Ludicrous!" blasted the captain. "You dare launch an attack on the tower!" he stated as he looked upon them, recognising one of them as a disciple.

"You!" he shouted at Lily. "What are you doing?" he ordered.

Lily remained silent, preparing herself. They could indeed feel there were some strong mages here.

"Heresy!" shouted the Captain. "You fools have sealed your own deaths!" he said as he ordered forward some of his soldiers. "The Three Stars will make short work of you!" he laughed as three mages stepped forward. "Destroy them!" he ordered.

Three elite mages sprang forward to engage Nex, Lily and Flowen. Flowen braced, receiving the attack of the first, a male mage.

"Freeze!" he shouted as a hurricane of Ice erupted from his hands and engulfed Flowen like an avalanche.

"You're going to beg me for death, little girl!" said another. An older woman who thought fit to attack Lily on the premise that she was the least threatening. She raised both her arms and summoned two copies of herself and they attacked the poised

Lily.

"I hope you're fast!" chuckled the third of the three stars as he began to jog on the spot and pump himself up confidently. Nex realised he was merely seeing the after image of a man who was no longer there. He turned to find the mage's punch connect with his jaw with force. Catching him off guard with his impressive speed, the mage continued to pummel his foe with his magically enhanced body.

"Chilly! slurred Flowen as he released a slice of his sword, cracking the ice that hurtled towards him.

"Wha-!" said the ice mage in shock as he prepared to release multiple attacks of ice. The barrage hit Flowen, one attack after the other as he defended, destroying each spell with his sword.

"I can see it!" he said as he sprang forwards, evading the attacks, smashing the hilt of his sword into his opponent, sending him flying into the wall behind, defeated.

"These copies are intricate!" said Lily, impressed as she battled the copies. When she seemed exposed, the mage herself attacked from her blind spot, only to receive the hilt of Lily's magical sword, sending her flying upwards and crashing into a higher part of the wall.

"TOO SLOW! TOO SLOW!" laughed the last of the three stars as he smashed Nex from each and every direction with his fists.

"Oh?" said Nex as he seized the blur by the neck, and raised the struggling man above his head. "Caught you!" he said with a sinister smile, releasing a blow into his gut to exhaust him.

Before the captain could comprehend what had happened to his elite mages, Flowen released a green wave that crashed into his remaining soldiers and defeated them all with one blast. As the captain then prepared to draw on his own power, Flowen summoned an intimidating stalactite, ten times the size of the man, to grow and rise across the room before coming to a stop between the captain's eyes.

"We just have a quick question,"

"You owe me that week's stay," whispered Lily to Nex as they approached.

"Wha!? I never agreed!" he protested.

"Don't care."

"Has anyone used the eye recently?" asked Flowen slowly, the captain unable to take his crossed eyes off the tip of the stalactite that was piercing the skin on his nose.

"N-no. No one has used it, I swear!" he cried in complete fear.

"I don't think he is lying…" trailed Nex casually.

"I'm not! I swear by the Maker!" cried the captain. "It takes a huge amount of power to use! If someone had used it, you would know!"

"And…?" encouraged Flowen.

"T-t-there were supposed to be people coming to use it. General Kleese and…and…a Sentinel! that's all I know I swear!"

Of the large, circular room, there was nothing of note around them besides the decimated Mantle soldiers. The seep of magical aura ran up the walls of the tower all the way to the eye as the source of its mystical power. This was all Nex needed to understand that this constant flow, combined with an enormous amount of personal magic power by the user, could operate the Eye. As soon as the dense, magical flow penetrated the top floor it ran towards the centre of the room like an inverted waterfall, being drained into a large, simple, silver fountain. Other than the large glass that allowed for vision in all four directions, there were no other notable features.

Although they did not need to witness it, they could all agree that the eye was a simple pedestal housing a small amount of black, gloopy looking liquid that's churns could be heard from all the way down here.

"It looks like it takes an enormous amount of magic power to use the eye," said Lily. With that, a sharp prick pierced them all as they sensed it.

"They have come," said Flowen as he looked North, sensing a great threat approaching them.
Lily and Flowen looked to each other worryingly but with a strange excitement, their shoulders feeling heavier under a dooming pressure.

Nex thought wisely for a moment as he sensed something more than his companions. He weighed up their options looking up to the floor above for inspiration.

"On second thoughts, I'm going to have a quick look at the eye," said Nex as he rummaged through the captain's pocket to find a small, dragon-stone gem. "Don't worry, I'll join you before the battle starts."

Both Lily and Flowen were excited to test themselves against the might of the threat that approached before Nex could join the fray. Deep down, they both wanted him to praise them for the efforts they were about to put in.

CHAPTER THIRTY: EYES OF DEATH

The dust and debris and bodies of the defeated moaned as it all settled. The littering soldiers stirred in their slumber and prayed that Lily and Flowen would leave the tower and take an interest in the new threat. Thankfully, they did, and they prepared themselves to exit the circular tower's northern exit and face the inevitable search party.

The northern door to the tower had been annihilated by Flowen's initial attack. The oaken door had splintered and now was left to die on their steel hinges. Lily and Flowen stepped out to greet the mages who had come all this way to hunt them. They came to a halt and looked upon the great powers that stood before them. The wind was strong now, the air brisk and uncomfortable. Nature anticipated the clashing of foes and ordered all its children to retreat. Ahead of them, the source of the tragic power was clear.

The Mantle and The Sentinels had come, in the form of incredible power. General Kleese stood tall, his gold and white Mantle military overcoat hoisted onto his shoulders, revealing his crossed muscular arms, displaying an immense strength that was only to be supported by the radiance of combat he gave off. Standing just behind him, were two great, towering figures. Giant suits of armour, hollow and impenetrable.

Flowen could not help but break the silence. "What the hell are they?" he asked, turning his head in surprise at the colossal figures.

"That's…from the Sentinel Vault," Lily gasped in surprise as she looked upon the creatures that stood before them as insurmountable and formidable as if they were a mountain.

Kleese spoke. "To think I must conquer both East and South. Henrys' failure was an unimaginable blow to the Mantle. But I wouldn't be true to my hymn if I said I was not merciful to those who repent and submit themselves to their faith."

"Kleese…" said Lily. "One of the Mantle's three Hymns, General Kleese, the Hymn of Mercy."

"Both his Holiness and General Vereoris were heartbroken when they heard the reports of your betrayal. I will assume this maleficent creature beside you is the one you now serve. Perhaps the one who fell Henrys himself." Kleese looked at Flowen thoroughly as the distaste began to show on his expression. "Demonic creature."

"There is no time for this farce," said Lily, Flowen remaining silent. "We have learned a great truth in recent days. My brother and I owe our reunion to one man and we have rightfully pledged ourselves to him. We have been beneath Eayr and witnessed the Kursed. We will force the Sentinels to heed their call and quell the taint."

"Yes, yes, I thought as much," trailed Kleese with disinterest. "You have tasted a mead too sweet and too rich for your own good and so, in your haste, you have betrayed his holiness. As you know…" he said as he brought himself closer, "We have quite the relationship with the Sentinels now, they have told us of impending threats but assured us nothing of concern will arise."

"They are lying to you," said Lily, clenching her sword with frustration.

The giant of a man stood proud and strong with muscles as

large as his magnificent magic power. Similar to Henrys, he wore the magnificent armour of the highest command of the Mantle. Kleese was golden and bright in his magic and he projected his aura over the whole battlefield with might and authority. His hostility was not as sinister or direct as that of the Sentinels they had met and was indeed filled with a mercy of sorts. In his heart, he believed what he was doing was right, and that he must uphold the peace of Ares and order beneath the Mantle. Kleese had a lovely, dark shade of skin that was lighter than that of Vosk's. From his complexion one could tell his heritage stemmed from both East and West. When such instances did occur the usual outcome of such breeding resulted in fine warriors. Barren and bare of hair, he wore only deep, inked designs on his chest, neck and shoulders.

"You both appear to be blessed by cursed swords…I can feel their hunger from here. To think you would house Illyrium blades. Perhaps the Goliath will prove to be at a disadvantage…"

"Have you come with no army?" asked Lily as she looked past him to see no reinforcements.

"Indeed. It seemed excessive for my men and Vereoris' to have such little time for recovery. There is no need for the entire might of the Mantle to defeat you. We will conquer Myphos after you have been granted his Holiness' mercy."

"So, they are not far behind you…" grasped Lily as she secretly pondered his mistaken use of the word 'we'. There was yet another spike in the atmosphere as high above them Nex had activated the eye accidently. It would appear that normally such a practice involved multiple mages all versed fluently in the rune which Gitterung bestowed upon the eye, however, with his clumsiness in the face of intricate magic, he had operated it himself. The activation of the magical item alerted every soul in Ares like an invisible shockwave of telepathic energy.

Following this, Nex plummeted, far and fast to clash with the ground beneath them with tremendous skill and fortitude. His agility ensured there was only a small crunch of the earth beneath him. He wore an awkward look on his face like he had just stubbed his toe. This indicated clearly to his companions that he did not mean to activate the eye, but in his eagerness and haste, had done, and caused them even more unnecessary trouble.

Lily and Flowen accepted their comrade's arrival and behaviour without pause or surprise. Kleese however was shocked to see such a feat. This one had obviously used the eye and yet, his magic was senseless *and* he had fallen from a tremendous height, one even the most advanced of mages would take with utmost caution. Kleese concluded that Nex's absent power was a result of the use of the eye.

"You…" trailed Kleese, "If I could not see you with my own eyes I would not believe you to be there. There is no mistaking it. And another cursed blade? Quite the trio. But to think you would have used so much of your magic power to use the eye. I can barely sense a presence from you since you have drained yourself almost completely. Perhaps you should have reserved such power for the battles to come."

Across the open expanse, where the hills clash and the forest begins to flourish, around one thousand paces away, there was another foe. Skilfully and stealthily with a guile matched only by the deadliest of hunters, a Sentinel had his bow drawn back to the point of calamity, a thin, ethereal black arrow true and unwavering in its sling. With the slightest of movements, the arrow was released and with all the force of a swooping dragon combined with the beauty and delicacy of a butterfly's wing beat, it sliced through the air at it's one, single target. In an instant it collided with an unsuspecting Nex as silently and as deadly as intended.

Undetected by both Lily and Flowen, they turned in shock as they shielded themselves from the catastrophe. Kleese, who had clearly been part of the plan to conceal one of their party, waited as he felt a presence begin to seep from the atmosphere. Nex released his aura.

Clamped firmly in his right hand which had reached over his left shoulder, Nex held the miasmic arrow which would have pierced, and probably passed straight through his lower neck. With a slight grin and a leftward turn, Nex looked to the area where the arrow had come.

"Impossible..." trailed Kleese at the sight.

"So there was another?!" asked Lily in realisation, looking in a few directions before freezing onto the same spot where Nex's glare rested. With his plan foiled and his location revealed, Raiku breathed deeply and released his concealed magic power. More sinister and more destructive than any Sentinel they had previously faced they could all feel its tenacity. The great oak that had once housed him covertly now warped and shuddered, its branches withering and cracking as he drew the life out of them with his immense, dark magic.

Raiku approached, and with a demonstration of his immense speed, joined Kleese's side in no time at all. With a sinister smile that someone powerful was before him to test his new power, Raiku spoke directly to Nex.

"To think you could catch the fastest of all my arrows whilst I had completely sealed my presence. There is no doubt in my mind that you are the monster we have been sent to find."

"*Almost* completely," corrected Nex as he gestured with a small gap between his forefinger and thumb, "But you'll find that the last steps to perfection take longer than that of the years you have already spent mastering your techniques until now."

Nex was being civil in tone but his words stung deep to the formidable Sentinel who could defeat ninety nine percent of the world population with the exertion of his magic power alone. Although with an unchanged expression, Raiku was now as annoyed as he was intrigued with the mysterious leader of rebels before him.

"What gave it away?" asked Raiku.

Nex brought his right index and middle finger together to point at the colossal suits of armour behind them. "One: Goliaths follow only the command of a Sentinel. Two: I could feel almost every part of you. Three: he said 'we'. Although I should be grateful you didn't send the Dural."

"Oh?" expanded Raiku at Nex's impressive knowledge of the legendary weapons of the Sentinels. "Then you will also know that a Goliath is completely immune to magic. Countless runes are cast inside the illyrium armour granting unparalleled magical fortitude whilst remaining completely magic resistant. Not even dragon-fire can melt it's armour completely."

"I know," stated Nex with knowledge. "But if they are made by magic, then they can be destroyed by it."

Raiku and Kleese looked upon the three silently, pondering their power and capabilities. As Flowen remained silent until the very end, his composure combated that of the Goliaths, who unless commanded, would not think, speak or move.

"No matter," said Raiku finally, "You will all die here, and your trouble will cease."

Raiku turned, nodding at the Goliaths to begin their attack. The great, soulless twenty pace high suits of armour stepped out, and walked towards them, shimmering silver armour with gold intricacies glistening in the light like the once untainted Sentinel armour.

Goliaths were impervious to magic. Lily and Flowen were not yet strong enough to pierce the Goliath's scales with their magical, cursed swords. Only pure, unaided strength would work against them. Nex nodded to his companions that he would take on the two impossible creatures alone, leaving them to choose their own opponents. With Lily's knowledge of Kleese she would probably be the best to face him. This left Flowen to tackle the corrupted Sentinel.

"This is but a mere hurdle for what is to come. To grow, you must know defeat, but you must also overcome it." His words spurred his comrades into battle with high morale. Flowen nodded in agreement and allowed Nex to wander forwards into the Goliath's path.

"There is no need to hold back, Raiku," said Kleese as he loosened his shoulders and prepared to unleash his full strength.

Lily and Flowen released their magic power, exerting themselves more than they had ever before. Their opponents reciprocated by exerting their great power too. Kleese and Raiku were on a completely different level from the two young mages, and they knew it.

The world around them began to shake and tremble. Forces like these did not meet commonly. What was to follow would be catastrophic. Lily leapt forward to attack. She knew of Kleese' magic and prepared for it. Flowen gathered his strength and unleashed a great strike of his own across the advancing Sentinels chest. That left the two towering metal giants to Nex…

Lily was struck in mid-air before her attack could connect and she was hurtled to her left from Kleese's spell. Her reflexes were just fast enough for her to block the spear with her katana. She crashed to the ground and managed to roll out of it, facing him once more. He remained still, his enormous arms still firmly crossed. Above each shoulder two golden portals with intricate magic circles circulated and out of them began to slither another four hefty, golden lances. They all fired from the portal with a magical force as if they were loaded into a heavy ballista. Faster than Lily had ever moved before she barely managed to evade the barrage as Kleese repeated this attack over and over. Disappearing from the smokescreen she emerged, high, her sword ready to cleave down upon him, only to be met with another strike from elsewhere.

Flowen put an incredible amount of power into his first strike to test his opponent. It was after a moment he had realised the effect of his attack. He looked upon Raiku who remained unscathed and was met only with a grin. From his lower back, Raiku withdrew his twin blades and prepared to engage in a melee with Flowen and his cursed sword. The two continued in a ferocious battle of blades, each displaying an incredible amount of skill and swordsmanship. It did not take Flowen long to employ a secret technique of his blade. The hidden ability for Akuma to change its length ten-fold. With this, Flowen was able to cleave at the land from afar and defend at close range with a blade that retracts in less than an instant. Raiku was skilled with his twin blades, enough so to even best the last Arcon himself in battle, but Flowen was something else. He and Akuma were one. It had only taken two or three hundred strikes before Flowen began to dominate Raiku in their melee. But Raiku's true strength did not lie in his practice with the sword. No. His skills lay elsewhere.

The dust around them scattered, the air became thin, and the darkness gathered around him in a gale. The black smog manifested at his summoned hand. Taking the form of the bow he had previously released his magic began to develop. From the handle it grew, up and up, stretching wide. "Ghandiva's Bow!" he summoned. This was his magic: A Darkness. In his left hand he gripped a destructive longbow, summoned through magic.

Unlike Flowen and Lily's katana's the bow had no physical form, and was purely and completely magical. It was around seven paces, thick and dark. It looked extremely heavy and yet he held it like it was weightless. He sniggered at the advancing Flowen, hoisting the bow toward him and drawing back on the invisible string with such precision and speed it was undeniably beautiful. As his hand travelled backwards, the bow began to spring, and as similar to how the bow manifested, an arrow began to form, sucking up the murky darkness that seeped out of the air and the ground.

At full draw, Raiku released the arrow, and it hurtled towards Flowen, the aftermath of the shot ripping up the ground in its wake. 'Such a fast draw!' thought Flowen 'But I can already see it!'

Unfortunately, this did not matter. The spell was so powerful and destructive that even though he could anticipate it, he neither had the time to dodge nor the power to defend completely. "Shit!" he cursed as he prepared his defence for a direct hit.

The Goliaths walked slowly towards Nex sensing his non-existent magic power. Devoid of ambition, fear, want or struggle they towered above the slender, young mage but they did not discriminate against his delicate, mortal frame nor his lack of power. They did not wait for conversation or analysis of its enemy and so they merely pulled back and released a physical punch at Nex, who spun to the side to dodge. Despite their large frames, the Goliaths were fast and unrelenting but of their two worst opponents they could ever face, one was before them.

Lily rose from the ground again, her left arm bleeding from a deep wound sustained from evading one of Kleese's many spears. But there were no signs of pain across her face. Both adrenaline and courage poured through her pains, increasing her threshold tenfold. To defeat this Great General, one of the Three Hymns himself, was drive enough for the young mage.

She remembered the intense training with Nex and the power he forced her to withdraw during their battles, and re engaged. She was faster now. Her power was becoming greater, and she could react to the summoning of Kleeses spears in a shorter time, giving her enough ground to close the distance between them.

"Futile!" he roared. "My magic allows me to summon the spears of Hyperion, the Titan King. Anywhere my eyes see I can summon one of his uncountable spears. You cannot possibly break through this defence!" laughed Kleese with his arms still crossed at the futility of Lily's struggle. It was no surprise, while Henrys was indeed powerful, Kleese had mastered his own magic in his own right and grown more powerful than the Hymn of Faith. Kleese's lost magic, 'Hyperion's Gate: Vault of Infinite War' was a formidable form of Lost Magic.

Flowen had also found it difficult to close the gap between himself and Raiku. The long-range attacks of his bow required a great deal of power to defend against and even with the enormity of Akuma's shapeshifting abilities the swings were too slow to catch the pluck of Raiku's fingers. But a cursed sword and demonic attributes was not all Flowen had in his arsenal. He would fight magic with magic.

"Horror Demon's: Bone Skewer!" he roared as he summoned the gnarly spikes from beneath Raiku, who dodged upwards to find himself in the path of Flowen's strike. Raiku raised his bow and blocked the great sword with its magical limbs before spin kicking Flowen away. The two relentlessly attacked each other with a fury of spells and close combat attacks.

The two monsters converged on Nex like two teigu against one elk. Despite being only minute compared to them he fought them with fists and kicks as if they were just obscenely tall men. Power-kicking one in the chest with enough force to force it back some fifty paces, he slid through the second and landed a blow to the back of its right leg, forcing it to kneel. Feeling no pain nor fear, the goliath turned quickly and swiped at Nex, who dodged, leaping over its attack. But as he landed it quickly followed up with a backhanded slap which Nex was unable to dodge. He absorbed the impact with his arms and parried the Goliath, forcing it backwards unbalanced. The impact was tremendous, the clash of the two forces created a wave that blasted across the battlefield forcing the other Goliath to fall back in its tracks and Kleese to raise his arms to guard from their battle. There was a saying in these lands: what happens when the immovable meets the unstoppable? Easy. If Nex is either one of them, then he will move the other.

Lily used the force from Nex's strike to propel her towards her target with much greater speed and was able to land a blow on Kleese.

"How is he still alive?" roared Kleese to Raiku in frustration, gesturing to the magicless man going toe to toe with, not one, but two Goliaths, a feat he could obviously not accomplish.

"He sealed his own magic power! He is the true threat!" shouted Raiku as he desperately avoided Flowen's cursed sword. For a brief moment, Lily, Flowen, Kleese and Raiku all looked at the battle in amazement. It was a wonder why Nex had not bothered to release his magic power in this incredible battle. The way he fought the two Goliaths strongly implied his physical strength was greater than each of theirs combined.

Lily continued to battle Kleese, and as she closed the gap between them, she sensed something was awry.

'He wants me to get close!' she thought in a flash as a discreet smile spread across Kleese's face. He summoned a single spear right behind her. She had only a moment to react. Just, with a millimetre to spare, she just managed to place Tsumikiri to block. It did not make solid contact, but the tip of the spear sliced into her side taking with it a small amount of flesh.

"Lily!" called Flowen as he rose.

Nex found himself in a situation he hadn't been in for a long time. If only he could remember…

Raiku raised his bow and fired a single dark arrow into the sky. "Ruined Cosmos!" A single, simple shot carried with it an enormous power as it drifted slowly and simply through the air devoid of any haste. Nex and Flowen knew this attack was different from his others. Just as the arrow rose and entered the edge of human sight, Nex, Lily and Flowen noticed the hundreds of specs raining down on them.

Lily stumbled to defend but It was hopeless. Even if she had all her strength, she could not defend against such a spell. Unable to evade, she braced for the blow. Inconceivably, Nex was already at her side raising his free hand to shield her from the rain of powerful, magical arrows that shook the earth as they fell.

CHAPTER THIRTY ONE: THE SENTINEL

The earth fell silent as the aftermath began to clear. Nex exhaled, free from any damage, shielding Lily from any harm. In his defence Flowen had activated his demonic powers and his rupture of green aura stunned them all.

"Demon!" gasped Kleese in revelation at the blind mage.

Flowen's being changed. Like he was beneath the cliffs in his dank, dark cave on his demonic throne. He had allowed the ancient demon within him to surface. Whether it was his new power or the desperation to grow stronger to protect his family, he had tapped into something he did not know he possessed. This time, however, he was in control.

The pressure he emitted pushed him into the ground whilst the gravity around him began to reverse. The force of the power he exerted forced the air away. Nature conceded at his power.

"Demon…" uttered Kleese again. "You unholy abomination!"

"This may perhaps prove interesting after all!" said Raiku as he disbanded his bow. Nex had already begun to heal Lily. He reached down and offered her his hand, pulling her up to her feet ready for his smart retort.

"I thought you were going to fight seriously?"

"Oh, shut up. I'm just getting warmed up." She brushed off the dust from her armour.

"You know it is basically cheating for me to heal you all the time," stated Nex.

"Oh, please," she protested, "he barely scratched me."

Lily could feel the pressure coming off her brother. He had increased his power and was beginning to leave her behind. This was something she could not allow.

"Healing magic?" questioned Kleese as if he was being cheated. "What is this creature?"

"Iaido-no-Shinken!" roared Lily as she summoned the magic of one the Seven Battle Gods, Himeros. She was like lightning, her sword so fast that Kleese could not defend against it fully, Lily's blade slicing across his abdomen and taking effect.

Nex returned to his prey, hunting the two Goliaths simultaneously with his strength. This battle resembled more of a fist fighting tournament where two large brawlers are pitted against an unsuspecting boy from the country, who then beats them both with his overwhelming natural ability.

With his demonic powers released, Flowen pushed Raiku onto the back foot. Even against a corrupted Sentinel it was Flowen who was the abomination. Raiku was not Nex, and Flowen found his movements more sluggish and more wasteful than that of Nex's, the master combatant.

Raiku, with all his years of training and experience had not faced a demon hybrid. He was struggling to keep up with Flowen's incredible strikes in which his foresight now found use with the amplification of its user. Finally, with Kleese on the brink of defeat, Raiku brought it upon himself to turn the tide of this battle.

"I'll commend you," said Raiku with a smile. "I did not think it would come to this." He turned to Nex for his next announcement. "To survive the Goliaths is an impossible feat. But now it is time you witnessed the full power of the Sentinels."

Raiku focused, and engaging his legendary mode, he embraced his Sentinel powers fully and erupted with a flaring scarlet energy. "This is true power!" he roared over the storm as his aura began to consume the very atmosphere. "This is death!"

Flowen's demonic form, satanic and horrifying, shuddered at the power. The fear was paralysing to all. Raiku reached out with both hands and laughed menacingly as he sought to attack the tower directly.

Crumbing and rumbling, Nex turned to see the colossal tower lean at the magic as it began to collapse. Raiku was going to pull the tower down on top of them.

"Hahaha" he laughed menacingly. He reached out with both hands, disregarding his magical bow and employing his personal Sentinel power. The aura he emitted was so pungent that neither Lily nor Flowen could penetrate it without being reduced to ashes.

"Rupture!" he roared as he activated his magic as he collapsed the enormous tower at its roots.

Nex turned to face it, raising his hands. With all his power, he held the incredible, unliftable structure still, almost half fallen.

Even Raiku, with his unleashed Sentinel power, could not comprehend the strength Nex demonstrated. It was one thing to fell the tower from its base, but to hold the enormous structure at bay with its mass leaning over them? That was another thing entirely.

But it did not matter now. Raiku's attacks had only just begun. He summoned his darkness and fired a second spell, this time at the three companions directly "Dark Apocalypse!" he roared again as he summoned an incredible spell of death.

Nex knew this spell. It was a legendary art used by ruthless and dark mages who wish only for death and power. The spell strips away flesh and magic and consumes all those caught within its effect in its withering storm of darkness, leaving the cracked bones to fall away in the wind.

Lily, who had drained an exponential amount of her power in her campaign against Kleese, did not possess the minimum requirement of power to survive the attack. The odds of the battle had shifted greatly. Nex had to make the decision in an instant.

Infinity Magic: Calamity Breaker!" roared Nex. He reached out and summoned two incredible, golden magic circles in front of his comrades that would shield them completely. Neglecting the immeasurable weight of the collapsing tower and making no attempt for his own defence he simply smiled softly with his decision and looked upon Lily who streamed tears back at him.

Nex became engulfed by the magic, its blackness burning the flesh off his very bones, melting his skin as the tower fell upon him. Even in the absence of his presence his spells remained true and strong protecting his comrades until the very end. The great tower fell, and its collapse could be felt all across all of Ares. Such a force was unmistakable.

Flowen gathered his remaining strength and raised himself, focusing his rage on his fallen comrade. He engaged both Raiku and Kleese ferociously, attacking and parrying the two simultaneously with a combination of Akuma, his demonic power and his Horror Demon Stalactites. Lily joined the fray too and the two battled the four foes responsible for Nex's untimely death. But their power was decreasing rapidly and soon they would surely be bested. Even with Kleese weakened by Tsumikiri, Lily and Flowen could do little against the two Goliaths let alone the rampaging Sentinel who kept bathing the battlefield in spells of darkness and death.

Defeated, they fell to their knees and looked to one another with a frustration and anger that neither of them had ever felt in their lives. Even with Kleese's magic drained from the cut sustained from the Tsumikiri, Lily and Flowen could not best them. Outnumbered and outmatched, this battle was over.

Raiku relaxed, and sealed his Sentinel gifts whilst the two Goliaths returned to his side in clear victory. They were all close to one another now. The scorched earth connecting them with the rubble of the fallen tower stacked upon a fallen Nex. The wounded Kleese walked slowly over to Lily and hoisted her up by her golden hair whilst Flowen objected verbally in his weakened state.

Kleese summoned a spear that slowly crept from over his shoulder and pierced the surface of the skin on Lily's neck. "While I may be merciful…" he began. "To cut my skin with such an un-holy blade riddled with curses and evil is a sin that cannot go unpunished. You will die. That is my mercy."

"Lily!" roared Flowen "I'll kill you!" he threatened Kleese. "Brother…" muttered Lily.

"Lily!" Blurted Flowen as he looked upon his sister's blood covered face.

Raiku nodded to Kleese, giving him his approval.

"Lilyy!!!!!" shouted Flowen.

Lily refused to close her eyes. She wanted her last sight to be that of her brother, of whom she had been separated from for so long and could die knowing she was complete. If she were to fade away from this world, at least she can do so looking at someone she loves. But just as the blade pierced into her neck, the cold steel was nothing compared to the animosity erupting from the rubble of the great tower. The pressure grew exponentially, to a point where it could not be measured.

Raiku and Kleese shuddered.

"This is…" muttered Raiku as his eyes narrowed in on the tower's remains.

This was like nothing they had felt before from their comrade. Not like the time beneath the mountain nor the time against the Sentinels. The air was so still and so thin it became painful to breathe. The lungs became like coarse parchment dried through the winter. Gravity shifted to a single point. An inconceivable weight pushed on them like the Maker himself stood before them and judged them unworthy with his glare. This was a terror none would hope to survive.

The rubble began to shift as Nex clawed his way out, completely rejuvenated and with unrelenting fury. As he had been ignited before by his rage, he summoned his true, cobalt blue Sentinel power that smoked through his eyes.

"I remember…" said the One Thousand Voices. The cobalt blue surrounded him. His aura erupted explosively spiking with tremendous power.

"Impossible!" stuttered Kleese in hopeless horror stepping away from Lily in terror.

"It cannot be!" roared Raiku. There was no mistaking this power. The power of Sentinels. "This is…"

"Lily!" shouted Flowen as he sprang to her and wrapped her in his arms to shield her from the god among them.

"Impossible!" roared Raiku again in disbelief and infatuation, "It is the Sentinel power but…complete."

"But- How can this be?!" questioned Kleese frantically turning back to Raiku. "That's…"

"Despair!" said One Thousand Voices. Raiku turned to the Goliaths and ordered them forward.

"Destroy him!" The Goliaths reflected its master's desperation and now sprinted at full speed towards the new threat, the ground trembling beneath their feet. Dismounting the rubble with a hefty thud, cool and collected, Nex proceeded to greet his enemy in kind. When the first Goliath came upon him it released an incredible punch, the force of which could have dropped the tower all over again.

Nex, who was now sprinting to meet it with the full brunt of his fury, retaliated with a punch of his own. The two fists connected in mid-air and the shockwave forced Kleese, Lily and Flowen to fall to the floor at its impact. With Nex's fist firmly planted onto the Goliaths, the shimmering of its armour gave away the breach in its perfect, impenetrable hide.

The Goliaths armour rippled and crimpled up its arm until it reached its shoulder, shattering as the reverberations of impact desperately caused the atoms within to explode at the containment of such inescapable energy. It was like it was made of glass and, in that moment, the undefeated and unfeeling creature felt fear for the first time.

It raised its left arm and attempted to smash it down on the human in pure hopeless desperation only to find Nex release another blow to its chest, the force of the punch removed the entire head and torso of the Goliath in one, leaving the empty, metal vessel to fall to the ground.

The second had not yet met Nex but it did not need to. It could already feel itself becoming weightless and its limbs non-respondent to its will. Nex, grappling at the air with his magic, crumpled the entire Goliath as if it were a can of vegetables. Now half the size, the hunk of metal fell to the floor.

Kleese was lost for words, fear had successfully consumed

him. For a mythical weapon such as these, undefeated and unrelenting, to be defeated by a human in such a manner, was declared impossible.

"Gah…" uttered Raiku.

"Forgive me," said One Thousand voices. Nex raised his Shirasaya out in front of him to symbolise the use of his most powerful weapon.

That's…" trailed Lily and Flowen.

Nex sprang with immense speed. To the surrounding eyes he disappeared, moving so fast the eye could not follow, an explosion of wind from the impact of his movement and a crater of cracked earth beneath where he once was with trails of his signature cobalt blue magic in his wake. In that instant, he reappeared in front of Kleese. Nex was already there, the tip of the sheath struck firmly into Kleese's gut.
"Sealed sword third form: Crashing pillars of heaven," he said. Even famed for his considerable defensive strength and muscle fibres that resembled the composition of iron, Nex broke through his armour and abdomen like a knife through warm butter beneath an oil lantern.

'Impossibly fast!' they all thought. Lily and Flowen still could not comprehend that, even with all this magic power in front of them, fluttering in the wind was the small piece of parchment that remained on the string around the bandages that fastened his Shirasaya shut. This sword was yet to be unsheathed.

Nex rose from Kleese and looked upon the one, remaining foe. Fear and desperation soon spread across Raiku's expression. With eyes wide he re-released his Sentinel power and began to summon his bow. It was almost as though Nex allowed him the time to make such pre-battle preparations. In an expert, singular movement Raiku had summoned a great arrow and drew back the ethereal string. But he felt the sheath of the sealed Shirasaya strike his drawing arm and the spell was completely negated.

Raiku sprang back and managed to recover despite the great pain that shocked not only his arm but his senses, too. Releasing a flurry of dark spells frantically towards Nex to conceal a partial withdrawal, he released gust after tornado after barrage of spells. With one great strike, Nex cut the very magic itself apart with the sealed sword.

"Infinity Magic..." began Nex as he brought his right hand in front of him in its signature movement, his middle and forefingers poised to the sky whilst his thumb held the remaining fingers down.

"Noooooooo!" Screamed Raiku defiantly as refused to accept such a possibility. He, the Arcon's right hand, the second most powerful Sentinel in all the world, would know defeat at the hands of some commoner absent of name or glory. Any hopes and dreams of progression amongst the Ten Kings would surely be just as annihilated by Nex's spell as his body was about to be.

"Trinity Abyss!" Nex released a top tier spell, just as he normally did, but the magic power he poured into it was more than he had in any previous attack they had witnessed. The three pillars of light around Raiku that quickly began to orbit his person, their speed increasing, getting faster and faster until they became one golden light, moving closer and closer before erupting through him with a mighty howl. Raiku, was defeated and the plains in which this battle had taken place fell silent. But for only a moment did the air become breathable and nature itself sigh with relief.

For another unnatural presence had arrived. Nex turned to see standing near the collapsed tower was a final, mysterious mage. He was in pitch black robes that themed Flowen's attire.

Lacking any flare or expense he was very simple with plain, knee high armoured boots and a black cloak to engulf him. He had thick, long black hair and a small, stubbled beard. He was handsome and stoic, perhaps totalling an age in the mid-forties. Unkempt and seemingly uncaring of his appearance and his intrusion, he spoke free of hostility.

"What's going on here?" he asked in a tempered tone. "Oh? My tower?" Though free of anger or malice the man who spoke demanded their attention. Even with the storm of Nex's power upon them, gushing and whooshing around the area like a typhoon, it was nothing compared to the man who stood casually next to his fallen tower.

This kind of power was impossible. A god perhaps? A Titan who has taken human form? Acting with caution was their only hope for survival.

"Your...tower?" muttered Lily in awe at the mages claim, witnessing his tremendous power first-hand that was incomparable to Nex's.

But Nex's awakening did not source him only his power. A cloud of irrepressible memories and emotions had filled his mind. A past long forgotten, cursed to endure and tortured to live, Nex, as he was, could not contain it all. Armed with animosity and a desire to return to the creature of darkness he once was, Nex would destroy all who faced him in defence of his allies.

As his many years of battle had taught him, he had a very specific imprint upon his body. An imprint that declared all creatures of power to be his enemy. He had no intention of greeting the mysterious figure with words. Sensing an impending explosion of malice from Nex's aura which would only increase, Gitterung knew, too, that there was no room for discussion.

He raised his right hand and presented his palm. With a spell he need not speak, he intensified the gravity around Nex one hundred thousand times over. This simple indication pummelled him into the ground and defeated him. Buried by the force and with his mind slipping away from consciousness, Nex's magic power slipped away from him, letting the wind sweep back in with its subtle gust.

"By the Maker, what a creature," stated Gitterung to the remaining mages.

"Nex…with one strike…?" gasped Lily in disbelief as she clambered around, Flowen hurrying over to her in wary of this unknown mage.

"I am Gitterung," he stated. "I came because you destroyed my tower," he said plainly, but without fury.

"Gitterung…" trailed Lily in awe of his legendary name.

"Odin's…Ten Kings…" muttered Raiku as he clambered upwards.

"It seems you were battling one another, and this one," he said as he looked to Nex, buried into the ground "uses Infinity Magic. Quite the find."

Raiku and Kleese raised themselves and barked at Gitterung, weary of his power.
"You should not…interfere."

"Yes, yes" he agreed. "It would be unwise for me to involve myself in the squabbles of the Aresian Empire. After all, it will be nothing but dust soon."

"Mind your tongue!" snapped Raiku in defence of the corrupted Sentinels and his master. "Though powerful you may be, Gitterung, do not make light of our new power."

Gitterung chuckled slightly at the retort glaring at the two through his dark, unkempt hair. "Power this one easily bested. Frankly, I don't care. I came for my tower and I see it is destroyed and now I happen across a great battle that has found its conclusion." With disinterest to the 'powerful' mages before him, the corner of his jet black eyes caught sight of the remains of the Goliaths, one missing its complete torso and the other crumpled like parchment. For whatever reason, this brought a slight startle to one of the Kings of Odin.

Kleese looked to Raiku to tell him that this was not a fight they could win at full power let alone with the injuries they had both sustained and the lack of magic that remained within them. Witnessing Gitterung destroy the monstrous Nex with a little exertion worried even them, a high General and the Second-in-command Sentinel. Retreat became more and more attractive by the second.

"Fear not," he spoke again as if to read the minds of all, "A dragon would not hunt a fly. What we are meant for is nigh on the horizon. It is of little consequence what your organisations scheme to accomplish. At The Dawn, we will be there," his words resonating through the air with power and gravitas.

The Sentinel Temple, filled with great and powerful magic, had an ancient flame of magic etched into tirs core: The Nexus. This ever burning, now crimson flame could Recall any member of the order who resonated with it. In this instance, Raiku would Recall to the Nexus to ensure his survival. If they were to attempt to strike their enemies, would Gitterung intervene? Did he seek some form of revenge against his tower? It was a risk neither of them dared to take.

"So be it, Gitterung," said Raiku as he made his decision. His body and that of Kleese's and the two Goliaths' remains began to fade away into a scarlet smoke as the teleportation spell pulled them home to the Capital. Through clenched teeth bitter with rage and resentment the two returned to the sanctity of the Nexus. Only our heroes remained, and the incredible mage, Gitterung.

"As for you two, we have watched you both carefully. Odin himself has taken an interest in you. Two Kings must be replaced. Before the Dawn, when you are ready, we will return." he added as he looked down upon the blind demon and the Mantle assassin. He looked to his tower in ruin without any emotion or disappointment. "That took me an age to build, you know..." he said in slight disappointment as he let out a sigh, revealing a more human side to the monster that he was.

CHAPTER THIRTY TWO: SOUL FRACTURE

There was not much to eat or drink in the days where the three young children were housed in their steel cells. Whittled down to two from three only the girl with the glistening moonlit hair and the balding one remained. Taken for ritualistic training, the third never returned.

"Say," spoke the soft voice of the young girl. "Does it hurt?" she asked, holding her arms in discomfort at the pain from her previous ritual, one of them broken and in a sling.

"Hmm…" thought the young boy as he looked into his hands, pondering the right words to say, finding only the truth as the viable option. "I am sure we will get used to it," he lied in effort to comfort his friend.

"Soul fracturing is the most painful experience for any living creature to endure. Each time enacted the soul splits. The severing of the soul, something purely spiritual and phantasmal, is unnatural. It is something Eren could no longer endure."

"But to be broken so many times…." she cried, "can we even be human anymore? Can we still be alive?"

The young boy looked at his friend with a kind smile. "Of course, we are! Here, see?" he said as he crawled low from the straw bedding on the cold cobbled floor to push his arms through the gaps in the rails.

"You're warm," she said, holding his hand.

"Now, see?" he said as he brought the temperature of his body down below zero.

"So cold!" she exclaimed but holding on tightly. "Eek!" she yelped as she drew back. The young boy had released a small, tingly spark from his skin that sent a gentle spark to the young girl.

"Ah!" she shouted.

"See?" he said in clarification.

"Pain, emotion, warmth, 'freezing cold', shock, shortness of breath, this is the proof you are alive. You know I must become strong but no matter my destiny, I promise I will always protect you always."

The young boy repositioned himself into a more serious seated position before he spoke his next words. "To be born with our souls already fractured naturally is rare, even among us, *that* is why we are here. That is what makes us special. And once we are done here, we will go on our endless adventure!"
"Hmm," she agreed with a soft smile as she examined the palm which had been shocked.

"To be strong...to protect" she pondered.

"When we are free, I promise, we will never set foot on this mountain again!"

"When we are free..." she trailed in excitement, a glisten of hope in her eye.

"Free to travel the world. Every night, we will light a fire and be one with the trees and creatures of the wilderness. Wherever we go we will look to the goddess of the moon and thank her for the gift of life and freedom!" he assured her.

The young girl's eyes lit up at the mention of the great moon above them. "Oh, I love the moon. I am certain that Amaterasu watches over us, even now!"

"Mhmm," he confirmed. Below the moonlight that beamed into their cells they both sat with their backs against the wall beneath the only windows in their un-homely space. Reaching through the bars they held each other's hands in comfort.

"Do you think you're in trouble?" she asked, rubbing her broken arm.

"It was worth it," replied the boy. "The moment I felt his arm snap I knew it was worth one hundred nights of back to back rituals!"

"I'm sorry for causing you so much trouble," she said.

The young boy thought of his day of training, and how his instructor had broken his young friend's arm. In retaliation, this young boy had overpowered his instructor comfortably, and returned the favour.

"You could never cause me any trouble. You are the only thing in this world that matters to me."

"I don't think that's true anymore! I have seen the way you look at her. You're just as excited to see her as much as I am. I wonder if she'll come back?" asked the young girl.

"Hmm, I wonder…" trailed the boy. They both thought of the guest who had visited them a few months prior and continued to do so frequently since. When the three prisoners had become two, a small, yet beautiful young girl had somehow managed to enter the compounds of the temple undetected. Between the back of the cells that faced the great, vying oaks of the perilous mountainside was the perimeter of the temple laid high with ancient stone. But here, in this town that rests high up the mountain, nothing was not magically enchanted.

The elders themselves had bestowed the town in protection. Even the strongest of wild creatures could not enter. But this young girl, a slip of the size of the young boy, even rivalling the malnourished, moon haired young girl had been visiting them in the dead of night. With golden hair like that of the purest sunlight and eyes with crimson that outshone the purest of ruby she was mystical and mysterious, and the only friend of the two young prisoners.

"Yes, yes!" said the young boy with a smile. "If she says she will come, she will! She's always true to her word, always."

"But I was thinking…" said the young girl softly with unease. "Do you…d-do you think…" with all her might, she could not get out her true feelings. Timid and tame was her nature, to thrust a suggestion on her kind-hearted friend seemed impossible. But, of course, he was accommodating. He already knew what was on her mind.

"Perhaps we should ask her to come on our everlasting adventure with us?" he pondered as if the thought was his own.

"Yes!" she exclaimed quickly as a beautiful smile crossed her face, a rare sight for him, which he adored above all else in this world. "Definitely! I do really hope she wants to come!"

"WHAAAAAAAAAAAAAAAAAAT? Of course, she would! Who wouldn't want to go on an everlasting adventure with people as cool as us?!" he exclaimed, his excitement pouring out of him on this rare occasion.

"We don't have any other friends. The Elders have never let us meet with the other children of the village."

"It's their loss, I'm sure. You and I are, by far, the two coolest people I know." said the boy.

"Then we should ask her," she said, making up her mind.

"Definitely," he agreed.

Two more moons passed and with the time came more gruelling rituals and magic training and yet neither of them had awakened. But, true to her word, the young girl returned to them in the dead of night.

Customarily these days, both prisoners would peer out of their small, steel barred windows to await their young friend's appearance. And, after what felt like an eternity of watching, springing down over the enchanted wall, the young girl fell, her long, golden hair trailing in her wake. She landed with ease making not even enough sound to startle a butterfly and began to the bars where her friends waited with uncontainable anticipation and excitement.

"Good evening," she spoke softly to them both with a decorum and accent that only a royal education could provide, concealing a small wicker basket behind her with both hands.

"Anna!" they both whispered as loud as they could without being heard. "Good evening!"

"I have brought you both some food from a feast we had this evening," she stated as she brought her wicker basket to their attention. "Here."

She opened the lid and from the basket withdrew, quite possibly, the finest treats of this world. First, small, sweet cakes glazed with sugar and ornamented with different slithers of fruit.

"These were known as 'cup-cakes'."

Then, she withdrew what looked to be a large 'normal' cake coated in powdered white sweetness centred with the whipped milk of a pure white cow which was lathered with the mush of the blackest of dark berries. She called this a 'sponge'. Finally, in long, tall, wooden containers sealed at the top with iron lids, the smoothest and most fruity liquid. It was a combination of fruits no one had ever heard of and sugar all doused with the freshness of a great waterfall.

As her manners dictated, Anna had not eaten her portion, and had brought it with her so she could share in the lushness with her two, dear friends. For there was no greater enjoyment to a feast if they could not all share in it together.

"Thank you!" they shouted in unison, through the bars, bringing their hands together and bowing their heads with sincere gratitude. The young girl did the same whilst they were met with a coy smile from the golden-haired Anna.

"How are you both, my dear friends?" she asked as she handed them over and they ate their food together, resting it on the small window ledges.

"Anna!" shrieked the young girl unable to contain her excitement and, with great fortitude, refusing to eat her incredible food before asking Anna the question. "Would you like to come on our everlasting adventure?"

"An everlasting…adventure?" she asked, unsure of the term.

"An adventure, where we can go wherever we want and do whatever we want. We can see the whole world, just the three of us, that lasts forever!"

As she said this, Anna's face lit up with excitement. They could see in her eyes that she was overjoyed with their proposal. But after a short time, the smile dropped from her face. The differences in their worlds were truly vast and although it seemed like the two prisoners were the only ones who could not be free, Anna too, lived in a prison of her own.

"I…don't think I would be allowed…" she admitted.

"By the Gods," began the boy, "when we are free, there will not be a reason in this world to keep our feet firm on the soil. We will wander, we will travel, and we will see everything!"

"But…My father would not allow it," said Anna.

"But if it's what you want, would he listen to your request?" he asked. "Surely-" he stopped himself from saying any more.

"He has a duty…" she began, "and, one day, that duty will be mine. We cannot escape our Maker's design."

"But-" began the silver haired girl before she was interrupted.

"Of course!" said the boy. "If you have your own destiny and dreams then they are yours to follow. It is that freedom to choose which is most important."

Anna looked up to him in adoration. He was right. True, he was only sparing her feelings and did not wish to rub salt in the wound, but, yet, he was right. All three of these young children were indeed prisoners in their own way and none of them could be free. If they truly wished for freedom above all else, they must be willing to cast everything they loved aside. This harsh reality was one that burdens these three children heavier than most.

"Perhaps, one day, your father might understand," said the boy in comfort. "And, it doesn't matter where or when or what, when you call we will always answer and there will be a place at our sides reserved only for you."

"Thank you…" said Anna. "I will definitely dedicate my thoughts to it. If I could only pluck up the courage to ask my father."

"There is no rush, as of yet. After all, we are both still stuck in here." He gestured to their cells with discomfort and protest. They, too, could not begin their lifelong adventure so prying into Anna's constrictions would not yield them any results.

The silver haired young girl was now making no waste of the

treats that Anna had brought them. She scoffed them down gluttonously as if they were to expire any moment from now. Of course, one would expect that Anna would have brought them fine bread or cured meats from her divine banquets, but as she quickly learned, those foods would be wasted on them. Both prisoners were vegetarian, as their whole village was, but also, above all else, they craved nothing more than sweet treats. Both, forever and a day, could live only on these 'sweets' as Anna called them.

"Eto, your arm!" said Anna as she raised her hand. Releasing a pure, ambient golden shine the malnourished young girl with moon kissed hair felt her arm begin to repair itself in her radiant spell before the young boy raised his hand in protest.

"Thank you, Anna, but the Elders will know. It will only make things worse…"

"Oh…" trailed the girl as she withdrew herself. "I didn't think."

"I'm sorry, Eto, but if she heals your arm now, the Elders will be convinced that it was you who healed yourself. If you cannot reproduce the spell in front of them it will only bring you more pain," said the boy.

"It's okay!" she smiled. "These cakes are so tasty I can barely feel it anymore."

"No," began the boy, "you're right. Sorry, Anna, would you please continue."

"But what about the Elders?"

"I am a fool. There is nothing more precious to me. I cannot turn a blind eye to her pain no matter what may lay ahead. I am sorry, Eto, how could I be so selfish?" he said.

"Are you sure?"

"I will say that I healed her. Anything that comes from it will be my punishment for being so blind. Please Anna, if you would."

She could feel the resolve in his voice as he spoke. She raised her hand and healed Eto fully.

"Thank you," he said.

"But N-" she began.

"No. You will not carry this pain, too. Now, enjoy these splendid treats that Anna has brought us! If you don't eat them then we will!"

They all laughed as they raced down the fantastic treats. "Tell us Anna, are there any interesting stories from the world around us?"

"Well," she began…

They could all be at ease, chatting and munching through the night until the sun blinked at them over the peak of the mountain, signalling that Anna must return home before anyone could become the wiser of her absence.

"Oh no! The sun is already rising!" exclaimed Anna as she scrambled and clawed at the evidence of her visit and stored it back in the small wicker basket. "I'm so sorry, I have to get back before my father knows I have gone!"
"Thank you so much for the treats!" said the boy, adopting his position of gratitude once again navigating the steel bars.

"Thank you, Anna! Come see us again whenever you can!"

"I will! Next week, on the full moon this time!" said Anna, already heading for the wall, her golden hair blessing the rear courtyard with its grace, before, with one spring, she leapt and cleared the whole, twenty-pace wall with ease. And like that, she was gone.

With her silver hair trailing down the wall the young prisoner sat back down to recover from their night of wonder. Despite the huge exhaustion of the ritual training they both felt revitalised by the great events of the night. The boy copied her in tune and exhaled slowly at the wonder of their friend.

"What a girl…" he said in awe. "You know," he looked to his friend, "you never talk so much when it's just you and I, but when Anna is here, you're the most talkative creature on earth."

"She is just…so lovely," she exclaimed.

"Mhmm…" he agreed, picturing her face in his mind.

"I cannot wait for our adventure to begin, now! To see the world and everything in it. How truly marvellous," said the girl with the moondust hair. "We'll always be together. You and I will be the greatest adventurers this world has ever seen! We will do such great things that even Amaterasu herself will bestow us with thanks! We will be the greatest Ankou to ever have lived!"

"That we will," he smiled.

As the two prepared for their day of training with their hopes and dreams held high, a darkness was to pass over them and their fortunes. Life, light and hope would all be extinguished in one fell swoop.

CHAPTER THIRTY THREE: WAVERING STARLIGHT

"Gah!" blurted Nex as he regained consciousness to find his head nursed gently on Lily's lap.

"Nex!" she spoke softly as he came about. This form of positioning was something only done between people of close bonds. Nex found extreme comfort on her delicate thighs as he caught her beautiful gaze.

"Hold on," said Flowen.

"Why?" she asked in protest.

Flowen turned his attention to Nex, who now began to rise to his feet and break away from Lily as he sensed the tension in the air.

"He is not just a Sentinel. There is something he is not telling us!" snapped Flowen, resentment and hostility in his voice.

"So?" said Lily, "he is still our friend"

"We can understand why you would keep your secrets…but just how many are there? How much is there that you are not telling us? We both almost died. *You* almost died! These people who we keep fighting, they are insanely powerful! Why have you kept so many things a secret from us? That mage, he said he will return. Nex, I am truly grateful to you for reuniting Lily and I, but I cannot hope to approach that man's power. I cannot protect Lily against the calamities you attract!"

"Flowen!" said Lilly with displeasure at her older brother's attitude.

"No Lily, He can't hide the truth from us any longer," said Flowen.

"I-" began Nex before Lily interjected.

"What does it matter?" she snapped. "It makes no difference to me whether he is a Sentinel or not. Whether he is a mage or not. Whether he is a God or a Titan or *Demon* or anything else. I love him for who he is and he is part of my family now, regardless of any secrets or past mistakes he has made. He is *our* friend" said Lily firmly as she broke towards Flowen and forced her words upon him. "Did he bat an eyelid in accepting me as an assassin? The countless innocent people that I have killed. Did he question the decisions you made, the people that you slaughtered in cold blood, the demon that you have become? No, he did not. And yet you have the gall to question him? Even if the Maker himself tries to prize us apart I will not leave his side!"

Flowen bowed his head in shame, processing the words that ripped at his skin more damaging than that of any blade. He spoke only in defence of his sister, of which he wanted to keep from harm.

"In a way..." began Nex, thinking he did, indeed, need to explain himself, "I am a Sentinel. But not like the ones you know. I was...I am-"

"You're right" said Flowen, disappointed in his previous behaviour "We are friends, regardless. I owe you much, Nex. More than I can ever repay. I defended your decisions before only to now go back on my own word. That makes me nothing but a hypocrite."

Lily took Nex's hand and held it between hers, smiling through her injuries.

"Do not let what I have done sway your decision. You are together now and free. I could never take away your freedom due to such a minor deed of mine. If you wish to part I will bear you no ill will. You are my friends and I want you to be happy."

"I...am sorry, Nex," apologised Flowen. "It was wrong of me. I do not follow you because it is only what my sister wants. I am grateful, yes, but you are my friend."

There was a long silence as the cold wind and air came between them. Nex approached Flowen and placed his hand on his shoulder. "Thank you."

"We sure got our asses kicked though, right?" said Lily, her warmth radiating to lift the hearts of both men.

"Oh, right!" said Nex as he raised his free hand to Flowen and emitted a healing spell on both his companions. "This should take the edge off."

"Ah!" sighed Lily in relief as the spell healed her wounds.

"That's very handy," admitted Flowen as his body became lighter, too.

"It's definitely cheating," added Lily.

"My head is ringing from that tower. Who was that, anyway?" asked Nex as he looked towards the collapsed tower for the mage that defeated him so easily.

"I think," began Lily, "It was Gitterung."

"Yeah." agreed Flowen.

"As in the same guy that built the tower?" asked Nex curiously.

"Yeah, although he didn't seem too heartbroken," said Lily.

"Did he say anything? Where is he now?" he asked.

"He said that 'Odin' has taken an interest in us. He also referred to something known as 'The Dawn' and he assured as, above all, that our paths would cross again," said Flowen.

"I am not surprised. If everything you have told me about the Ten Kings is true it was only a matter of time for you both," said Nex as he thought back to his reasons for approaching the two of them in the first place.

"He finished you in one attack, even whilst you were using your Sentinel Powers!" said Lily in astonishment.

"I didn't think I'd ever see you lose…" trailed Flowen at Nex's incredible power.

"Well I definitely feel like someone just dropped a moon on me!" laughed Nex to his companions, the atmosphere just like it always was with the three of them.

"I underestimated the power of those mages. They were all really quite strong, " admitted Nex.

"I told you!" snapped Lily in excitement, an opportunity to point out that he was wrong.

The three had not moved since Nex's defeat at the hands of Gitterung. Around them, the green fields and magnificent tower was now a large wasteland of exerted power. The ground was hard and scorched from the various magical attacks. The great tower was now nothing more than rubble strewn across the landscape. If anyone inside was to have survived they would have surely escaped through the Southern exit so as to not enter the clashing of titanic forces.

"So, what now?" asked Flowen as the great battlefield began to rest. Nothing was around them. All life was empty and still.

"I must reach the Nexus within the Sentinel temple. I can extinguish that flame and bring an end to this corrupted Sentinel order. There is also something I must uncover from their ancient library. Once that is done, my struggle against the Kursed will begin. But first, beneath the mountain, there was a voice. Did you hear it?" Nex asked.

"We could not ignore it. I can still hear the evil ringing inside my mind," said Flowen.

"The seals are broken. There is no time for us to be fighting amongst ourselves," said Nex

"The Kursed..." added Flowen in thought.

They all exchanged a depressing glance before Nex spoke once more. "The Kursed have returned, and with them, the reincarnated generals, The Seven Dreads. After the great war, with this fate unavoidable it was ordered that seven mountains be hollowed out at the hands of Titans. Each Dread would be entombed, deep beneath it. They have now been reborn and now commune with their Immortal King. The Kursed will not truly rise until their fallen God has been awakened," said Nex.

"The Seven Dreads?" asked Lily. "What...are they?"

"Creatures consumed by the Kursed. Titans, humans and even Gods. Each is second only to the Immortal King. And the one who spoke to us, she announced herself at the mountain pass. She calls to me now," said Nex as he bestowed ancient knowledge upon his allies.

"You can hear her?!" exclaimed Lily. "I am a Sentinel. I can hear the cries of the wicked. The corruption of the Sentinel order is due to the heart of Asashima, a Kursed artefact. What they do not know is that they have become the very evil they were sworn to destroy. This sin is mine to bear."

"And this Kursed General survived the collapse of the mountain?" snapped Lily as she stepped forth in protest.

"Sentinel magic is the only power in this world that can destroy the Kursed once and for all. Anything else will only lead the creatures to reincarnate into new flesh. Now, I must ask of you both something that no ally should ever ask of his comrades." he said shamefully, his gaze falling to the ground.

"Infinity Magic, a sealed sword that can dispel magic with one swing, One Thousand Voices, the Sentinel Magic from the ancient tribe of the Ankou. How can you be human?!" asked Lily in awe of Nex's traits.

"I am not only the creature you see before you. I am the Nexus of humanity. I am the Sentinel."

"We will do as you ask," assured Flowen, trying to swiftly recover from his earlier insubordination.

"Right," confirmed Lily. "No matter what you are, we will fight, too."

"A dread is not something either of you are ready to face. It is a battle that I cannot risk either of your lives. The Kursed do not kill, they consume and devour. Even if I fail in my task, I will return. But there is also a threat to our North. The forces of the Mantle are to collide with the remnants of the rebel army. I can feel it. You must try to warn them all what is coming. Otherwise, there will be no world left for them to rule If another old God rises again as the Kursed King or Queen. I, and I alone, will silence her screams. Should I succeed I shall not be far behind you and you. I will always sense you here," Nex brought his fist to his chest over his heart.

Indeed, their bonds allowed them to sense each other, no matter the distance. This was also due to a subtle enchantment Nex had placed upon them in secret.

"We will continue North," she stated as Flowen nodded in stern agreement, "and we will wait for you to join us. Our victories so far cannot be ignored."

Nex thought for a moment as he processed their words. They knew the power of their opponents, yet without fear or hesitation they would move forward.

"If only I had your courage when I was young," said Nex in admiration.

'Tss, ' said Lily, kissing her teeth. "Who do you think we got it from?"

"Try not to fall too far behind. I want to go somewhere nice and have a few drinks sometime soon," said Flowen. "I'm sure in the meantime there will be plenty of small fry before we hit any more big fish."

"Kleese said the whole army of the Mantle was coming for the Southern Kingdom. There is no doubt we will run into them before we reach the capital there. It is unlike Piaus or Thusien will venture south which leaves only Vereoris as the likely intercept. We must hope that the rebellion has some power houses themselves. There's no other chance of us defeating the Hymn of Wrath," declared Lily, carefully surmising the options before them strategically.

"In defence of Myphos they will attempt to invade North. To the east, there is a place where the two armies would likely meet. This will allow the forces behind them to fortify at the border for the true battle. It is a bold tactic but it has proved to succeed throughout their history as an independent kingdom."

"That's a good idea," agreed nex.

"It sounds like they are going to get smashed anyway…" admitted Flowen honestly.

"You two have already become so strong and yet you have merely scratched the surface. Rally with the Southern Kingdom's forces. They will likely be grateful for assistance in the form of you two," said Nex, still in awe of them, remembering the days back when he did not have the courage to act, despite all his power.

"When we meet again, we will be even stronger," said Lily with a smile as she wrapped her arms around Nex.
"Without a doubt!" added Flowen.

"Then I'll meet up with you in a few days!" shouted Nex as he began to jog back towards the rubble of the great tower. "Don't go too far ahead without me!" he added as his voice slipped away into the wind as he made distance between them.

Nex was facing reality. Their enemies were indeed very powerful. The mages of this era are indeed strong. He had to reach the Sentinel flame that burned within the Nexus. But Nex knew that he had to stop the Kursed above all else, even at the cost of his most precious friends. Seeds of doubt were flourishing into roots deep into his weary mind.

"See you!" waved Lily with a smile as she watched Nex disappear. She and Flowen began Northwest toward the most direct route from the South in Nex's stead. Meeting with that mysterious young mage had already changed both of them beyond comprehension. Now, they both possessed far greater power than they had ever had. But, more importantly, they had found something to live for. It was not power or fame or riches or title, they had something to protect and something to fight for. They were as scared and fearful as Nex thought, but they moved forward with courage and the lust of challenge. Battle had never tasted so sweet to either of them. Fighting for something other than themselves...

CHAPTER THIRTY FOUR: THE SEVEN DREADS

Lily and Flowen continued north still laughing and jeering at the stories each had to tell and living this new life of theirs free of the burdens of guilt and purpose. A lifetime of memories missed that spared none for the future. Reunited they would never let go of one another. They both discussed to great lengths all their secrets. Their bond was cemented and renewed as if they had spent no time apart. Finally, they began to discuss the mage responsible for all of this and his safety as he was to indefinitely battle something far worse than the two of them could ever imagine.

"How is it that Nex knows so much about these blades? To find them in all the world and to even lift the curses. I have sensed it for some time now, but even his Shirasaya resembles Akuma and Tsumikiri in ways I cannot describe. It is not a sister blade but a parent?" said Flowen.

"He is rather reticent. He thinks that with each detail he tells us he burdens us. But it is quite the opposite. We are happy to take some of that burden from him. You can see it in his eyes, he knows more about the three cursed blades than anyone. It's almost as if he plucked the stars from the sky and made them himself!" Lily and Flowen looked at one another and laughed awkwardly.

"They are thousands of years old…" he stated in worry. "It could be a coincidence"

"I would have thought that a few weeks ago," admitted Lily. "But nothing is a coincidence with Nex. He is always on about 'destiny this' and 'fate that'. Of all the world, our swords were in Ares. Further to that, the ones who held them just so happened to be you and I. Nex told me that it is not just a principle of compatibility with these swords. It was both their destiny and ours to be united. It's not that the sword was waiting for someone of its choosing. It was that, for all those years in the Mantle's ownership, with hundreds, if not thousands of mages trying to steal this blade for their own, the blade was simply waiting for me, and me alone."

"Is that true?!" said Flowen at the story. Could such a thing be true? Was Tsumikiri destined for Lily and Lily alone? And was it a coincidence that he held the second blade? He, who shares the same blood as Lily. His sword did not have the luxury of choosing a wielder from the myriad of mages. Housed, deep beneath the cold stone of a cottage where he spent some weeks of his life, the sword whispered into his mind. Was it sheer chance that he was there, at that time in all of History, with the sword buried beneath him?

With half a day between them it was certain that at this time Nex would soon be engaging his mortal enemy, the dreaded general of the Kursed army buried millennia ago beneath the Eayr Mountains. But they were soon to have their own perilous battles ahead of them. They continued north towards where the armies of the southern kingdom were sure to meet the Mantle's advance. But over the hills and across the fields where they could see what looked to be the encampment of the southern kingdom's army, a small group of three stood between them.

These Sentinels blocked Lily and Flowen's advance but had been sent as a forward party to pierce an unsuspecting army. Little did they know, this was the path of our heroes.

This was a battle that Lily and Flowen must overcome if they are to hope to begin to approach what it is that Nex and Odin had seen in them. Something alien to the siblings was that Nex placed them in high esteem. He saw that they would become great mages under his stewardship and that it was their destinies to release this. So, lost in their previous worlds they had all but forgotten how humans can help each other grow. Nex had more faith in them than they did in themselves and this faith and hope ignited them.

"We can take them!" said Flowen as they summoned their swords to battle the great Sentinel warriors. 'They feel weaker. Their auras are less menacing. I can breathe more freely under the weight of my chest. Are they weaker than what we have faced so far? No. we, have grown stronger.'

Back over the roving hills and scorched battlefields to the south beneath a pouring storm, Nex found himself in the presence of the one he hunted. He had intercepted her as she clawed from beneath the rubble under the mountain, her horde not far behind her. Those powerful enough to remain close to protect her had already been annihilated by Nex. Only she remained, beckoning her horde to follow.

The Kursed are a manifestation of evil itself. It is true that they are living creatures. They will feel fear for their lives, and they will breed and live for themselves unless ordered to do otherwise. But deep inside them is a hunger that they cannot ignore, a desire they can never be free of. However, the Kursed do not have souls like you and I. Born of the tainted and rotten flesh poured into the world by all the races they are but the will of one Immortal. To increase their numbers, they began to consume the living. But they consume not only the flesh for their brood-mothers, but also the soul. That soul, which is then converted into life energy, deletes the being of the creature it once belonged to. Therefore, it can never pass on to the afterlife and re-join the Maker or be reincarnated. All victims of the Kursed are consumed and destroyed, forever.

Powerful creatures will have the fortitude of the soul to maintain their being, but even they will still be slaves to the desires of the Immortal King who will lead them. There may possibly be only one person on this world who knows the truth behind Sentinel Magic. Its cobalt blue is the essence of the soul itself. As the flesh of Kursed is also made from souls, normal magic cannot slay them. Sentinel Magic is the only way. This method destroys the Kursed permanently. However, what happens to the souls next is-

"Akeidna," stated Nex to the tall creature before him. The Titaness could not resist the call to be reunited with her creator and so she fell to the corruption but both she and Nex shared a dark taint between them. Vanquished millennia ago, she has been reborn from the filth within this hollowed mountain, her old, rotten flesh is given new life. This great Titan stood before Nex, its full strength not yet rejuvenated as it warned him of their power.

The Kursed taint poisoned the air and gutted the entrails of all nearby. The desire for Nex to cut open his own abdomen and hurl his innards was the feeling which these Dreads, generals of the Kursed army, bestowed upon mortal creatures.

"For five thousand years...we have fed on the magic of this world. Chakravartin's whispers still reach our ears. Our father wills this. He wills us all to become one. I could never truly understand as the creature I once was, but now..." she said, "Wwe will deliver him the imperfect world he has always desired." It spoke to Nex in terrifying Kursed words that none could understand, the stench of its rotten flesh poisoning the air and banishing life. But Nex was fluent in the Kursed tongue and understood their threat.

"You looked much better as a Titan. I will return you to the dust," declared Nex. "This third life of yours has already been lived too long." Nex slowly but powerfully began to release all the power within his essence that he could muster.

The hollowed mountain, empty of all life, housed his tremendous aura in preparation to battle the Kursed Titan. The two exchanged a long silence. The creature before him was a disgusting configuration of a humanoid figure with traits of both Dryad and beast towering Nex considerably with its Titan heritage. For all the dangers in this world this dead flesh could not reach the surface. Nex wielded an immense power. Hopelessness, fear, despair and darkness became consumed by Nex's blue aura as he took them all for his own.

"She awaits you, in the kingdom she has built over the moonless aeons," said the Kursed General.

"It does not matter who you dig up. I will kill them all," said One Thousand Voices as he suppressed his worry and fear behind a façade of bravery, the wind howling at his words escaping through the cracks around them.

The Kursed creature parted its foul lips in a smile like motion and began to hiss with laughter. What was left of its once beautiful visage was now only despair.

"Nexus…" it breathed heavily in the common tongue as it raised its long, slender arm to point at Nex with its index finger, "There…is no…Maker…here…to save…you."

Nex had an extensive knowledge of this creature and the world's previous battle against the Kursed, something had not yet been revealed to Nex's companions about his long and distant past. But for now, in his current state, it was all he could do to defeat this creature. He prepared himself for the decaying Titan as it readied itself. Kursed creatures possessed immense aura. The Senses, no matter how well trained, could not ignore their presence. But with all the life and flesh and power and darkness and soul energy broken down amalgamated into one, pure, putrid form, the Kursed's capabilities were endless. They were evil incarnations of nature. The yang to its yin.

But this was not a battle of lightness and darkness nor was it a battle of life and death. Nex's aura was just as dark as the enemy he faced as it warped from blue to black. Like a gushing of the infinite cosmos itself, a blackness where no light can break through, they matched one another. A cataclysmic battle was about to rage. Nex brought his sword to him, the 'sealed' piece of parchment flailing frantically in the wind at the terrific power of the Kursed Titan released, he blinked, and allowed the cobalt blue to smoke from his eyes with all its glory.

"Let me show you," said One Thousand Voices, "you will never see the Maker again."

The Kursed General was angered by these words beyond conveyance. As a primordial deity with a will as strong as the immortals they desired one thing and one thing above all, to reunite with their father.

With his true, Sentinel power unleashed he began to battle the great creature. The vibrations of such a battle could be felt all the way to the north, where three corrupted Sentinels fell to the floor in defeat at the hands of Lily the assassin and Flowen the Horror Demon.

"Are you hurt?" asked Flowen as he noticed his sister's discomfort from an area on her left collarbone.

"I'm fine, brother," she replied with a pant at their hard-fought feat.

"These Sentinels are rather troublesome," said Flowen as he straightened himself.

They looked down upon the three Sentinels whom they had

just defeated. They were strong and relentless, their Sentinel powers full and true to their master's wills. But Lily and Flowen had become a greater power. Under their new teacher they had learned much and their teamwork was formidable. Whilst by no means easy, they had bested a troupe of powerful Sentinel soldiers.

"I hope Nex is okay," she said, sensing his disturbing presence in the distance.

"I am sure he is already on his return," declared Flowen as he gripped his bicep in triumph. "He's strong after all! They won't be able to flank this side of the army, at least. But you can be sure there will be more. Though something far more terrible awaits us ahead.

CHAPTER THIRTY FIVE: WAR

Lily and Flowen left their defeated opponents behind and approached the large encampment of the Southern Kingdom, Myphos, from which they had spent the majority of their adventure in.

"Enemies spotted! Western side!" shouted a scout guarding the perimeter of the camp. "Stop!"

Lily and Flowen raised their hands high above their heads indicating they were surrendering with ease. Any form of hostility towards this army would spell them as enemies and that was not their intent.

"We are not here to fight!" shouted Lily as an entire brigade of soldiers surrounded them, spears poised and ready for battle.

"Unarmed!" shouted a soldier who circled to the rear. "On your knees! Get down."

The Assassin with the Mantle's insignia lowered herself slowly to her knees in surrender whilst the blind demon, oozing with a dark aura followed suit. The patrolling guards slowly and cautiously stepped forwards and placed silver manacles around the wrists of both before hoisting them up to their feet. Whilst they may have declared they had no intention to cause harm their auras were supreme. The guards knew they held tremendous power.

"We did not come here to fight!" said Lily at the discomfort of the manacles. "We are here to help."

The soldiers took little notice of what Lily and Flowen had to say. Clearly it was some form of ruse to gain access to the camp. Hoisted through the ranks towards the centre where the leaders presumably were, they stopped before a large tent before entering slowly.

"Captain!" said the one who led them, "we found these two on the western perimeter!" he reported.

From his wooden chair a huge figure rose to his feet and walked over to the two powerful mages. Bork towered them both in an attempt to level the playing fields of their two tremendous auras. "Who are you?" he asked inquisitively, knowing the two mages could have easily bested the guards who had brought them here and even run amok in the army's encampment. "Why are you snooping around a battlefield?"

"There was a Sentinel scouting party to the West. We put them down before they advanced at your flank. It seems you would have been hit from that side, at least," stated Lily, the other guards scoffing at the disbelief of the story.

"Hmm…" thought Bork loudly in ponder of the young girl's words. "Have you defected?" he asked, unable to ignore the insignia on her armour.

"Defected?" she asked.

"Have you come to fight for us instead?" asked Bork.

"Fight…for you?" she asked in confusion.

"You would not be the first from the Mantle who has joined our resistance. We have had healers, priests, and soldiers all from their ranks who have defected. They have abandoned the rotten Mantle and seek to correct them. Myphos is far from united, but our forces grow strong."

Lily had never pondered the idea. With the corrupted Sentinels governing the country and the Mantle following suit there would indeed be those who cannot abide by that law. Now, they fight against them.

"I am no longer affiliated with the Mantle. Both the Sentinels and the Mantle are our enemy," she said as she gestured to herself and her Demon of a brother.

"We have come to aid you in your battles, nonetheless. We have been sent to break through to the capital in wait for our comrade," added Flowen.

"You do realise there is an entire army ahead of us, boy? Or can you not see through those bandages?" asked Bork. "The entire Mantle army, North, East and South have converged in a single effort here. They campaign for Myphos at all costs.

"We must reach the capital. Neither the Mantle nor the Sentinels truly know how dire the situation is."

"Dire?" asked Bork as he gestured around himself. "Everyone in all of Ares is aware of how 'dire' the situation is around here. Perhaps it is you who has not fully grasped the severity of what is happening."

"We will be breaking through the army with or without you. If you will not accept our aid, then you'd be better off letting us go," declared Lily.

"Hahahaha" laughed Bork loudly, his great voice carrying through the camp. "You have spunk! I like that. You two would make a great difference here. Then I will update you on how things are going," he finished.

Through their words, Bork could feel their conviction and determination. He could not ignore their tenacity and he took note of how they took little regard for their safety in a potential enemy camp.

"Have you met them in battle yet?" asked Lily, moving forwards.

"Captain!" protested a guard. "You cannot believe what they say!"

"We could indeed sense a battle to our West and the then dulling of some power. Whatever their reasons it would seem they did indeed battle the Sentinels. Their power will be invaluable to us."

"Here," said Lily as she presented her unlocked manacles back to the guard who had cuffed her.

"What?!" gasped the captain as he received them and then Flowen's too.

"Haha!" laughed Bork at the two mages. As an assassin Lily had little trouble picking the locks. With an infinite armoury of pointed objects at his disposal and a miasmic vision of all things, Flowen was also not fazed by simple, metal restraints.

"To answer your question, yes," said Bork, turning to the large table behind him and pointing to the map, "we have already clashed today. They were most likely looking to test our forces. As you can imagine we are vastly outnumbered and severely outgunned. There are perhaps four of us who could potentially match a single Sentinel in power. But in a one on one scenario we would need tonnes of luck. With you two, that would total six adversaries for the Mantle's forces," indicated Bork whilst he pointed to various locations of the battlefield on the map.

"We have a third. He is likely to not be far behind us. I can vouch for his strength first-hand. He is invaluable as a soldier and his power as a mage is far greater than ours combined. My name is Lily, and this is my brother Flowen. It's a pleasure to meet you all," stated Lily as they both bowed in the proper introduction, respectfully.

Bork raised an interested eyebrow at the beautiful young Lily's claim. To praise someone powerful at their level, who she spoke of must be strong. "I am Captain Bork. I lead the resistance here in Eos."

"But what are we facing?" she furthered.

"There is no doubt that the three armies are being led by General Vereoris alone. The Hymns of Faith and Mercy are not here. They do not seem to have left the capital," said Bork. "There are also multiple Theinite's from each individual army."

"Theinite?" asked Flowen , unfamiliar with the term.

"They rank below the General in their armies, each with a command of one thousand soldiers each. With a force as large as this I would imagine there are a fair few of them. Each are rather powerful. Not Sentinel level but not far off and there are far, far more of them," clarified Lily. "Also," she turned to Bork, "Kleese will not be coming. He was defeated at the tower of Gitterung yesterday."

"Hmmm," thought Bork aloud. "First Henrys and now Kleese? We had some reports he was going south to the tower, but we could not confirm he had even left the capital. There's a lotta mystery around the Mantle and the Sentinels at the moment. Apparently, there was meant to be a joint mission. Wait! Does that mean the Sentinels were defeated there as well?"

"Yes. Both were defeated and both fled," clarified Lily.

"But the rumours said it was Raiku who went south. The Arcon's right hand man!"

"He and Kleese returned to the Nexus. They will still be recovering," said Lily.

"Then there is no doubt in my mind. It must have been him!" concluded Bork loudly, referring to the mysterious young mage whom he had witnessed defeating Henrys some week prior. Lily and Flowen looked at one another before speaking.

"Yes…It was our third companion. He defeated them," said Lily.

"Could It be?! Are you with him? You were with Nex?" asked Bork as he placed each of his enormous hands on both Lily and Flowen's shoulders. "How is he?!"

"You know Nex?!" she exclaimed with tremendous surprise.

"How is that young lad!?" laughed Bork.

Ah…" said Lily awkwardly, "He is fine."

"That's great, that's great!" he chuckled as he patted them. "I knew I had a good feeling about you two! But unfortunately, we may not have enough time for his return. Battle for today has ended, but the Mantle will strike again early, as the sun rises. If he has not returned by then we will have to begin without him. But if he has put his trust in you two, there must be a good reason for it!"

"We are unsure as to when he will return. He is battling a kursed General beneath the Eayr mountains," said Flowen.

"A Kursed General?!" exclaimed Bork in horrifying surprise as he paced around. "Do not fret, young ones. He will come!"

"It is unlikely there will be any soldiers of accountability. If we hit them full force right off the bat, we are bound to get their attention. I assume you have already begun to retreat south in preparation to cut them off at Ember?" asked Lily, already knowing the answer.

"H-how? Y-yes," answered Bork, stunned by her strategic prowess. "The majority of our forces are in the process of retreating. We advanced North of the border with only a small number as a guise of holding a larger army. Myphos itself was difficult to unite under one banner and has not yet collected itself into one army. Our efforts here are to bide time for a larger army to gather to prevent them crossing in Myphos. The King resides south of the river with his daughter. The town of Ember, after successfully repelling the Mantle's first attempt, has since been transformed into a military city. It's unrecognisable."

"Then we will hit them hard here, biding time for retreat whilst also giving the false impression that we are confident in both strength and number," said Lily, deciding as if the army were her own.

"You really know what you're doing, eh?" said Bork, probably more inexperienced than she.

"Wow, little sister. Colour me impressed," said Flowen as he tapped her back in admiration of his younger sister's strategic planning.

"There is little chance they will actually believe our ruse, but they will not be able to ignore us. That will give us enough time," she added.

"We might just stand a chance if the Hymn of Wrath doesn't show up. At first light, we will counter their advance! I have other matters to attend to before the battle, I'll see you two young'ens on the front lines tomorrow. Please, get some rest until then," said Bork as he began to leave. "Help yourselves to any of the refreshments here, friends of Nex."

Lily and Flowen had not rested for quite some time. They had many battles under their belts since the last time they had the luxury to relieve themselves of strain and stress. If it were not for Nex's magic they would have collapsed long ago. As the night passed, they waited for Nex to join them. But, from the darkness, he did not come.

"I can feel him, out there," said Lily.

"I can too. Even now, I can sense he is still battling."

"I cannot help but think we should have gone with him…" she trailed.

"Now who is it that doubts his power?" asked Flowen. "He feared for our safety. He did not fret when we faced the Sentinel and the General of the Mantle. But this foe, this one struck fear into Nex. I could feel it in his presence. He is scared of this battle. And if what he says is true, we would have been a hindrance in the way of his magic. Only he can slay the kursed."

"Perhaps you are right…" trailed Lily. "But still, even knowing that I cannot do a thing, I would want to be with him regardless."

"You are very kind Lily. I am glad that, even though you have spent your life murdering from the shadows, you have a kind and thoughtful heart."
"Hey! You could have put that more delicately!"

"But then you wouldn't react like this. I can still tease my little sister, you know," protested Flowen.

"I want to see him again…" she trailed under her breath.

Flowen heard, and smiled to himself. "Tomorrow."

When the sun began to creep over the horizon, the encampment of the resistant Southern Kingdom was uneasy and racked with nerves. Whilst what they did was admirable and provided tactical strength, the likelihood of survival, let alone victory, was low. They lacked in both power and numbers to repel yet another day of battle. Only then, in retreat, would they hope to live another day.

Lily and Flowen were fresh and revitalised and prepared themselves at the camps most northern border. They were eager for battle for a myriad of reasons. To fulfil Nex's wish, to tell the

Sentinels and the Mantle that the Kursed were to come and to inspire those around them that even in the face of such tyranny they would not falter. Those who did not succumb to tyrannical rule must be rewarded! These reasons, combined with their desire and lust to fight strong opponents, made them the keenest of all in this resistance they had now officially become a part of.

"There you are, you two!" shouted Bork as he emerged from further back in the preparing ranks. "This is Captain Vanor and Captain Kain. We three are the last to ensure the full retreat, and thus, to hold off the Mantle until then. These are the two I told you about. They are his companions. Their power is invaluable."

The army began to emerge. Soldiers formed ranks and from the tents and clearings emerged not only defected Mantle soldiers and priests and mages, but adventurers and hunters and mercenaries. The combined effort of all would attempt to halt the invasion at any cost.

"This is it, Men! Everyone, forward!" roared Bork, a man who stood like a giant over his fellows. The banners of the Southern Kingdom rose and the army began forward.

CHAPTER THIRTY SIX: CONVERGENCE

The battle raged on. Both sides clashed with ferocity and determination. One, to fight for what they believed was right, the other, fighting through desperation to protect their homes and their freedom. War was sadly more than common in Ares. The province baskedin war and bloodshed since the beginning of time, and found its namesake from the God they worshipped. When words failed, if they even arose at all, the clashing of swords and magic would ultimately decide who was right.

The powerful write history and the truth of the weak is forgotten. The Mantle outnumbered the rebellion one hundred to one. If not for the strength of the three captains, who could best one hundred men and counting, the battle would have been lost before it had begun. However, the Mantle too possessed mages of their own renown who indeed held fame in their own right, through research or rank. The adventurers, by way of a fee, also fought fiercely on both sides, utilising their formidable powers and weaponry to combat their opponent's soldiers. Whilst their involvement was frowned upon by their peers, they were within their rights to accept any job for Aur.

However, Lily and Flowen acted as deterrents. They could be classed as 'anti-army individuals'. With a swing of his sword and a blast of Flowen's magic, the open battlefield would become a graveyard of merciless spikes as far as the land allowed. Flashing like green lightning faster than the eye could follow and causing calamity in her wake, Lily cleared them all. This one-versus-many technique earned an individual the title of an anti-army combatant, a fearsome and terrifying trait for one to bear over the opposition.

After only a short time of battle, between thirty to forty minutes tens of thousands of Mantle soldiers, including high ranking mages and leaders, had been defeated. The rebellion had now enabled a large-scale retreat whilst only a few factions remained to help Lily and Flowen's effort to push forward. Inevitably, this would draw out the leader of the army. But this battle was only the beginning. Above them, encompassing the whole sky above them, an eye opened. With a pupil of deep crimson and an emblem of ouroboros on a pure white conjunctiva, this divine eye gleamed down upon them menacingly, swallowing the entire battlefield with its glare, there was nothing it could not see.

"What the hell is that?!" exclaimed Lily as she finished bringing down a large squadron alone and moving to relocate with her brother in fear of the huge magic power.

"An eye?" questioned Flowen at the enormity of such a thing. It emanated such a sinister and malicious intent. Whatever it was, it looked down upon them with a murderous gaze.

"That's not good!" shouted Bork to what remained of the men fighting.

"It isn't! Bork, now is the time for your retreat!" said Lily turning back to him.

"No, we ca-" he began before Flowen spoke over him.

"This is the turning point," stated Flowen as he looked past the remains of the Mantle first wave to their encampment. It seemed that someone had taken an interest in the delay of their army.
But that was not the only thing that they could sense. Flowen

was the first to feel it, with his mystic might and spiritual gaze, he sensed strong auras from both East and West converging on their position. Lily soon followed, picking up the tremors of aura. But, both menacing and disastrous in scale, could be recognised. Neither East nor West was the aura of Nex.

"It's time for you to leave," confirmed Flowen to Bork and the remains of the resistance. "You will not want to be far away when whatever is coming gets here."

"This is where we part ways. You have been a great help to us!" Bork gritted his teeth in frustration. They were right. Despite his wish to stay and fight and to support them, there was none among them who would be able to make a difference. It would be a wasteful death.

"ALL UNITS: RETREAT!" he roared, battle-axe held high over them all in victory. He waved them past, all who were near to hurry them along. In a scurry, the retreat began, but the eye above them did not move. Focusing on Lily and Flowen alone, it had no interest in the retreat of the rebellion.

"Things are about to get serious," said Flowen to his younger sister.

"I think i'm just about warmed up," she sniggered. "It's not Nex."

"From the East is an enormous aura. The west is prominent too, but pales in comparison. What worries me…" he trailed as he looked to the North. "A monster worse than them all awaits us ahead."

From ahead of them The Mantle's encampment held not one, but three disastrous auras. The hostility of which could topple a kingdom. The eye above them, finding all that it had sought, vanished at its master command. In their bones they could all feel it. North, West, South and East would converge upon one another. This was no longer a war between armies, but a battle between monsters.

From the West arrived three women clad in armour like that of Mantle females but golden like the light of a star adorned with the most expensive finery and jewels. All with long, golden hair that could reach the waist they each presented differently to create some individuality and uniqueness between their near identical appearances. But the insignia they all bore resembled the Mantle's but was somewhat different. Their emblem consisted of a simple design of closed lips with a sword piercing down through them combined with the radiation of the Maker's streak to glisten them with faith. Therefore, it was identical to the Mantle's but in place of the All-Seeing Eye of the Maker's gaze there were the Maker's lips, sealed shut. Each of the beautiful women held a powerful weapon in their grasp. One, a huge scythe that matched the intimidation of Akuma. The second, twin cut blades shaped like flames each, as long as a Katana. The third, held a tremendous sharpened lance that, in full length, was around ten paces, the soldier's small hand housed on its guarded hilt. It was like an amalgamation of a lance, spear sword and rapier all moulded into one. It was very unusual. Their beauty was enough to stun both Lily and Flowen. They were surely the perfect representation of a female warrior-goddess.

"The Pontifex must be playing at war," said the first, beautiful woman.

"Piaus should never have held onto his position for so long," said the second aggravatingly.

"Perhaps we should return with the information we have now rather than questioning Piaus? There is clearly something wrong in Ares," concluded the third. "Have our Eastern Allies waged war on their own Kingdoms?".

Lily and Flowen recognised their speech. Indeed, these three beautiful women were not from Ares. In fact, they had journeyed over the western sea. Whilst they resembled the Mantle, they looked to be questioning allegiances.

The middle woman stood forward and presented herself to Lily and Flowen. "My name is Teresa. This is Isla and Sophia."

"Teresa is right," stated Isla, "There is no question that the corrupted Sentinel order and the Mantle of Ares have fallen into darkness. We must investigate the Nexus and report only once we have gathered all relevant information."

"I can't say I expected any less from you, Isla," said Teresa. "You should not give up so easily, Sophia."

"Perhaps not," said Sophia.

The three soldiers stopped before Flowen and Lily and analysed them with little interest.

"A demon with no eyes," said Teresa.
"And a Mantle assassin," said Isla.
"You two are indeed powerful" finished Sophia.

"You too, are quite beautiful," observed Flowen, complimenting them for their beauty.

"Perhaps the two of you can enlighten us?" asked Teresa, leading to more questions. "We can see you are no friends of the Mantle. What has become of Ares?" she asked.

"Of the Mantle?" asked Isla.

"Of the Sentinels?" asked Sophia.

"Do you guys…always talk like that?" asked Flowen as he gestured to their in-tune speech physically with his finger.

"The Sentinels are corrupted, and the Mantle seems to have followed suit," said Lily. "You are Sisters of Silence?"

"Yes. We are from across the sea," stated Teresa simply.

"We have come to investigate this corruption from our own empire," said Isla.

"We are The Sisters of Silence," declared Sophia.

"Sisters of Silence?" questioned Flowen.

"The Mantle equivalent on the Western Continent," informed Lily to her older brother.

"Although our goal lies in the Capital we could not ignore the powers that drew us here," said Teresa.

"Both you two…" said Isla.

"And the others that are to come," finished Sophia. They of course referred to the approaching dooms from both sides.

Whilst they did indeed radiate powerful auras themselves equal to that of Lily and Flowen, the remaining Western and Northern threats were leagues apart. The battlefield was bare and scorched from battle, but of what little remained of the dead and unconscious and weakened soldiers regained themselves as their instincts took control of their bodies. Clambering around in desperation they began to claw at their surroundings and struggle to their feet to return to their comrades in the Northern encampment. What approached was so terrifying it could rip a man from near death into desperate survival.

High above them, where the white clouds gather and the sun pierces through the sky, the land became cloaked in darkness as if the moon itself was falling upon them. The pressure of the world around them became almost unbearable for the strong mages as, swooping down upon them, a great black dragon came.

With its boned hands protruding from its wings similar to that of a common wyvern the great Titan smashed down upon the land.

In anticipation both Lily and Flowen and the Sisters of Silence had braced themselves for the imminent battle, but, even combined, what could they hope to do against this mythical creature? Despite being cataclysmic in power and gigantic in size this young dragon was uninterested in the humans below its long, powerful, serpent-like neck. Almost completely swallowed by its blackness the Sentinel armour on its back dismounted and dropped some forty feet to land on the recovering ground. The Dragon brought its long neck around with great reach to place its head in front of its temporary foster mother and await a stroke of approval.

Daisy could not contain her gratitude and petted the mythical creature with one hundred percent enthusiasm. "Good boy, good boy!" she said with an enormous smile across her face. The dragon flared its nostrils and breathed heavily in reward.

"A Dragon!?" exclaimed Flowen at the impossibility. With his magical gaze he could not see the dragon, only an infinite aura of pure black like that of a violently erupting volcano.

"Well, that was much faster," stated Galatea as she too petted the good boy. Vosk, with one hand thanked the Dragon with one quick pat of gratitude before entering the conversation of strangers.

"Please be at ease, we mean you no harm," he stated. "We were on our return to the Nexus but diverted due to the unusual amount of power gathered here."

"We cannot Recall via teleport. We have been cut off from the Nexus," said Galatea whilst Daisy had not yet finished patting her new child's head.

"Sentinels?" said Lily in surprise at the uncorrupted appearance, "How are you unaffected?"

"Uncorrupted?" asked Teresa.

"We have not yet seen a Sentinel to compare," stated Isla.

"There are those who have remained uncorrupted, then?" finished Sophia.

"Greetings, Sisters. No doubt you have come to investigate the rumours surrounding both The Sentinels and The Mantle. Unfortunately, we three were situated on a mission in the Eastern Kingdom of Haraura. We only learned of the corruption when brothers of our order came for us. After our battle we have endeavoured to return to the Nexus for ourselves, but we have met countless problems on the way. In the darkness creatures of death and destruction have come. Without the true light of the Sentinels and the Mantle things in Ares will only deteriorate. But the threat yet worsens…" finished Vosk.

"I see," said Teresa, bringing her hand to her head in thought. "So, there is little you can tell us."

"But we are fortunate that you three have survived," said Isla in comfort.

"Do you know of any others?" asked Sophia.

"It is possible it was the distance between us and the Nexus at the time," admitted Vosk before presenting the second possibility. "But we have no knowledge of any other parties like ours away from the Nexus. We have also thought it was the nature of our mission with the Arcon had given us. The Hollowed mountain may have prevented the spell from affecting us. At this time, we simply do not know. Forgive me, but I do not know you. I am the Sentinel Heleic Vosk, and these are my primus': Galatea and Daisy. We are the Sentinel Vanguard. Who are you?" asked Vosk finally to our young mages.

"I am Lily, this is my brother Flowen," she said plainly, with no other titles to support their claims.

"Hello!" said the blind Demon enthusiastically with a wave as he looked upon them all with his magic.

Vosk, Galatea and the recently joined Daisy took their appearance in finally concluding unanimously that they were quite the unusual pair. "I see. Very abnormal," he stated.

"You can't just say things like that! Those bandages are cool! Do you see through magic, then?!" asked Daisy in excitement as she walked right up and into Flowen's face.

"Uh, y-yes," he confirmed.

"Excuse me?" said Lily in surprise at her brazenness.

"Oh, I apologise." corrected Vosk.. "A Mantle Assassin and a demon? That is quite an unusual sight for one, let alone paired up."

"Former assassin," Corrected Lily.

"Former Demon," added Flowen.

Behind them all the Dragon took little interest in the going's on. Whilst sentient and capable of human speech, this century old dragon probably understood them to a degree but was still an infant and years from developing the skills in which to converse. As such, its behaviour was akin to that of a child, waiting for its mother to finish a lengthy exchange.

"It would seem we all have the same goal, then," stated Lily finally to the three parties.

"Who, exactly, are you?" asked Galatea.

"Where to start…we have been beneath the mountain of Eayr and witnessed the broken seal and, whilst it may be complicated and difficult to believe, we have seen the Kursed and know of the Titan General who has regenerated there. Our companion remained to prevent her escape from the mountain kingdom. He has sent us ahead of him in an effort to create a path to the Sentinel Nexus and to warn both the Mantle and the Sentinels."

Vosk, Galatea and Daisy looked to one another in disbelief. "You have been beneath Eayr and seen the Kursed?" asked Vosk as he turned in thought. "Then it was not only our seals which were weakened. A vanguard was to be sent to each but, given the distance of ours, we were released preemptively on our mission. We have not been able to contact any of the other teams via a scrying orb."

"I see," said Teresa.

Flowen waited for Isla to speak and Sophia to finish, but it never came.

!They didn't do it!" he said childishly as everyone else moved on.

"But wait, your companion has remained behind? That's suicide!" said Vosk loudly. "The three of us barely escaped alive! The Dread beneath Ibis was had not fully awakened and yet we barely slowed his advance at the cost of all our combined power."

"We only survived because of him. But believe us when we say, if anyone was to succeed, it would be him," said Flowen.

"It does not matter how powerful he is. If he has not taken the Sentinel flame from the Nexus then he is powerless against them," gasped Vosk stepping closer to them.

"To further your questions from earlier, he is a Sentinel," said Lily.

"What was his name?" asked Vosk with desperation. "Please, tell me!"

"Nex." They both said in conjunction.

"Nex?" questioned the three Sentinels looking at one another. "There is none in our order with such a name? Are you sure?" they asked.

Lily and Flowen both laughed back to them lightly. "Yes, we are sure. But he is not like any Sentinel we have ever seen. He said he is not a Sentinel of Ares."

"Hm…" thought the Sentinels. "It is quite possible he is from a neighbouring order. But if he was of such power he would have been made Heleic. Tell me, what magic did he use? Perhaps that will aid us."

"Hmmm…" thought Lily bringing her finger to her lips, "Ice, Lightning and Infinity Magic so far…" she said.

"Impossible!" they gasped. "We have heard of no such Sentinel. There is only one creature in all of Ares who uses Infinity Magic."

Flowen, Lily, the three Sisters of Silence and the three Sentinels and even the young, mythical Dragon felt the spike of power around them. Their skin began to crawl as if to escape their very muscles. Their instinct told them to even retreat was impossible and no matter how hard they willed their bodies their limbs would not respond to the commands of their brains.

"This power…" stuttered Flowen.

"It's…more powerful than Nex" clambered Lily.

"And so the monster has finally come?" said Vosk.

A power so menacing that even taking one's own life became not just a thought, but a compulsion to spare them from the possible threat they were to face. A presence so evil and sinister even the Dragon gritted itself to release its breath in desperation of escape. It felt like death himself was reaching from behind them to grasp their spines and wrench them from their bodies. General Vereoris had come and cursed them all with a presence that etched its existence into their very souls.

CHAPTER THIRTY SEVEN: THE HYMN OF WRATH

Flowen and Lily's eyes expanded to the point of imminent explosion at the being that stood before them. They could not comprehend its power.

Long, silver, moon-dust hair stretched down to the woman's waist. Her silver armour was more intricate and more beautiful than the three Sisters combined in every conceivable way. Her petite figure, dainty and humble, overflowed a menacing evil that brought all those around her to the verge of death. Her soft, supple face, so delicate and innocent, bore a sinister smile that only the most despicable creatures could adorn. Trimmed elegantly with a small golden lacing, her narrow, star metal greaves caressed her legs upwards before sealing themselves off on her upper thigh, concealing a small heel in the foot. The knee held a small, golden intricacy that pleased the eye, veining off fluidly to its decorated ilk. Her curvaceous hip bones effortless held the separated plates of her legs, resting on the tiny space provided by the concaving bones. Her breast plate began at the bottom of her rib cage, clamping her torso tightly in its embrace, revealing her lower stomach and arms, but providing a less discrete housing for the upper female endowment. Casing her perfectly, it stretched up to her neck and guarded everything below her. Her subtle shoulder plates rose violently outwards in a threatening manner, poised for attack, clamped down as a separate part of the armour that fastened to the torso. Her gauntlets were more like gloves, matching the eloquent design and bending with its hundreds of tiny different components at the knuckles to enable full flexibility and movement. They covered down from the fingertips to the bottom knuckle in the thumb, leaving an inch and a half gap between the armour on her wrists. From her bicep down was the cover of black, magical sleeving that cuddled her arms, latched like piping, guiding her flesh. Some of the uncovered canvas of her skin was covered in a tight, night black underlay rendering her revealing flesh obsolete to those prying eyes. Finally, draped over her as if bestowed unto by a God was the Military overcoat that boasted her ultimate rank. Like Henrys and Kleese before her, mounted upon her small and modest head was the matching hat of authority.

"Vereoris..." spoke Teresa with tremendous difficulty as she examined the monster and the creatures that accompanied her.

"Our short discussion must come to an end," said Veroeris to the incredible mage beside her. "And all too long it was"

"You cannot ignore The Ten Kings." said Gitterung, the great, black mage. "Our words do not come without warning"

"Oh," she said so softly with warmth, "it has been quite some time since anyone has whispered my name with such hate and resentment," she said as behind her, a crimson dragon almost five times bigger than the black one that had carried the Sentinels, snarled at the black mage's insult. "It truly fills me with joy!" she said as she raised her hand to signal the dragon's obedience. "How nice it is to finally see you all again, Teresa, Isla, Sophia."

"A woman?!" asked Flowen in surprise of the monster before him.

"Did I not say?!" said Lily, obvious to the fact. Lily and Flowen had not forgotten Gitterung. How his power swallowed that of those at the fall of his tower and how he defeated Nex with a simple wave of his hand. But, even he, beside Vereoris' limitless power, could sense almost nothing from the mage. Vereoris was so powerful and terrifying that she commanded respect from even one of Odin's Ten Kings?! Perplexing thoughts and confused theories cascaded between them like a tidal wave as they did their very best to conceal their worry.

"You," said Fowen as he looked at Gitterung with malice and vengeance of his friend.

"I have seen these before…" said Gitterung to the monster beside him that even he was weary of. "although there was another, if I recall."

"Oh?" said Vereoris with curiosity, "and how did you fair?" she asked.

"An unusual one, even if I do say so myself. But Odin has asked for their audience, eventually. Their companion however, does not interest him," said Gitterung bluntly.

"I see…" trailed Vereoris in thought, "but he does interest me a great deal. Vosk, Galatea and Daisy is it? It is good to see that some Sentinels remained free of Thusien's curse."

"General, now is not the time for pointless war. All of Ares is at risk. The Kursed have returned!" said Vosk, cutting to the chase.

"So I have heard," stated Vereoris as she gestured to her side, indicating Gitterung as her informant.

"Then you know it is of paramount importance that we all band together!" urged Vosk.

The Hymn of Wrath let out a long sigh from her small lungs. "Before my time in Ares I spent many years doing various different things. I have seen human kingdoms rise and fall, men become kings and kings become gods, and in the grand scheme of things, they all return to dust in the end. I even helped in the conquering of kingdoms for the Sisters of Silence in the western provinces across the vast sea. When the thrill ran dry, I returned here in hope that their time had come. But, I was decades too soon. Now, finally, the darkness stirs and with it, my heart awakens again. If Ares is to come to an end, I shall simply leave it in ashes."

"You cannot be serious?" shouted Galatea over her.

"What are you?" added Lily.

'I can't even move!' thought Flowen in desperation. 'Are they allies?' he thought as he tried to look between them, the pressure of the area now almost at its climax.

"Oh?" said Vereoris, shifting her attention to Lily with intrigue. "I do not believe we have met?" she said. "I kept a careful eye on you in your time at the Mantle. I knew at once that Tsumikiri sought you. How close we must have been in the shadows of passing and yet you know nothing of me. But, of course, I know of you. Tsumikiri....Akuma. None other than you can hold those blades. And you, Lily, have a lingering sin on your lips that I cannot, with all my might, ignore," she stated.

The general reached out slowly, and the already thin air at her palm, cracked with a scarlet lightning that erupted and whipped the air. From nowhere there came a thin, but intricate, rapier.

It was incredibly well made, so much so, it was surely beyond the skill of any human craftsman. "To think *only* this one would answer me," she said as she showed them all her blade. "I cannot begin to explain the nostalgia you have brought me for you could not comprehend the depths of my connection to these star metal swords. Thank you. But, unfortunately, neither Akuma or Tsumikiri are the blades I want."

Lily and Flowen could both sense it. The fourth and final, legendary blade infused with curses crafted by the master smith was contained within the Hymn of Wrath's hand. She sought a fourth? What could she mean? Was it the blade that Nex carried?

"But, oh my! How much have you two grown under his stewardship?" she asked, her malice and bloodlust decreasing so much so that she could only almost be described as human.

Flowen and Lily were taken aback by the accuracy of her words. She spoke of Nex, and yet he was not there. "I was thoroughly disappointed when I learned that he was not with you today!" pouted Vereoris, devoid of sympathy. "One mustn't get a lady's hopes up."

All looked at Vereoris unsure of what she was saying and the casual demeanour she adopted. The usually disinterested Gitterung hung on her every word with intrigue. Lily and Flowen remained silent, their eyes attacking Vereoris.

"It seems he's made quite the impression on you," stated Vereoris through her tightened face with bitter resentment. "All is coming to pass. Let us see if he mourns your death, at least."

With all his might Flowen moved in front of his sister in her defence.

"Do you dare oppose us all? Even *you* cannot win this battle!" declared Vosk.

"You cannot hope to face us all?" asked Isla. They all turned to face an enormous Dragon, a King of Odin and the Hymn of Wrath. Lily, Flowen, Vosk, Galatea, Daisy, Teresa, Isla, Sophia and the great, young black dragon prepared to face their foe.

"Do not worry," Vereoris spoke gently, "the King of Odin was just about to leave." She gestured Gitterung away as if he were of no significance. The suspense was incredible. They were prepared to face all three with their numbers and yet she insisted Gitterung was not to fight. Her dragon would surely defend its master.

But the colossal black beast that had brought the Sentinels was younger in adolescence than them all. Out of desperation and with a great bellow, one that cracked the trees and forced the very magic inside the planet to subdue itself beneath the surface, it released a relentless breath of crimson flame. Flowen and Lily and The Sisters of Silence could feel their armour begin to bubble and melt at the unparalleled heat of dragonfire. The Star metal Illyrium of the Sentinels fared well, it would take several minutes of continuous dragon-fire to melt the Illyrium down.

At this distance, despite being terrified, they were all safe from its heat. For almost twenty seconds of pure catastrophic power the young Dragon released its howl towards General Vereoris and the mage Gitterung. When it retracted its neck for breath it finally revealed that Vereoris' own dragon had reached out its wing to protect them all.

"Tss," began Vosk in disbelief.

"When you finally get your own dragon, you get pitted against another? Typical," hissed Daisy.

Vereoris glared at the Dragon with her crimson eyes, threatening the god of the skies with her might.

"Tempest!" she summoned crimson lightning to her which hit the dragon in an instant beneath its long neck, piercing the chest of the great creature. Crashing backwards the beast scurried to its feet in desperation, and with a great beat of its wings, took flight and retreated into the sky.

Flowen was upon her in that instant. Unphased, his huge sword found itself clamped between her delicate fingers.

Reigning him in, Vereoris released a simple blow to send him flying. The great Dryad, daughter of Titans, Galatea was behind her ready to release a spell of destruction about the Generals back. Vosk and Daisy were also upon her, their swords ready to cut her clean in half, Daisy's pitch-black darkness consuming the area around her. High above, Teresa, Isla and Sophia prepared to crash down upon her with their huge weaponry whilst Lily, faster than all of them, was below her left arm, ready to push Tsumikiri through her left abdomen and out of her right shoulder. As every detail transpired Lily caught sight only of Vereoris' crimson pupils in the corner of her eyes, looking to the young assassin in wait. What followed was a tale of complete disbelief.

One could not do justice to describe the events as they transpired for none would believe just with how much ease General Vereoris, the Hymn of Wrath, bested her foes simultaneously, free of mercy and effort. She was fast. Faster even than light. Maybe, even faster than time.

Totally defeated, unable to contest her strength even without the aid of her mighty dragon or that of the King of Odin, the seven adversaries did everything in their power to rise again to face her.

Even with their combined might and magic they had exhausted themselves upon her in a hopeless struggle. She had no need to display her unmatched swordsmanship nor her weightless agility or fire another magic attack. She bested them all with one, free hand.

"Oh, I apologise," she said softly. "Were you not ready?"

"We-" began Lily before Vereoris interjected. Vereoris withdrew her star metal rapier slowly from the sheath and spoke over her.

"The curses placed on these are unlike any other in this world. It's almost as if they were made to be a hindrance to the user," she said with criticism. "Pynagol has its own curse, of course. A rather relentless one that forces me to endure great pain whenever I wield it. But I revel in such ecstasy, it helps me remember. It reminds me of times my memories cannot do justice."

"And its power?" asked Flowen, raising himself.

"You will know of it soon enough," said Vereoris as she brought it to her side. "Akuma…although I can see that no curse resides on that blade no longer"

"Thankfully…" admitted Flowen, "I don't think I would stand a chance otherwise. "It is true that while I may have a soul that you can indeed wound, the difference in our power is fathoms deeper than you can possibly understand," she declared.

"Whether I can understand it or not. It makes no difference," said Flowen as he fully raised himself to his feet. "I will protect my sister." With his free hand, he pulled Tsumikiri to himself from Lily's defeated grasp and attacked with all his magic.

The stalactites erupted from everywhere, spearing the sky. Vereoris dodged each one before firing herself towards him directly. She met his cursed sword with his and the two entered an incredible frenzy. Their skills were out of this world. Both wielded the blades like an extension of themselves with nothing to waste. Their movements pure and precise landing exactly where they were destined to. Flowen poured his power into his magic as the stalactites erupted and just when he thought he had her, the enormous spike that could pierce through the tower of Gitterung itself, became trapped in her fingers like she held a butterfly.

"You're much faster than I thought you would be, and to think you could use both Tsumikiri and Akuma at the same time," admitted Vereoris. "Your skill with the sword is probably the highest in this kingdom. I can think of only a few who rival you. I, myself, only took up the sword recently."

Her words could not ring true for she was soon to overtake Flowen's gifts. He released his full Demon power and poured everything into his next barrage of attacks. As he had increased in tenacity, she responded in kind to combat him until finally, she began to pour her magic power into her strikes.

Her sword was much faster now. So much so that Flowen could only follow one in every three strikes with his magic. She cut him over and over and over again until he could no longer stand from the wounds she had inflicted.

Lily attempted to use her words against the black mage, who seemed to be of reasonable understanding.

"Please, Gitterung. What use are Odin's Ten King's if not to prevent the destruction of Ares?"

"You are quite right, young one," said the middle-aged black mage. "Odin tasked me to relay a request to Vereoris in hopes she would cease her actions here. With each drop of blood that is spilled on any battlefield they grow stronger. These words of mine fell on deaf ears," he stated.

"The Kursed…" trailed Vosk from the ground.

"Then, please!" pleaded Lily. "Stop her!"

Flowen spurted blood from his mouth as he faced his final defeat from Vereoris. He had done well against her, surpassing his limits and forcing her to tap into her enormous power. Vereoris stood above them all in complete triumph. In the presence of her aura their bodies became numb and unresponsive.

"I…cannot" declared Gitterung, stating that not even he, one of Odin's Ten Kings, could stop her onslaught.

"So young...so beautiful," said Vereoris as she adored the burning look of hatred in Lily's eyes. Vereoris licked her lips in satisfaction. This sadistic feeling was her true nature. This suffering was her addiction. She reached down to grab Lily by her beautiful Golden hair and hoisted her into the air.

"I wonder how he would react if I killed you right now?" she asked the helpless Lily.

"Lily!" roared Flowen through a mouth of blood.

"Stop this, Vereoris!" ordered Vosk as he, Galatea and Daisy rose to their feet from her magic. Even Galatea and Daisy, as gifted as they were, could not heal those who were not almost touching them. The gap between their healing and that of Nex's was large.

"Go...to hell!" laughed Lily through bloodied teeth in the face of doom. Vereoris plunged her sword into Lily's abdomen so that she would cry over the wind in tremendous pain. Skilfully done, this wound would inflict a great amount of pain whilst keeping the loss of blood to the minimum for a continuation of the torture. She released it slowly in preparation to pose another question to the helpless young mage.

"Stop this!" ordered Vosk as the Sisters rose too.

"He cannot hear you!" screeched Vereoris as she held them all at bay with her presence, her sadistic emotion boiling inside of her as she released even more malice. With a second plunge her rapier went straight through her right shoulder, severing all the nerves in one go, but again, skilfully allowing for more pain to follow.

"You are not the first he has forsaken but you may well be the last. Let your cries ring out across the cosmos for the Maker to hear and writhe, in undying torment, on the false hope that Nex will save you from me."

But through the dust and debris he came. His presence was undisputable. None in all of Ares could ignore it. Nex had come.

CHAPTER THIRTY EIGHT: THE STAR METAL FLOWER

He was unlike he had ever been before them. His power was overflowing, erupting ferociously and untamed. He walked slowly under the weight of his own power, his cloak ravaged and held in the wind. His anger burned endlessly like the dragon-fire they had just witnessed. The world retreated from both Vereoris' icy presence and Nex's malice in search of warmth and sanctity. But it was not to be found. The hallowed silver moons glistened down upon them begging them not to fight. The cold air of the night was unforgiving as it toiled through their lungs.

"Hello," she spoke softly over the wind, her voice igniting the chemicals inside the brain.

Nex looked upon the woman as if she were a goddess that only the Maker himself was capable of such a craft. Her beauty was unrivalled. Her skin was flawless with divinity and she exhumed a golden light that blinded the eye. She had long, moon-dust hair that danced in the wind behind her. Her face was soft, caressed with beautiful red lips and a sinister smile. Akin to the females in the Mantle she wore similar attire but more radiant than humanly possible. But, through the inescapable thoughts rushing through his head he knew he recognised the unforgettable visage as that of the young woman with the basket of apples outside the trinket shop in Rook.

With him Nex had brought an unbearable stench. Heavy and

sickly their stomachs, already on the verge of the unimaginable pressure and animosity that Vereoris exhumed, turned at the stench. Now visible through his aura they could see Nex, and his condition. On his right hand he only had his thumb, index and middle finger remaining. His right leg held a wound that swallowed his entire thigh with a ghastly gash. On his face, a strike that ran from his hairline to the side of his mouth truer than even the straightest of arrows, cleanly slicing through his left eye.

Nex had sustained heavy damage from his previous battle. The stench that he carried was recognisable instantly by Vosk, Galatea and Daisy as that which they had retreated against beneath the hollow mountain. To Lily and Flowen, it reminded them of the perilous, unwinnable, unforgettable disaster that befell them beneath the Mountain Kingdom. To Teresa, Isla and Sophia, who were alien to the stench, thought the smell must be of a beast of unimaginable evil and corruption. Vereoris and Gitterung brought their hands to their mouths in disgust.

"This creature…" trailed Vosk in disbelief.

"So…sickening…" said the three sisters from the ground.

"A Dread?!" said Daisy, preparing herself. It was the duty of Sentinels and Sentinels alone. Any Kursed creature could only be slain by their magic. Even Vereoris, with all her power, would prove useless against a Kursed beast lacking the knowledge of magic used to destroy flesh and soul. Without conferring or hesitation, the Sentinels, now somewhat healed due to Galatea's magic, sprang for Nex with intent to kill.
Vosk dived straight in, his Sentinel vanguard, Illyrium sword slicing down through the air only to find that even he, Leader of the Sentinel vanguard, potential Heleic of the old order, did not have the strength to press the blade through Nex's dense aura. Unable to break through, the force overwhelmed him,

and he was flung backwards harder than any blow he had ever received, breaking countless bones. Daisy and Galatea met similar fates, With everything they had poured into one swift attack they met nothing but aura, so fierce it began to eat away at their star metal swords with its intensity before pummelling them deep into the cold ground. Whilst Nex harboured them no ill will, he simply cared only for his companion's survival. Any who opposed him would be dealt with, without prejudice or discretion.

"Mhmm," said vereoris softy. Despite Nex's incredible presence and portrayal of power, the petite, angelic mage remained unphased.

"This man..." trailed Gitterung at the mage who reeked of death. "He is not like he was before." Gitterung could feel the change. But he did now know if this was the great mage he had already defeated at the remains of his tower or if he had been corrupted and consumed the Kursed taint. Nex was so consumed by power and hatred whilst soaked in the rotten flesh of the Kursed, it was impossible for Gitterung to tell whether he remained human or not. This power was that of Dread General. His senses urged him to attack before anything could progress, and he did.

He reached out with both hands and released a tremendous spell without restraint, pouring all his power into it. A magic circle erupted above Nex and shifted the gravity exponentially that even those around felt like their souls were being pressed out of their bodies despite the psell not reaching them. Even a Titan would surely be crushed under the strain. This was the true power of one of Odin's Ten Kings.

But the shift in gravity did little to affect Nex. True, his shoulders felt heavier, but this was not a handicap. Gitterung was taken aback by how little effect his magic had. Shifting gravity to that of a multiple of around one million, this was the maximum amount of exertion Gitterung could accomplish. If Lily or Flowen were to even place a finger in the area-of-effect their limb would be removed from existence.

"If I was you, I wouldn't bother," said Vereoris, still in control of the battle. "As he is now, even you wont come away unscathed."

Gitterung looked upon death itself. A battle that even he, one of Odin's Ten Kings, the most powerful mages in all of Reath, contemplated victory. He turned to look at Vereoris in horror before he faded away into the wind like ash.

Nex was ravaged from his previous battle within the hollow mountain. He reeked of blood and death, stained onto his very soul. But his power had not diminished nor would he allow his wounds have any bearing on his performance.

"INFINITY MAGIC: Hyperion's spear!" roared Nex as he summoned above his shoulder a golden spear of light some fifty paces long and threw it at Vereoris with such calamity it could fell a dragon from the sky.

The incredible spell collided with the unguarding Vereoris and blinded all. But there was no diminishing of her presence.

"So, it's true…" spoke Teresa softly through the mist, initiating shocking gasps.

"Infinity Magic." said Isla.

"…and It had no effect?!" said Sohpia.

"You, of all people, should know that you cannot harm me with that magic," added Vereoris as she examined the dust that was attempting to settle on her impeccable armour. "Perhaps you need to be more *physical*. "Infinity Magic-" she began to everyone's disbelief.

"Ame no Murakumo!" From her, a sword of miasmic energy

gathered itself in less than a moment and cleaved horizontally through the air to collide with Nex who did little to defend. "I am aware it has no effect on you, either."

"He's...unharmed?" they all surmised as Nex took little from the blow. The truth behind their exchanges had now been revealed. Infinity Magic, the highest tier of magic known to this world, when wielded by one user against another, had no effect.

Nex could sense no limit to her power. She far exceeded him in terms of disposable spells and attacks and now his greatest form of Magic would do nothing against her. As consumed as he was with fury, he knew that for her to remain unscathed from an attack like that was something he could not take lightly. He needed to collect his thoughts and conclude on the best course of action.

"Let's see how much you can remember..." trailed Vereoris as she stepped forward to him and in a flash was upon him with a killing blow of her rapier. The sound of her eccentric, star metal Pynagol clashed with the simple structure of Nex's sheath, which he had summoned to his defence in incredible haste. She followed with relentless attacks as the two entered a melee, faster than she had with Flowen, each displaying an indescribable amount of skill, agility, and power. The shockwaves from their battle kept any spectator on their knees. It soon became clear after each delivered multiple successful blows to the other that Nex was superior, forcing Vereoris to stagger back and recover.

"It seems your physical abilities are completely restored. I had not been bested with a sword in a very long time," she stated as she composed herself, still unharmed.

Nex was wary. This was everything he had. Every fibre of his power had been summoned to ensure her defeat. Who could have possibly imagined the leap in ability between the two generals he had already faced? With her army out of range Nex considered her magic. It was surely devastating. As they broke away again, he used the opportunity to reach out and heal his comrades.

"Infinity Magic: Amaterasu's grace!"

How so very predictable," said Vereoris as she stepped forwards and released the true power of her blade. She was upon him in an instant and slashed across his abdomen with an enormous strike that struck through Nex and sent him crashing for hundreds of paces through trees and rocks and walls and the solid ground of the farmland they were in. But before Vereoris could taunt at his shortcomings Nex was behind her, his eyes burning with the cobalt blue power of the Sentinel. Nex's attack, as powerful as it was, met nothing but air.

Vereoris was a safe distance away. It was clear Nex had poured a lot into his attack that he needed a moment to recover.

"That wasn't even close," she said as she raised her hand towards him. "Soul Extinction." She summoned her colossal spell. It erupted in an instant, a cyclone of crimson darkness that was not evadable. Nex took the full force of her god-like spell.

"That would have turned them to ash had you not saved them," she stated as she looked upon the scorched Nex's unharmed friends. He had sacrificed his own defence so that they would not be harmed.

"SNOW QUEEN!" roared One Thousand Voices. This was nothing like he had ever conjured before. Surely the uninhabitable lands of drastic North and South were covered in an ice warmer than this?! The air tried to escape the gathering of his magic. Life could not exist in this space where he was. He summoned it to himself and released it like a barrel cannon of ice at the General.

The calamity of the spell was tremendous. The force pushed forward intensely and forced her back along the ground further away from him. The frozen blue barrel of ice ended. Carved into the ground before him was the result of his magic. A wound in the earth that time could never heal. They waited, all of them, their breaths held in tight, for the smoke to clear.

"So disappointing..." trailer Vereoris from amidst the smoke. She slashed at the air with her blade and cleared the area of all debris. "To think that is the best you can muster in these trying times."

Nex straightened himself, and with the exertion of his true Sentinel powers purged himself of the putrid presence of Kursed flesh he had been drenched in. He was now as human as any monster with this sort of power could be. To all those around them they could only feel the unmeasurable presence of the two. None of them possessed the power, wisdom or skill themselves to be able to tell that Vereoris' aura dwarfed Nex's like a torch to a raging forest fire but his body began to move on its own. Against his will his right hand crept around him slowly and hovered over the hilt of his Shirasaya, preparing to finally unseal the blade.

One Thousand Voices escaped Nex's mouth as he spoke. "No..." This was the turning point. Vereoris' expression changed, to a cold, evil stare. Her magic spiked as she lost control of her emotions. She looked at Nex as if to take his head in one blow. By a fraction of a morsel, she managed to contain herself as she spoke.

"You cannot defeat me. Nor can you save your precious friends," she declared. "If you forsake them now, I will accept that as an apology. The only way you can hope to face me is if you release that blade."

Nex's hand halted and eased. She wanted him to draw his

sword. For whatever reason she urged him to do it. This was indication enough it should not be done even if the mystical power that had come over him yearned for it. Even for the companions he now held dear and loved with all his heart, he could not unsheathe the sword, even if it meant their deaths.

"I will die for them before I unsheathe this blade," said Nex as he met his breaking point.

Vereoris smiled as if she was filled with nostalgia and braced to receive Nex's strikes. He vanished, moving so fast it was as if he teleported, but a cobalt blue streak of dark magic trailed in his wake as he attacked her, his sword still sealed away but devastating, nonetheless.

"Sealed sword fourth form: collapsing universe!" This strike was the second of Nex's hidden techniques more deadly than any magical spell he had released. As the name implied, a swing of this sealed sword could make the very space around him fold and overlap so his sword could enter different pockets of time and reality all to converge on the central point of his target. As if all was frozen in time, Vereoris deflected the blow with her own sword and even employed her hands and forearms to combat the simultaneous blows through time and space at speeds so minute and microscopic they arguably never occurred at all. But such defence did not come without cost. Each following strike was deadly, and every blow exchanged dealt considerable damage to the other. Countless barrages and blows later, Vereoris emerged with a simple drop of blood beneath her eye. She wiped it off slowly and poised it onto her tongue. The blood belonged to Nex.

"You taste delicious!" she stated as the sensation poured through her. She was unable to contain herself. "Soul: Extinction!". Vereoris with an outstretched left hand released a crimson black vortex down onto Nex, shredding through his magic defence like arrows through paper. The spell was incredible. Focused on Nex, it had also destroyed the land over one hundred paces behind him and yet she did such damage effortlessly. But now Nex could not move. Somehow, he was frozen to the spot. Was it her last attack? Or was it something else? Something inside him prevented him from moving even a hair on his body.

"Aha..." she spoke softly as she stepped towards him. "Finally."

Horror and despair stepped closer and closer until she was upon him herself, her silver boots weightlessly striding across the ground. The pain was sharp and intense, easily leagues above any recent thing he had endured. He could feel his blood thickening into paste as it boiled, churned, and clotted in his veins. His lungs began to poison the air that circulated around his body spreading like an uncontrollable epidemic. This horrific torture had not come from the curse of Vereoris' blade but from the touch of her lips themselves.

She embraced him with a long, soft, passionate embrace and through all the pain Nex could only stare eyes wide at her sealed eyes. As terrifying as it was, he was blessed. The Goddess herself touched her divine lips to his, a mere human.

"Gah!" he gasped as he fell to one knee, now free to move. Vereoris took little notice of his response. She was transfixed with the residue left on her lip. She touched it with her finger and her tongue.

"Maybe this is enough to spur you into action..." she said as she stepped backwards. "Pure misery in its purest form. It's the only thing I can do for him."

Even with all his conviction and sacrifice he knew he must not draw his sword. If he did, a fate would befall the world, the likes of which can never be repeated. But for his friends, for their survival, he would do it!

Nex had given in. Around him, the ground broke at the acceptance of his will. As his hand drew with intent towards the hilt of his Shirasaya. He began to erupt more and more with a dark, sinister power full of despair and malice as his intention came true. It bore its fangs all those who would oppose his might. Titans, Gods, Humans and even the Maker himself would shudder at the terrifying power that poised itself like death incarnate at Nex's enemies.

Now, with his hand gripping his hilt tightly and ready to withdraw, Nex was almost complete, the surging cobalt blue light erupting from his eyes and glowing through the mystical, war-torn bandages.

But it was one unaffected by the animosity of his dark aura. One who his hatred and anger had not been poised against who had moved closer. It was the cold, star metal blade that slipped through his back and between his shoulder blades that defeated him.

He shut down, his mind plunging into darkness with no chance of recovery. Lily withdrew her sword from his chest slowly in remorse for what she had done. Vereoris sheathed her cursed sword and dispersed it and smiled the most sinister smile any creature could adorn in her victory.
Nex was stricken with grief and betrayal. He turned slowly to look upon her traitorous face streaming with tears that glistened in the moonlight. In her eyes he saw the complexities of her soul and understood what it meant to them in these very moments. Softly, Nex smiled back at her anguished face.

Through her remorse and grief Lily then, with one easy slice, severed Nex's left arm. Now, unable to keep the blade in his possession, Vereoris summoned it from his lifeless grasp and caught it outstretched to receive.

She began forward to the wounded mage where a single

tear had managed to escape from his oceanic, blue eyes and plunged her hand into his chest mercilessly to crush his stricken heart.

Above them, high in the sky, the daughter of the moon wept her stardust upon them as Vereoris brought her soft lips to his ear and whispered gently so that only he could learn, "That's the second time I have ripped out your heart, my love."

The End

Printed in Great Britain
by Amazon